The Traitor's Son

Path of the Ranger Book 1

Pedro Urvi

COMMUNITY:
Mail: pedrourvi@hotmail.com
Facebook: https://www.facebook.com/PedroUrviAuthor/
My Website: http://pedrourvi.com
Twitter: https://twitter.com/PedroUrvi

Translation by:
Christy Cox

Edited by:
Peter Gauld

DEDICATION

To my good friend Guiller.

Thank you for all your support since day one.

Content

MAP

Prologue

With loyalty and courage, the Ranger will guard the lands of the Realm and defend the Crown from enemies both internal and external, serving Norghana with honor and in secrecy.

There is no soldier, mage, wizard or beast who does not fear the skill of the Ranger, for his true arrow will bring death to them without their even being aware of his presence.

Excerpt from The Path of the Ranger,
the dogma of the Norghanian Rangers.

Chapter 1

"My father was no traitor, and one day I'm going to prove it!" Lasgol shouted. He threw his head back to avoid the huge fist which brushed past his nose.

"Your father's the biggest traitor the Kingdom of Norghana's had in a hundred years!" Volgar yelled. He lunged his arm in a cross-punch that Lasgol dodged by ducking his head.

"That's a lie!" he said. He stepped back to get out of the giant's range, careful not to slip on the snow which covered part of the cobbled square.

"You dirty son of a traitor, I'm going to break your head open!"

Lasgol moved further away. "Leave me alone. All I want is to trade my furs and the meat from my kill, then I'll go." He gestured at the satchel on his shoulder, where he was carrying the half-dozen hares he had caught in his traps.

Volgar spread his arms wide. "I've told you often enough. Only honest and honorable people can trade here. You can't come to the village square to contaminate it, you stinking traitor. This is a respectable village. Give me your kill and get out of here, then maybe I won't crack your skull."

"No way! And who are you to forbid me to do anything? I belong to this village just as much as you do." Lasgol glanced around. He noticed that Igor and Sven, the two thugs who were always with Volgar, were approaching him from behind to bar his escape-route. In front of him was the bully, to his right was the fountain, a little to the left was the trough for the traders' horses, and behind him the two sidekicks. They had him surrounded.

"Don't you dare oppose me! I'm going to have to teach you a lesson!"

"You'll have to catch me first!" Lasgol said. He was looking in every direction, searching for a way out. Volgar had intercepted him at the furrier's door, opposite the tradesmen's houses in the village square. Now he could see quite clearly that he had been ambushed. They had been waiting for him. It was too early for that monster even to be awake. But today was market day, and they knew Lasgol would have to come to sell his kill.

Volgar threw a left punch, but he saw it coming and dodged it with a feint. He had to go on avoiding the blows and not let himself be caught. If he stopped to exchange punches they would tear him apart. That much he had learned when he was only ten. He still recalled the tremendous beating he had been given. If they managed to catch him, he would suffer the same fate.

"Stay still and fight!" the giant shouted, his face red with rage at not being able to grab him.

"In your dreams!" Lasgol said. He was moving nimbly around his rival, being careful not to slip too much on the snow. He knew he had no chance of beating that hulk. Although they had both just turned fifteen, Volgar was twice as broad as he was himself and a head taller. There was no-one his age as big and ugly in the whole village. And even worse, although his big body was decidedly fleshy, particularly his belly and abdomen, he also had a lot of muscle. His brute strength was enormous, and the bully knew how to use it to terrorize everyone, even those who were older.

"I'm going to yank your head off!" the bully yelled, and a cloud of steam came out of his big mouth. It was quite cold that winter morning, even though spring was on its way. But here in the north of Tremia it was always cold.

"Like father, like son! Traitor and coward!"

"My father didn't betray the realm, and I'm no coward," Lasgol yelled back as he searched around for help. The furrier had come to his door and was watching the fight with arms folded. Since a Norghanian hardly ever intervened in somebody else's fight, nobody at all would move a finger to help him. He was the son of Dakon Eklund, the Traitor Ranger. He saw the smith put aside a sword he was hammering on the anvil and came out to watch. The butcher and his two sons came over from the other side of the square, and after them several neighbors from the little mountain village. They were not coming closer in order to intervene, they were coming to see him given a good beating. They would cheer if that was what happened. They all despised him for who he was. They treated him like the plague.

"Your father betrayed King Uthar, he sold him out to Darthor, Black Lord of the Ice," Sven said behind him. "You ought to be thrown out of the North. You're soiling our land with your stinking presence."

Lasgol looked at him with half-closed eyes. Nothing he might say or do would prevent him from getting a beating. "Leave me alone, I haven't done anything wrong."

"I'm getting tired of this!" Volgar cried. "Grab him!" His two buddies were waiting for his order. In Norghana, one-on-one fights were traditional and always respected. Volgar, however, had lost his patience, something that happened quite often.

"So who's the coward? You need your friends to defeat me one-on-one? You're the one who's a shame on Norghana."

"Grab that traitor! I'm going to beat him to a pulp!"

Igor tried to catch Lasgol, but he managed to get away. Sven tackled him and almost brought him down.

"When I prove my father's innocence," Lasgol said, struggling to get away, "you'll have to swallow your words."

"You can swallow this!" Volgar said, and launched a right hook. Lasgol tried to dodge, but Igor grabbed his arm and Sven his waist. The punch hit him in the face like a hammer. His lip exploded with pain and his head whipped back from the tremendous force that almost left him stunned.

"I've got you!" Volgar said to his two buddies. "Hold him tight!"

Lasgol shook his head. Dazed, he saw the giant lunge at him. If he reached him he would batter him to a pulp. He freed his arm with a strong tug which Igor could not manage to resist. With his arms free, he hit Sven in the back with his forearms to get rid of him. Sven, in an attempt to hold on to him, caught the satchel and fell backwards with it.

"My kill!" cried Lasgol.

"Hold him!" yelled Volgar, and Igor tried to grab him by the neck.

He freed himself by leaping aside and saw Volgar's fist fly past his eye, hitting nothing but air. Sven was smiling in triumph on the ground, and for a moment Lasgol thought about getting his satchel out of the other boy's hands. If he lost his kill he would be in big trouble. But he forgot about it. He had to get away from there before they tore him to shreds. He took two steps forward to gain momentum and jumped to the fountain. Igor followed him. From the fountain he took a long leap to the trough.

"Stand still!" Volgar yelled. "You cowardly squirrel!"

Lasgol kept his balance without falling into the water and took another leap, this time to the porch of the nearest house. He hung from it, holding on tightly. He could feel the cold and damp of the snow through his tanned leather gloves. He had to take the greatest care over his next move so as not to slip and fall on his back.

"Where d'you think you're going? Stop!"

Lasgol swung from the porch, then with one fluid movement gave a leap and climbed on to the wooden roof. He was about to make his way along it when Igor's hand closed on his ankle. The gaunt thug tried to pull him down with him by using his own body weight. Lasgol threw himself flat on the roof and held tight. But Igor was tugging at him and he was beginning to slide. If he did, it would be the end.

"Bring him down!" Volgar yelled, and Sven tried to help.

Panic threatened to overcome Lasgol. But he managed to clear his mind. With his left boot he kicked repeatedly the hand that held his right ankle, holding on at the same time with all his might. Igor moaned, let go of his ankle and fell to the ground. Lasgol got to his feet and climbed to the apex of the roof like lightning.

There were murmurs among the spectators.

Volgar was red with fury. "Come down from there!" he yelled.

"Come and get me if you can."

He saw Igor and Sven trying to climb on to the porch. Volgar would never make it, he was too heavy, but the other two would manage to if it occurred to them to think and help each other up. Luckily thinking was not something the three of them did very often. But just in case a miracle happened and they decided to use their heads, he was not going to stay and find out.

"That's it. See you never!"

The giant's face turned so red it looked as though it would burst like an overripe tomato.

"You'll regret this!"

Lasgol turned and slid down the other side of the roof. With great care he began to jump from roof to roof, crossing the village high up. He had to be very alert because the snow on the roofs were treacherous. If he slipped, he might fall all the way down and break his skull. He focused all his attention on each jump. The fur-covered leather boots he was wearing were not slippery, but all the same he did not entirely trust them. He had a couple of moments of panic when he nearly lost his footing and fell, but with an enormous effort of concentration he reached the last house at the northern end of the village and dropped to the ground. Then he ran and vanished into the forest.

Once he was sure he was not being followed and was safe, he climbed to the top of a huge fir-tree by the river. Climbing up to high places was something he loved to do. Ever since he was little he had felt attracted by heights. Perhaps it was the feeling of achievement when he reached the top, or perhaps it was the amazing views, or perhaps it was the peace he felt when he was alone at the top. Probably all these reasons combined, and maybe others he was not even aware of. The point was that whenever he could, almost instinctively, he ended up at the top of something, whether it was a tower, a hill, or as in this case, a tree. Besides, the fact that it was covered in snow, so that the ascent was more difficult, motivated him even more.

He took a deep breath of the forest's aromatic scent. This relaxed him. He felt a pang of pain in his mouth and wiped the blood off his broken lip with the sleeve of his worn winter tunic. As he did so he realized that one sleeve of his old sealskin coat was nearly torn away. He sighed and then smiled. He would have to sew it himself. The things you learned when you were poor and hated. He could already sew, weave, cook, and a host of other things he had been forced to learn out of sheer necessity. He glanced at his thick woolen pants with their covering of fur and saw that they were still in good condition. If he had to replace them it would have been complicated, but that was what happened with fights in the North: you ended up beaten, with your clothes in tatters.

He felt his face and legs in case he had any wounds he had not noticed. *Nothing serious,* he thought. It was not the first time he had been beaten, nor would it be the last. It was something he was used to. Beatings barely hurt anymore; what really hurt was the scorn. Not so much towards him —that he bore in silence— but toward his father Dakon. He had grown accustomed to it and it hurt less and less as time went on. He could not however, bear it when they slandered his dead father. That he would never get used to.

Three long tortuous years had gone by since that fateful day. The day of the King's Betrayal, the day of his father's death. The day

Lasgol's life was torn apart forever and became a nightmare he could not wake up from, no matter how hard he tried.

He heard a faint sound to his left and turned his head slowly. A squirrel was watching him curiously. Seeing it, he remembered the kill he had lost. He sighed and shook his head. He had been coming back from collecting the traps he had set in the underbrush when he had been ambushed. Now he had to go back to his master's home without the coins he should have gotten. That was going to cost him dearly. His master Ulf would make him sleep outside, or something worse. Sleeping outside in the midst of the cold winter in the most northerly realm of Tremia, famed for being frozen three-quarters of the year, might have been considered an inhuman punishment in the eyes of half the civilized world, but it was not so in Ulf's. Unfortunately Lasgol had already endured it.

He put his hands over his mouth and mimicked Ulf. "It's good for the character," he told the squirrel, imitating Ulf's deep, hoarse voice. "A Norghanian must be able to sleep even on a block of ice. Not for nothing are we the People of the Snow."

The squirrel ran off, leaping from branch to branch until it disappeared among the trees. He smiled as he watched it into the distance. *I must stop speaking out loud. I sound crazy.* But what can you do when you have no friends and everybody avoids you, insults you or tries to beat you? He shrugged. His father had taught him to avoid self-pity. "Always keep a positive attitude, no matter how difficult the situation. Always look ahead, and be optimistic." Most likely his father had not foreseen a situation like this one. But he would follow his advice, just as he had always done.

He glanced up at the sun among the clouds, which were threatening a storm. *I'd better face the punishment as soon as possible.* He climbed down from the tree as fast as he could. He always did it like that, going up as well as going down. He was training his muscles and his coordination. Strong hands and sure footing were essential, particularly for someone like him who was not strong. Lasgol looked at himself and shook his head. He was not the archetypal Norghanian, if anything the opposite. The Norghanians were tough, fierce men, tall and strong like the oaks of the North, doughty warriors trained in the use of the axe and round wooden shield. Their skin was as white as the snow that covered their land, with eyes as pale as the northern sky, and hair blond as the weak rays of the sun from their country. Although Lasgol was blond and blue-eyed, he was not tough or fierce. He did not know how to use the war-axe and shield, and above all he was not tall or muscular, rather the opposite.

He shrugged and smiled, because there was one thing he most certainly was: very fast and agile, more so than anyone else he knew. For this reason, whenever he could he trained his body to make the most of his advantages to build up the strength he lacked. *They may all be as tall and strong as bears, but I've never seen a bear catch a squirrel.* He burst out laughing and turned back to the village.

When he arrived, he made sure there was no danger waiting for him in the streets and made his way to Ulf's house. He took the main street, which was wider and would allow him to escape more easily in case of fresh trouble. He passed his old home and stopped to look at it, as he always did. It was a building of wood and stone in the Norghanian style, surrounded by a modest wall, bigger and more luxurious than the other houses in the village. Both the house and the several acres of land and forest behind it had belonged to his father. It had been the family property, but not anymore.

The village of Skad was a mining community in the northwest. Most of the houses in the village were simple, and the only one that looked as if it belonged to a rich merchant, or perhaps a nobleman, was his father's. There was a reason for this: his father had been neither rich nor a nobleman, but nor was he an ordinary man either. He had been First Ranger of Norghana. It was a feat very few men had been able to achieve. They could be counted on the fingers of one hand.

He sighed. longing for the good times when he, his mother Mayra and his father Dakon had lived there and were happy. It pained him to remember so little of his mother, who had died when he was a little boy. His father used to tell him about her, to keep her memory alive. Unfortunately he had lost him too. It seemed like a whole lifetime since the incident, but it had only been three years.

"What are you looking at?" came a voice. "Have you forgotten all over again that this isn't your house any longer?" He came back to reality. From the old entrance in the middle of the wall a guard was gesturing for him to go away. Beside him another guard was glaring sourly at him.

"Go on your way," the second one said.

"I'm not doing anything wrong."

"I told you to go, my lord doesn't want to see you around staring at the house like a stuffed dummy. It makes him angry."

Lasgol was about to reply but he thought better of it and bit his tongue. When his father had fallen into disgrace, the King had stripped titles and land from him and his descendants; such was Norghanian law. Lasgol had lost his father, his home and everything they had owned. Count Malason, the lord of that county, had handed over house and lands to his second cousin Osvald, nicknamed *The Whip*, for his love of that instrument, which he always wore coiled around his waist ready to be used, and who was in charge of managing the two mines in the area, of iron and coal.

"All right, I'm going."

He walked to his present "home". It was the old house of a retired soldier which stood by itself in the northern part of the village. It was small and had seen better times, but it was solid and the roof still held. What was most important was that the fireplace gave out enough heat so they would not freeze to death when the temperature plunged, which often happened every winter. He stopped in front of the door and hesitated between going in and turning back. He was afraid of Ulf's rage. He began to turn around.

"Hey, boy! Is that you?" came Ulf's deep, hoarse voice from inside the house.

Lasgol stood still. How could he have heard him?

"Where's my medicine?"

Lasgol sighed. He opened the door and got ready to take his punishment.

Chapter 2

Lasgol eyed his master with his head bowed and his shoulders drooping. Ulf was past his middle years, big and ugly as a bear. His hair and beard were red, and always unkempt. He was one-eyed, and wore nothing over the empty socket of the other for all to see, which increased the ferocity of his appearance. The first time Lasgol saw him, he thought this must be a bear of the southern woods. He still thought so every time Ulf yelled at him, or rather roared. He leaned his huge body on a staff, since he had lost a leg in the war against the Zangrians. That was why Lasgol was there. The huge warrior could not look after himself on his own. Thinking about it, Lasgol shivered. If Ulf Olafssen knew what he was thinking, he would tear his head off with a roar.

"Where's my drink, lad?" Ulf growled.

"Well… sir…" he tried to explain.

Ulf's face began to turn red. "Well what?"

"Volgar and his buddies, they set on me in front of the furrier's…"

Ulf took no notice of this. "Why are your hands empty?"

"They took the game from me… I couldn't sell it… and without coin I couldn't buy the Nocean wine from the cellarer."

"For the Five Ice Gods' sake!" Ulf exclaimed. He raised his left arm and waved it as if in a fit of rage while with his right he leant on his staff, struggling to keep his balance.

"I'm sorry… I didn't see them until it was too late."

Ulf came to stand a hand-span away from him, bent over and shouted in his face like an enraged beast. The lad did not move an inch. He knew he had to stand his ground whatever happened.

"Excuses!" he thundered into Lasgol's face. "You're making excuses to me! What do I always tell you about excuses?"

"A Norghanian doesn't make excuses…"

"Exactly! A Norghanian doesn't make excuses. A Norghanian does exactly what he has to do, but he never makes excuses!"

"Yes, sir…" Lasgol closed his eyes tight. Ulf's shouts were so loud that he thought he would end up deaf.

"Thirty years in the Royal Norghanian Army, and I end up with the worst lad in the kingdom!"

"I'm sorry, sir."

"Who took you in when they threw you out in the street when you were only twelve years old?"

Lasgol bent his head and swallowed. He knew what was coming, and against it he had no defense.

"Who put a roof over your head, offered you a place by the fire to keep warm and fed you so you wouldn't die of hunger and cold in the streets?"

"I'm sorry," the boy repeated. He avoided raising his head so as not to meet the old soldier's furious gaze.

When he was in his cups, which he often was, Ulf was difficult to deal with. His nasty side came to the surface. But when he was hungover and there was no wine for him, it was almost worse. Rage overwhelmed him, and he would turn into a savage ogre who would not be soothed until he got his liquor. Nothing Lasgol might say or do would quiet him, nothing but bringing him his *painkiller*, as he called it. There was nothing that the boy could do except wait out the storm as best he could.

"Who let you stay and protected you when they all wanted to throw you to the forest wolves?"

"You…"

"Who took you on as a servant in his own house?"

"I'll bring some wine," Lasgol assured him.

"I should think you will bring me my wine! By the white bears of the north, you'll do that!"

"I'll go right away."

"Go, and don't come back without my wine or else you'll be sleeping outside, and I think there's a storm coming tonight." He closed his one good eye and bent over to touch the stump of his right leg. "Yes, there's definitely a storm on its way, one of the violent ones that mark the end of winter. This old soldier of the snows knows it. It hurts, and the pain never brings anything good…"

Lasgol nodded without raising his head. He crossed the kitchen and went to the back of the house, where Ulf kept the weapons. The old soldier had set up a wooden armory against the stone wall. He took a good look at the weapons. There was an infantry soldier's sword: Ulf's most prized possession, since the Norghanians used axes for fighting, and having a sword was a symbol of belonging to the army and either having reached the rank of officer or else belonging to one of the elite units. Beside the sword were three axes: a short one for throwing, a long one for fighting and a huge two-headed one that took two hands to wield it.

"Don't you even look at my weapons! To be able to bear them you have to earn them with the sweat of your brow, with years of sacrifice and service to the crown!"

Lasgol did not turn around. He hated the crown and everything to do with it after what had happened to his father, but he said nothing. It was not a good idea to enrage the old soldier even further. A negative comment about the king or the army and Ulf would bite his head off.

"And don't you imagine I don't know you want to handle them. But for that you have to be a true Norghanian, and you're just a skinny brat!"

Lasgol sighed. Ulf had forbidden him to touch his weapons. Once, when the old soldier was not home, he had tried to grasp the great axe, and to his surprise and horror he could barely lift it off the floor. For a man to fight with such a weight in his hands seemed impossible, however bearing in mind that the men of the north were as big and strong as bears, he understood the reason for that colossal weapon. It could probably bring down a house with just four strokes.

On top of the armory were the two bows: the short one for hunting and the longbow for war. He passed his hands over both, as if greeting them. Those two magnificent weapons were not Ulf's, they were his own. Ulf hated bows. According to him they were for cowards. Men ought always to fight hand to hand, face to face, and not from a treacherous distance. This was a widespread belief in Norghana. Archers were frowned upon, and the Rangers even more so. And he himself was the son of one of them. And not just of any one but of a First Ranger, the best among them.

"Don't get your hopes up, laddie," came the hoarse, disdainful voice.

Lasgol did not turn, but took the short bow and the quiver full of arrows hanging on one side.

"You're too weak to be a good soldier, you haven't got the bulk. At your age you should already be twice the size."

Lasgol looked back over his shoulder. "I don't want to be a

soldier," he said softly.

"Well, you'd better not want to be a bloody Ranger. Those cowards camouflage themselves in the landscape so that they can kill from afar without being seen. And all those things the villagers say about how the Rangers are mysterious, that they can disappear in plain sight as if by magic, that their enemies don't see death coming...it's all nonsense! There's nothing magic about them!"

"They're the king's elite group," Lasgol said, knowing this would enrage Ulf.

"They're cowards!"

"The King holds them in great esteem."

"Bah! He uses them to track and hunt down men and vermin. They're nothing more than his bloodhounds. Either that or for spying missions. But in the open field, face to face, a soldier would tear them to pieces."

The boy remembered what his father had told him so many times. "That's not their purpose. Their job is to protect the kingdom from internal and external enemies, and to serve the king."

"You're not going to tell me you want to follow in your father's footsteps, are you? Look how he ended up."

The comment stung Lasgol, and he half-closed his eyes. "No, I don't want to be a Ranger. I don't even want to serve the king or Norghana."

"You're talking like a bloody traitor! There's no greater honor for a Norghanian than to fight for his kingdom and for his king!"

"Not for me..."

"You ungrateful weasel! Take your bow and go before my patience runs out!" He hurled his staff at the boy. It hit the wall on his right, hard. Lasgol headed for the door.

"Where do you think you're going?"

"Hunting..."

"By the mines of oblivion! You're the worst servant in the whole north! Bring me my staff!"

Lasgol obeyed. "Here it is, master."

"Now get out of my house and don't come back without my drink!"

The boy left at once for the northeastern woods. He did not have much time, and he needed to hurry. It would be a long walk, it would take him almost half a day to reach the woods where there was good game. With a bit of luck he could be back before nightfall. He needed a good kill, or else he would not get the coin he needed. Unfortunately his traps were empty and it would take two or three days for them to be full again.

Stepping lightly, he went on into the forest. The walk in itself didn't bother him. The snow and cold, somewhat more, although his old coat, tunic and the woolen jerkin he wore under it provided enough protection, so long as a storm did not catch him by surprise. He was used to moving through the snowy woods. In order to get a good catch he had to, although he did not usually go very far. He was cautious. The woods and the cold could betray the most experienced hunter. The slightest mistake might end in death. Although he was inexperienced, he had a great respect for the hostile lands of the north.

It was his habit to leave before sunrise to reach the good hunting grounds early. Once there, he would scout the area in search of fresh tracks, which was one of the things he enjoyed most. Once he had found them, he would set the appropriate traps in the best spots. Then he would hide somewhere high up, upwind so as not to be discovered, and wait for a large catch. Recognizing animal tracks and choosing the right places to wait and catch them was an art. An art Lasgol had learnt from his father.

He hastened on through the forest, leaping over roots and low brush with the lightness of a cat. Unfortunately he would not be able to go so fast further on. The snow covered the high forests and would make his progress more difficult. Today he would not have time to reconnoiter the area, so he would have to go to one of his favorite spots, where he could always find some medium-sized prey, such as a deer. That would be more than enough, if he was lucky. Wild animals were wary and could detect men from leagues away in the high woods.

It took him a while, but he finally headed up the last slope. His legs hurt from the effort and his lungs were burning as he went on through the birches with the snow up to his knees. He could feel the damp cold biting his legs, but he was already very close, and that cheered him up. From the hill he looked down at the stream which crossed the hunting ground. He smiled; he had arrived. He looked up at the sky. Through the tops of the trees he could see the sky growing darker, threatening a storm. The temperature had begun to fall. *This is looking bad. I'd better hurry.*

He went down to the stream and began to search for animal prints on the shore. He soon found the first ones and bent down to study them: they were those of a silver fox. It was probably doing the same as he was himself: searching for the trail of some smaller animal. He was not mistaken; a little further on in the snow he found the trail of a hare running into the forest. He kept looking. Time was getting short, he could feel the cold on his face now. The tanned leather gloves protected his hands from the cold, but not from the wetness of the snow. He had to be careful not to get them wet. Once he had done this, and the temperature had fallen so far that he had to return home. When he got there, two of his fingers were frozen and he nearly lost them.

He readjusted the furs that covered his legs from ankle to knee. They reinforced the protection of his winter boots, which were an absolute necessity for walking in the snow. Boots and furs alike were treated with seal fat to stop the damp from penetrating.

A trail a little further on caught his attention, and he hurried to study it carefully; it was a reindeer. There was no doubt about it. His father had taught him to recognize most of the prints and trails men and animals left in the woods. Few escaped him, although he sometimes made mistakes as he was not infallible and still had a lot to learn.

He let himself be carried away by nostalgia. Tracking was his father's favorite pastime. Dakon had taken him tracking for the first time when he was just four years old. He could still remember it, although the memories were fading with the passage of time. Since that first day they had spent many moments in the woods as tutor and pupil, as father and son Lasgol had enjoyed those days immensely, every single one of them. Since his father spent such long periods of time away from home to serve the king and the rangers, spending time with him on those expeditions in the woods when he was a young lad made those moments all the more precious to him.

He had never known when his father would leave or when he would be back. He would go without telling him. One morning Lasgol would wake up and he would be gone, and then on some other evening when he would be about to go to bed, his father would walk in through the door. No matter how many times he asked, his father never told him anything about the Rangers' missions. *The*

Rangers and their secrets… always with their secrets… In fact Lasgol had spent most of his childhood with Olga, his father's long-time servant, a wonderful old woman, who had raised him like her own grandson. Stern but sympathetic, and above all filled with love. She had taught him discipline, taught him to work, and to value things. He had dearly loved that iron-willed woman. Unfortunately Olga had died the summer before the fateful incident and had not lived through what happened next. It would have broken her heart. Lasgol gave thanks to the Gods of Ice for having spared the good woman that torment.

He sighed. When his father came back from his missions, the first thing he would do was take him to the high woods and test him by choosing trails that were almost imperceptible, or else very confusing. He had enjoyed every moment of those journeys with his father immensely, and tracking had become what he enjoyed most in the world.

"What is tracking?" his father had once asked him.

"Searching for the trail of something, finding it and following it?" Lasgol had answered.

Dakon had smiled. "Yes, that might be the correct answer, but it's much more than that."

"Much more?"

"Yes, my son. It's solving a small mystery."

"I don't understand, dad."

"Every time we go into the woods and find a trail, you need to treat it as if you were solving a mystery. What man, or what animal, left this trail? What was it doing here? How long has it been there? Where is it going now? And most important: why?"

Lasgol had stared at his father in fascination. "I'd never thought of it like that."

"The next time you follow a trail, look at it from this perspective, ask yourself those questions. They'll help you, not only to track better, but to make the experience a much more satisfactory one."

"I will, dad."

And ever since that day in his childhood, Lasgol had always remembered those questions when he was on a trail. As in many other things, his father was right: not only was following the trail easier, but in addition he thoroughly enjoyed it. He checked the reindeer prints on the snow again. It was a young doe, not very big, moving agilely. It would be hard to catch. Lasgol wondered at the things a trained eye could read in the tracks. He smiled.

He adjusted his quiver, checked his bow and grasped it in his left hand. It was time to hunt down the prey. He crouched, then very slowly began to follow the prints the animal had left after coming down to the ravine to drink. He took very careful steps, not wanting to make the slightest sound, lest he frighten his prey. As he moved forward he stopped to check the direction of the wind. If the animal scented him he would lose it. He advanced very patiently, closing in on his prey without it being aware of it. He could not see it, but he did not need to, the prints were guiding him.

As he went deeper into the forest an odd feeling came over him, as if he were being watched. He looked around, but he was completely alone: he, the forest, the snow which covered everything and an ever-darkening sky. Lasgol sometimes had odd feelings. In fact, for the last week those feelings had been more frequent. This worried him; there was usually a reason for his 'feelings', and they were not always for good. *Don't imagine things, it's the storm, it's almost upon me,* he said to himself. He shook his head and went on.

He passed over a fallen tree buried under the weight of the snow and checked the prints. They were fresh. He was very close. He scanned the forest with alert eyes, but he could only see the snow. He went on slowly until he reached a half-buried boulder. He skirted it and stopped, standing as still as though he were part of the boulder beside him. Twenty paces away, among the trees, was the reindeer. It was browsing the bushes, half-buried in the snow, that still survived in the cold.

He hid behind the boulder and checked the wind. *I'm downwind. I'm in luck. It won't detect me.* He took a deep breath and got ready. Very slowly, with a long-drawn-out movement, trying to make it imperceptible to the animal, he took an arrow from his quiver and nocked it. As it was a young doe he would not get much for the horns, but he would do better with the meat and skin. He focused on the shot. *Come on,* he said to encourage himself, *I can do it.* Archery was not his forte. He was good with traps but not much use with the bow; that was something that ate at him. He practiced every day, but did not seem to get any better. Not having anyone to help him, he did not make any progress. He was sure he was doing something wrong, but could not puzzle out on what it was.

He tried to relax. *It's close,* he said to himself, *I can do it.* Five paces further back and he would certainly have missed. But at this distance he had a chance. He considered approaching closer – the closer, the better the chance that the shot would not go astray – but rejected the idea. The risk of being spotted was too great. No, he would have to hit it from where he was. He made his decision, inhaled deeply and at the same time tensed the string until the feather of the arrow tickled his cheek. He aimed. Again that sense that he was being watched came over him, and a shiver ran down his spine. It almost broke his concentration, but he held it. *Now,* he said to himself. He breathed out and at the same time loosed the arrow.

There came a dull blow, and the reindeer fell sideways on the snow. Lasgol stood up in delight, his arm raised. *I did it!* He ran to the animal and crouched down beside it. It was dead. *What a great shot! I won't be sleeping in the street tonight!* He had hit the doe in the head with such force that it had died instantly. The embarrassing thing was that he had been aiming at its heart. *I definitely need someone to help me with the bow. The hunters would be ashamed of me. Maybe I should throw rocks at them instead. That way I'd be sure not to miss.* But he soon got over his annoyance. He had made his kill, which was what mattered.

He was so happy he did not realize that the temperature was beginning to fall sharply. A gust of wind whipped his face, and he looked up at the sky. *Very dark. Too dark.* The storm was almost on top of him. He had to leave at once, he was about to prepare the kill to carry it home when he became aware of something that made him stop. A pair of eyes was watching him. They were fixed on him. He froze. Ten paces away, between two birches, a gray wolf was stalking him.

He eyed the wolf shyly, his head bent. He must not move suddenly or he risked being attacked. He thought of using his bow, but hitting an attacking wolf was beyond his ability. By the time he had aimed, it would be on top of him, and in any case, surely he would miss. He thought of the knife he carried at his waist. It was a skinning knife, too small to face a wolf with, besides, he did not know how to fight, least of all against a wild animal. Fear began to tighten his stomach. *I can't let it smell my fear or else it'll attack me.*

He tried to keep himself calm. The wolf gave a long growl, wrinkled its nose and showed two huge fangs in a clear threat. He knew it was about to leap on him. There was only one choice left: he must retreat little by little, without turning away, and hope it would not attack. He took a deep breath, gathered his courage and began to step back, crouching, his eyes on the wolf. It went on growling, more aggressively now. He glanced at the fallen doe. If he left it there he would have to sleep outside and he would freeze. Very carefully he began to tug at the carcass.

The wolf leapt forward and growled angrily. Lasgol was paralyzed. His heart was beating so fast he thought it would burst out of his chest. The wolf wanted the carcass. But he needed it himself. He let it fall. *Go away. I need it. It's mine.* He waved his arm to scare it off. But the wolf took another step forward and growled, snapping its teeth in the air, showing its fangs. Lasgol felt so afraid that his knees almost gave way.

He recovered. With one hand raised toward the wolf and his gaze fixed on its wild eyes, he insisted. *Go away! This kill is mine!* A green flash ran through his head and arm. The wolf took a step back and whined. Lasgol went on staring at it, his eyes fixed on its own. *Go away!* he insisted, while his hand remained steady. Another green flash accompanied the mandate. The wolf howled. Then it lowered its head and flattened its ears. It turned, then went slowly back into the forest.

Lasgol stayed still. He had scared the wolf off, although he did not quite know how. But this was not the time for wondering. He picked up the carcass, slung it across his shoulders and began to run, with the first flakes of snow already falling on his head.

I'd better hurry back, before the snow turns to ice.

Chapter 3

Lasgol arrived in the village after nightfall, with the storm hard on his heels. He was very tired. Breathless. He stopped in the middle of the village square beside the fountain. Leaving the kill on the ground, he bent over with his hands on his hips, trying to get his breath back. All the muscles in his body were aching, but he was happy. He had done it. He had the kill and had reached the village before the storm broke. As his father used to say: *He who seeks his goal with soul and claw attains it. Never give up.*

He glanced around him. The last villagers were running to the shelter of their houses and farms, and by now the square was almost deserted. The lights of the houses lit up the doorways, and the oil lamps which the bailiff would soon put out did the same for the square and the little inn. His eyes turned to the furrier's house, then the butcher's. The sensible thing to do would be to prepare the carcass, then sell meat and skin separately. He looked back at the sky behind him. It was so dark that any moment now the storm would break out. He would not have time to go home, prepare the carcass and then come back. It was too late.

The furrier leant out to close his shutters.

"Wait, please!" Lasgol begged him.

"I've already shut up shop," said the furrier, looking annoyed. It was the same annoyance he showed whenever Lasgol brought him furs, although he generally accepted them. Business was business, and coin did not recognize the sons of traitors.

Lasgol hurried to the window. "I've brought something good."

The furrier eyed him doubtfully. "Let's see what you have. And make it quick. The storm's almost on us, and I want my dinner."

Lasgol put his bow aside and showed his kill.

"Not bad," he said, and started to close the shutters. "Come back tomorrow with the skin."

"Sir, I need the money now."

"Sure, and I need a good wife." Everybody knew that the furrier's wife was an unpleasant woman who made his life impossible. He probably deserved it.

"Please..."

"Enough of your *pleases*, I don't buy unprepared carcasses, you know that, everybody knows it. Do your job and come back tomorrow."

"But..."

"No buts!" and he closed the shutters with a bang.

Lasgol sighed. He was not going to give up. He ran to the butcher's door and knocked urgently; the storm had broken. Rain and snow began to whip around him, driven by frozen winds. Nobody answered.

He knocked again and waited. Nothing. He turned to go. What else could he do? And then the door opened.

He turned back. "I've brought a good carcass."

The butcher, a large fleshy man, appeared at the door. He was bald, with a thick fair beard. He looked at Lasgol up and down with unfriendly blue eyes.

"I'm closed for today. You interrupted my dessert."

"I'm sorry..." Lasgol showed him the carcass.

"You haven't prepared it."

"I know," Lasgol pleaded desperately. "But I need coin now."

The butcher nodded as if he knew exactly why.

"No exceptions. I don't do other people's jobs. Game's sold ready prepared, or else not at all."

"Please... sir..."

"Come back tomorrow." The butcher's massive frame turned and shut the door behind him. To leave no doubt about his intentions, he locked it.

Lasgol bent his head and sighed. The storm was already lashing the village, and what was even worse, the wine cellarer was closed by now. He could not get the wine. The freezing winds ruffled his hair and he felt the moisture of the snow on his face. From his wrist he took a leather strip, and pulling his blond hair back he tied it in a queue. That way he would see better. *Never give up*, he said to himself. He half-closed his eyes and looked round the square. There was only one place still open: the inn. Without stopping to think twice, he ran to the door. The wind was blowing so hard he found it difficult to move. The cold penetrated his winter clothes and the snow soaked his face and hair. He thought about the night he would have to spend outside and shook his head.

He opened the door of the inn. At once a bright light and a strong rancid smell struck him in the face. He turned to one side, then after he had recovered he looked round the room. He recognized several customers. Drill, the local drunkard, was arguing with Bart, the innkeeper. At a table three miners were playing cards and downing beers. Apparently they had not noticed that the storm had arrived. A little further back Ulric and his two sons, better known as "the loggers" were finishing their dinner.

"Close the door!" came the cry from a gaunt man with sharp features. Lasgol turned quickly and shut it.

"Much better," the man said. By his clothes he looked like a merchant, and Lasgol had never seen him in the village before. He must be passing through.

"What do you want?" Bart asked him sharply. Lasgol did not flinch. He was used to being greeted like that wherever he went. Although to be honest, the inn-keeper was impressive. He was more than six feet tall, and thickly built. In the village they said he had cracked many skulls in the course of stopping squabbles in his establishment. Not an unlikely thing to happen, given that the Norghanians loved their beer and their brawls. Lasgol could not understand his fellow countrymen's enthusiasm for fighting to see who was left standing at the end, and boasting of being the strongest and most daring. He had been told that in other cultures, like that of Rogdon, fighting was frowned upon. Perhaps one day he would be able to go west, to the Kingdom of Rogdon. He would not mind in the least leaving the village and seeing the world.

"Did Ulf send you?" Drill asked in a voice that left no doubt that he had drunk more than he could hold. That, and the fact that he was leaning on the counter so as not to fall. Lasgol improvised. He knew Ulf was a regular there and that Drill was one of his drinking buddies.

"Yes, sir," he replied, trying to sound sure of himself.

Drill looked at him in surprise. "*Sir?*" he repeated with a smile. "Aren't we well brought-up?" His front teeth were missing; he had lost them in a bar fight, something quite common among the Norghanians. Bad teeth and iron fists.

"What does Ulf want?" the inn-keeper asked.

Lasgol approached the counter and deposited the carcass on it. "He wants a trade-in: the kill for four bottles of Nocean wine." He said this as seriously as a gravedigger, although inside, his stomach was turning.

"So what's Ulf thinking of, then? Here we only take coin for drink, not dead animals!"

"It's a good kill, sir, and very fresh. I've just come down from hunting in the high woods."

"Well then, prepare it and take it to the butcher. It's no use to me as it is."

"He's closed until tomorrow…"

"Then go tomorrow."

"Ulf told me he needs the wine now, sir."

"Is that what that old crosspatch told you? Well, you can tell him we don't give credit or do trade-ins here. The gall of it!"

"Please…" the boy pleaded.

"I said no. And don't get me angry."

Lasgol sighed. He was not going to be lucky tonight.

"I'll give you three coins for it," came a voice behind him.

They all turned toward the voice. Lasgol saw a man sitting at the back, in a corner, in the shadows between the two walls. His back was against the corner, and the shadow made him almost invisible. Lasgol could have sworn he had not been there when he had come in. He squinted, but could barely make out a silhouette. The man wore a hooded cloak that covered his body completely so that he blended into the shadows.

"Thank you… sir…" Lasgol stammered. He had no idea who this mysterious person might be.

"Bring me the carcass," the stranger said.

Lasgol set it on the table in front of him. He noticed that even now, two paces away from him as he was and in the light of the inn, the man was barely discernible within the shadows of the corner.

He gave Lasgol three coins. The hand the boy saw was gloved in leather. The movement was so swift it took place in the blinking of an eye.

"Can you lend me your satchel?"

"Of course, sir."

Lasgol passed it over. The man nodded and said nothing more. Then he turned to the innkeeper and put the three coins on the counter.

"I'll give you three bottles of the Nocean wine Ulf likes," Bart said.

"Only three? For three coins the cellarer gives me six…"

"This wine is better than the cellarer's. Besides, it's more expensive here. I have to make a business of it too."

"But… the difference…"

"Take it or leave it," the inn-keeper said. He knew very well that Lasgol had no choice but to accept whatever he offered.

"Well… all right then…"

"You're not thinking of cheating the lad after all his work hunting this reindeer, are you?" the stranger interrupted.

"Me? Cheat? This is an honest establishment!"

"I'm sure it is, but for three coins you should give him at least four bottles."

"Four?"

"It's enough of a margin," the stranger said. His voice was so cold that it sounded like a threat.

The inn-keeper stretched to his full height. He was about to reply, looking offended, but did not dare. "All right then, four," he said, and turned away. After a moment he came back with the bottles.

"Here, take them and get out of my sight."

"Thank you," Lasgol said. Then he turned to the stranger. "Many thanks, sir." The stranger gave him a slight nod. Lasgol did not know what else to say to him. He did not understand why the stranger had helped him, but he was grateful. Nobody ever helped him in the village. With anything. He turned and left the inn.

He ran through the deserted streets amid the snow and freezing wind. He reached home with the storm at its height. The temperature was still falling, the wind growing fiercer.

"I've brought the drink, sir," he announced.

"High time!" Ulf grumbled, sounding bad-tempered. He was always in a bad mood when he did not have any wine.

"By the gods of the ice! There are only four bottles!"

"It's all I could manage…"

"Late and not enough!"

"But…"

"No buts! Tonight you'll sleep in the shed!"

"It's not fair…"

"Since when does justice dictate things in the frozen north? Here the strong ones rule, not justice."

"Yes, sir." Lasgol lowered his head, knowing that unfortunately

Ulf was right. In the north a strong arm was worth more than being in the right, a lot more.

"To the shed, I said!"

"With the firewood?"

"Yes. You didn't do what I told you to, and a soldier always does what he's told. That way you'll learn your lesson."

Lasgol wanted to complain that he was no soldier and neither were they in the royal army, but he knew it would be useless. Ulf was still living as if he had never left the infantry. Although to be fair, he had never really left it. He had been retired because of age and injuries.

"At your command, sir," Lasgol said resignedly.

"Well, go on then, out. I want to enjoy my wine in peace and quiet."

"May I take a blanket to keep warm?"

"No blankets. I've spent hundreds of nights out in the open without a coat on campaign. That's how you build character, that's how a soldier's forged."

"Yes, sir," Lasgol said sadly. He went out, closing the door behind him.

The storm welcomed him with freezing arms, and he tried to dodge it. He ran to the back of the house, where the wood shed was. It had three flimsy walls, and a roof that was not much stronger. But the frail structure offered some protection against the storm. The freezing wind came through the cracks and the open front, whipping his face and body mercilessly. He stared at the wood he himself had spent half the fall chopping and piling there ready for the harsh winter, and scratched his nose. *I've got to do something about this open wall.*

An idea came to him, and he smiled. He began to move a pile of logs, arranging them to block off the open face of the shed. It took him a while, but he did not mind; he got warmer as he worked. In the end he managed to create a wall of logs which blocked much of the open wall, and huddled behind it. Surrounded by logs on all sides, he wrapped his fur coat around him and settled as comfortably as he could. He even managed to lie down. He had the impression that he had built a tiny wooden house for himself. Although if the wind blew too hard, it would probably collapse on top of him.

The storm continued to lash the house and shed, but the improvised shelter held. He was cold, but he knew he could bear it.

I'm a Norghanian, and for Norghanians the cold is our brother, he told himself to keep up his courage. He gave a snort. He did not deserve to be there, at night, alone, in the midst of a storm and exposed to the cold. He knew that. But such was life: unfair most of the time. He sighed. It was a lesson he had already learnt, cruelly, thanks to what had happened to his father. *Life's unfair, but it's no good lamenting and weeping. You have to keep going. Never give up, and keep going.* He had learnt that from his father. With that thought in his mind, and remembering his father, he fell asleep.

The next morning, as soon as the first ray of sun penetrated the storm, he went into the house and revived the fire. He was frozen to the marrow, and it took him half the morning to feel warm enough. Ulf was sleeping happily after enjoying his wine. His snores were so loud it almost sounded as if another storm was raging in his room. Outside, the real storm went on for two more days. It was the last one of the winter.

Three days later Lasgol accompanied his master, Ulf, to the village. This was in an official capacity. It was the Spring Festival, and Ulf was in charge of the fights. The warrior was resplendent in his dress armor, so that Lasgol barely recognized him. He looked like a true Norghanian hero. He wore the winged helmet of the infantry, a long coat of scaled chain mail which reached to the knees. Over this he wore a long breastplate in vivid red with white diagonal marks which identified him as belonging to the Thunder Army. But what caught Lasgol's attention most was the Shield of Norghana in the very center of the breastplate: the majestic eagle with its wings spread, the ensign of the realm, in shining albino white.

It had taken Ulf an eternity to put on all that armor that morning. He kept it spotless, taking care of it as if it were made of gold, as he did with his precious sword and round shield. Lasgol was carrying the sword and the shield for his master in his role as his servant. Both of them weighed a ton. He wondered how anyone could fight with anything as heavy as that in each hand. He could barely hold them up! Surely they would be exhausted after three blows. On the other hand, seeing the size of Ulf, and others in the village who were equally big, he guessed they could manage a weight which was beyond him.

"Heavy, eh?"

"Yes, very."

32

"To be able to wield sword and shield you have to be a true warrior."

"And very big and strong…"

"Hah! Very true, but there are some who are bigger and stronger than me among our people. One day, when you're a man, you ought to travel to the north of the country, where the cold's so intense it freezes your thoughts. There you'll find men a head taller than I am, and so strong they can fell a tree with three strokes."

Lasgol thought Ulf was exaggerating. Although it was not his usual way. He might grunt and grumble, but he did not exaggerate. Then the boy looked at his face, and the warrior stared back at him with an expression that left no doubt: he was telling the truth.

"Yes, I'd like that," said the boy. In fact he had never even left the county. The furthest he had been was Count Malason's castle, with his father. The Count had invited them because at the time he and the First Ranger were friends. As his father spent most of his time away, Lasgol had not had the chance to travel. And when his father returned, they normally spent time together in the village because he never knew when he would be summoned again, which was usually quite frequently.

"Today's going to be fine," Ulf said as he limped along beside Lasgol. He looked up at the clear sky of the first day of spring with his good eye and repeated: "Today's going to be fine."

Lasgol watched him out of the corner of his eye. He could not tell whether his master was happy because he had already had his morning drink or because they were on their way to the Spring Festival. Probably both. And when Ulf was happy he treated him well, so that Lasgol too was happy that morning. Ulf was going to act as judge in several of the fighting tests. He was the village's leading expert in the art of fighting.

"You should take part. A Norghanian always competes. And particularly a Norghanian soldier."

"Me? Oh, no thanks."

"If you win in one of the tests they might stop treating you as if you had some contagious disease."

"I shouldn't think so, sir. Besides, which of the tests could I compete in?"

Ulf scanned the surroundings. The pens for the different competitions were dotted across the field.

"Let's see. The unarmed combat will be in the center … no, you're too skinny, they'd crush you with a couple of blows. Sword and shield are out, seeing as you can't even lift them up. Hmmm … throwing the short axe? Because we can certainly rule out combat with the two-handed axe."

"I don't know how to throw the axe, sir. I only use it to chop wood."

"A Norghanian is born with an axe under his pillow! I knew how to fight before I could talk!"

"I'm sorry…"

Ulf shook his head and uttered a string of rude words. "There, on the left, is the Archery competition. You know how to use a bow. It's not very worthy, but at least it's a weapon."

"Yes… but I'm not much good…"

"By the Ice Golems! Haven't you got any skill worthy of a Norghanian?"

Lasgol shrugged. "I'm pretty good at climbing."

"Is that a skill? It's no use at all!"

"I'm quick and agile."

"Yes, like a hare! You'll be somebody's dinner!" Ulf gave a snort and let fly another long string of curses.

"We'll leave it at that. Stay beside me and try to learn something."

They found the square swarming with people. All the miners and farmers of the area had come to enjoy the Festival. The celebration of the First Day of Spring was one of the favorite public events of the region. Winters in Norghana were bitterly harsh and the arrival of Spring was a real event. It meant calm after a long period of freezing storms. It was celebrated in all the villages of the realm which were large enough. In the others, the villagers went to the nearest towns where it took place. Nobody was left unable to enjoy the celebration.

Gondar Vollan, the village Chief, came over to them. After him came his assistant Limus Wolff.

"Ulf," said the Chief in greeting. He gave a slight bow.

"Gondar," Ulf replied, and bowed in his turn.

Gondar gave Lasgol a disgusted look.

"And this bastard…" he began.

Ulf stared at him hard out of his one eye. "He has a right."

"… Well, all right then," the Chief conceded. "But you'll have to answer for him." He jabbed his finger at Ulf. "I want no disturbances

34

at the Festival. At the slightest sign of trouble, you take him away from here."

Ulf nodded.

Lasgol bent his head. He knew nobody wanted him there, he knew that everybody wanted him to stay at home, or disappear, himself included: but Ulf would not allow it. As far as Ulf was concerned Lasgol was his servant and had to go with him and always help him, whatever anybody might say, whoever he might upset. Ulf did not care about that and would confront anybody who thought otherwise. Ulf was many things, and not all of them good (as Lasgol knew very well), but he was one thing above all else: he was a man of honor.

Lasgol watched Chief Gondar. He was always impressed by him. He was as big as Ulf but considerably younger. He was said to be a formidable fighter. In his youth he had won the competitions year after year. On being named village chief he stopped competing and went on to become a member of the jury, together with Ulf. They were the two best warriors of the village and (it was rumored) of the whole region.

"This year the competitions are going to be good," Gondar was saying. "There's new blood to fight the veterans."

"That's great," Ulf said. "Last year it was rather bland."

"I know. It almost made me want to compete again, to liven things up a bit."

"A Chief can't compete..."

"I know, I know, envy and that sort of thing..."

Ulf nodded. "Is everything ready? I'm looking forward to a good show."

Gondar's assistant nodded. "Everything's ready," he said in his thin, almost feminine voice. Limus was a small man, with the face of a mouse. Rumor had it that he was extremely clever. He was in charge of all the administration of the village, on behalf of the Chief.

Ulf was looking around. "I see this year you've opened the coffers," he said. The whole square was filled with stands where merchants and farmers sold and bartered their wares. The craft shops too were open and decorated, from the forger to the furrier, taking in the wine cellarer who would make his sales of the year. As always, the inn was at full capacity during the festival. The crowded square was a seething mass of people and conversation. Cries of joy and displays of cheerfulness could be heard everywhere. Lasgol guessed that like good Norghanians, they would have been drinking for a while already. A delicious smell of roasting reached his nose, and his stomach roared with hunger. On one side of the square two whole cows and three pigs were being roasted on open fires. His mouth watered.

"In order to reap, you have to sow" Limus said with a smile. His eyes shone with intelligence. "Last year was a bad one, but this year looks as if it's going to be good. We need to encourage commerce and business. This Festival will set its seal on the year. It's very important."

Ulf looked at Gondar blankly. The Chief shrugged. "Commerce, taxes and all that sort of thing."

"Ah," Ulf replied, still at a loss.

Lasgol looked at them. They were as big and strong as bears: good fighters, but as for intelligence… little Limus had more than both of them put together, several times over. Lasgol smiled at the assistant, who noticed this. He nodded in acknowledgement, although his face showed that Lasgol's presence annoyed him.

"Come on," Gondar said. Anticipation was clear on his face. "Let the competitions start!" They moved away to preside over the first round: Archery, the one Ulf liked the least, and probably Gondar too.

Lasgol very much enjoyed that competition, Helga, the village huntress, had won it three years in a row. But to the annoyance of the village women, who adored her, this year a seventeen-year-old boy beat her with a shot that left everybody open-mouthed. Helga had hit the bull's eye in the finals, and everybody was sure she would win again, but Olstrom's arrow had hit exactly the same spot as her own. It had narrowly avoided splitting hers in half. Ulf and Gondar had to measure and argue for a long time because both shots were practically identical. In the end, Limus decreed that Olstrom's arrow was a hair's-breadth nearer the center than Helga's, and he was crowned champion. The men cheered and took Olstrom away on their shoulders, while the women booed.

The morning sped by amid competitions, songs, beer, food and varied exchanges of views. Lasgol was enjoying himself, to his own surprise. He could see that everyone was looking at him in disapproval, but nobody dared to confront him, as he was with Ulf and Gondar. At the first hour of the afternoon they headed for the axe competition and passed Volgar and his buddies Igor and Sven, who stared at him as if they wanted to strangle him. But Lasgol winked at them with a mocking smile, knowing they could not touch him. The sight of the extreme frustration on the faces of the three bullies alone was enough to make his day worthwhile.

The axe-throwing competition began. It was a skill which had always fascinated Lasgol. He did not understand how they were able to throw an axe so that it spun in the air and hit the target with such force. He had tried it by himself several times, and generally he could not manage to make the edge strike first. The competitors were mostly mature men, but this year they were joined by a couple of younger ones. They took their places ten paces away from a target on a tree, then threw five times each with a short axe. Lasgol wondered at their skill. None of them failed a single throw. He enjoyed the show, as did the hundred spectators who cheered their favorites, consuming large quantities of beer at the same time.

The final was between the veteran Usalf and the surprise of the year: Mistran, one of the younger ones. It was decided in the last throw. Usalf threw his axe with a powerful whiplash of his right arm and hit the center of the target. The spectators broke into applause and cheers. Then there came silence and Mistran (whom Lasgol knew because he was only a year older, even though he did not deign to speak to him any longer) threw with precision, but not enough strength. The axe buried itself three finger-breadths below Usalf's. The crowd broke into cheers for the champion.

Ulf crowned Usalf winner of the competition amid applause and cheers, and Gondar handed him ten coins as a prize. Smiling from ear to ear, Usalf treated everyone to a round of beer.

The festival went on all evening and everyone's spirits soared, because the celebration was turning out to be a success. Finally the moment came for the top two competitions: the fight with axe and shield, then the one with sword-and-shield. The first one, the audience's favorite, was a demonstration of physical power. The colossal blows they hurled at each other left Lasgol wide-eyed. Brute force prevailed here. The axes struck the shields with such violence that the spectators cried out in fear. The winner was Toscas, a miner as big as a troll, and just as strong. He had destroyed the shields and the arms of all his opponents with tremendous blows. Lasgol knew after watching the competition that he would never be able to wield axe and shield. One of those blows would have split him in two.

But the sword-and-shield competition was different. This was Ulf's favorite. Since the elite soldiers such as he had been, did not use the war axe for fighting, but rather, the sword, and its use was hard to master. It required grace, something few men of the north could boast about, or simply lacked altogether as the pile of broken shields attested to.

The first fights resembled those with the axe, as nobody was a master of swordsmanship, but when Nistrom's turn came everything changed radically. Axel Nistrom was a mercenary who had retired to the mountains a couple of years before. Nobody knew much about him; he was very reserved. He lived in a cabin outside the village, away in the woods to the east of the village. One thing however that everybody knew, was that he knew how to weld a sword. He was neither very tall nor very strong, but very athletic. His hair was salt-and-pepper, his eyes small and brown, his nose hooked. His movements were easy and confident. At his waist he always carried a sword and dagger.

"Watch and learn," Ulf said to Lasgol.

The boy had already noticed that this man was not like the others. "Yes, sir," he said.

Nistrom used skill rather than strength. He moved from side to side with swift, smooth movements, dodging his opponents' brutal blows. Not only that, he counterattacked with feline agility when he saw that an opponent had launched a clumsy blow which left his body unprotected or off-balance. What most impressed Lasgol was the way he disarmed his opponents with feints and almost imperceptible twists of his wrist. Swords and shields flew through the air before the astonished eyes of the crowd.

Ulf nodded. "That one certainly knows how to fight."

"He surely does," said Gondar. "I hope he doesn't go wrong... it would cost us several men to bring him down. He's from the south of the realm... and you know what I think of the southerners..."

"Yes, that they're a bunch of snakes," Ulf said with a smile. "That mercenary has been in the army, there's no doubt about that. You'd better keep an eye on him, just in case."

Gondar winked at him. "I'm already on it."

Nistrom won all the fights easily and was proclaimed champion. Gondar and Ulf gave him the title, as well as the prize in coin.

Although everyone looked at him warily as a stranger, Lasgol liked him. He was one of the few who still deigned to greet him when their paths crossed in the village. Perhaps it was that not being local, he had no idea who Lasgol was. Or perhaps he knew and did not care, although this was much less likely. Whatever the case, whenever they met (which was not often) the mercenary spoke to him, and for Lasgol that was the greatest of compliments.

After the fight the music started in the square, and everyone danced and drank until well into the night. After several mugs of beer, Ulf gave Lasgol's shoulder a slap and said: "We'd better go home now. If I have one more you might have to drag me all the way, and I don't think you'd be capable of it."

"Yes, sir," Lasgol said gratefully. He knew there was no way he could drag that giant of a man anywhere.

It took them a while, as in any case Ulf walked slowly with his staff under his arm, and with a couple of beers on top of it he was doubly slow. But finally they arrived home. Lasgol was about to hang Ulf's shield and sword in the armory when once again he had that strange feeling that he was being watched. He stood still in the middle of the room and scanned the shadows. At the far end, wrapped in the dimness, almost invisible, was something, or someone. Ulf noticed nothing.

Lasgol pointed into the shadows. "Sir, be careful!"

The old warrior followed his pointing hand, unable to see what Lasgol was drawing his attention to. "What's the matter?"

"I hope I'm not intruding," a stranger said as he emerged from the shadows, wrapped in a hooded cloak.

Ulf took out a knife with his left hand and held it at the ready. Lasgol, startled, dropped the shield.

"I came to return your hunting bag," the stranger said. Lasgol realized then that it was the stranger from the inn.

"You... but... who are you?" he asked in puzzlement.

"He's a bloody Ranger!" Ulf barked. "That's what he is!"

Chapter 4

The stranger revealed himself and gave a slight bow. "That's right,"

"What the hell are you doing in my house? Get out of here right now!"

"I'm on a Royal Mission. This isn't a courtesy call. You can put your knife away."

Ulf eyed him with his one good eye half-closed. "Your kind gives me goose bumps," he protested, shaking his head. But he put away his weapon.

"That's natural, the Ranger said quietly. He did not seem offended." It happens to a lot of people."

"Always in the shadows," Ulf murmured. "Lurking…"

The Ranger nodded at him. "For coming out into the open and facing the enemies of the kingdom we already have the brave soldiers of the infantry. The Thunder Army?"

Ulf tilted his head back in surprise. "How did you know?"

"You have the look of those who lead the way."

"That's right. 'We are those who clear the way, those who pull down walls, those who take fortresses,'" Ulf said, reciting the motto of the Thunder Army. He relaxed a little. "If you're on an official mission I'll offer you my hospitality. Lasgol, light an oil lamp and set the fire."

"Yes, sir," said the boy. He ran to put Ulf's sword and shield back in the armory, and then do what he had been told.

"Something to drink?" Ulf offered.

"No, we Rangers don't drink. Alcohol clouds the mind, and that leads to mistakes, some of them lethal."

"Bah! Nonsense!"

"The fish dies by its mouth…"

"What a lot of bull that is!"

"It might be, but there's a lot of truth in it," the Ranger said, and showed his hands in their gloves of tanned leather.

Lasgol had already learned that liquor was a bad companion after living with Ulf.

"Well, I've offered you my hospitality. Now, tell me, what do you want?"

The stranger strolled over to Lasgol, who looked at him closely now that he had the chance. He wore a hooded cloak which covered his whole body and reached almost to the floor. It was an unusual dark green, streaked with brown, and blended with the shadows. Wrapped in it he seemed a sinister spirit of nature. Under the hood was a pale face with intense brown eyes. Lasgol could not see his whole face, but he looked young.

The Ranger pointed at the boy. "I've come for him."

Lasgol tilted his head back. "For me?"

"Yes, You've turned fifteen. You're of age."

Ulf swore. "You can't be serious. Him? After what happened to his father? He's just a scrawny weakling!"

The Ranger ignored these protests. "Do you know the *Recruitment?*" he asked Lasgol.

The boy shook his head. It sounded vaguely familiar, but he did not know why. His father must have mentioned it when he was little, but he could not remember.

"Every Spring, the Rangers recruit new youngsters to strengthen our ranks."

"And to replace those who've died," Ulf put in.

The Ranger was silent, his eyes fixed on Ulf. He had not liked either the comment or the interruption. Ulf noticed this, and helped himself to a glass of wine to get out of the way.

The Ranger went on: "The youngsters who are recruited must be fifteen springs old, or else have their fifteenth birthday within the year. To be able to belong to the Rangers, a Royal invitation must be received. These invitations are sent only to relatives of Rangers and to people of special interest to the Crown. I'm a Recruiter, and I've come to give you your invitation as the son of a Royal Ranger."

The Ranger handed him a rolled parchment. It bore the seal of the crown. Lasgol opened it and read:

By Royal Decree and by means of this letter we communicate to Lasgol, son of First Ranger Dakon Eklund, the invitation to join the Corps of the Rangers of Norghana.

With loyalty and bravery the Ranger will care for the Realm and defend the

Crown from her enemies, both internal and external, serving the country with honor and secrecy.

Signed:
His Majesty King Uthar Haugen of Norghana.

He read it and a whirlwind of emotions overwhelmed him. He did not know whether to cry, laugh, get angry, or yell.

"Are you… inviting me to join the Rangers?"

"I'm carrying out my duty as a Recruiter. I've watched you for a while. Physically and emotionally, you're suitable. Therefore it's my duty to hand you the invitation."

"But I don't know how to fight, and I'm not strong…"

"Those aren't the main qualities we look for in a Ranger. Although they're always welcome if we find them in a candidate." He indicated himself. "We Rangers are nimble, swift, slippery, and light. I've assessed you in your environment. You're suitable."

"You've been watching me?" Lasgol asked. He remembered the strange impressions he had been having for some time.

"Yes, for two weeks."

"Evaluating me?"

"That's right."

"But… but I've done nothing more than what I always do."

"It's been enough. In some cases, if there are any doubts, the candidate spends a trial period on arrival. I've seen and witnessed enough: in your case that won't be necessary. Your skills and character comply with the requirements."

"Hah!" snorted Ulf, unable to keep quiet.

"I thought this visit had something to do with my father, not with me."

"In a way it has. You're the son of a Ranger. That's the reason why you're receiving the invitation, because of your father."

"I see…" Lasgol said, and was thoughtful. "What does joining the Rangers involve? There are lots of things my father never told me about."

"That's understandable. Rangers never reveal their secrets." The stranger bent to look into his eyes. "The first thing you need to understand is that the Rangers are the protectors of the crown and of the realm. We're the King's elite group."

Lasgol nodded and listened without blinking.

"For four years you'll train with the Ranger-Instructors at "The Camp", in the north of the realm. In the Secret Valley. At the end of each year your competence will be evaluated. If you're competent you'll be allowed to pass to the next year. If not, you'll be expelled. At the end of the fourth year you'll be granted the title of Ranger and you'll be in the service of the King. In some cases, those who are most outstanding are invited to spend a final year at a place known to only a few, where they'll be trained in advanced and secret matters. Those who graduate become members of the Elite Rangers and serve the King directly. That was what happened to your father, who became First Ranger of the Realm of Norghana."

"Hmmm… it's not going to be easy, is it?"

"It will be tough, both physically and emotionally. Only those with strength of will and courage will end up becoming Rangers of Norghana. And a handful will become Elite Rangers. It's not for everybody…" The tone in which he said this and his gaze seemed to Lasgol to be warning him that it might not be for him.

"It doesn't sound very encouraging."

"The reward is. The Rangers are a brotherhood. We look after our own, we protect each other, you'll always have a home, you'll always have companions and friends. And what's more important, you'll have a purpose in your life: making sure the realm is safe from all kinds of enemy."

There was a silence, which none of the three broke for a long moment. In the end Lasgol spoke. "What do you think about my father, about what happened?"

The Ranger took a step back and crossed his hands behind his back. "What I think has nothing to do with my mission."

"I'd like to know," Lasgol insisted.

"All right then, as you wish. Your father was First Ranger. The best among all the Rangers, and because of that he must be admired. But he committed high treason, and therefore deserved death and our eternal scorn. The king's enemies must be captured and executed. It's one of the main tasks of the Rangers, whether those enemies are external or internal. That your father was one of us is a dishonor we will always carry with shame. A stain on the honor of the corps that can never be erased."

"Does everybody think like you?"

"I can't speak for everyone, but yes, it's the general feeling."

"And tell me, why would I join the Rangers, when they all believe my father was a traitor and a dishonor to the institution?"

The Ranger nodded slowly. "My duty is to hand you the invitation if you're suitable, and so I have. The decision whether to join the Rangers or not is your own."

"They'll all hate me there for being who I am, even more so than here…"

The Ranger nodded. "Yes, that's so. I'm not going to lie to you."

"And in that case, do you recommend me to go?"

The Ranger crossed his arms over his chest. "I can't recommend you one way or the other. It's your decision and yours alone."

Lasgol was not happy with the reply. "Would you go if you were me?"

The Ranger tilted his head to one side and thought for a moment. "No, I wouldn't. Your life there will be more complicated than the one you have now in this village. You're the son of Dakon the traitor… that will always haunt you, and you'll be treated as such. Nobody there will forgive you, and they'll remind you of it pretty harshly."

"I guessed so."

"Your answer to the invitation?" the Ranger asked, with a gaze that expected a decision.

Lasgol pondered. Since what had happened to his father, he hated everything to do with the kingdom, with the crown and particularly with the Rangers. The invitation had taken him by surprise as he certainly had not expected this. He needed some more time to think about it, to make the right decision.

"Can I think about it?"

"Of course. It's a decision that will change your life forever. I'll be in the village for two days more. At dawn on the third I'll be on my way. If you accept, join me outside the village, by the mill across the river. Bring the invitation, signed with your blood."

"Signed with my blood?"

"The old way. A cut in your thumb. You press it on the parchment. Many of the candidates can't read or write."

"Oh, I see. All right then. Thank you."

Lasgol knew how to read and write; his father had insisted that he learn, because it would be very useful when he grew up. In the village, hardly anyone knew how, and those few who could, like the cellarer or the smith, had only a very basic knowledge of it, more to do with numbers and accounts than with reading and writing: just the bare necessities for their businesses. Not even Chief Gondar knew how to read and write, which was why he needed Limus, who was an expert in the arts of writing and accounting.

"If you decide to come, bring only a travel satchel. We Rangers travel light."

Lasgol nodded.

"And don't bring anything of your father's with you. It wouldn't be welcomed."

Lasgol frowned and looked at him blankly. He had nothing of his father's. They had taken everything away, even his clothes.

"I don't have anything that belonged to my father…"

The Ranger gave Ulf a strange look. The old warrior lowered his eyes and looked away at the fire. There was a pause, then the Ranger said:

"Remember, two days. I'll leave with or without you." Without another word he went out of the door.

"Wait," Lasgol called after him. "What's your name?"

The answer came in a whisper. "My name is Daven Omdahl."

Lasgol's gaze was lost in the night after the Ranger's departure.

"Shut the door or else we'll freeze to death!" Ulf snapped out.

Lasgol came back to reality. "Oh yes, right," he said, and rushed to close the door.

"And bolt it. I don't want any more surprise visitors in my house."

Lasgol nodded and did as he was told. He turned around to find Ulf looking at him with his one eye half-closed. He made an unfriendly gesture.

"You're not thinking of going, are you?" he asked menacingly.

"I… I don't know…"

"If you think things are bad for you here, you've no idea what's in line for you there. They'll all have it in for you, from your fellow candidates to your instructors. Every day they see you, your presence will remind them of your father's betrayal and the dishonor of the corps. They'll have no pity for you. Every day will be hell."

"I didn't say I was going…"

"Let me tell you that if you go, it would be the greatest mistake of your life. Here you've got a roof over your head and food on your plate. I might be a big pain, but what you'll find there will be much, much worse."

"I can't stay here forever... I've already turned fifteen. I'll have to find a job..."

"If you want a future, enlist in the army. Do it under another name, leaving your own behind. That's what you need to do. Now that's a future that'll make you into a man. Not the bloody Rangers and their secrets. I've been a soldier all my life and I haven't regretted it a single day."

"But I don't even have what it takes to be a soldier. You remind me of that yourself all the time."

"Not for the Thunder Army or the Snow Army, where the best infantry is. Certainly not for the Invincibles of the Ice, who are the elite of our army. But in the Blizzard Army, the support army, there are archers, light cavalry, messengers. You'd find your place there. You'd make a good messenger."

"But... I'd have to hide who I am..."

"No buts!"

"I'll think about it..."

"There's nothing to think about!" Ulf roared. "By all the snow leopards, you're pig-headed!" He left the kitchen in a huff, still cursing.

That night Lasgol was unable to sleep. Confusing thoughts whirled in his head. He had two days to decide whether to accompany the ranger or not. His heart told him not to go, and his mind agreed. Why suffer unnecessary torture? He had a hard-enough time with Ulf in the village. He had always wanted to leave, but had never had the chance. Little by little, the idea of joining the army began to seem more attractive. At least he would have a future, a profession. If he gave up being who he was, he would have no trouble and they would teach him how to fight like a true Norghanian. Yes, perhaps that would be the best option.

Thoughts kept bombarding him, non-stop. Finally, when he was on the point of falling asleep, a barn owl hooted in a nearby tree. For some reason it reminded him of the strange look the Ranger had given Ulf, and Ulf's reaction, which had been even stranger. He was someone who never looked aside or backed away from anything, even if he was not in the right. Ulf was like a bull, charging blindly.

Hmmm... there's definitely something very weird going on here.

Chapter 5

Lasgol rose with the first light of day. He had barely slept at all, and was very drowsy. He washed with cold water, poured from an earthenware jug into the basin. This woke him up properly. He wiped the sleep from his eyes, then the rest of his body in front of the embers, which he stirred into life again with a fresh log. Ulf liked to get up and find the house warm. He was still asleep. His snores shook the house.

The boy dressed and attended to the household chores, careful not to wake the old man. He cleaned, brought fresh water and wood from outside, prepared breakfast and picked up the clothes Ulf had left strewn everywhere. As they stank, he took them outside and washed them in the stream behind the house. He did not mind doing the housework; when he was a child he used to help Olga. It was like a game they played daily. Now it was a duty, but he did not mind as often this reminded him of better times, when his father and Olga were alive and he was happy.

Once his chores were done, he took his bow and hunting satchel and went to the forest to check the traps. The snow was beginning to melt with the arrival of spring and the woods were waking from their long winter sleep. They would soon be bursting with life.

On his way to the village, on the wooden bridge over the river at the northern entrance, his path crossed with that of Dana and Alvin. They were with their father Oltar, the miller. Lasgol had known Dana and Alvin since they had been five. They were the same age, and they had always been friends. Always, that is, until the fateful day of his father's betrayal. Since then they had not spoken a word to him. He had lost all his friends, and of all of them the loss of these two hurt the most. Alvin had been like a brother. They went everywhere together, they had been inseparable. And Dana… Dana always took his breath away with her gentleness, her beauty… His subconscious betrayed him, and he nodded in greeting as they passed. Both looked the other way.

"How dare you greet us, traitor's blood?" Oltar rebuked him, deeply annoyed.

Lasgol glanced at them for a final moment, hoping for a gesture, a glance, something that resembled sympathy. But all he saw was scorn. He sighed, bent his head and went on, feeling deeply hurt.

When he reached the village he stopped and looked round the square to make sure Volgar and his two buddies were not waiting for him. He took his time, hiding in the shadows of the buildings and watching the square. That was something else he was good at: hiding. He had learned to do it with his father, to hunt and set traps in the woods, and he had now perfected his technique in the village to escape the bullies. The moment he saw a shadow he tried to blend in with it. And if it moved, he followed. It had saved him from quite a few beatings.

Chief Gondar was talking to the blacksmith. He was ordering something for the village, and they seemed to be arguing about the price. Limus was shaking his head. Lasgol did not want them to catch him listening to the conversation and withdrew into the shadows. The smith raised the sword he was forging, the Chief's assistant kept shaking his head and the argument went on. Lasgol guessed that Limus was haggling over the price, while Gondar was applying pressure as chief of the village. In the end the smith seemed to give in, because he went back into his house in a fury. Gondar gave Limus a congratulatory pat on the shoulder. The gaunt assistant almost broke in two.

Lasgol followed Limus to the Chief's house and went to stand behind him as though he were his shadow. "Good morning," he said.

The Chief's assistant turned abruptly round and looked him up and down. He did not bother to hide his displeasure. "What do you want? If it's not official business, I don't want to talk to you."

His rejection did not surprise Lasgol. "It is official," he said.

"Very well, what is it? Quick, I have a lot to do."

"It's about Dakon, my father... about his belongings..."

"You were informed in writing of the Royal Order. All his belongings were confiscated by King Uthar."

"Yes... I know that... I don't mean those..."

Limus frowned. "Then what do you mean?"

"Personal belongings..." Lasgol was trying to get some information. It was just a shot in the dark, but he might be lucky.

"Personal belongings?"

"Yes..."

"Those found in the house were auctioned."

"And was there anything else?" Lasgol asked in desperation.

Limus looked at him curiously. "Anything else? You mean the Rangers' package?"

Lasgol had to hold back his enthusiasm and pleasure at his own success "Yes," he said baldly so that Limus would keep talking. He himself knew nothing about any package.

"It was handed over to you."

"To me?"

"Yes. Well, it was delivered to your house."

Now Lasgol understood. It had been Ulf! He was about to curse the man out loud, but he restrained himself.

"When was this?" he asked, trying to appear calm.

"Hmm, let's see, it arrived about six months after the incident. The Rangers sent his belongings to his closest relative, which is to say you. That's the tradition. They sent it to the Chief, and I delivered it personally as you were no longer living in your old house."

"I see…"

"Is there a problem?"

Lasgol shook his head. "No, none," he lied. It would be no use explaining that he had never received the package. They would not help him. If he wanted to get it back, he would have to do it himself.

"Anything else?" Limus asked impatiently.

"No, nothing. Thank you."

Limus glanced at him, annoyed at the waste of his precious time, and left in a hurry.

Lasgol sighed. Ulf had kept the delivery from him. He did not know why, but he had to find out where it was and see what was in it. Yes, that was what he would do. With determined strides he set off to the inn to check whether Ulf was there. If so, he would have time to search the house.

Suddenly he heard a racket. Through the southern entrance of the square an old man on a cart drawn by two mules was arriving. Both the old man and the cart were unusual and unmistakable. He was dressed entirely in red and green: half in green, half in red, to be exact. He wore studded boots, thick red woolen trousers and a belt. On top he wore a tunic, a coat, gloves and a pointed green woolen hat. You could see him from two leagues away. On the cart was a sign that read: "Raelis' wonderful world", and a dozen bells hung

50

from it. With every turn of the wheels they rang, announcing the arrival of the cart.

Lasgol knew at once who it was: Raelis, the traveling tinsmith. The cart reached the square and stopped by the drinking-trough for the mules. Then it turned into the center of the square. A crowd of people began to gather round this eccentric character. The tinsmith was very popular in the village. He followed a route that began in Norghana, the capital of the kingdom, calling at several mining towns in the region, this one among them, before he headed north. He was a crazy old charlatan, but everybody listened to him with great expectation as he always brought news and rumors both from the realm and from other, more distant regions of Tremia, and his strange wares delighted the younger people. Lasgol knew that both news and wares were of dubious "quality" but his visits were always deeply interesting, given that nothing of any importance ever happened in the village and the closest thing to an exotic object was Gondar's staff of command.

"Gather round, gather round, everyone! Girls and boys, men and women, old people too! Miners and Kings! All of you gather round!" he repeated dramatically as the people began to draw near.

"Come close and admire my valuable merchandise! Form a circle so that you can see better!"

The crowd followed his instructions and formed a wide circle around the tinsmith's cart. The two mules that drew it were used to crowds. Raelis gave them some carrots so they would not become impatient.

"Delicious, aren't they?" he said to the animals, forgetting for a moment where he was. "We like our veggies, don't we, my friends?"

The village people had all gathered around by now, and Lasgol took the opportunity to get closer without being noticed. Raelis was still talking to the two mules; he had completely forgotten where he was and what he was supposed to be doing.

"Raelis, what news of the capital?" asked Bart, the innkeeper.

"Yes, what news have you got for us?" echoed the furrier.

Suddenly Raelis realized he had the whole village around him. He spun round, emerging from his trance.

"Oh, yes! News! Yes, I bring news!"

"Well?" the smith asked impatiently.

"The King has put the Rangers on the alert."

"Why?" Gondar asked.

"It's rumored… they say… that in the north… evil stalks again… that the one who wanted to kill our king and take over the kingdom has returned."

The crowd fell utterly silent. They were all hanging on every word. Lasgol strained his neck to miss nothing. This interested him enormously. It had to do with his father's death.

Raelis went on dramatically: "The freezing north wind whispers of the return of Darthor, Black Lord of the Ice…"

At the mention of the Corrupt Mage's name the villagers cried out, and fear spread among those present like a breeze taking hold.

"Those are just rumors," Gondar pointed out. "Besides, if Darthor reappears, King Uthar will defeat him again."

"Will he be able to?" Raelis said, and paused for some time. All eyes stared at him. "The Black Lord of the Ice is very powerful, supremely dangerous, the incarnation of the corruption of the ice. He almost did the unthinkable: killing the King of Norghana. And he almost succeeded."

"But he didn't. The traitor who helped him was found out and executed. King Uthar and his Ice Mages rejected Darthor."

When Lasgol heard this he felt a stab of intense pain in his chest. The traitor in question was his own father.

"Yes," Raelis went on, "but the crown paid a very high price. Several of the Royal Ice Mages died… Uthar himself was badly wounded and hasn't recovered… some say he'll never recover… And at the same time they say Darthor has become stronger. He won't be denied again."

"Don't try to scare people!" said Ulf, who had limped over from the inn. "If the King's Mages don't stop him, the Generals of the Three Norghanian Armies will."

Raelis smiled. "It's possible, yes… this old wandering tinsmith only tells what he's heard…"

"What other news is there?" Limus asked. Lasgol had the feeling that with this comment Gondar's assistant intended to deflect the conversation.

"Other news … yes there's more…" Raelis scratched his head. "The kingdom of Rogdon has sent emissaries. The powerful realm of the west wants to strengthen their alliance with us, the Kingdom of the North. A peace treaty."

"Surely to face off the growing power of the Noceans in the south," Limus guessed.

"Yes, so say the rumors. In the distant South the Nocean Empire goes on conquering the desert towns and expanding its power. An alliance between West and North is good for dissuading the South from looking in the direction of our territories."

"And the East?" Ulf asked. "What news of the East?"

"In the East, the Five City-States continue their eternal disputes. Too busy to look at the rest of Tremia." Raelis covered his eyes with his hand. "And now that we've visited the news, who wants to see my enchanted wares?"

There was a stir among the crowd, who all of a sudden had forgotten about Darthor, Black Lord of the Ice, in favor of the extravagances Raelis was about to try to sell them, most of which were utterly useless. But not in Lasgol's case. The news had affected him deeply. There was a sorrow in his soul which would barely let him breathe.

My father didn't betray King Uthar and didn't join Darthor. I never believed it and I never will. I don't care what they all say. Nobody knew my father as well as I did, he would never have sold out his lord the King to the Corrupt Mage. Never!

He left the square, deeply troubled, and headed home at a run. Once there he hurried to Ulf's room. He had some time; the old warrior still had to limp all the way home from the square. At the foot of the bed was a huge iron trunk. Here Ulf kept his most precious possessions, such few as he had. Lasgol had never seen what was inside it. Ulf always shut the door to his bedroom whenever he needed to rummage for something in the trunk. Lasgol had always been intrigued by what might be inside. Once he had dared to look through the keyhole, but Ulf's massive body blocked the view of the trunk completely. He could not see anything, and not willing to risk being discovered, he had never tried again.

But today I'm going to look, I really am! If the package is in the house it has to be here. He squatted down and tried to open it. The trunk was locked, as he had feared. *Where would he keep the key?* He searched the old pinewood closet. Nothing, only well-worn clothes, boots, coats and so on. He went to the chest of drawers and searched through it, drawer by drawer. Nothing. He left the room and looked round the kitchen and the common area. He would not hide it there, because

Lasgol was always around, particularly in the kitchen, which Ulf hated to go near.

He looked at his own tiny room at the back of the building, against the back wall. No, he would not hide it there. Then where? Aware that time was running out, he began to search the house desperately. But he could not find the key. Where would a crippled old warrior hide a key? And then an image came to his mind. The boots in the closet! He went back to Ulf's room and opened the closet. There were three kinds of old boots, all of them single apart from the regimental dress boots. In this case both were there. He put his hand in the boot that Ulf would never wear again. And to his surprise, he touched something metallic in the toe: the key!

Smiling broadly, he took out the key in triumph. He fitted it in the keyhole and turned it. The trunk opened with a click. Lasgol glanced behind him: he was still alone. He opened the trunk. The first thing he saw was a Norghanian war-axe. It was of very good quality, probably a gift. He put it aside carefully and searched. The sound of coins made him pull out a leather pouch. When he opened it, his eyes widened in astonishment. There was enough coin there to buy the entire inn. Lasgol thought it must be Ulf's retirement pay, for his services to the crown. He put the pouch back in its place and went on looking.

Finally his hand met something solid and wrapped at the bottom of the trunk. He took it out and as he had guessed, it was a wrapped package tied up with string. It was unopened. On one side someone had written:

Belongings of First Ranger Dakon Eklund.
Village of Skad, Malason County.

There was no doubt about it now. This was the package containing his father's belongings. He cut the strings with his skinning knife and opened it. Inside was a hooded cloak in a strange shade of green streaked with brown, together with a blood-red wooden box with eye-catching gold ornaments. It was certainly striking, unique.

He picked up the cloak and examined it: it was his father's Ranger's Cloak. Wrapped in it were the tunic, pants and gloves he had normally worn. The tunic had a hole the size of an apple in the center of the chest. He held it up against the light and saw that there was a similar hole at the back. He held up the cloak and saw it too had a hole in the same place, as if something had gone through from side to side.

He puzzled over this. Then suddenly, horrified, he realized that this must be what had killed his father. He dropped the clothes with a shaking hand. A shiver ran down his spine and turned his stomach.

He turned his attention to the box. Carefully he lifted the gold bolt that closed it and opened it. His eyes widened in surprise. Inside, protected with hay, grass and linen, completely covered, was something unusual.

An egg!

He could not believe it. He blinked hard in case this was some kind of hallucination, but no, it was an egg, and it was right there in the middle of the box. Carefully he drew aside the hay and linen and picked it up. He held it in the palm of his hand and looked at it. *What are you? Why are you among my father's things? I never saw he had anything like this. It doesn't make sense.*

Sitting on the floor, he studied this odd discovery. It was all white, a white which almost hurt his gaze. He was familiar with the eggs of the birds of that area, and this one resembled none he had ever seen before. It was bigger and heavier than that of any of the birds of the surrounding woods. He was puzzled. *What can it be? Could it be a reptile's? Yes, it could be, something big. Snake, lizard or something of the sort. Or perhaps a huge bird…* He stared at it intensely. *What is this egg? Why did my father keep it? What for?* The more he looked at it the more questions he wanted to ask, the more he wanted to find out about the object.

For a moment he thought it might be a gift his father had been saving for him. He sometimes brought him unusual things he found on his trips. But this was genuinely puzzling. Why an egg? In any case, after so long whatever might be inside must be more than dead. He put it to his ear and concentrated. He could hear nothing. He put both hands around it and felt its temperature. It ought to have been cold, but for some strange reason it was tepid, on the warm side even. *This is really strange! And it makes less sense all the time.*

He was staring at it there on his hand so intensely that for a moment he thought it was going to crack. But no, something even stranger happened. The palm of his hand shone with a flash and the egg stood on its end in the center of it.

It stood up! He almost fell backwards from the shock. *But how?*

He was left staring flabbergasted, not knowing what to do or even think. The egg was perfectly upright on his palm. A word came to his mind. One they all feared, one that was never uttered aloud in the North: *Magic.*

Very carefully he put the egg back in its box, and as he did so he noticed a small inscription inside the lid. He closed his right eye and brought his left close to it to see it better.

The eyes of the realm, the king's protectors, the heart of Norghana.

He recognized the saying. His father had repeated it to him many times. *The eyes of the realm, the king's protectors, the heart of Norghana: The Rangers.*

He did not know what to think of all of it: clothes, egg, everything was too strange. There was a lot more here than met the eye. What he did not doubt in the least was that his father had not betrayed the crown, had not joined the Black Lord of the Ice. In fact he had never really had any doubts, in spite of what everybody, from the King to the village bullies had told him. *I have to find out what all this means. My father didn't betray the king. He didn't plot with Darthor to take over the kingdom. I'm sure of it. There has to be some explanation and I need to find it. I'm going to prove my father was innocent. Clear his name.* And in order to do this, everything pointed in the same direction: The Rangers. *The Rangers are the key to solving the mystery of what happened to my father.*

A sharp squeal followed by a crack made him turn his head. The front door had opened. Ulf was back home. Lasgol hid the box under his tunic and picked up his father's clothes. He stood up, turned around and waited without moving.

Ulf reached the door of his room, and his face changed.

"By the white abyss!" he thundered furiously.

Lasgol went on standing there in front of Ulf's enraged stare, with the air of someone who feels he is in the right.

"How dare you? How?" Ulf yelled.

Lasgol crossed his arms over his chest and half-closed his eyes. "Why didn't you give me my father's things?

"That's none of your business! How dare you search through my things? My things! My room! My trunk!" His face was so red that it looked as though he had caught the sun badly.

"I've just taken what's mine. The package belongs to me."

"That doesn't give you the right to do what you've done!"

"I wouldn't have had to do it if you'd given me what's mine."

Ulf was getting more and more beside himself with fury, so that his face seemed on the point of bursting like a ripe tomato. "You're going to pay dearly for this! You're going to be sleeping in the street for a whole week! Without a coat!"

Lasgol shook his head. "No. That's all over."

"What do you mean, *all over*? Nothing's ever *all over* here! This is my house! You're my servant, you do what I say!"

"Not anymore. I'm leaving."

Ulf's face changed at once. "What do you mean, you're leaving?"

"I've decided to join the Rangers."

"That's stupid!" Ulf protested. But his face, instead of fury, now showed a mixture of rage and concern.

"I've made my decision. Tomorrow I'm leaving with the Ranger Daven."

Ulf was calmer now. "You're making a big mistake."

"Maybe, but it's what it seems to me I have to do."

"Stay with me one more year. At sixteen you can join the army. It's the best option for you. Believe me. I wouldn't lie to you."

"It's not that I don't believe you, it's just not what I want to do."

"If it's because of this incident, we'll forget about it." Ulf's voice was more soothing now. "Tomorrow it'll be just as if it had never happened."

"Thanks. But it's not because of this. I have to follow my own path, and it leads me to joining the Rangers."

"What for? Why? There's only pain and suffering for you with them."

"Because of my father," Lasgol said simply.

Ulf leaned on his staff. In a calm voice he said: "It's precisely because of your father that you shouldn't go. You're going to the place where he's most hated, and just as they hate him, they'll hate you, for being blood of his blood."

"I'll prove them wrong."

Ulf threw his head back. "So that's what it is. Now I understand what you want to do. I understand, you have a good heart, and a brave one, but you're wrong. It's precisely your good heart that's leading you down the wrong track. You want to believe your father's innocent, but let me assure you that he wasn't. King Uthar himself

57

was a witness to his betrayal. Your father was his friend. His guilt is beyond any doubt. You have to accept this for your own good, before it ruins your life."

Lasgol shook his head. "My father was an honorable man who'd never betray the realm. I knew him better than anybody. Nothing will make me change what I think of him. I don't care what they say he did. I know it wasn't like that."

"You're defending the indefensible."

"I know it couldn't have been him. There has to be another explanation."

Ulf gave a deep sigh. "Love blinds us. We're human and we let ourselves be fooled by deep feelings. But those feelings don't allow us to see the truth."

"He'd never do anything like that, never. He was the most honest man in all Norghana."

"Even the bravest and most honorable men might commit unthinkable acts. There are many forces more powerful than courage and honor."

"My father would die before he did anything like that."

"And *die* is what he did."

Lasgol clenched his fists, and his eyes moistened. Ulf's reply had hurt him. But he swallowed hard, and with an effort he managed to hold back his tears.

"And I'm going to clear his name."

Lasgol passed Ulf as he left the room. He stopped beside him, looked at him one last time and said: "Thank you for giving me shelter, for everything. I'll never forget it."

This time it was Ulf's one eye that moistened. He nodded slowly, accepting defeat. "Good luck, Lasgol."

"Thanks Ulf, I'm going to need it."

Chapter 6

With the first light of dawn, Lasgol was up and ready to leave. He shouldered his traveling bag, took his short bow and quiver and left the room. As he went through the common area, all was silent. Ulf was asleep in his room, although strangely enough this morning he was not snoring.

Lasgol sighed and went to the door. Hanging from the bar that bolted it he found a small leather pouch. Inside it were ten coins. He felt a tightening in his chest and his eyes moistened.

"Thank you…" he said. But Ulf did not reply.

He left the cabin and with a bitter-sweet feeling in his heart went to his meeting with the Ranger Daven. The morning breeze was cool and smelled of spring: of nature and life. The sky was clear; it was going to be a nice day. This cheered him. He sighed and relaxed. A tiny smile came to his face. He had made his decision: he was going to join the Rangers. A difficult decision, but one he felt was right.

At the riverside he set off across the old wooden bridge. He could not see Daven yet. The mill was further on, round a bend in the path, but he would soon reach it. He looked back one last time and saw his father's old house in the distance, and the village square a little beyond. Many mixed feelings came over him. Good memories of his childhood mixed with horrible experiences during the last few years. He sighed again. Today he was starting on a new path, leaving all that behind. *Let's hope my new life, however hard it may turn out to be, helps me reach my destiny, and may that path, be a good one.* He glanced up at the sun and felt its warmth on his face. *Yes, I'll make it one way or another. I promise you that, Father.*

He went on. When he was halfway across the bridge he noticed someone lying face down at the far end. Fearing he might be hurt, Lasgol hastened to help. When he was only a step away, the body moved and suddenly got quickly to its feet. He stopped in surprise.

"Where do you think you're going, you traitor?" came Volgar's unpleasant voice. There was a malicious grin on his bully's face.

Lasgol was so startled that he jumped backwards. What was Volgar doing there? The bridge was not very wide, and the other boy was holding his arms wide to block his way, shaking his head at the same time. This looked bad, and Lasgol started to feel worried.

He tensed. "Let me through," he said.

"No way. You're not going anywhere. You're going to pay for the other day at the square. Nobody makes a fool of me in front of everyone else," and he thumped his fist against the open palm of his other hand. Lasgol knew very well what that meant. He was in for a beating.

He turned to escape the way he had come, and found Igor and Sven crouching behind him. *It's a trap!* His stomach took a leap and all the muscles in his body tensed into alertness. He had been so sunk in his own thoughts he had not even realized the ambush they had set for him. He had to think of some way of getting out of there, fast.

Volgar stepped forward. Lasgol saw him coming and had only a moment to decide whether to try to dodge him or run towards his buddies. He decided on the first. He moved sideways quickly, at the same time propelling himself forward, eluding Volgar's attempt to grasp him. For a moment he thought he was free. But suddenly the bully's hand closed on his satchel and pulled hard backwards. Lasgol was about to let go of the satchel, but inside it was his father's box with the egg. He could not let it fall into the hands of those brutes. He decided to fight for it. He spun around and tugged the satchel hard to free it from Volgar's iron grip.

It was a mistake. Lasgol did not have anywhere near enough strength to free it from the big boy's grip. While he was still trying desperately, tugging with all his might, Igor and Sven jumped on him. Suddenly he felt the weight of both on his body, and he fell. He writhed with all his might, but could not manage to get free. They were on top of him and their dead weight alone was too much for him. He was pinned to the ground.

"You're mine, traitor!" Volgar cried in triumph. He dropped the satchel and got down on one knee to hit him more comfortably.

The first blow caught Lasgol full in his right eye. He felt a sharp pain and thought he would end up one-eyed, like Ulf. The second blow was on his nose, which burst with pain. Blood began to stream from it. There were tears in his eyes, and now everything in his vision was blurred.

"You're going to get the beating of your life!"

Volgar went on hammering his face with his enormous fists. The blows hurt so much that Lasgol thought they must be hitting him with a club. But he only had one thing in mind: he had to escape somehow or else Daven would leave without him. And if that happened, he would never be able to join the Rangers and everything would be over. That thought, that anxiety, made the following blows feel muffled.

He tried to wriggle out of Igor and Sven's grasp, but they had him tight and did not let go. They were not even trying to hit him; their job was to keep him trapped, and they were doing it perfectly. Now Volgar was hitting his body to stop him moving.

"This is what we do to traitors in Norghana!"

The blows left him breathless, and he began to cough and shake uncontrollably. It seemed to him that everything was lost. Daven would leave without him. He could not let him do that, he had to reach him. With a tremendous effort he turned over under the weight of his captors and began to crawl away, with them on top.

"Pin him down! Don't let him escape!" Volgar shouted.

Igor and Sven used all their strength to keep him held down. But Lasgol was crawling to the end of the bridge with all his might. *I have to reach the Ranger.* It was all he had in his mind amid the terrible pain he was feeling.

"Stop!" came Volgar's cry of rage as he flung himself onto him.

He took the final blow in the back of the neck. He felt the impact, the pain, and then darkness took him.

*

He came to, utterly dizzy. He tried to stand, but a sharp pain through his entire body prevented him. He was lying on the bridge. He peered through his swollen eye and saw that nobody was in sight. He finally managed to locate the sun, and by its position in the sky he guessed it was almost noon.

"No..." he began, but the pain in his broken lip forced him to stop.

Anxiety came over him. It was too late! Daven would have left without him! He would not be able to join the Rangers, he would never be able to find out the truth about his father or clear his name.

He felt so miserable he almost threw up.

What am I going to do now? he thought desperately. He tried to stand up again, but could not. The pain was too intense and he was still very dizzy. Volgar had carried out his promise, he had given him the beating of his life. Carefully he felt his legs and arms. They hurt, but nothing was broken. Then he felt his body, and the pain was unbearable. *I might have a broken rib. I won't know till I manage to stand up.* He touched his face with enormous care. It was swollen and bloody. *My nose doesn't seem broken. I've been lucky.* He groaned with pain.

Very slowly, he dragged himself to the river and washed his wounds. The coolness of the water felt good, and his dizziness passed. But when he washed his wounds the pain became more intense. It smarted, and he howled. Very carefully, groaning as he did so, he managed to wash. Finally he got to his feet. He breathed deeply, in and out, until he was sure he had no broken ribs. *I must be made of clay, I can absorb any number of blows and still recover. That's a useful kind of skill very few people have,* he thought with a grin. But as he did so his lip split again.

Suddenly he remembered his satchel. He searched around desperately and saw it beside the bridge, almost in the water. He opened it fearfully to see if the box was there. It was! Inside it the egg was still intact, as if nothing had happened to it: not even a scratch. He felt enormous relief. He had no idea what that egg was or why his father had had it, but it seemed to him that he had to protect it. Or maybe it was because it was an egg that it stirred those feelings in him. *Whatever it is,* he consoled himself, *I must keep it safe. And if I'm being a fool: well, it won't be for the first time, or the last.*

He put it back in the satchel. It seemed that Volgar and his two buddies had only had one thing in mind: to give him a tremendous beating. Satisfied with that, they had left the satchel alone. Or maybe they thought they had killed him and panicked. Yes, that was probably it, they had got scared and run away, the cowards.

He waited a little longer until he was in a fit state to walk. He knew there was nothing to be done, that the Ranger would have left hours before, but he set off, limping, to the meeting-point. *At least nobody'll be able to say I didn't do everything I could to get here.* With his body battered, feeling intense pain at every step, he went on with his gaze fixed ahead.

When he reached the mill he stopped in his tracks, open-mouthed.

Daven was still there!

He found him stroking a beautiful gray horse. The Ranger looked hard at Lasgol and shook his head.

"You're rather late. That's a very bad habit."

Lasgol wanted to explain everything that had happened, but all that came out of his mouth was: "I'm sorry, sir."

"You shouldn't stop to fight when you have an important appointment," Daven said with a touch of irony.

Lasgol was paralyzed. "Did you see it?"

"I'm a Ranger. Nothing within a league escapes my sight."

"But... then... why...?"

"Why should I?"

"They were three of them... against me... bigger..."

"Yes, big and stupid. You should've been able to get rid of them."

Lasgol shook his head. He could not believe Daven had not helped him.

"But I'm an apprentice..."

Daven shook his head. "Not yet. And it's called an *initiate*." His voice took on an official tone. "Have you decided to join the Rangers?" he asked. There was a shade of disapproval in his voice, as if that was not what he wanted.

Lasgol who had given up that option, was surprised.

"Can I still do that?"

The Recruiter nodded. "I don't recommend it, but you can, you have a legal right to. Think about it carefully. What happened today will happen again, and it'll be worse there ... are you sure?"

Lasgol thought for a moment. His body hurt like fury, he could not see properly and he could not hear properly from one ear, but he would go on, no matter how great the obstacle.

"Yes, sir," he said, trying to sound as sure and dignified as possible. "And don't worry, I'm made of clay."

Daven raised his eyebrows and bent his head. "Made of clay?"

"Just saying, sir."

The Ranger eyed him with amusement. "Did you bring the invitation signed with your blood?"

Lasgol handed it to him. "Yes, sir, here it is."

"Everything's in order, then," the Ranger said when he had

inspected it. "Last chance to change your mind."

"I want to be a Ranger," Lasgol said firmly.

Daven gave a deep sigh. "Very well, but don't say I didn't warn you." He put the invitation away in his tunic and gave Lasgol a nod.

The boy nodded in turn and almost instantly, he felt better. He had signed the parchment and given it to the Ranger. It was done. He concealed a sigh of relief so that Daven would not notice.

"Now if you want, we can go after those three bullies and settle the score."

Lasgol looked at him in surprise. "Really?"

Daven nodded. "The Rangers take care of their own, and now you're one of our own."

"But before that ..."

"Before that I wanted to see how you behaved in a demanding situation. And you've passed the last test. It takes a lot of courage to do what you did. Do you want us to chase them?" His face had turned hard and grim.

Lasgol looked into his eyes. He was not joking. At a word from him, the Ranger would hunt them down. And Rangers were extraordinary man-hunters.

"What'll you do to them?"

He indicated Lasgol's face and body. "Punish them according to their crime." His tone was cold and cutting.

Lasgol felt a twinge of fear. "No. Don't do anything to them."

"Are you sure? Most people in your place would want justice. You're within your rights."

Lasgol shook his head. "Let them go. I want to look to the future and leave all this behind."

Daven's eye lingered on him for a moment, as though weighing him up. At last he nodded.

"Very well. Let it be so," he said, as though giving judgment.

"Thank you."

The Ranger searched in his saddlebags and gave him a small ceramic jar covered with linen, and a leather pouch.

"It's an ointment that'll prevent your wounds from getting infected. In the pouch is the powder of several medicinal roots which will make the wounds heal better. Spread it on once you've applied the ointment."

Lasgol was speechless. He felt less and less able to fathom the

Ranger. First he had not helped him, and now not only was he offering to give the three bullies what they deserved, but was also giving him medicines. He shrugged and applied the ointment and powder as he had been instructed.

When he had finished, the Ranger put them away. "Can you ride?" he asked.

"Yes, sir. My father taught me. But I'm not very good, I haven't been able to practice these last few years…" He shrugged apologetically. What he really meant was *not at all*, because he had not been near a horse for the last three years. Soldiers like Ulf did not have horses. Horses in Norghana were a privilege and cost a great deal of coin.

"It doesn't matter. What matters is that you can ride. Otherwise you'd have had to ride with me, and that would've delayed us too much." He put his fingers to his mouth and whistled. A white pony, long-haired and robustly-built, came to his call.

"This one's for you," the Ranger said, indicating the pony of the snows.

"For me?"

"Yes. A Ranger is nothing without his mount."

This surprised Lasgol. His father always rode Flyer, who was a magnificent black stallion, from Rogdon, from the land of horses, but Lasgol had never imagined that all Rangers had horses.

"Oh. All right then, sir." He approached the pony and stroked its neck and mane. The pony replied by shaking its head and giving a snort. Norghanian Ponies were large and very strong.

"Now he's your responsibility. There's no greater shame for a Ranger than to lose his mount. Remember that."

"Yes, sir. Absolutely." For the first time in a long time the boy was happy. He had a horse! He could not have been happier. The beating was completely forgotten. He stroked the horse's ear and murmured into it. The more he looked at it, the more impressive and beautiful the robust pony seemed to him.

"You need to give him a name."

"Whatever I like?"

"Yes. So that he recognizes you."

Lasgol thought about it for a long time and finally decided.

"I'm going to call him Trotter."

"That's a nice name."

"Thanks," said Lasgol, and stroked the horse. "You like your name, Trotter?"

The pony nodded and licked his hair. Lasgol was so happy he was on the point of breaking into a dance, except that his body was in such a state that he would have fallen on his face.

"On we go, then. We have a long journey ahead of us."

"Where are we going?"

"North. To the Camp."

"The Camp? In the village they say nobody knows where it is. Except the Rangers, of course."

"It's because nobody can reach it. It's in the Secret Valley."

"Nobody, sir?"

"Nobody who isn't a Ranger."

"And where is this Secret Valley?"

"If I told you it wouldn't be a secret any longer," Daven said.

"Yes... of course...I...."

The Ranger glanced at him in annoyance. "Do you always ask so many questions?"

"Oh ... I'm sorry, sir."

"Ride behind me, watch what I do and learn. Ask only when it's absolutely necessary. I'm not one for chit-chat."

"Yes, sir. Sorry."

"The journey will be hard. I trust you'll be up to it and that I haven't made a mistake about you."

"Oh, I will be," Lasgol assured him, trying to hide his own doubts.

"Remember, you're coming of your own accord, against my advice. Don't forget that."

"I won't do that, sir..." The warning hurt him. But it would not make him change his mind.

Daven gave him a nod and spurred his horse. Lasgol did the same, and they set off. The journey, just as Daven had told him, was long and tough, at least for Lasgol. For Daven it seemed to be no more than a stroll in the woods of the realm. For more than two weeks they rode with barely any rest. They only stopped when the horses were too tired to go on without putting their health at risk. They barely slept, and Lasgol had almost slid off his horse when he had fallen asleep on his pony. For some reason the Ranger did not follow the paths of the kingdom, choosing instead to penetrate into thick forests and climb steep hills, then descend into uninhabited plains.

Lasgol had the feeling that either the Ranger did not like people and paths, or he was trying to dissuade him before they even reached the Rangers' fortress. Still, no matter how tired he was, no matter how much his backside hurt, and no matter how hungry and thirsty he was, he did not once ask the Ranger to slow his pace, much less stop to rest. Every once in a while Daven would turn to check that he was still on the pony, then carry on.

There was no conversation from the second day on. Lasgol was too tired even to speak. When they rested, he concentrated on gulping down the serving Daven gave him from the supplies they carried. The truth is that the serving was very meager. If that was all the Rangers ate, he had no idea how they survived in the mountains. The physical demands were much greater than could be made up for with so little food. The only good thing about the journey was the way his wounds healed. The ointment and powder he applied every three days had worked wonders; the wounds had disappeared without leaving any trace.

Lasgol bore the pace as best he could, and on the fifteenth day Daven stopped at the top of a hill. He pointed downwards. Lasgol went to stand beside him and looked. A wide, winding river of gray water flowed towards the south-east. In a bend three boats were moored. The first two were assault boats, light but with little draft. The third was a cargo boat. What were they doing there?

"We're here," Daven announced, and at the sound of his voice Lasgol jumped.

He meant to ask: where? But he thought better of it and kept silent. Daven waited for a moment for the question, and when it never came he nodded and his lip twitched slightly. He nodded to Lasgol to follow him and carefully started down the hill toward the boats.

As they approached, Lasgol began to understand what was going on there. In front of the two lightly-built ships was a large group of people, about a hundred. In front of the cargo boat were their horses, enclosed in a pen. They headed for this. Here Daven stopped his mount and greeted several men who were looking after the horses. They were all dressed as he was, with those same unusual hooded cloaks which covered them from head to feet. They were armed with bows, and Lasgol guessed they would be carrying knives under the cloaks. In fact they looked sinister... secret... they were Rangers.

"You're here at last, then, Daven," said one of the men.

"The boy had doubts," he said with a nod towards Lasgol. "I had to wait till he made his decision."

"Is it him?"

Daven nodded. "Get down, Lasgol," he said.

The boy did as he was told. He took hold of Trotter's reins.

The man came up to Lasgol and without a word took the pony's reins. Then he spat at the boy's feet. Shocked, Lasgol drew back.

"The traitor's son," said a second Ranger. He too spat at Lasgol's feet.

Trotter snorted and shook his head, as if he were not happy. The Ranger took him away with the other horses.

"You'd better go with the rest of the candidates," Daven said to Lasgol. Then he dismounted and gave his horse to a third Ranger, who gave him a dark look as he took the reins. "Cursed traitor's blood," he muttered under his breath.

Lasgol took a deep breath. And started to walk away.

"Second boat," another Ranger said to him. "The other one's full, traitor. Or you can turn back. You're still in time."

Lasgol did not answer or turn around. He kept going with his eyes fixed on the ground. In the group of candidates were fifty or so boys and girls, all of his own age. There were more boys than girls. Half a dozen Rangers were watching them without a word. When Lasgol reached them, one stared at him from head to foot.

He pointed to the group. "Wait with the others."

Lasgol nodded and went over to the group. He was not at all sure what to do or say, and since he was who he was, he decided it would be best not to say anything. He moved a little aside and stood watching how the other youngsters interacted. He soon identified the bullies, which was not too difficult, since most of the others were neither particularly tall nor particularly big. This surprised him, as he had imagined they would all be the size of Gondar or Ulf. It seemed after all that it was true that the Rangers looked for other qualities. He also identified the ones from noble families. They were easily spotted thanks to the expensive clothes they wore and the way they strutted. It was also clear which ones belonged to poor families, like himself. With the girls it was harder to tell who belonged to which class.

"What a varied collective we are, aren't we?" came a voice to his left.

Lasgol turned and saw a boy, standing apart like himself, also watching the group. He was very thin, and shorter than he was himself. In fact he looked quite puny, particularly for someone who wanted to be a Ranger.

"Varied collective?"

"A group of very different people," the other replied with a smile.

"Oh. Well, yes."

The boy held out his hand. "My name's Egil."

"Mine's Lasgol."

"It's an honor and a privilege to make your acquaintance in such an illustrious setting."

"Hmmm… same here… Do you always speak in such a flowery way?"

"Flowery? Hah, I suppose I do. I have a great weakness for reading and the arts, and that tends to influence the way I express myself in conversation." He showed Lasgol the book he was carrying

"I see…" Lasgol was finding it harder and harder to understand how this boy could be there.

"I believe we're soon to embark and set out toward our glorious destiny as Rangers, ascending the River of No Return to the Secret Valley."

"River of no Return?"

"Sounds ominous, doesn't it? I consulted several maps of the realm before I set out and there's no reference to its source. The only thing they say is that it ends in the sea of ice. I also consulted several tomes concerning Norghana's geography, and there isn't a single reference." He raised one eyebrow suspiciously.

Lasgol shook his head. "Wait, you prepared for the journey? Are you sure you want to join the Rangers?"

Egil smiled at him. "Surprising, isn't it? It's a long story, one for some other, more propitious occasion. Or perhaps I'm a Shifter…."

Lasgol looked blank at this. "A Shifter?"

"A shape-shifter."

"I'm sorry, I don't know what you're talking about."

"Where have you been? Haven't you heard about the metamorphics?"

Lasgol shook his head.

"A person or being, who can change shape, or adopt that of someone else, or that of an animal, without it being detectable."

"It rings a bell, yes…"

"They're part of our mythology. There are many examples of powerful creatures adopting the shape of mere mortals. The Shifters are part of our culture. Myth or reality, they exist in the stories our grandparents tell their grandchildren around the fire."

Lasgol put his hand to his chin. "Ah… like when the Gods of Ice turn into Snow Panthers to visit men?"

"Exactly."

Lasgol nodded. "That much I had heard about."

"Well, I'm a Shifter," Egil said with a smile. "At the moment in my lesser form, but later on I'll turn into a Giant of the Ice." He began to laugh.

Lasgol could not help himself and joined in the laughter.

"Do you believe Shifters exist?" he asked after a moment.

Egil nodded. "To be honest, basing my view on myth, folklore, and the tomes I've been able to consult on the subject, I'd say it's very likely that they do."

"And they can't be detected?"

"So it's said. Not by natural means. As long as they keep the shape they've adopted for the human eye, they're impossible to tell apart. I've read that they're capable of deceiving animals, even bloodhounds, so that it's extremely difficult to identify them."

"What kind of creature are they?"

"That's a good question. Some people say they're beings with powers, others that they're just men with inexplicable skills. But of course those are just guesses, there's no proof. It's a subject that fascinates me."

"Yeah, I can see that."

"When I return to my natural form, you'll see," Egil said, and winked.

Lasgol laughed and nodded.

"Whichever way, I believe my presence will add a note of color to the candidates, in clear contrast to certain others, like for example that big fellow over there." He nodded towards a group nearby.

"Move over, you idiot!" said the bully, massively-built, as he pushed another boy who looked much weaker. The boy was thrown backwards and brought down several other people with him. One of them fell against the group who were standing beside Lasgol and Egil. A blonde girl bent down to help the boy who had crashed into them. Then she turned to the bully.

"Hey, you!" she shouted, and started to walk towards him.

Lasgol watched her. What was she going to do? She was surely not going to...

The girl went to stand in front of the bully and she faced up to him. Her blue eyes were fixed on his gray ones. She was tall and wiry, with long blonde hair which she wore in several braids. Her brow was furrowed and her face grim, so that he could not tell whether she was pretty or not. But the bully was at least a hand-span taller, and two hand-spans wider. This girl was about to get into trouble.

"That wasn't a very nice thing to do," she said with her arms akimbo.

"And what do you care?" he asked disdainfully.

"I decide what matters to me or not."

He took on a superior air. "This is no place for a girl."

Her expression changed to one of disgust. "That's what you think, you oaf!"

He frowned. "Oaf? If you don't shut your trap you're going to learn a lesson."

"Well, you're not going to make me shut it. My name's Ingrid, and I say what I want, where I want."

This was going to turn nasty very soon. Lasgol stepped forward to help the girl.

"You shouldn't be among the candidates. What are you doing here?" the bully said. He jabbed the girl's chest twice. There was no third time.

"This," Ingrid said, and launched a straight right-hander to his jaw. The bully fell backwards like a felled tree. He did not get up again.

Lasgol was frozen halfway. There were cries of surprise, then silence fell among those who were watching the confrontation. Ingrid turned and went back to the group beside Lasgol, who was gaping at her with his mouth wide open, unable to take his eyes from her.

"You want to say something too?" she asked him threateningly when she realized he was staring at her. She readied her arm for another punch.

"No! Nothing! I wasn't going to say anything," he hastened to say. He made soothing gestures.

"That's what I thought," she said, and lowered her arm.

Lasgol watched her, half-terrified, half-delighted. At that moment the order came for the Rangers to embark.

Egil moved to stand beside Lasgol and whispered in his ear: "I think it would be wise for us to befriend this damsel."

Lasgol looked at him and nodded. He had the clear feeling that they would be needing all the help they could find, and rather more than that.

Chapter 7

They embarked. Lasgol smiled as he studied the boat with avid eyes. It was the first time he had ever set foot on one. He had seen them on the coast, but from a distance. He had never had the chance to look at them in detail, and they had always fascinated him. He had grown up in the forest and could not understand how those fragile single-sailed structures of wood were capable of navigating rivers, still less the icy sea.

Egil, beside him, must have read his expression. "Is this the first time you've seen an assault craft?"

Lasgol nodded. Judging by the expressions on the faces of many of the candidates who were crowded together by the mast, glancing around the boat with fearful eyes, he was not the only one.

"They're fast, even though they're rather fragile, and they can't carry a lot of cargo. They're the ones the incursion troops prefer. I'd guess they're used in secret missions, because they're fast and silent."

Lasgol glanced around. "I don't understand how it can carry all of us and not sink. There are forty or so of us candidates, plus a dozen Rangers."

Egil chuckled. "Don't worry, it won't sink. I'd guess it could hold double the load safely."

"Are you serious?"

"Yes. I'm always serious. Humor isn't one of my fortes, you'll come to realize that." He smiled and shrugged. "At sea things would be very different. Waves and storms might sink it. But here on a river we're safe, I can assure you. You can rest easy."

"But... the water almost comes up to the edge."

"It's called the gunwale, in maritime terminology. The front part where the Rangers are standing is the prow. The head of that beastly sea-snake you can see is the figurehead. It's the custom to decorate these vessels with the heads of abominable beasts. Supposedly they scare the enemy. The rear part" (he pointed to the back) "is the stern. As you can see it's decorated too, in this case with the snake's tail. But the really important thing about that section is that it's where the helm that steers the boat is."

"Do you know everything?" Lasgol asked in surprise.

"Everything? Of course not. I read a lot and I learn as much as I can. There's nothing worse than a mind full of air." He chuckled, but Lasgol did not see the joke. "You see? What did I tell you about my sense of humor?"

"I'll get used to it," Lasgol replied, and winked. Egil was strange, but he liked him. He did not seem to bear any malice and he knew a great deal. Lasgol took a good look at him. Even though he might deny it, he probably knew everything.

"Vessels of this kind are clinker-built, and very stable because they have a draft of only eighteen inches."

Lasgol stared at him blankly.

Egil smiled. "Let me explain: the bottom of the boat is built with overlapping planks, but she only sits in the water about a foot and a half deep. That allows her to be very fast. For the same reason she can't carry much of a load. Imagine a nutshell in a puddle. It's very similar. If you blow on it the nutshell moves, but if you put a pebble in it, it sinks."

"And why's it so narrow? Wouldn't it be better if it were wider? So it would be more stable, I mean....."

"Assault boats of this particular type are about sixty-five feet long and nine wide, with only eighteen inches draft. In other words they're long and narrow and they don't sink low in the water, which makes them very fast. But you needn't worry, she won't sink, I promise you."

At that moment one of the Rangers turned to address the candidates.

"Your attention, everybody!" he said in a deep, powerful voice. He was middle-aged, and his face showed traces of many battles.

Conversation stopped at once.

"I'm Captain Astol. This single-sailed beauty you're on is my ship. There's none better, nor faster, in all Norghana. You'll respect her as you would your own mother, and me as if I were your own father, while you're on board. Anybody who fails to respect this simple rule will end up stark naked in the river. It's as simple as that. Do you understand?"

There was a timid murmur of "ayes", together with nods, but nobody dared speak out loud.

"I'll take that as a reply. Time to leave. Those of the Fourth,

Third and Second years have already left. As is the tradition those of the First year will be the last to leave and the last to arrive. Listen carefully to me, because I'm not going to repeat myself. Sit down in pairs. Twenty pairs on each side."

The candidates looked at each other, not knowing who to pair up with. Lasgol and Egil exchanged glances, nodded and were the first to sit on the bench beside them.

"Come on, we haven't got all day!"

The candidates began pairing up as best they could, and went on sitting down on the benches until they were all seated.

"At last!" the Captain protested. "Now each pair will take an oar. Off you go!"

Everybody hastened to obey.

"Nobody is to start rowing until I give the order. Sail!" he called out, and two of the Rangers hoisted the sail.

Lasgol bent his head and whispered to Egil: "Are we going to row?"

Egil glanced up at the sail and nodded. "We're going up-river and there's no wind. We'll have to row."

Lasgol was puzzled. He had imagined the wind would carry them. But no. It was not going to be a relaxed journey; they would have to work hard.

The Rangers took their places along the boat and explained how two people needed to hold the oars between them and synchronize their movements, following the rhythm that the Captain would set. It did not look too complicated, and Lasgol smiled at Egil. But the smile was wiped from his face as soon as the Captain gave the order to row. The result was utter chaos. Everyone rowed at a different rhythm, several nearly lost their oars and one of the candidates, a redheaded girl with a face full of freckles, fell backwards off her bench. Her partner tried to help her stand up, but the oar, borne by the current, hit them and knocked them over again. It was almost comical, except for the terrified face of the redhead as she tried to stand up, stepping on her partner and holding on as best she could to the oar, which seemed possessed and moved in every direction.

"By all the sea snakes!" cried Astol, waving his arms.

The candidates tried to master their oars and row as one, but it was a disaster. The Captain's cries almost deafened them all.

"You take the far end," Egil muttered in his ear. "The inertia is

75

greater thanks to the lever effect, and it requires greater strength."

Lasgol did not fully understand, but he nodded. "All right," he said. They switched places so that Egil was sitting by the gunwale and Lasgol by the aisle, holding the end of the oar.

They tried, with some difficulty, to row as one. But if managing the long oar was complicated to begin with, keeping the same pace as the pair in front of them was impossible. Particularly because in front of Egil was a hulk of a boy more than six feet tall, with shoulders as wide as those of Lasgol and Egil put together. He rowed as if he were in a competition and with every stroke lifted his partner into the air. He meanwhile was clinging on to the oar for dear life,

Egil patted his shoulder to call his attention.

"Aaah!" the giant cried out in terror and flung up his arms. As he let go of the oar his partner was thrown off and rolled along the aisle as far as the mast.

The giant turned half-way around. He had the face of a true Norghanian warrior: square rocky jaw, straight blond hair down to his shoulders. His appearance alone was enough to spread fear. Lasgol thought he was going to snap back angrily at little Egil for startling him, and he prepared to come to his defense. But in the eyes of the giant, blue as the sea, was not anger but something very different: fear.

"We're not in a royal competition, my lord oarsman," Egil said with a smile.

Seeing the smile, the giant's eyes brightened and the fear vanished from them. His rough face softened.

"Am I going too fast?" he asked mildly. "It's just that I don't know what I'm doing. I grew up in a farm, with cows and lambs. I don't know anything about boats or oars."

"Same as me," Lasgol replied, trying to calm the giant. "I've got no idea either."

His partner sat down on the bench again and glared at him.

"I'm sorry... I didn't realize... I didn't want to... I got scared..."

"Just take a bit more care, or else you'll kill me,"

"I'm sorry..."

"Count to five and then row," Egil said. "You'll see how much better things go."

"Oh, all right then, we'll try."

At once things improved. The giant's partner was so grateful that he nodded to Egil in acknowledgement. It took them half the morning to learn how to row with a minimum level of skill to keep the boat on a stable course. Astol ended up losing his voice. The Rangers offered their help and advice to the inexperienced rowers, and thanks to them they gradually got the hang of it.

The three boats followed the river upstream. They advanced slowly, and the Captain's cries fell on the rowers like a winter storm. Luckily the weather was favorable, the breeze mild and the sun warm on them, so that the shouting and the effort became more bearable.

They rowed all day and moored at nightfall. They were allowed to disembark to stretch their legs. They lit fires at a prudent distance from the boats and dined from their supplies, which offered two choices: smoked fish or dried meat. Afterwards they went back to the boats to sleep on board. According to Captain Astol one had to love one's bench and oar, and nothing united them more than spending the night with them.

The first two days were hard. It turned out that rowing required an intense effort which their untrained bodies were not used to. Lasgol and Egil chatted as much as they could to forget their aching bodies.

"It'll be dark soon and we'll be able to rest," Lasgol said as they rowed.

Egil sighed. "Yes, very soon I hope. My sublime mind can no longer deceive my bruised and battered body."

Lasgol, who was slowly getting used to this flowery way of speaking, half-understood him.

"Then we'd better have a chat. Tell me about yourself. That way you'll be distracted."

"Very well. Let's see, I'm the third child of the illustrious Duke Olafstone, lord of the Duchy of Vigons-Olafstone, a man of high lineage and noble birth, joined by blood to the house of Vigons, a contestant for the crown."

"You're the son of a Duke?"

Egil nodded. "Of one of the most powerful Dukes in the realm."

Lasgol gave a long whistle. "In that case you're rich. You'll have grown up among servants and luxury." The moment he had said this, Lasgol realized how wrong it had sounded. "Sorry, it slipped out without thinking."

"Don't worry," Egil said with a smile. "Everybody thinks the same. But there are a couple of unusual circumstances about my person which it might be appropriate to explain." There was an odd expression on his face as he said this.

Lasgol tilted his head. What could those be?

"Although I'm of a house which is both noble and powerful, it was heir to the crown, which puts it in an awkward position. The house of Vigons on my grandfather's side, to be more precise. Our dear King Uthar and my father Vikar don't enjoy an especially friendly relationship. The King has obliged my father to renounce his rights to the crown and adopt the name of the Olafstone family instead of Vigons, since the latter bears the right to the crown. My father has sworn fealty to Uthar, like the other Dukes and Barons of the kingdom, but in reality they're rivals."

"Rivals? Why?"

"Because should Uthar die without offspring, and as of today there still is none, the crown could pass to my house, to my Father."

"Oh! Yes, I see...."

"And that tremendous political tension makes itself felt at home. My father lives under constant pressure, and that's passed on to his children. Well, that and the fact that my father isn't exactly a very amiable person. The opposite, if anything. He has a very strong character. Some say he's blown off more than one head with his shouting. According to him, men without character aren't even worth the clothes they wear. And – well, nor are those who aren't capable of knocking down a door with their heads."

Lasgol's eyes widened. "You said children? Do you have siblings?"

"Yes. I'm the last of three. In all senses." He smiled resignedly. "They're big, strong, true Norghanians. Me, well.... you know..." He glanced down at his own slight body.

"Muscles aren't everything, you know."

"They are in Norghana. And in my father's house even more so. If you're not capable of fighting like a raging bull to defend your house, you're not what my father expects."

Lasgol nodded understandingly. "I don't have any siblings. It must be nice to have someone to grow up with..."

"It was, when we were little. Then everything changed. My brothers are my father's pride, and little by little they turned into his image. They stopped playing with me and started wielding weapons, and from then on they never had the time or inclination to play again. My father found the best martial instructors of the realm for them and made them practice day and night."

"Are they going to join the Royal Army?"

"Oh, no!" Egil shook his head. "My father doesn't trust the King, or the other Dukes, and vice versa. He won't let his children serve him. He wants them with him, to rule the Duchy. Every Duke and Baron has a small army at his service, to rule his lands."

Lasgol was thinking of Ulf. "I thought that King Uthar had an army of soldiers."

"He does, but it's not a very large one. It costs a lot to maintain." There was a glint of intelligence in Egil's eyes. "It's more efficient if his lords, the Dukes and Barons, have one and pay for it themselves."

"Oh. I didn't know anything about this."

Egil winked. "Don't worry, that's what you have me for."

Lasgol laughed. Then he became thoughtful. "But in that case what are you doing here? Why aren't you in your father's duchy?"

"Ah. The explanation for that is both simple and sad."

Lasgol looked at him, intrigued.

"The King requires a proof of loyalty from all his Dukes and Barons. It's always been like that, since the dawn of the realm almost a thousand years ago. Every one of them has to send one of his children to serve the monarch, so that they won't be tempted to betray the King."

"Because he'd have a hostage for each of them."

"Exactly. And I'm that hostage. My father sent me to serve the Rangers because I wouldn't be accepted in the Royal Army, given my physical condition."

"Hm, I see... and the sad part?"

"The sad part is that he sends the son he doesn't love, the weakest and least skilled with weapons, the son he's ashamed of."

"Don't say that..."

"Well, it's the truth. My father's a hard man, cold as the mountains in the north. When he saw that I'd never be like my two brothers, he lost interest. He focused on them. Basically he rejected me. From then on he's rarely spoken to me, and when he has it's always been to order me to do this or that. Never a kind word. So I found myself alone and took refuge in books. Luckily my father's castle has a huge library which my father built for my mother. I've spent most of my life there, more or less on my own."

"And your mother?"

"She died of the white fevers when I was only five."

"I'm sorry… my mother died too when I was little."

Egil smiled. "There you are, we have something in common."

"I'm really sorry about your father."

"Don't worry, there's nothing to be done about it. There's no love between us."

But from the sadness in Egil's eyes Lasgol had the impression that he did love his father, even though the latter had rejected him. Lasgol was touched by the trust Egil had shown to him in telling him all that. He thought of sharing his secret with Egil… that which he had kept hidden and which he had sworn not to use again, after his father's death. But he did not dare.

By the third day of their journey Lasgol had really begun to enjoy the experience. His hands and arms ached, but the landscape was truly impressive. The river gleamed like crystal, the nearby fields where the snow had melted were covered in intense green. The woods were still covered by a thin layer of snow which would soon turn to water and flow down into the earth. In the distance were the defiant, majestic mountains of Norghana, covered in snow. A landscape which left him breathless. Egil had told him they were heading northeast, so that the weather would turn a bit colder, but bearable as it was spring.

Egil, on the other hand, was not enjoying the journey so much. The effort was beginning to take its toll on his puny body. Lasgol made sure he did most of the daily effort on the oars himself, but even so, there were too many hours of continuous work for Egil. By the seventh day he looked like a corpse slumped over the oar. He was very pale and had ugly shadows under his eyes. Nor was he the only one. Lasgol saw at least a dozen more boys who looked like ghosts. And of the rest, only half were bearing up under the effort.

"Do you feel all right? Do you want me to call for help?"

Egil shook his head.

"Are you sure? You look bad."

"Don't worry, there's more to me than meets the eye."

"I don't want anything to happen to you."

At that moment Captain Astol yelled: "At your age I was capable of towing this boat with a dinghy up-river! All by myself!"

The untimely comment filled Egil with determination.

"I won't make myself into a laughing-stock."

"But it's too much effort."

"It isn't too much for you, so it can't be for me."

Lasgol wanted to deny this, but he knew he would never convince him. There was a gleam in Egil's black eyes that clearly indicated that he was not prepared to give up.

"All right," he said reluctantly. He searched for some way of encouraging Egil and taking his mind off the torture his body was undergoing. "Tell me your favorite subject."

Egil's face lightened up.

"Mages..." he said, and his eyes gleamed.

"Mages?"

"Yes. Do you know there are people who have the Gift? Or the Talent, as they call it here in the North. They can do things that would be unthinkable for ordinary people like you and me." He said this with such excitement that Lasgol was sure the subject fascinated him.

"Dakon... my father ... told me a little about it."

"It's truly fascinating," Egil said, his eyes bright. "Only a very small percentage of the population is born with the Gift, or the Talent, and those who find they have it and develop it could become great mages of incredible power, able to save a kingdom or ruin it."

"My father told me that the Mages have incredible power, that they're capable of bringing down buildings and causing huge losses in entire armies."

"And that's quite true. The Ice Mages who serve the King can manipulate the element of water and turn it into ice or any of its other forms in nature, and use it to cause devastating effects."

Lasgol stared blankly at him.

"They're capable of freezing people where they stand, of creating lethal storms, of freezing the very air we breathe. They say an ice mage can freeze you at a glance."

"But you said it's only a small percentage of the population, right?"

"Yes, it seems it's passed through blood from parents to children, but not always. According to the compendiums on the subject which I've been able to study, for someone to be born with the Gift, some ancestor must have been born with it as well. The Gift runs in families, in the blood. It can't be acquired or transmitted in any other way except through blood, in other words from parents to children."

"That's really interesting. I didn't know that."

"Yes, there are very few of them. In all Norghana there can't be more than a dozen, and not all of them have the same power."

"They're not all very powerful mages?"

"Well, no. It's odd. Let me explain, because it's something which fascinates me. In some people the Gift manifests itself very powerfully. Most of them study the elements, and when they find one they have a greater affinity with, such as water, they specialize in it."

"Becoming Ice Mages."

"That's right. Or Mages of Fire, Earth or Air. They master the elements and they're extremely powerful because of the skills they can develop. There are some who can create volcanoes, earthquakes, and even hurricanes as they wish."

"I see... but not all of them, I hope..."

Egil laughed. "Not all of them. The Gift is rather arcane. Not much is known about it. It doesn't show in the same way in everyone. The most common kind is the mastery of the four elements and the skills derived from them. But there's written proof of many other kinds of Talents... of which very little is known. For example, in the far South, in the lands of the deserts, they say there are Sorcerers who specialize in the magic of blood and curses. They can make a person die just by looking at them and laying a curse on them, or making their blood boil."

"That's horrible."

"So it is. The Nocean Empire has Sorcerers of Blood and Curses. The Kingdom of Rogdon has Mages of the Four Elements, who aren't specialized in any single one but can use skills developed out of the four elements. Our kingdom, Norghana, has Ice Mages, who specialize in the element of Water. From what's said in the tomes I've been able to study, specializing in just one element turns the skills that have been developed into much more powerful ones."

"That makes sense. Mastering one subject is easier than mastering many."

"And not much is known about all the types of magic. Then there are Shamans in remote parts of Tremia, our beloved continent, with unknown skills."

"Shamans..."

"Yes, witches."

"I see…" Lasgol was delighted, and a little afraid, at the sound of all this.

"But the strangest thing is that there are also other manifestations of the Gift, and not much is known about them."

Lasgol was deeply interested. "Such as what?"

"Mages and Sorcerers are the best known, and there are well-documented tomes and compendia about them. But as for others…people with the Gift…who aren't as powerful or striking as mages and sorcerers: not much is known about them, but they exist."

"That's odd… you mean people who have the Gift, but don't show it openly?"

"Either that, or whose Gift isn't as powerful as that of a Mage of the Four Elements, or a Blood Sorcerer, but who have the Gift all the same and have developed it so as to have their own specific skills."

"That's interesting… What kind of power do they have?"

"There are those who can manipulate other people's minds. Just think, they can make you do things you'd never do."

"That's awful!"

"Exactly. They call them Dominators. They're very dangerous, as they can affect their victims' minds, making them believe things that aren't real. They say they can make you fall asleep wherever you happen to be, or take your own life… and what's much worse, make you take somebody else's life."

"But that's horrible!"

"Yes, they're very dangerous… I read in some book that they mark their victims."

"Mark them? How?"

"With a Rune on their flesh, so the domination will be stronger and they won't be able to resist."

"Horrifying!"

"Yes. Then there are the ones who develop skills to give their bodies special powers and turn into lethal assassins."

Lasgol nodded. "That makes sense."

"Others are able to develop skills connected with Nature, such as interacting with beasts or melting into the forest."

"I like the sound of that."

"But the fact is that someone with the Gift can develop different skills. The tomes of knowledge concentrate on the commonest ones, the ones there's proof of, but there's no limit. If I had the Gift, which unfortunately I don't, I'd spend my day developing skills to see how far I might be able to reach. The wonders I could achieve would be unbelievable."

Lasgol laughed. "If you had the Gift, I'm sure that in just a few years you'd be the most powerful mage in all Tremia."

Egil laughed with his friend. "I can assure you that instead of going to serve the Rangers I'd be off to serve the Ice Mages or other Sorcerers. I'd try things out, learn and turn myself into a force of nature." He smiled and flexed his weak arms.

They were silent for a moment, thinking about the implications of it all.

"If you had the Gift, what kind of Mage would you be?" Lasgol asked.

Egil thought about this. "A Dominator of Mages. That way I could use any type of power and control other people with the Gift."

Lasgol nodded, laughing. "Very smart. But if you came across a person who had very little of the Gift?"

"Then I'd use him to lead me to a powerful mage, and I'd dominate that one."

Lasgol laughed outright. "All right, you win!"

Egil smiled. "In fact we know very little about the people with the Gift. We know there are very few of them and that they hide because they're feared and rejected. From what I've read, it's been proven that there are people with different degrees of power, capable of developing different skills. But not much is known outside the circles of the Mages, and they work in secret."

"You mean like the Rangers?"

"Yes, not so different from the Rangers. Everything secret. Remember that people hate what they don't understand. Most of them fear and hate the Mages, everybody who has the Gift. Hatred and fear lead to persecution, and death. That's why they hide."

Lasgol nodded. "Everything you've told me is fascinating."

"It is, isn't it? I'm crazy about the subject. What wouldn't I give to know someone with the Gift and try things out with him, or her."

"Put that way, I'm not sure anyone would let you…"

"You know what I mean," Egil said, with a flicker of amusement.

Lasgol smiled. "Sure." He thought about trusting his secret to

Egil, he would probably understand. But he had promised himself to keep it a secret, to bury it inside his soul. No, he would not trust anyone. He had enough problems as it was to add another one. One so big.

That evening, after the conversation, Egil barely ate. They were beside one of the fires, and he fell asleep. Lasgol covered him with a blanket. When they went aboard for the night, he carried Egil on his back. On the gangplank he met Ingrid. The blonde looked him up and down, then at Egil, limp over his shoulder, and shook her head.

"You need to take care of your own strength," she said, disapprovingly. "He's not going to make it."

Lasgol was annoyed at this. "We'll see."

"Yeah, sure, we'll see," she said, and went on past him with her head high and her back straight.

Lasgol watched her as she went up the gangplank. He admired that girl's strength; she was more whole than he was himself, more whole than most of them, but he had not liked her attitude. He went on board and laid Egil down as comfortably as he could. Dawn came, and the Rangers woke them to start the day. Lasgol woke Egil up. He still looked terrible.

"I think we should warn the Rangers. You're not well." He wished Daven were on the boat with them so that he could talk to him, but unfortunately he was not. He did not know whether he had boarded another boat or gone on another mission.

"I feel better. Don't worry," Egil said. But Lasgol did not believe him.

The Rangers handed out water and breakfast. Lasgol made Egil eat.

The Captain gave the order and they began to row. At midmorning Egil fainted and almost fell off his seat. Lasgol seized hold of him and held him up.

"Rangers, help!" he called when he saw that Egil was clutching the oar with his gaze distant, as if he did not recognize him. Something was very wrong with him.

"By all the freshwater mermaids!" the Captain protested.

A Ranger came up to them. "Help!" Lasgol cried, deeply worried about his friend.

Everyone stopped rowing and turned around on their benches to see what was happening.

The Ranger, a weathered man, looked at Lasgol with interest. And he recognized him. His eyes widened and gleamed with hatred.

"What do we have here?"

Lasgol was about to say something, but the Ranger raised his hand to silence him. In a very loud voice, making sure everybody could hear, he said: "Well, if it isn't Ranger Dakon's son, the son of the great traitor!" He spat at Lasgol. "There's no help for you."

Lasgol felt an immense rage burning in his stomach.

Murmurs of surprise and questions began to spread throughout the boat. A moment later the rumor had reached everyone, and the murmurs were now of disapproval and scorn.

Tears came to his eyes.

"The traitor's son, among us," said one. "Incredible, how dare he," said another. "He ought to be thrown out. Or better still, give him a beating and teach him a lesson," said someone else. The murmur grew into an uproar, then came several insults out loud. Now they all knew who he was. And they hated him.

Lasgol clenched his fists tightly. He clenched his jaw and held back the tears as they went on tarnishing his name and his father's. He raised his gaze to the Ranger and pointed to Egil. He kept pointing at him without saying a word.

The Ranger noticed at last. "Move over," he told Lasgol, and bent to examine Egil.

He raised his arm. "Over here, he's got a high fever," he said, and immediately three Rangers came to help. They carried Egil away, semi-conscious, to the Captain, and he was examined at the prow. Several potions were prepared, which he was made to swallow, then he was rubbed down with cold water. Everybody was watching, and they forgot about Lasgol for a moment. The Rangers looked worried. The Captain ordered the boat to moor. The other boats stopped alongside. Two horses were readied on the cargo boat. Two Rangers rode, and they made Egil ride with one of them. They tied him to the Ranger so that he would not fall off, then carried him away at a gallop.

Lasgol prayed to the Ice Goddess that they would be able to save him.

Chapter 8

On the tenth day the river forked, and Captain Astol followed a northeastern course. Lasgol was rowing by himself. He felt lonely. At night he no longer left the boat for the warmth of the fires to avoid the insults and fighting talk of the other candidates. He took his share of dinner and went back to his rowing bench, ignoring comments, looks and provocations.

In the darkness of the night he rummaged in his satchel and took out the box which contained the strange egg. He was becoming more and more fascinated with the object. He was no longer afraid of breaking it by accident. This was because one evening it had slipped from his hands. Shocked, he had dived to the floor to save it, but had not been able to catch it in time. After hitting the floor it had rolled between the benches. When he finally recovered it he had inspected it closely, expecting to find it broken or cracked. But no, it was intact. This was unusual enough, but the feeling he had when he held it in his hands was even more so. That first time, at Ulf's house, he had not realized. But these past evenings, as he watched it intently, he was aware of a strange feeling in his stomach, as if he were nervous, which was not normal for him. And when he felt something strange, there was usually a good reason for it.

The boat entered a narrow pass. It seemed as if a god had struck the mountain with an axe, cleaving it in two to let the river through. On both sides the walls were extremely high, of pure vertical rock.

"We're going through the Gorge of No Return!" the Captain announced.

As soon as they had crossed it, two watch towers appeared on either side of the water. Rangers on guard stood on them, bows at the ready. A little further ahead was a wooden pier which gave access to what appeared to be a small village. They steered towards it and moored.

"This is the Foot of the Camp! Journey's end!"

Lasgol looked around him. They had entered a gigantic valley surrounded by a huge mountain range. He looked back. It seemed impossible to enter the valley except by following the river, passing through the gorge. He was beginning to understand why nobody knew where the Rangers' base was. He put his hands to his eyes and scanned the distance. The valley seemed to be endless, and on both sides of the river were great forests. The landscape was unusual, but what most caught his attention was the strange mist which covered the forests, as if it had descended on the valley and refused to leave. Above the mist could be seen the crowns of the trees, still covered in snow.

The order came to disembark and assemble in front of the houses. The village turned out to be nothing of the sort. It consisted of warehouses and buildings where the Rangers stored all manner of supplies. It was the base-camp, where supplies and food were brought upriver. One of the buildings, a little more solid, had a tower attached to it, and on it were several Rangers on watch duty. This was the command post. The Captains of the three vessels went in there to report.

Lasgol had the feeling that the gigantic valley which opened up before them belonged to the Rangers. They were allowed to stretch their legs, something which they all appreciated. While he waited, a little apart from his group, Lasgol watched the other group which had just arrived. He counted forty more candidates. In all there were about eighty of them. He wondered how many would hold up, and for how long. Already the boat journey had had its effect on several of them, and they had not even reached the main Camp yet.

The two groups mingled and exchanged greetings and gossip while the Rangers busied themselves with administrative tasks. Out of all the candidates, one in particular spurred Lasgol's curiosity. It was a girl with long wavy hair, black as a starless night. Enormous green eyes in a fierce and lovely face held whoever looked at them in their spell. For a moment he stared at her, forgetting where he was. He would have liked to go up to her and find out who she was, but as he was who he was… better forget about it. Besides, she was surrounded by three huge boys who were vying for her attention. At one point in their conversation he heard her name: Astrid. A pretty name. He would remember it.

Suddenly he felt a tingling he recognized: it always happened when he had the feeling that someone was watching him. And he was not wrong. A tall, athletic boy from the other group was staring at him: more than that, his gaze was fixed on him. A very unfriendly gaze. The boy strode toward him, leaving his group behind. Lasgol suddenly felt nervous.

The other boy came to stand close up against him, barely leaving any space between them. He said coldly: "They say it's you." He was trying to intimidate him. He was almost a hand-span taller than Lasgol, and considerably stronger. But there was agility in him; he was not burly but athletic. His blond hair was short, and his ice-blue eyes pierced Lasgol.

Lasgol frowned. "Who says what?" He was not prepared to cower.

The boy gestured towards his group. "They're saying you're the son of Dakon Eklund the Traitor." It sounded like an accusation.

Lasgol held his gaze. "And what does it matter to you who I am?"

"Answer the question," the boy said. His eyes narrowed threateningly and his arms tensed. Lasgol's sharp eye noticed the muscles in those arms. A confrontation was not in his best interest.

He took a deep breath and decided not to look for any more trouble than was absolutely necessary.

"I'm Dakon's son," he said proudly. "So what?"

The boy's eyes widened. They gleamed. His gaze was now one of intense hatred.

"My name's Isgord. You and I have an account to settle."

"What account?" Lasgol asked blankly. He had not been expecting this.

"You'll find out," the boy said, then turned on his heels and left as determinedly as he had come.

Lasgol was left feeling confused. Restless. The boy's tone and manner had seemed to him a very real threat. He was used to insults and slights, even people pestering him, but it was rarely personal, it was simply hatred. He had to pay for all the evil done by others. Hatred always looks for a scapegoat. But this threat had been different. The hatred was real, he had felt it as if he had been stabbed with an icy dagger. He would have to be careful. *Isgord*: he would remember that name.

"What's this, making more friends?" came a soft voice with a definite touch of irony in it.

Lasgol turned and recognized one of the boys in his group. Until then he had never spoken to him. He recognized him because he too usually stayed away from the rest. In the evenings beside the fires he sat alone and watched the other candidates. More than that, it seemed he was studying them one by one. Lasgol had not often seen him speaking to anybody, even though he was good-looking and seemed to be able to take care of himself without anyone else's help. He was tall and thin, with long black hair which he wore loose down to his shoulders, and intense green eyes. He looked tough and at the same time strange, almost sinister.

"I do what I can," Lasgol said, pretending to smile.

The boy nodded toward Isgord, who had already gone back to his own group.

"A popular guy," he said, in a tone which revealed a certain envy.

Lasgol looked more closely. Yes, he looked like a popular guy, everyone was around him trying to attract his attention. Especially girls.

"If you want some free advice, stay away from that one."

"Because…?"

"That one was born to be a First Ranger. Nothing and nobody will stop him."

"How do you know that?"

"If you keep your eyes open, you can pick up a lot."

Lasgol nodded. "He was the one who came over to me."

"Even worse. He has some beef with you."

"But I don't even know him."

The other boy shrugged. "Be careful with him."

"Why are you warning me?"

"Because you've got too many problems already and today I'm feeling generous. It must be having my feet on dry land again." He smiled, and this time his smile looked sincere.

"Thanks. What's your name?"

The boy's expression turned mocking. "We're not going to be friends. Don't fool yourself." He turned around and left, with a chuckle.

Lasgol snorted in disgust. "Isn't there a single normal person here?" he muttered to himself. And the worst thing was that this was just the start. He looked up at the clear sky and felt the warmth of the spring sun on his face. It soothed him.

The Captains came out of the command post and called for attention.

"Everyone listen to me!" said Astol. "It's time to work those lazy muscles!"

The candidates got ready to obey the Captain's orders.

"The Rangers have unloaded the horses," added another Captain. "It's your turn now. Unload the supplies and take them to the warehouses!"

Lasgol was glad of the work. While they were busy, the candidates stopped staring at him and pestering him. It did not take them long to finish. Once everything was unloaded the three boats set off downriver, leaving them there: with no way of getting out of that enormous valley. He heaved a sigh. *Now there's no going back.*

"First group, with me!" one Ranger said. He recognized Daven's voice.

"Second group, with me!" said another Ranger whom he had not seen before.

Daven led them to the horses and ponies. Each one found his own mount. Lasgol greeted Trotter affectionately and was received with a joyful snort and much head-shaking.

"I've missed you too," Lasgol told him with a smile, and stroked his back and his cream mane.

"Those of you who can ride, do so. Those who can't will have to go on foot, leading your horses."

They started up-river, following the bank, going deeper into the valley. Daven was at the head of the group and Lasgol fell back to the rear. The other group left later. Most of the candidates were on foot, with only a third of them riding. Lasgol was happy to be riding Trotter again. The pony had nibbled his ear and he was sure he had recognized him.

They went on for two days without leaving the course of the river. Lasgol murmured endearments to his horse, who snorted in reply and shook his head up and down.

On the third day, Daven addressed the group.

"Stop. Dismount," he ordered. "The rest of the journey to the Camp will be on foot." Lasgol stroked Trotter's neck and the pony shook his head happily. The boy took the reins and followed the group. They went on toward the misty forests.

"Mind your step," Daven warned them. "The mist is thick, and it'll get even worse further inside."

As soon as they were among the fir trees, the redhead who had had problems with her oar tripped over the leg of her pony and fell on her face, so awkwardly that she started to roll downhill. She tried to find something to hold on to, but was unable to. A tree abruptly stopped her fall. Laughter burst out among the group. Daven helped her up while she wiped herself clean of grass and mud. She had had quite a fall.

They carried on into the forest until sunset. The fog was growing thicker every moment, so that the ground was barely visible, with roots and low brush making it more difficult. It was not particularly cold, but there was a dampness in the atmosphere which made them hug their clothes around them. Lasgol glimpsed a deer in the distance, together with several squirrels. There were also colorful local birds. This made him feel more relaxed. The fog might be strange, but the wildlife was at its ease, which meant there was no immediate danger.

They stopped at last. "We're here," Daven announced.

Looking ahead, all Lasgol could see was the edge of a massive forest, dense and thick, forming an impenetrable wall. The trees were so close to each other and the vegetation between them so thick that there was no way through. He had never seen anything of the sort. It spread for leagues in both directions around them. It was a palisade created by nature. Or had Man played a part? If that was the case, he could not explain how. Equally, he could not think of how they were supposed to go on, least of all with their mounts.

"Arrived? Where?" said the sinister boy who had warned Lasgol.

"At the Rangers' Camp."

"Is that a joke?"

"No, it's no joke," Daven said. His voice was serious. "This is the entrance to the Camp. What you can see in front of you is the outer wall. It surrounds the whole enclave. It protects it. It makes it practically inaccessible: a natural barrier."

"All you'd need to do is set light to it," the boy said dismissively.

"Big mistake: it's very damp here, and those trees and bushes are soaked. They'd never burn. I see you haven't been paying attention, because the tops of the trees are full of snow. Even if the fire were to take hold, the snow would fall and put it out."

The boy made a bored gesture and said no more.

Daven gave three long whistles. For a moment nothing happened. They were all looking around expectantly. Suddenly there came a grating sound. To the astonishment of the group, three of the great trees in front of the Ranger moved back to leave a way through.

There were muffled sighs and cries of surprise. Even a few loud cries of "Magic!" Daven went first, followed by his horse. The pass was just wide enough to let them through.

"Follow me!" he said.

They went in after him, one by one. Lasgol went last. When he had passed through, the trees blocked the pass once more, as if they had a life of their own, or else as if some sort of arcane art was involved. He stopped a moment and looked at the ground, searching for traces and found something: ropes. He followed them with his gaze and above, among the tree-tops, he thought he saw something unclear. He could not tell what it was because it blurred into the foliage. If he had had to bet however, he would have sworn there was a Ranger hidden there who had activated a mechanism of ropes and pulleys. He could not stay to investigate, he had to follow the group.

What Lasgol saw as they went into the Camp made his jaw drop. He had always imagined the Camp would turn out to be a castle, or a fortress in military style. Nothing could have been further from the truth. The Camp was an immense open area with great forests, rivers and lakes interconnected by open spaces as far as the eye could reach. Around it all: the impenetrable barrier they had just crossed.

As they went on he realized the Rangers had taken over much of the valley and built their refuge here. At first he could not see any kind of building. To the east was the oak forest, surrounding several calm lakes. To the west, firs took their place and the forest was thicker. To the north were wide, empty green fields with clumps of trees between lakes and rivers. It was a beautiful landscape, and Lasgol was deeply taken with the place. They went on further, and at last the first buildings appeared. They were made of pine: simple, as though respectful toward their environment. They had been built using local stone and wood.

Lasgol could make out different workshops. A forge, a tanner, a carpenter, and a butcher, judging by the shape of the buildings and what he could see in their doorways. He also saw a low, very long building. He did not know what it was, but it looked like a warehouse.

"Follow me," Daven said. He turned away from the workshops and headed north, following a small crystal brook.

Suddenly, after passing through a plantation of trees, the stables took shape. They were huge, with more than five hundred horses in them. Behind the buildings was a wide-open area of green fields where several hundred Norghanian horses and ponies were grazing.

"Hand over your mounts," Daven ordered as he leapt down and handed his reins to a stable boy.

Lasgol and the other candidates did the same. The half-dozen stable hands took the horses away one by one.

"Don't worry, they'll take good care of them."

Lasgol said goodbye to Trotter with a caress which the pony seemed to appreciate, and he wondered who those stable hands might be, as well as the people in the workshops, since it was clear they were not Rangers, nor were they candidates. He would have to find out later.

Once the horses had been left in the stables they followed Daven and crossed a bridge over a pond with colored fish. Around the pond, forming two half-moons, were several cabins that looked as though they were there to house people. A little further behind was what looked like a small village of wooden huts, with a lake at one end and a forest at the other. Lasgol guessed they were entering an area where the Rangers lived.

"Don't stop to look," Daven said. "You'll have time to see everything later." He led them to an enormous building, long and narrow, like a ship. The roof was high and sharply pointed. At one end of the wooden house was the carved image of a bear, with one of a wolf at the other. The door in the middle was decorated with natural motifs. It was strange to find this building in the depths of the forest, but what made it even stranger was that it was built on an island in the middle of a lake.

Lasgol stared at it, his mouth hanging open. In that landscape forest, lakes and green fields interlaced, creating a beautiful and fascinating world.

"This is the Command House," Daven said. "Fall in."

They bent down on one knee and stared ahead, as they had been taught the way Rangers did it. They waited a moment and out of the corner of his eye Lasgol saw the other group arriving. They were made to fall in beside them. In the first row was Isgord. He looked back, saw Lasgol and gave him a glare of pure hatred. Lasgol sighed and ignored him. He looked around. The Camp was huge, they could see no end to it in any direction. It was a whole world in itself. Lasgol was lost in wonder.

Night was beginning to fall, and the shadows began to fall on the forests. The doors of the long building opened and five figures came out to meet them. They crossed the wooden bridge over the lake and came to stand in front of the two groups. They were dressed like Rangers, but there was something different about them, something mysterious... powerful. Lasgol watched them without missing a detail. Their faces were covered by green scarves. Only their eyes and foreheads were visible, with their noses and mouths hidden. There was no way of recognizing them.

The presence those Rangers emanated was a very powerful one. He could feel it, as if they were projecting it toward him, and it struck his chest and face. He might have been the only one who felt this, because of his secret. Sometimes he felt strange things which others did not, and now what he was feeling was something both powerful and strange. Whatever the case, clearly those five beings were very special and there was something strangely different about them... they gave out an almost mystical aura... no, it was not mystical, it was arcane, dangerous. He felt a shiver run down his back.

Who are they? Where have they brought us to?

The figure in the middle stepped forward.

Lasgol felt the hair on the back of his neck stand on end.

Chapter 9

The stranger looked at the candidates for some time; all eyes were on him. Lasgol knew this was the Camp Leader, although he could not have said what gave him that impression. He made a swift movement with his right hand, then from behind his back brought out a long wooden staff ornamented with silver. He grasped it with his right hand and stood it upright on the ground. It was as tall as he was: over six feet. In the other hand he carried a tome with green covers and gold engravings. He showed it to them all: *The Path of the Ranger.*

With a lethargic movement he pushed back his hood and lowered the green Ranger's scarf, revealing his head and face.

"Welcome," he said, firmly but kindly. He was an elderly man, around seventy. He wore his hair shoulder-length, long and straight. It was completely white. What drew attention to his face were his eyes, of an intense emerald green, and a well-tended snow-white beard cropped to an inch or so. Despite his age, he emanated agility and power.

Lasgol was surprised. He had not been expecting this from someone as old as that. He studied him carefully. The power he projected did not feel evil to him. He relaxed.

"I am Magnus Dolbarar, the Master Teacher Ranger, Leader of the Camp," he said, and unfolded his cloak. On his chest hung a large round wooden medallion with the image of a tree carved in its center. Instead of a chain, it was strung on a braided cord. He showed it to all of them. "This medallion identifies me as the highest authority in the Camp. The Instructor Rangers wear similar medallions. They are carved from a century-old oak, which grows in the heart of the camp, a mystical and holy place for all of us. It represents our spirit, since we Rangers are like the century-old oak: we grow strongly, honorably, protecting the earth, and are one with nature. Don't worry, you'll soon learn this and other truths of the Path of the Ranger, which are the mantra and code of honor we follow." He waved the matter aside. "I bid you welcome. From this moment on you are accepted as Initiate Rangers. I hope and wish that you will find a home and a family among us, because that's what we, the Rangers, are, one family, with a sacred duty which we carry out honorably: to protect the kingdom from all danger."

Daven gave a slight bow which Dolbarar returned, then he left, disappearing in the direction of a group of buildings behind a pond toward the east.

Dolbarar went on: "In order that you can become Rangers, a difficult path lies ahead of you. I am not going to lie to you, it's not going to be easy; not all of you will make it. The Path of the Ranger is a difficult one, but deeply gratifying once accomplished. For four years you will follow it under the watchful eyes of the instructors. At the end of each year you will be assessed in accordance with the grades you have achieved. Those who pass the year's tests will be able to go on to the next level. Those who fail will be expelled. There will be no second chances. That is what the Path requires, and thus the Rangers walk it."

Lasgol swallowed. This did not look as though it was going to be at all easy.

"And now let me introduce you to the Four Master Rangers." Dolbarar continued, indicating the four figures who accompanied him. "They are the highest manifestation of the Four Schools."

The candidates stared at them, enthralled.

"As Master Ranger of the School of Archery: Ivana Pilkvist, 'The Infallible'." Dolbarar waved his hand, and the figure on his right stepped forward and pushed back her hood and scarf. It revealed a woman of no more than thirty, with her blond hair tied back in a queue. She was beautiful, but with a cold, Nordic beauty. Her eyes were gray, with a lethal gleam. Lasgol shivered at the sight of those eyes. She wore a wooden medallion like Dolbarar's but rather smaller, with the image of a bow in its center.

"The specialty of Archery is reserved for those with a falcon's eye and steady hand," Ivana said, and went back to her place.

Dolbarar indicated the figure to his left. "As Master Ranger of the School of Wildlife: 'The Tamer' Esben Berg." He beckoned, and the figure on his left stepped forward and removed hood and scarf in his turn. He was a middle-aged man, big as a bear, with abundant brown hair and thick beard of the same color. His face could hardly be seen among so much hair, but he had large brown eyes and a flat nose. On his chest he wore a wooden medallion with the carved face of a roaring bear.

"The specialty of Wildlife is reserved for those who have an affinity with animals," he said. He bowed slightly and went back to his place.

Dolbarar gestured toward the figure further to the right. "As Master Ranger of the School of Nature, 'Erudite' Eyra Vinter." The figure took a step forward and uncovered her face. She was revealed as a woman of around sixty with curly salt-and-pepper hair and a long, crooked nose. On her chest hung a wooden medallion with an oak leaf carved in its center. The old lady curtseyed to the initiates.

"The specialty of Nature is reserved for those who understand the secrets of Mother Nature, from botany, through healing with ointments and medicinal plants, to the making of traps that will enable you to survive in the frozen mountains and forests."

"And finally," Dolbarar announced, turning to the last figure, "as Master Ranger of the School of Expertise: Haakon Rapp, 'The Untouchable'." He beckoned, and the figure to his far left stepped forward and revealed his face and head. He was a tall and slender man in his early forties. His skin was dark and his head clean-shaven, with small black eyes above a beak-like nose. On his chest he wore a wooden medallion with a Snake carved in the center. Ivana's gaze had been lethal, but Haakon's was sinister, arcane. Lasgol felt uneasy at the sight of him.

"The specialty of School of Expertise is reserved for those who make a tough yet flexible weapon of their bodies, make silence their ally, shadows their dwelling, and stealth their way of life." He was silent for a moment, then went back to the others.

Dolbarar spread his arms wide and addressed the initiates:

"Each of the Four Master Rangers will choose those candidates who will form part of their particular School. They will do so according to your innate abilities and the progress you show. If you are not accepted into any of the four specialties, you will be expelled and you will not do the final year."

Lasgol swallowed again. He had no idea which specialty he wanted to belong to; all four sounded fascinating. But at the same time they seemed very difficult, so that he feared he would not be chosen and would end up expelled. Besides, he was the son of the Traitor. Surely none of the Four Master Rangers would want him with them, which meant that he would be fated to be expelled. *There's nothing I can do about that now. I'll go on and we'll see what happens.*

"But those who are accepted," Dolbarar went on, "will progress and have the chance to join the Advanced Specialists. That will depend entirely on you, on how hard you work and how strong your will is to reach the end. Those chosen will be presented at the end of the fourth year, and will train at a secret location for a fifth and final year. I hope to find several candidates for this extra year among you."

This caught everybody's attention. Many had heard talk of the famous Advanced Specialists and of how difficult it was to belong to them. Lasgol knew some his Father had mentioned, but not all of them.

"Who knows, among you there might be a future 'Mage Hunter', or perhaps a 'Beast Whisperer', or a 'Stalker', a 'Chameleon', or my favorite: an 'Indefatigable Explorer'."

Murmurings among the initiates indicated that yes, they all wished to become part of the Rangers' Elite. But from what his Father had told him, Lasgol knew that only a handful ever make it to elite specialists.

"And that concludes the introductions," said Dolbarar with a smile. "The thousand questions buzzing in your young minds will have to wait until tomorrow."

One of the Rangers went up to him and whispered something in his ear.

"Excellent. I've been told that everything is now ready. It's time to celebrate the arrival of the new initiates. Follow me. This evening is one to be enjoyed. Tomorrow you'll start a new life, but don't concern yourself about it now. Tonight is a time of celebration, since for yet another year the initiates have arrived, and this must be celebrated."

Dolbarar motioned them to stand and follow him. He led them toward a grove of trees, followed by the Master Rangers. Night was falling, and as they walked Lasgol saw several older boys lighting oil lamps that hung from the tress. He guessed they were the Ranger Apprentices of the second or third year.

When they entered the grove, they found an empty field with a dozen fires. All kinds of delicacies were roasting on them, from venison to pheasant. Lasgol's stomach rumbled loudly. On tables made from great tree-trunks a great banquet had been prepared: spiced soup with meatballs, grilled vegetables seasoned with pepper and garlic, roast trout, stuffed turkey with garnishes as the main meat course, with honey sauce and spiced mashed potatoes. And if that were not enough, there were fruits and berries on another table for dessert.

"Come on now, sit down and enjoy your dinner," Dolbarar said to them. "You've earned it." He and the other Rangers took their places at a table set a little apart from that of the Initiates.

They ran to take their places and enjoy the meal. Immediately boys and girls slightly older than themselves began to serve dinner as if they were servants, although they were obviously Second- and Third-year students.

Dolbarar turned to the Initiates who were staring in amazement at the dishes being served.

"Now let's all eat!"

Both groups of Initiates hastened to take their seats and enjoy the meal. They were exhausted, but more than that, they were famished. Lasgol sat down at the end of the table, fearing they would pick a fight with him, but nobody paid any attention to him. They threw themselves on the food and gobbled it down as if there were no tomorrow. The apple cider and water washed the meat and spiced mashed potatoes down their throats. Everything tasted glorious to Lasgol, and by the look of immense delight on the other boys' faces he guessed the meal was truly splendid and it was not just the hunger they all felt.

But if the roast and side dishes were delicious, what followed left them all speechless.

"My favorite part of a meal: dessert!" Dolbarar announced.

They were served fruits and berries, along with blackberry pie, cream and honey. The desserts were so delicious that for a moment Lasgol thought that he was asleep and it was all a wonderful dream. The apple pie was spectacular.

They ate until they were ready to burst, enjoying every delicacy. Finally Dolbarar stood up and addressed the Initiates.

"And now it's time to go and rest. I know your tired bodies will appreciate that. The First-year Initiates have the cabins at the southern part of the camp. On the door to each cabin you'll find the names of the six people who are to live in it. It's not a random list, it has its importance. I wrote that list myself, based on the reports sent to me by the Rangers who had spent time evaluating you before delivering their invitation. Those six people will form a team for the rest of the year."

A murmur began to spread among the Initiates. They all eyed each other, wondering which group they had been allotted to.

Dolbarar's voice turned more serious. "The teams will not be changed, whether you like them or not, whoever you may be. As of tomorrow you are all Initiates, your previous lives are completely unimportant here. Nobles and farmers are equal here. Men and women, tall and short, strong and weak: you are all equal here. The team is now your family, and this is important because here we work as a team, we learn as a team, and we fail or succeed as a team. The six people in each cabin form a team and you will, or will not, pass to the second year as one. Individuals have no place among the Initiates. You'll be evaluated in all disciplines as a team. You will have to pass all your tests as a team."

The murmurs and outcries spread. This surprised Lasgol, who had always assumed that his studies here would be individual and that he would have to pass the tests on his own. It did not make much sense, since after all Rangers operated alone most of the time. They rarely did so in groups, according to what his father had told him, which was not much.

"I hope I have made myself clear."

The tone in which he said this was so stern that a solemn silence fell on all the Initiates at the table. Nobody dared say anything.

"Very well. I see I have explained myself. It's time to meet your partners for the rest of the year. Go to your cabins, and goodnight to all of you." He waved his hand toward the south.

Isgord was the first to rise and make his way toward the cabins. A path lit by oil lamps marked the route. After this a dozen boys and girls of the second group went after him. They were presumably hoping they would be with him. The others got up and went hastily toward the cabins. They were all nervous, anxious to find out who their partners would be and whether their team would be a good one. All, that is, except Lasgol. He knew that whichever team was his lot, he would have a bad time of it. They would hate him even more because he was in their team.

He was the last to rise. He started walking, slowly and reluctantly. On the way he glanced timidly at Dolbarar, who gave him an odd, almost mischievous smile. Lasgol breathed out heavily. He was in for it now.

There were fifteen cabins, forming a semicircle. They were small, built of stacked pine-trunks, like those of woodsmen. The roofs were still covered with snow that was reluctant to melt. In front of the cabins the Initiates ran from one to another searching for their names on the pieces of parchment nailed to the doors. Groups were beginning to form in front of each cabin. Lasgol waited until they were all more or less complete. When he saw there were only a couple of people still looking for their team, he went closer.

There was no need for him to search. He identified his group immediately. Not so much because there was still one missing but by the looks of intense frustration on their faces. He went slowly closer, knowing he would not be welcomed. Because of this he prepared himself inwardly for rejection. *I'm here for a reason, to clear my father's name. I don't care how bad a time I have to go through. I'll do it.* Straight away he recognized the first person looking at him as he approached. Her arms were crossed over her chest and she was glaring at him icily. On her face was a look of absolute disappointment. It was Ingrid.

She was shaking her head in disbelief. "I can't believe they've put me in this group."

Lasgol stopped in front of her and looked at the others.

"Well, I can easily believe it," said the strange solitary boy who had warned him about Isgord. "They've put us in the losing team."

"It isn't such a bad team," said a big strong boy. He turned towards Lasgol. It was the giant who had been rowing in front of him on the boat.

"I don't think it's so bad either," said the redheaded girl who had had a series of mishaps during the journey.

Lasgol noticed that there was one missing. "And the sixth?"

The door to the cabin opened and a head popped out. "I'm the sixth," said Egil. His face was as white as a ghost's.

"Egil!" cried Lasgol. "Are you all right?"

He smiled, leaning on the door jamb so as not to fall out of pure weakness. "The fever's going down. I'll be fine before long."

Lasgol hastened to Egil and hugged him tightly.

"You gave me quite a scare."

Egil smiled. "Well, you can imagine the one I had myself. Don't squeeze me so tight, I can barely stand."

"Oh, sorry." Lasgol helped him to sit down in the porch.

The unsmiling boy eyed them all one by one, as if he were measuring them, almost judging them.

"Yes, the best of teams, sure. On the one hand we have the famous Traitor, beloved by all, someone the instructors are sure to help at every moment, and of course help his team as well. And with him his puny friend who couldn't even reach the Camp by himself. And alongside" – he pointed at the redhead – "the clumsiest girl in the kingdom, either on the water or on dry land."

"Hey! That's not fair. I only had a couple of accidents…"

"Oh, sure…"

"Let her be," the giant put in.

"And next we have the biggest and strongest boy in the camp. Which would be fantastic for any team, especially this one, which needs it so much, except for the slight inconvenience that he's scared of his own shadow." He made a sudden move as though he were about to hit the giant, who leapt backwards and covered his head with both hands.

"And why don't you try doing that to me?" Ingrid snapped at him.

"Don't worry, Princess, there'll be others who'll take you down a peg. There are some who are stronger and tougher than you are."

"Boys, you mean?"

"Yes, and they'll beat you to a pulp because of that pretty little mouth of yours."

"We'll see about that. I'm not afraid of any boy."

"As you see, we make a fantastic team. This Dolbarar has surpassed himself."

The others protested at this, but he took no notice.

Annoyed, Lasgol asked him: "And what about you? What makes you so much better than the rest of us?"

"Me? Who said I'm any better than you? I'm bitter and lonely. I ought to be the black sheep of the team. But beside you lot, I'm more like the one-eyed man in the country of the blind."

Ingrid waved her hand bad-temperedly. "In that particular case I'm with you. Dolbarar's outdone himself. We don't stand a chance."

Chapter 10

Dawn arrived, and Lasgol found it hard to wake up in spite of the light streaming in through the windows and a strange sound ringing in his ears. He sat upright in the bunk and searched around for the origin of the annoyance.

It did not take him long to find out what it was. The door to the cabin opened and a Ranger came in playing a small silver bell. It was not particularly loud, but on the other hand it was extremely shrill and pierced their eardrums.

"Up you get, all of you! Fall in outside the cabin!"

Lasgol jumped from his berth on to the wooden floor, which was covered with a huge bearskin. He looked to see how Egil was in the lower bunk.

"Looks as though we've got to go out."

"I've been granted leave to rest," Egil said.

"Oh, okay then," said Lasgol, and smiled. "Take care of yourself, you'll soon be fine."

He took a good look at the cabin. It was divided into two by a solid wall of pine logs. One half was for the girls and the other for the boys, with separate entrances. Each half had a fireplace, a rustic table with benches facing a sink-kitchen and a small bathroom. They had thick woolen blankets for the coldest days and furs on the floor to make it cozy. Although it was small and functional, Lasgol found it very welcoming.

In the other berth, the giant had been obliged to sleep on the lower cot in case the structure collapsed under his weight and squashed the grumpy boy, who did not trust it at all. A trunk for each of them had been left by the bedsides. Lasgol had put his traveling satchel in it, and to his surprise had found two complete changes of clothes and a hooded cloak, like the ones the Rangers used, but in a striking red.

"We're not going to get lost in these," he commented.

The giant put on his own. It barely covered him.

"Mine doesn't fit," he said resignedly.

"Your problem is that you're as big as a mountain and just as cowardly," the grumpy boy said.

"Hey!" the giant protested. "I'm not trying to pick a fight with you."

"It's to wake you up a bit, but I can see it's useless."

"Leave him alone," Lasgol said.

"Don't you interfere, Traitor," he said, emphasizing the last word.

Lasgol shook his head. What a malicious person this was. And with this thought he realized he did not know their names.

"What's your name? I'm Lasgol Eklund."

"I'm Viggo Kron," the boy retorted with a murky glance, "and as far as I'm concerned, you'll always be Traitor."

"I'm Gerd Vang," the giant said. He looked annoyed.

"Get dressed and come out! Quick!" called a deep, powerful voice from outside.

They streamed out of the cabins and lined up in front of them, one knee on the ground, gazing ahead as they had been instructed to.

"Good. I'll introduce myself. I'm Oden Borg, the Master Instructor of the Rangers."

Lasgol took a sideways glance at him. He was a strong man, although not a very big one. He was about forty, and his face was unfriendly. His long copper hair was tied back in a queue. But the most striking thing about him was the gaze of his intense amber eyes. It was a very hard gaze. It pierced the soul.

"I'm in charge of all the courses. I've already called the Fourth- Third- and Second-year students and got them started. Now it's your turn, Initiates. That's you, in case you'd forgotten. I make sure the rules are always followed. Anyone who fails to follow every single one of those rules will be expelled. Is that clear?"

Everybody nodded, and there were some timid "yesses".

"I asked whether that was clear. I didn't hear the answer."

"Yes!" came the answer, much more loudly.

"That's better." He put his hands on his hips. "First rule: when you hear the bell, wherever you are, you drop what you're doing straight away, take your places and fall in. Anyone who doesn't will be punished. And believe me, you won't like my punishments one little bit."

Listening to him speak, Lasgol felt his skin crawl. It was his tone of voice: grave and deep, with an icy firmness that froze the blood.

"My job in the camp is to make everything flow like the water in the river. And it's going to flow, you can take that from me."

Viggo made a face. Gerd was looking at Oden apprehensively. Lasgol had not the slightest doubt that not everything would flow and that they would soon be in trouble with him.

"First of all, we follow tradition. We Rangers have traditions and ways of doing things which were established more than a hundred years ago. They're collected in the *Path of the Ranger,* which we abide by. We respect them and keep to them. Always."

Lasgol was beginning to notice that Oden liked to emphasize his sentences with the word *always*.

"First tradition: the Drawing of the Badges." He took out a leather bag and showed it to the teams. "There are badges in this bag. Each team will be named after the badge it gets in this draw. This year we have fewer teams than usual, I can count thirteen instead of the usual fifteen. It's a good thing I'm not superstitious, but even so, I'd say it's not a good beginning to the year. Let's go on. Each team now has to choose a captain. At the end of the season you might change him or her, at the Seasonal Tests. And yes, the captain is important. So choose well. Off you go, I'm waiting."

They all looked at one another, not knowing what to do; nobody really knew the person next to them. After a moment of doubt, arguments broke out in all the teams.

"I don't want to be Captain," said Lasgol. "I don't think it would help the team to have me as Captain."

"You really don't think so?" Viggo said sarcastically.

Gerd shrugged. "If you like, I could …"

Viggo rolled his eyes. "You? I bet you're even scared to put your hand in the Master Instructor's bag."

"Don't be like that," the redhead scolded him.

"I'll be Captain," Ingrid said with absolute confidence.

Lasgol and Gerd nodded in agreement. So did the redhead.

"And why you?" Viggo challenged her.

Ingrid raised her fist. "D'you want to fight for the job?"

Viggo smiled, and his eyes shone with a cold, dangerous flash. He put his hands to his waist. "If I fight you, I'll hurt you." The way he said it made Lasgol's hair stand on end. "But I don't want the job. You can have it." He gave her a bitter smile.

"Whatever you say," Ingrid said, and lowered her arm.

"Come on, we don't have all day!" Oden called to the teams.

Isgord, of course, was already with Oden. He looked at Lasgol, as if he were defying him to accept him as Captain and vie with him. Lasgol snorted in disdain and ignored him. Ingrid went to join the other captains in front of the Master Instructor.

"Good. Now, following the tradition, each captain must choose a badge. Come closer. Take one out at random, without looking inside the bag."

Isgord was the first to put his hand in. He handed Oden the badge he had picked. It was silver, the size of a plum.

"The White Eagle!" Oden announced. "Your team will be the Eagles."

Isgord's partners broke out into applause. There were four boys and a girl. Two of the boys were tall, strong and athletic, the other two shorter and sturdier. The girl was blonde and snub-nosed; she looked tough. The whole team looked like a tough mouthful to chew.

"That one has everything in its favor," Viggo said resentfully.

The next captain got the badge of the boar. "The Boars!" the team shouted joyfully.

The boar was followed by the bear, the wolf and the owl. When they reached the team of the Owl, Lasgol leaned forward to get a better sight of the Captain, almost without realizing. Nor was he the only one. The Captain was a girl, with long jet-black hair and eyes that took one's soul away. It was Astrid. Lasgol watched her, spellbound.

"She's pretty, huh? Her name's Astrid," Gerd whispered to him. "I met her the first day, before we boarded. She was kind to me. I liked her."

Lasgol looked at Gerd and nodded. He blushed.

Viggo had been watching them closely. "Don't even dream of it, Traitor," he said.

Lasgol frowned and ignored him. Of course he would not dream of it. He knew who he was and what they all thought about him, and this girl would be no different. In any case, he would not have time for girls. He had enough trouble as it was already.

Master Instructor Oden went on with the ceremony. The next team picked the fox, then it was Ingrid's turn. She went up to Oden, put her hand in the bag and gave him the badge.

"It's sure to be the skunk," Viggo said.

"Quiet," the redhead snapped. "I want to hear."

"The Snow Panther!" Oden announced.

They were all stunned. They had not expected anything good.

"Yoohoo!" cried the redhead delightedly. Gerd joined her, and even Lasgol muttered "Great!"

Ingrid turned to them with shining eyes and a gesture of triumph.

The ceremony continued until all thirteen teams had received their badges. Then Oden ordered the Captains to put the badges on the cabin doors, which had notches ready for them.

"Good," said Oden. "That's the end of the first tradition. Now you'll head to that building." He pointed to a large flat-roofed wooden building with four wings. It was not far from the cabins, and had a view of a small lake. "That's the dining room-canteen. You'll have breakfast, then we'll begin your training. If it was up to me, I'd make you hunt for your own food, but unfortunately Dolbarar doesn't allow me to. Come on then, we haven't got all day!"

When they reached the canteen they saw that it was divided into four sections for the students, plus a fifth for the Instructors. They were clearly marked by colors: red for the first year, yellow for the second year, green for the third year, brown for the fourth year. They sat down at large tables lined with benches, so that the teams were obliged to share. Most likely that was the intention. They all eyed one another warily and a little fearfully, except for the bullies and those who believed they were better than anybody else, who acted as if the tables were their own.

Breakfast was served by a group of second-year boys. This surprised Lasgol. Apparently the second-year students served those of the first, those in their third year in turn served the second-years and the fourth-years waited on the third-years. It was very curious and must serve some purpose, since nothing seemed to be done here by chance. He looked closely at the second-year boys and girls, who seemed much older than they were themselves, even though they had only been there a year. But of course it was a whole year of instruction in the Camp.

A second-year boy was about to serve Lasgol, but instead of doing so he poured the whole dish on top of him. Lasgol gave a start and shook the food off his clothes. He looked into the other boy's eyes, and there was rage in them. He decided to avoid confrontation and said nothing.

Ingrid rose to defend Lasgol. "Hey!" she cried.

The boy looked at her. With an obviously feigned gesture of apology he said: "Oops, how clumsy of me."

"I'll make sure you're left clumsy forever if you don't get out," she said threateningly.

"Be careful who you defend," said another of the serving boys. "Traitors' friends are regarded as traitors themselves."

"I don't care what you think," she said, and glared defiantly at the two boys. They were both a head taller than her and stronger, but Ingrid cared nothing for that.

There came the sound of a throat being cleared loudly. It was Oden, who was watching from one of the Instructors' tables. The two second-year boys withdrew without another word.

"Thank you," said Lasgol.

"I'm the Captain. I'll defend my team."

Viggo jabbed his thumb at Lasgol. "I don't think that includes him."

"It includes even you," said Ingrid, eyeing Viggo with distaste.

The redhead laughed, and Gerd choked. The situation became less tense, and they turned to their breakfast. It consisted of berries, dried fruits and nuts, goat's milk, a slice of bread and a piece of dried meat. Lasgol loved it, and the bad moment passed, although he noticed the gaze of the older boys fixed on his back as if it were a target. It was more than obvious that he was not wanted there. He sighed and went on eating. It did not take them long to gobble down their meal.

"Don't choke," Ingrid told the redhead, who was eating with both hands as if someone were trying to take her food away from her.

"I bet you she drops the plate or something," said Viggo.

The girl stuck her tongue out at him. "I'm not going to drop anything."

"I wouldn't be so sure," said Ingrid. "I had to change beds with her because the first thing she did was climb up to the top one, slip and fall down."

"It was slippery and dark," she protested.

"Yeah, sure, the bed, really slippery," Viggo said ironically.

"What's your name?" Lasgol asked the redhead.

"My name's Nilsa Blom."

"Pleased to meet you, Nilsa. I'm Lasgol. The big guy is Gerd."

Gerd nodded at her. "The grumpy one is Viggo."

Viggo turned a wide, insincere smile on them. "Me, grumpy? I'm sweetness itself."

"Yes, Prince Charming," Ingrid said with a frown. "I'm Ingrid Stenberg." They all nodded in greeting.

"The sick boy in the cabin is Egil," Lasgol said. He smiled. "Well, now we've all introduced ourselves."

"For all the good it's going to do us," said Viggo, "I'd almost rather have gone on the way we were before."

"If you want to give up before you even start, that's your problem," Ingrid said. "I've come to fight, and that's what I'm going to do."

"Hear, hear," said Gerd. "Are you going to finish your bread? It's just that this portion's not really enough for me…"

Nilsa smiled at him. "Here, take my bread, I've got more than enough."

"And my nuts," said Lasgol.

The giant grinned. "Thanks," he said.

The silver bell sounded again, and they got up and left. Master Instructor Oden was already waiting for them outside. With him was another Ranger, who looked enormously strong and athletic.

"This is Herkson, the first-year Physical Instructor. I'm going to leave you with him. And remember, anyone who steps out of line will pay for it. I'm always watching you. All the time." His grim stare passed around the group, and he left.

"Every morning," Herkson said, "we'll work on your fitness, strength and stamina. Then in the evenings you'll be instructed in the Schools. Every day a different School. But the mornings are mine. I'll turn those weak bodies of yours into pure muscle. Get into your teams."

The groups assembled. Lasgol felt a little strange in the company of his partners, and he knew they felt the same way. He could see it in their faces. But whether they liked it or not they were a team, and there was nothing they could do except get used to it.

"Follow me to the lake," Herkson said.

At first the Instructor walked slowly, but then he picked up speed. They followed him in a long line, broken into groups for the separate teams. They crossed a wood, and when they came out into the open Herkson speeded up his pace until it was a steady trot. They crossed a river, and the trot became a run. Herkson reached the lake at a sprint. The initiates arrived after him, their tongues hanging out. He gathered them together at the southern end of the immense lake. From that point they could not see the northern end.

"Before we start with the physical work we have to warm our muscles up to avoid a lesion. I can see by your faces that a lot of you are totally unfit. That's bad, very bad. For a Ranger his body is crucial, that's what he owes his survival to. You'll live and die according to what your bodies are capable of. Don't you forget that."

"In that case we're screwed," said Viggo. He was holding his sides and panting.

"Shut up and learn," Ingrid scolded him. She was unaffected by the effort.

"Don't you tell me what to do, Miss Bossy-Boots."

Ingrid showed him her right fist. "Don't you call me *bossy*, or else I'll make you swallow this."

"Listen to me. Now you're going to do three laps around the lake. In teams. The rule is that the whole team must arrive together. You mustn't leave any of your group behind. If one of you falls, the others will help him or her to get up and go on. If one of you has to give up, the others have to do an extra lap."

"That's not fair!" someone said.

"Who told you life's fair? Who told you, you can question what an Instructor says? You can do an extra lap."

The protests and whispering stopped, until there was only silence and the singing of birds in the nearby woods.

"And now, warm up. Follow my instructions and you won't hurt yourselves. Make a circle around me, in teams."

Herkson explained the warm-up they had to do. For over an hour they learned the dozen or so exercises for stretching and warming the muscles of legs, arms, abdomen and back. Lasgol had never done anything like it, and felt as though his body were made of stone. Nobody could be any less flexible than he was. Well, maybe Gerd.

"How can they do the exercises so easily?" Gerd asked. He had seen that Ingrid and Nilsa had no difficulty, whereas he was suffering agonies.

"Because they're girls, chicken," Viggo said.

"So?"

Nilsa gave a giggle.

"Well, they're flexible and we're not."

"And strong," Ingrid added, with a warning look at Viggo.

He gave her a dismissive gesture and ignored her.

"Right then, that's enough," Herkson said. "Now run. Three laps. Off you go."

The teams set off at intervals set by Herkson. Their turn came, and at his signal they started to run. Ingrid went first, sure of her skill. Nilsa followed immediately, then it was Gerd's turn. Lasgol glanced at Viggo, who waved him ahead. He set off at a run, with Viggo keeping up the rear. They ran as fast as they could, but soon realized that the lake was immense and that it was going to take an enormous effort to run around it three times. Herkson set off after the last group. He passed everyone easily, watching every group as he went.

They completed the first lap, and the effort began to tell on the teams.

"Keep the team together, as one," Herkson said, as he passed them. "Don't leave anyone behind."

When they had run a lap and a half, Gerd began to lag behind. Lasgol was keeping up the pace quite well, but when he saw the giant in trouble he moved forward until he came up with Ingrid.

"Slow down a bit. Gerd can't keep up with you."

Ingrid looked at him in annoyance. Then she turned to look at Gerd, who was falling behind, red as a ripe tomato.

"All right," she grumbled, and slowed down.

Lasgol fell back to Gerd's side. "Come on, you can do it."

He was gasping for breath. "No, I can't. I'm too big."

"Don't worry. On you go. I'm with you."

But the effort was too much for Gerd. He completed the second lap and had to stop. Viggo stopped too. He did not look well.

"Wait," Lasgol called to the girls.

Ingrid slowed reluctantly. "We can't stop."

"Oh, the poor thing," said Nilsa.

Gerd, bent double, was throwing up.

"Argh, how disgusting!" protested Viggo. He gave a start as Gerd vomited over his boots, then ran to the lakeshore to clean them.

Lasgol put his hand on Gerd's back to comfort him.

"Take it easy, don't worry."

Ingrid folded her arms. "They're all overtaking us."

"Let him get his breath back," Nilsa said.

Ingrid shook her head. "We'll be last."

"Other teams have got problems too," said Lasgol. He had noticed at least two other teams falling back.

Suddenly Herkson appeared at a run and stopped beside Gerd.

"We're not going to leave anybody behind," he said. "He's got to finish, even if he does it walking. You all walk with him." He ran off.

"Great!" said Viggo. "We can finish at a walk. If I'd known, I'd have thrown up myself a long time ago."

"Great plan, smarty-pants, except that we'll be penalized."

"Penalized?" Lasgol repeated.

"This test counts. What did you think?"

"Oh," Viggo said, and shrugged.

"I'm feeling better," Gerd said. He was as white as a ghost now. "Let's go on."

"Are you sure you're up to it?" Lasgol asked him.

"Yes, let's go. I don't want us to be the last just because of me."

Gerd, very honorably, finished the exercise. He even managed to break into a trot several times, although he did have to stop to catch his breath for a moment because he was about to throw up again. Viggo leapt back like lightning. They ended up walking, but unfortunately, they were the last. Gerd collapsed in exhaustion, and Viggo did not look too well either. Ingrid and Nilsa, on the other hand, were untroubled. For his part Lasgol was tired, but well.

Herkson greeted them with a nod. "Get back to the cabins. The others have already gone. Have your lunch at the canteen and rest. You have classes in the evening. Tomorrow we'll do this again, so come prepared."

Chapter 11

They reached the cabin as best they could. Ingrid and Lasgol were carrying Gerd on their shoulders. Nilsa was helping Viggo, who could not even speak. The atmosphere inside was grim. Gerd was lying on the bear fur, stretched out. He had not managed to reach his bed. Viggo was already sleeping face-down on his bed; he had collapsed, exhausted, still dressed and with his red cloak on.

"How did it go?" Egil asked when Ingrid and Nilsa had gone out.

"Very badly. We finished last," Lasgol said downheartedly.

"Gerd?"

"Yup, how did you know?"

"His body mass is too big for this type of endurance exercise."

"I forgot how smart you are."

"Nonsense. It's a logical deduction. Someone as big as a mountain might bring down a wall with a single charge, but not run around it for half the morning. He'll get better. He's very strong, he just needs to train. He's probably never run a single day in his life. Someone his size doesn't often. Which reminds me of…"

"What is it, Egil?"

"My own size. Gerd and I are opposites, but at the same time very much alike. I've never run a single day in my life either…"

Lasgol could not hide his concern. "Don't worry, we'll practice, I'll help you."

"Thanks, you have a good heart. But I'm afraid we'll need a lot more than that if we want to survive this dramatic situation in which we find ourselves."

Lasgol shook his head. "We're not going to give up, least of all before we've even started."

Egil nodded. "You're right As soon as I regain the merest trace of my limited strength, I'll start training. But I have to warn you, don't build too much hope on it. My body is weak."

"But your mind is huge," Lasgol said with a smile.

Egil laughed. "Go have something to eat, you need it. These two aren't going anywhere. I'll watch over them."

Lasgol went to the canteen. Ingrid and Nilsa were there, sharing a table with the Owls. Lasgol's eyes met those of Astrid, who was watching him with a stern expression. He looked away at once and sat down in front of his two partners. Ingrid was not happy at all; her face was frowning and her gaze grim. Nilsa on the other hand smiled at him.

Ingrid was unable to hold back her anger. "And then they're always pestering us girls, the weak ones. Well, it's a pretty pair of feeble little men they've saddled us with."

"They did what they could," Lasgol said.

She gave a grimace of distaste. "Sure, and what good did it do to the group? The only good thing about today is that it's made it absolutely clear that the girls are superior to the boys in the Snow Leopards team."

"Hear hear!" cried Nilsa, and gave a badly-controlled leap which almost made her fall backwards.

"If any boy tells me that we're inferior again, I'll beat him into a pulp."

"You can count on me to help you!" said the restless Nilsa, who was already squirming on the long bench. How she still had so much energy was something that puzzled Lasgol. This girl was always on edge.

Lasgol was silent. Their exhaustion made itself felt and they did not talk any more, they just ate. The second-year boys who served them did not cause any trouble this time, but Lasgol felt the eyes of the other initiates stabbing him with scorn. But although that was bad enough, it was nothing compared with all the other students in the dining-room, the second-, third- and fourth- years and even the Instructors, all watching him, burying arrows of hatred in his back.

Nilsa, who could not be still one moment and was looking everywhere, noticed this. She leant across the table toward him.

"They're trying to intimidate you. Don't let them."

"I know... thanks..."

Ingrid raised her head and looked around threateningly. A few hostile gazes turned away, but not many.

"Don't worry, I already knew what to expect before I came."

"Seeing this... I don't know whether I'd have come in your place..." Nilsa admitted.

"The brave grow up amid difficulties," said Ingrid. "My aunt used to say that, and she was a great warrior."

Lasgol nodded. He would either have to grow up fast or look forward to a terrible time.

They were about to get up when three boys came toward them. Lasgol recognized the one in the middle. It was Isgord. With him were two fair boys, tall and strong. They were twins.

"You were last," Isgord said abruptly.

Lasgol gave him an uncaring glance and said nothing.

"And what's that to you?" Ingrid asked.

"The Traitor and I have a score to settle. I wouldn't want him to be expelled before we have a chance."

She stood up. "If you don't leave now, I'll throw you out."

Isgord smiled. It was not a smile of scorn or mockery but one of acknowledgement.

"I see you've made friends, Traitor. That's good. But she won't save you. Not from me."

Nilsa was watching the exchange with such intensity that the soup bowl she was holding dropped to the floor.

"Get out of here," Ingrid said. "Now!"

Isgord gave her a hard look. This boy was not afraid of her. He was not afraid of anybody.

"I'll be seeing you again, Traitor." He signaled to the twins. "Jared, Aston, let's go."

Lasgol watched them leave and wondered why he had such bad luck. Everybody hated him, but Isgord seemed to want to kill him.

Ingrid sat down again. "Hey, what have you done to that one?"

"Nothing. I swear it. I'd never seen him before I came here. I don't know what he has against me."

"Well, it's a shame, because he's very handsome," Nilsa said as she picked up her bowl from the floor.

Ingrid and Lasgol looked at her blankly.

"Well... he's... it's just that he's...well, he is, and he's tall and strong and athletic..."

"You've forgotten his eyes," Ingrid said sarcastically.

"Oh yes... those blue eyes..."

Ingrid rolled her eyes, got up and left, looking daggers.

"Thank you," Lasgol said, before the Captain had gone.

Ingrid waved it away as if it were not important.

He was about to get up from the table when he felt a presence behind him. He prepared for another attack.

A soft voice said: "They say the apple never falls far from the tree. Is that your case?"

Lasgol turned around slowly and was left speechless. It was Astrid.

"I..." he muttered, "no, or – well, yes."

Astrid narrowed her eyes and tilted her head. "Well, yes or no? It can't be both."

"No... I'm no Traitor, which I think is what you were asking me. But yes... yes, I'm like my father. And I'm proud to be."

Astrid's expression changed to surprise. And then to wonder.

"If you're like your father and you're not a Traitor, are you trying to tell me that you don't believe your father was a traitor?"

Lasgol nodded, unable to take his eyes away from hers.

"Interesting."

"I'm not lying to you."

She smiled slightly, but did not reveal whether she believed him or not.

"I wish you luck. You're going to need it."

"Thanks ..."

Astrid left, followed by her team. Nilsa smiled at him and winked.

"I believe you."

"Thanks, Nilsa."

"But then, I'm a really trustful person, or at least that's what they tell me at home. I don't think I'd be the best judge about those matters."

"You've judged me well. You can't be that bad."

Nilsa laughed. "You say that, but you could be lying."

Lasgol gave a bitter laugh. "You're right, you wouldn't know."

She jumped up, almost upsetting the table. "Come on, or we'll be late."

They left the dining-room, and Lasgol took a deep breath of the forest air. It comforted him. They went to the cabins to join the rest of the team.

They rested as much as they could, but evening came quickly and the bell rang. They left the cabin and fell in. Master Instructor Oden was waiting for them with his hands behind his back, looking unfriendly.

"I see the physical training has done you good," he said with a sarcastic smile. "Now it's time for herbal instruction. Follow me to the cabins of the School of Nature, where you'll be given your lesson. Every evening, after lunch, you'll be instructed in one of the four Schools, every day, each one alternately. And no, nobody is excused. If anybody's feeling poorly, I'll be delighted to show him the way out of the camp. Anyone?"

There was silence. Lasgol glanced uneasily at Gerd, but the giant held his ground.

"Very well, then. Last year I had a drop-out the first morning. They don't make Norghanians like they used to… Follow me!"

The lesson in herbalism turned out to be highly interesting and informative. Particularly Instructor Marga of the School of Nature.

"She's a witch, for sure," Viggo whispered to Gerd.

Gerd nodded. "She certainly looks the part. Do you think she'll teach us how to make poisons?"

"Most certainly. It'd be nice to poison somebody by accident" Viggo gave a nasty snicker, his eyes on Ingrid.

"Shut up and listen, you fool," she scolded him in a harsh whisper.

Viggo wrinkled his nose and made a face.

"This mushroom isn't poisonous," said Instructor Marga. "And you can use it to prepare a potion that will help you sleep."

Lasgol had to admit that she looked like a witch. She wore a black cloak and her face was that of an old woman, with untidy white hair. A large hooked nose and two warts, on her chin and cheekbone made for a decidedly ugly face.

"But there are some which are very poisonous, so if you don't know anything about mushrooms, and by the looks of you, you don't, don't even think of eating them."

They were sitting inside a building shaped like a horseshoe, and the instructor was walking around the inside, explaining the wonders of wild mushrooms in a hoarse voice.

After the lesson, which lasted forever, they had dinner in the canteen and then went back to their cabin. They were so tired that all they wanted to do was sleep. Ingrid and Nilsa said goodnight and went in on their own side. The boys went into theirs. Gerd and Viggo collapsed onto their berths.

"Lasgol…" Egil called out.

"Yes, what is it? D'you need anything?"

"No, I'm all right. It's something else…"

"Tell me, what is it?"

"Do you really think we'll make it? I've spent the whole day thinking about it, and the chances are so unlikely…"

"I'm sure of it. Now rest."

"Okay. Good night."

"Sleep well."

Lasgol took off his cloak and opened his trunk. He put it inside, and when he did, he had a strange feeling. The hair on the back of his neck stood on end. *Hmm, that's really strange…* He stared at the trunk, but there was little that could be seen in the light of the solitary oil lamp on the table. And almost unconsciously, his hand searched for the box with his Father's gift. He opened it carefully. The egg was still intact. He let out his breath, relieved. For an instant he had thought that something bad might have happened to it. He had been meaning to examine it for days, but it had been impossible. He took it between his hands and studied every detail. There were thousands of tiny black specks encrusted on its white surface. And now he was paying more attention, they seemed to form a pattern. *How curious… or rather how strange…*

Everyone else was sleeping, and he was already very tired. It would be better to put the egg back in its box and go to bed. But before he did that, he wanted to check something that had just come to his mind. He stood the egg upright on the floor, holding the tip with one finger. With his other hand he made it spin like a top. He knew it would not be damaged because it was hard as rock. The egg started to spin under his finger and the pattern he had identified began to appear before his eyes. He spun it faster and the pattern became a word: L-A-S-G-O-L.

My name! By the icy winds! What does this mean? He had to find out what was going on. He focused on the word he could see with growing clarity. His eyes were fixed on it while the egg spun under his finger. He felt a slight dizziness and closed his eyes. As he did, a green flash came out of his hand and passed into the egg through the finger that was keeping up the contact. The egg reacted by giving out a golden flash, and a discharge of energy hit Lasgol and hurled him to the floor.

Chapter 12

"Come on, wake up, please," Egil said. He sounded deeply concerned.

Lasgol did not move.

"It'd be better if you shook him a little," Viggo said. "Or a punch in the face might help."

"Leave it to me," said Gerd. "Lasgol, wake up!" He shook him by the shoulders with his huge hands.

Lasgol opened his eyes. His face was a total blank.

"What? Where... am I?"

"On the floor of the cabin," said Egil. "Are you all right? We couldn't wake you."

"Uh ... oh yes ... did I fall asleep on the floor?"

"It looks that way," Viggo said. He folded his arms. "You certainly like to make your life more complicated, what with the way these beds are so comfortable."

"We have to go," Gerd said. "The call's sounded." He went to the door, looking resigned.

"Yeah, sure... we can't be late," Lasgol said.

Egil helped him to his feet.

Suddenly he remembered the egg, and the discharge of energy! He looked around, searching for the egg. When he did not see it, he felt worry grip his chest.

"Are you looking for something?" Viggo asked suspiciously.

"I... well..."

"It wouldn't by any chance be a huge egg?"

Lasgol turned to Viggo. "D'you have it?"

"Me? No, the giant here must have had it for breakfast. He was famished."

Lasgol turned to Gerd in the doorway, his eyes almost bursting from their sockets. "Nooooo!" he protested.

The giant turned around in surprise.

"Don't take any notice of him," said Egil. "It's not true."

Viggo began to laugh.

"It's not funny! Who's got it?"

Viggo was in stitches. "If you could see your face, you wouldn't think that."

"I have it," said Egil, and showed it to him. "I found it on the floor."

Lasgol gasped in relief. He took the egg between his hands. It was intact.

"It's not to eat!" he said, jabbing his finger at Viggo, then at Gerd.

Gerd's face was red. "I wasn't going to eat it... well, actually maybe I was, but Egil told me we'd better ask you first."

Viggo was still laughing. He was having the time of his life.

"Nobody's to touch that egg!" Lasgol shouted.

Ingrid came into the cabin, followed by Nilsa. "What's all this about an egg?" she said.

"This one," Lasgol said. He showed it to her.

"What on earth do you think you're playing with? Stop being silly, we're going to be late and I don't fancy running an extra lap around the lake. Do you?"

Gerd left the cabin like lightning, looking embarrassed. Nilsa followed straight away, giggling, and overtook him.

"I'm coming, I'm coming," said Viggo. "It was really funny." He followed them, grinning broadly.

Lasgol turned to Egil. "Will you look after it? The box for it's in my trunk."

"Of course. Off you go now, don't worry."

"Thanks."

Ingrid and Lasgol set off at a run. They caught up with the rest of the teams at the lake. Luckily Herkson made the groups arrange themselves in order of their arrival the day before, so that the Panthers set off last. Because of this, they were not penalized for arriving late.

This second morning was not too different from the first. Poor Gerd threw up again, and they finished last once again. Although to add a positive note it took them less time than it had the day before, even though only a little. Viggo had suggested changing the name of the team from the Panthers to The Snails.

The afternoon did have one positive surprise. Master Instructor Oden made an appearance, and with his direct, abrupt style led them to the Archery Fields in a cleared area east of the camp center.

They found Ivana, the Master Ranger of the School of Archery, waiting for them. She made the thirteen teams fall in, going down on one knee and looking straight ahead.

"The School of Archery is essential for all Rangers. The things you'll learn in this discipline, the skills you'll develop, will make you better Rangers. Every Ranger needs to acquire the basics of this School. Anyone who fails to master this basic competence will be expelled."

Lasgol watched her, captivated by her cold beauty, fearful of failing and having to leave the Camp.

"On the other hand those who stand out, the best ones among you, will go on to be part of the Specialty of Archers at the end of the Fourth Year. I'll choose them myself, personally."

Lasgol glanced at Ingrid and she nodded. In her eyes he could see the conviction that she was going to succeed. He, on the other hand, knowing how mediocre an archer he was, only hoped he would be able to pass the basic tests to avoid expulsion.

"And as for the very special ones, I'll choose them for the Elite Specialty. That is, if there is one among you who's good enough. Will there be? It doesn't usually happen, but we'll see…"

Nilsa squirmed restlessly. More so even than usual. She could not stay still. Falling in was torture for her, but in front of Ivana it was even more so. Nilsa wished above all else to become a Mage Hunter, one Specialty of the Elite Archers. Nothing would make her happier than to free the world of the cursed mages and wizards. She had a profound wish and motive, one of blood.

Gerd gave her a friendly poke. "You'll be sure to make it."

"Oh sure," Viggo sneered. "She'd probably strangle herself with the string of her own bow when she was trying to tighten it."

Nilsa made a face, but was not going to let Viggo bother her. She needed to succeed in this discipline, and she was going to put all her attention and effort into it. Nothing was going to distract her. Nothing was going to make her fail.

Ivana went on: "A demonstration will give you a clearer understanding of what I mean. I've always said that when it comes to demonstrating something, words fall short beside a true arrow."

She signaled, and two Rangers appeared with bows.

"Show the initiates which School you belong to," she said.

The two Rangers opened their cloaks. Around their necks was a medallion identical to Ivana's, with the carving of a bow in the middle, but smaller.

"I'll get as far as wearing one of those," Ingrid said.

Lasgol nodded and smiled at her. He was sure nothing would stop her.

"Right then. Show them what the Archers are capable of."

The two Rangers moved a hundred paces away from each other. One of them raised his bow and held it over his head with both hands, a hand's-width apart. The other left his own on the ground in front of him. Everybody watched attentively. There was a moment's pause. Nobody spoke. There was a gentle breeze that smelled of moist grass. In the distance came the sound of fledglings tweeting, demanding food from their parents.

Suddenly the unarmed Ranger moved. He slid the tip of his leather boot under the bow on the ground and lifted it with a well-judged movement. The bow rose in front of him, spinning. His left arm shot out like lightning and caught it as it spun in midair. His right hand moved over his shoulder and took an arrow from the quiver at his back. In a swift move bow and arrow slid into position. The Ranger crouched until one knee was on the ground, then released the arrow. The whole movement had occurred in the blink of an eye. The arrow flew the hundred paces with a lethal whistle and embedded itself in the handhold of the bow above the other Ranger's head.

The initiates cried out, utterly surprised and stunned. Lasgol, gaping at what he had just witnessed, longed with his whole being to enter that specialty. To be able to do what those Rangers were capable of. Then he thought of how unskilled he was with the bow, and his hope sank down into the mud.

"If you want to be as good as they are, if you want to wear the medallions that hang around their necks, you'll have to work hard. Very hard. For three years. But if you do, someday you'll be able to do what you've just witnessed. And one of you, a special one – if there is one among you – will get to do truly amazing things."

The murmurs among the initiates were full of optimism. "I'll manage it," "I want to be like them," "I'll be an Archer" and other comments of the kind could be heard. The two Rangers came to stand behind Ivana.

"Remember this well," said the Master Ranger of the School of Archery. "Those who fail to master the basic level of skills will be expelled, they will never be Rangers. On the other hand, those who excel will be able to belong to the Archers."

And with that message Ivana withdrew, followed by the two men.

"I'm terrible with a bow," said Gerd.

"I'm not too good either," Lasgol agreed.

"Phew, what a team..." Ingrid snorted.

"And are you any good yourself?" Viggo asked her.

"Well, as a matter of fact I am. Not only that, I'm very good with sword, axe and fist. A lot better than most of those strutting peacocks." She indicated a group of boys who were discussing what they had just seen, as if they too could do it.

"Well," Viggo said, "if you're good with sword, axe and fist, that's because you've been trained. You should've gone to the Royal Army, that's where all those weapons are normally used, not here. So why are you here?"

"Because my father was a Ranger."

"*Was?*" Lasgol repeated.

"He disappeared... on a mission..."

"Oh, and he never came back?"

"No."

"Sorry, I didn't mean to..."

"It's okay. It was a long time ago, when I was a little girl."

"So in that case who taught you to fight?"

"His sister, my aunt Brenda."

"A woman?" Viggo said in surprise.

"Yes, a woman. So what?"

"Nothing, it's just unusual."

"My aunt belonged to the Invincibles of the Ice."

"Now that's something nobody'll ever believe!" cried Viggo.

"Are you calling me a liar? I'm going to punch your nose!"

Gerd stepped in between them. "Don't fight," he said.

"The Invincibles of the Ice are the elite of the royal infantry," Viggo said. "They don't accept women."

"You don't know anything about it!" Ingrid cried.

"I know you're lying. There aren't any women in the Invincibles."

Dodging Gerd, who pushed himself into her way to stop her, Ingrid tried to hit Viggo. Nilsa held her, while Lasgol did the same with Viggo.

"My aunt was an Invincible of the Ice! And I'm going to mark your face with what she taught me!"

"Sure, and I'm a Prince of a Kingdom of the East!"

Nilsa, Gerd and Lasgol had to struggle to contain the fight.

"What's going on here, Snow Panthers?" came a stern voice they did not know.

The spat stopped at once, and they turned to the Ranger beside them. Around his neck hung a medallion with the image of a bow.

"This isn't much of an example for a team. You'll only get yourselves expelled this way."

Ingrid and Viggo went quiet, and the others bent their heads in shame.

"My name is Ivar, Instructor in the School of Archery. Now fall in!"

The five bent one knee and looked ahead of them.

"Wolves, Bears, Falcons and Panthers, with me," said Ivar.

At once the teams assembled. Another three Instructor Archers took charge of the other teams. Lasgol was glad they were not with the Eagles, which included Isgord.

Ivar addressed the four teams: "The Instruction of Archery will be divided into two parts, one learning and the other practicing the subjects a Ranger needs to know in order to survive." He swept his gaze over the four teams. "What's a Ranger's main weapon?"

Ashlin, a girl from the Wolves, thin and dark, with a clever face, stepped forward.

"Yes?" said Ivar.

"All the Rangers carry a bow. It's their main weapon, and also a hunting knife and a short axe."

"Very good, the answer is correct. You'll learn to use all those weapons, and in more ways than one."

"How?" asked Osvak, a tall, strong boy from the Bears.

"You'll be taught, don't worry. Everything in its own time, and following *The Path of the Ranger*."

"What's that?" Gerd asked.

"It's the set of teachings the Rangers rule themselves by. We've been doing that for over a hundred years, and with very good results."

"Uh, thanks," Gerd said.

"I'll teach you to make your own bows," Ivar went on, "choosing the wood, the string and the appropriate components. The same with the making of arrows. So that if one day you find yourselves without your weapon, you'll be able to make one with your own hands. I'll also teach you how to make rudimentary axes and knives."

"Wouldn't it be a lot easier if they gave us coin and we bought one?" whispered Viggo into Nilsa's ear. She giggled.

"Shut up and listen!" Ingrid reproached him.

Instructor Ivar seemed to notice the whispering and gave them a warning glare.

"A Ranger must be able to survive by himself in the wild. The dangers facing you are many, and you'll find yourselves in some dire situations. Those of us who serve the realm live lives full of danger. The things you might learn during the time you're here will save your life more than once. Of course, I mean those of you who manage to become Rangers, which of course not everybody will."

The comment had an effect on Lasgol. He had been practicing with a bow since he was four years old, when his father had made him his first one and shown him how to use it, and he had not been able to master it. The memory filled him with sadness and his eyes became moist. He took a deep breath and tried to stay calm.

"Well," Ivar said, "let's see what I've been given to deal with this year. Each team, get into a line, with the Captain in the lead facing those trees." He pointed to four oaks fifty paces away with a large round target on their trunks. "Shoot at that target. Five times each, in rotation."

He gave each Captain a bow and a quiver, then moved back and watched. Ingrid examined her bow, then checked the direction of the wind. She took her time and finally released. Simply by watching her handle the weapon, Lasgol knew that she would hit the target. And he was right. She hit the bull's eye. She passed the bow and quiver to Nilsa, who was too eager and hasty and failed to get a good grip on the quiver. It fell to the ground, scattering all the arrows on the grass.

"I'm sorry," she said and began to pick them up. Ingrid covered her eyes in despair.

It took Nilsa a moment to put all the arrows back in the quiver, then sling it on her back correctly. Finally she was ready to shoot. And to the surprise of all the Panthers she did it well. She hit the target, although not in the center as Ingrid had done. She smiled from ear to ear and passed the bow and quiver to Gerd. He shot, and the arrow seemed to swerve to one side. It hit the target, but on the outer rim.

"Phew!" he breathed, relieved that at least he had hit something.

Lasgol was next. He tried to relax, but Ivar's eyes were fixed on him. He inhaled deeply, then breathed out three times. Then he aimed.

"Let's see what the Traitor's son can do, then" Ivar said disdainfully.

The comment distracted him. Rage began to burn his stomach, but he controlled it. He would not give him the satisfaction of making a fool of himself. He concentrated, breathed and released. The arrow flew off at great speed. It reached the target a hand-span off-center. An accurate enough shot, but worse than Ingrid's or Nilsa's. He sighed. It was not bad for his level of skill with a bow.

The last one was Viggo. Lasgol watched him curiously. Would he be good with the bow? The answer was not long in coming. His arrow struck beside Gerd's. A pretty bad shot.

"Again," said Ivar.

They all released five shots. The results were not very different. Ingrid hit the bull's eye each time. Nilsa tried to get close to the other girl's shots without succeeding, although they were still good shots. Lasgol came halfway. Gerd and Viggo had difficulty in getting their arrows to hit the target. Compared with the other three teams the result was not very good. The Falcons had six very good archers, while the Wolves' results were similar to those of the Panthers and the Bears' a little worse, which was surprising.

After the archery exercises Ivar made them sit in a circle around him. He pointed out all the mistakes he had noticed in the way each of them used the bow. It was amazing how much detail the instructor had retained. Lasgol listened with all his attention; maybe he would learn how to shoot properly at last. Then Ivar explained the importance of measuring the wind, the correct posture for getting a good shot and how to aim at a target at that distance. But above all, how to release the arrow without losing their balance, which seemed to be the great problem for most of them.

At the end of the lesson they went to the canteen and had dinner. They sat at a table with the Wolves. While they ate, Luca, the Wolves' leader, an athletic boy with brown hair and a pointed nose, came to speak to Ingrid. Lasgol was so hungry that he did not pay much attention to what they said. When Luca went back to sit with his team, Viggo questioned Ingrid.

"And what did he want?"

"Captains' stuff."

"What d'you mean, 'captains' stuff?'"

"That it's no concern of yours."

"Everything you plot with other teams is my concern."

"Who said I'm plotting anything?"

Nilsa, Gerd and Lasgol watched the exchange without stopping eating.

"You were planning something between you."

"Shut up and eat."

Viggo glared at her angrily. "I'm watching you," he said, and jabbed his finger at her.

Ingrid shrugged it off and went on eating.

Lasgol ate and tried not to look around, since he knew that the eyes of all the second-, third- and fourth-year boys were on him. It surprised him to see Dolbarar at the instructors' table dining with several of them and chatting animatedly. For some reason he had thought Dolbarar would have his meal in the great house, but it seemed he preferred to come down to the dining room. Ivana, the Master Ranger of the School of Archery, came in at that moment and sat down at the table beside Dolbarar. A little later the Tamer Esben, Master Ranger of the School of Wildlife, came in. He looked like a great bear indeed, and he moved like one. He sat down at Dolbarar's table and made an attempt to comb his unruly hair as he greeted the others. It appeared they all had their meals there, along with everybody else. Lasgol nodded involuntarily. He liked that point.

After dinner they went back to the cabins for the night. When they arrived Egil was waiting for them eagerly.

"How did it go?" he asked.

"Actually, quite well," Lasgol said.

"We didn't come in last!" Gerd said enthusiastically.

Egil smiled. His color was already much better. "That's really good!"

"You should've seen Ingrid and Nilsa," said Gerd. "They're really good with a bow!"

Egil smiled and nodded. "And you?"

"So-so," Lasgol said.

"It's true we weren't last today," Viggo said, "but that'll soon change, won't it, Egil?"

128

"What d'you mean?" Gerd asked blankly.

"Our discerning partner means to suggest that when I join the team, we will indeed trail the field," Egil said.

"Really?"

"Yes, my mastery with the bow is non-existent. I have never used one."

"Oh … well…. if it makes you feel better, I make us last when we run…"

"Thanks, Gerd, you're a good partner," Egil said, smiling.

Viggo snorted. "We'll see what we come last in next…"

"Look on the bright side," said Egil. "From now on, we can only get better."

Gerd, Lasgol and Egil laughed. Viggo looked from one to another, shaking his head.

The door opened. Ingrid and Nilsa looked at them in puzzlement.

"Why are you laughing?" Ingrid asked.

Egil looked at her. "Because as we're so bad, the sky's the limit!"

Ingrid put her hand to her eyes and shook her head. Nilsa burst out laughing.

Chapter 13

The following week things were more or less the same, except that Egil had now recovered and joined the team. And with this, the Panthers' results worsened even further. In physical training Gerd, who had improved considerably, was no longer last; now Egil took his place. They had to wait for him. With his far-from-athletic body and inexperience with the rigors of physical activity, he could not manage more than a single lap around the lake. Things were no better in the School of Archery sessions. He had no idea how to even handle a bow. His shots never reached the target, and not only because of lack of marksmanship but lack of strength. Lasgol meanwhile had decided not to have anything more to do with the egg again after the earlier incident, at least until he was able to understand rather more of what was happening.

That afternoon Master Instructor Oden appeared after lunch and told the thirteen teams to fall in: one knee on the ground, looking straight ahead.

"Today you'll begin your training in the School of Wildlife. It's a complex specialty, and 'accidents' can sometimes happen. For that reason, give the instructors your full attention. And don't do anything stupid. Anything at all. Is that clear?"

A murmur of "yeses" came from the teams.

"I only want to hear the Captains."

"Yes, it's clear!" the Captains called out as one.

"Good. If anybody finishes up wounded, human or animal, you'll remember me. You can bank on that. Understood?" he shouted at the top of his voice.

"Understood!" the Captains shouted back.

Oden led them to the woods north of the Camp limits. They had never gone so far into the dense vegetation before. The walk turned out to be refreshing, not just for the spirit but also the body, since the further north they went, the colder it was and the more snow and ice they saw. On a hill in the middle of a fir forest they found four long cabins decorated with portrayals of animals.

"There you are," Oden said, "the School of Wildlife. They're waiting for you." He walked back briskly.

In the space between the cabins five Rangers were waiting for them. As they came closer they saw that the Ranger at the center was none other than Tamer Esben, the Master Ranger of the School of Wildlife.

"Welcome to all of you, Initiates. I'm Esben the Tamer. They call me that because they say I have an innate ability to communicate with animals and dominate them. And they aren't wrong. This might be a strange concept for you, but the Rangers are among the few who practice this art, and I think you'll find it interesting, even fascinating. With a bit of luck there'll be some among you with the same aptitude. Unfortunately it won't be the case for the majority. This discipline isn't like the others, because part of it can't be learned, it's innate. Some are born with it, some not. Those who have it will be able to move on to the elite specialties. Those who don't will still be able to form part of this school if they pass the basic training."

He gestured to one of his helpers, who stepped forward and displayed the bear medallion. He put two fingers to his lips and whistled in imitation of a bird's call. Then he stretched out his arm. On it they could see a wristband of reinforced leather. Suddenly there came a shrill croak, and they all looked up. A great white eagle glided over their heads, so that they cried out and crouched down in fear. The eagle glided above them once again, then landed on the instructor's wrist and gave its powerful wings a final shake.

Lasgol gasped in astonishment as he watched the instructor stroking the majestic bird, which responded by moving its head. How could he manage to do that himself? *I wish I could do that with animals.*

The instructor shook his arm and his eagle flew up and away. Then the Ranger withdrew to his place.

Esben came closer to the teams. Seen from so near, Lasgol realized he was extremely big and strong. A true Norghanian, although with a certain animal look about him.

"In the School of Wildlife you'll learn everything about animals, domestic ones as well as the ones that inhabit the forests and mountains of our land. You'll learn to look after them, from ponies and horses to other, wilder animals. With me, you"ll learn to recognize the birds by their songs and the beasts by the prints they leave on the ground. You'll know where they nest, where they hibernate, where they hunt, and how they do it, because only in this way will you be able to move in the wild lands like one more animal among others. The Path shows us that the Ranger walks like one more creature of the forest."

He crouched down. "Captains, to me."

The thirteen Captains gathered around him.

Esben pointed to the damp soil. "Who can tell me what animal left this trail?

"A wolf?" Isgord suggested, although not very confidently.

Esben shook his head.

"Fox," said Jobas, the Captain of the Boars.

The Master Ranger shook his head again. He looked at Astrid of the Owls, then at Ingrid. They were the only two girls among the Captains. He asked Ingrid: "What do you think?"

Ingrid hunkered down, examined the print and sighed.

Lasgol, who had recognized it, wanted to whisper: "It's a ferret!"

Ingrid shook her head. "I don't know. I've been taught to fight, but I can't track."

Lasgol thought her reply would anger Esben, but he was wrong.

"That happens to a lot of people," he said, and smiled. His beard seemed to take on a life of its own. "Let me tell you that for a Ranger it's much more important to know how to follow a trail than it is to fight."

Ingrid was taken aback. "More important than fighting?"

"What use is fighting if you go into a forest and you lose track of your prey? I'll tell you what'll happen. The prey will get away, and if it knows how to follow a trail it'll go around you and kill you before you even know it's happened." Esben mimed releasing an arrow, then a knife cutting a throat.

"Oh, now I see," Ingrid said.

"I'm glad. Anyone who's certain what print this is, raise your hand."

A dozen hands rose, among them Lasgol's.

Esben noted those who had raised their hands. When he saw Lasgol he singled him out.

"You, the son of Dakon the Traitor. Are you sure you know what animal made this print?"

Lasgol did his best to stay calm. "Yes, sir."

"You'd better be very sure, because if you fail, I'll send you to clean the stables every morning for a month. And let me tell you, they stink."

"It's a ferret's," Lasgol said confidently.

"I see your treacherous father taught you something useful after all. What do you know about ferrets?"

"Ferrets are carnivores. They're excellent hunters. Above all, of rabbits and rodents, although they also catch small birds. They hunt in the morning and spend most of the day sleeping. They can be tamed and used to hunt because of their ability to get into lairs. They're intelligent and very curious. Like skunks, they give out a scent to mark their territory or when they're scared, although they don't smell as bad and the odor doesn't last as long. Their pelts can be sold to tanners."

"How many more animals do you know?"

"All the animals in my county, the County of Malason."

Esben nodded and clasped his hands behind his back.

"What you have just witnessed is what I expect of each and every one of you. And it won't be just a single county but all Norghana. Anyone who's unable to learn the same as the Traitor's son will be expelled."

Gerd, looking worried, whispered to Egil: "I'm not very good at remembering things..."

"Don't worry," Egil said. "I'm extremely competent at that. I'll help you."

Gerd gave him a relieved smile. "Thanks, pal."

"Does anybody know why the Rangers are called the King's bloodhounds?" Esben asked.

"Because they follow and hunt down the King's enemies," said Isgord.

"Exactly. A Ranger can read the trails of beasts and men, no matter how difficult the terrain. He can work out how many men camped at a site on a hill two days before, the kind of horses they had with them, whether they were soldiers or mercenaries, the supplies they were carrying, the direction they came from and where they were heading, what they ate, how much rest they needed, their state of mind, and much more just by reading the trail they left. That's what you'll learn in this School."

"I'd love to be able to know all those things just by looking at prints," Gerd whispered to Egil.

"It ought to be possible. It's a matter of relating the cause and effect of each print and guessing its meaning through the application of expert knowledge."

Gerd stared at him blankly.

"What I mean to say is that we'll be taught to interpret the prints and make the most plausible deductions about their significance."

"I didn't understand that any more than I understood what you said the first time."

Nilsa gave a friendly nervous laugh. "The wise guy means we'll be taught to read tracks and who or what might have left them."

"I'm not a wise guy…"

"Aren't you? Oh, well then, a know-it-all," said Nilsa with a laugh.

Egil made a face and laughed along with them.

"This is going to be a School where we'll learn a lot. I think we're going to be good at it," Lasgol said, smiling. It was certainly the School he would manage best himself.

"And now," Esben went on, "you'll be assigned an Instructor. In this School you'll be dealing with wild animals, so you'll have to pay close attention and be very careful. Follow the Instructors' orders, and that way we won't need any trips to the infirmary."

"Wild animals?" Gerd said, looking fearful.

"Yes," Viggo said. "I understand we'll be taught to dominate beasts, wolves, and bears even." He gave a sinister leer.

Gerd's face turned white.

"Don't listen to him," Nilsa said "He's exaggerating."

"No, redhead, I'm not exaggerating. You wait and see."

One of the Rangers with Esben came up to them.

"My name is Ben, Instructor in the School of Wildlife," he said. "The Eagles, the Boars, the Bears and the Panthers: with me."

Lasgol gasped. Those were the strongest teams, and unluckily for him Isgord was the Captain of the Eagles. All of a sudden his eagerness to enjoy that School vanished.

The teams gathered around Ben. Isgord glared at Lasgol with hatred the moment he set eyes on him. Lasgol ignored him.

"We're going to go into the forest, toward the northeast," Ben said. "Follow me in absolute silence. When I raise my fist, crouch and stay as still as stone statues. Is that clear?"

They nodded.

Ben did not waste a moment. Confidently he went into the forest. The teams followed, with the Panthers keeping up the rear. They walked in silence for half the afternoon. The tops of the trees were covered in snow and the ground was damp. It was cold, but the impressive cloaks they wore protected them from it and the cutting wind. Lasgol had no idea what material they were made of, but it was something he had never seen before. They were very sturdy but light, and very warm. Maybe Egil would know what they were made of. He would have to ask him.

They came to a hill, and Ben raised his hand. They crouched and stayed still.

The Instructor turned and whispered: "Tracks. Fresh ones. Each team, examine them, and then the Captain can tell me what animal made them."

All the teams came closer to inspect the prints, then moved back to compare notes. When the Panthers' turn came they all looked at Lasgol.

"What do you think?" Ingrid whispered, looking determined.

Lasgol studied the trail for a long moment in silence, concentrating deeply. Then he looked at the trees around.

Gerd was staring at him in fascination. "Why are you looking at the trees?"

"They're deserted."

"So?" Viggo asked.

"There aren't any birds or squirrels, and I haven't seen any kind of deer either for quite a while."

"Predators," said Egil.

"Exactly. They're wolf prints."

"How clever you are!" cried Nilsa excitedly.

Ingrid half-closed her blue eyes. "Wolf prints, then?"

"Yes. I'm sure of that," Lasgol said.

Ingrid informed Ben.

"Eagles and Panthers, with me. The rest stay here because you were wrong, and study those prints until you can remember every detail."

"We're good at something!" said Nilsa. She gave a leap of joy.

Ben signaled to them to follow him. Isgord led the Eagles, Ingrid the Panthers. They went on deeper into the forest. Ben stopped from time to time to examine prints, then went on. After a while he made them stop. He studied the soil and the vegetation around closely.

"Wait for me here," he told them, and went deeper into the trees following a trail.

"What d'you think he's looking for?" Nilsa asked.

"No idea," said Gerd. He was sitting with his legs crossed, and the rest of the team followed his example. "From what little my brother told me, those with the skill of Wildlife are capable of following any trail and communicating with animals."

"You have a brother who's a Ranger?" Nilsa asked.

"Communicate with animals?" Ingrid asked at almost the same moment.

Gerd looked at both girls. "Yes, I have an older brother who's a Ranger, that's why I was given the invitation. And yes, some Rangers are capable of communicating with animals, or at least that's what my brother told me on one of his visits. But you know what they're like, everything's secret. He's hardly told me anything about what goes on here."

"I'm sure he didn't tell you any more so as not to scare you," Viggo sneered.

Nilsa wrinkled her nose. "Leave him alone."

Viggo raised his hands in surrender.

"What School is your brother in?" Egil asked.

"The School of Archery. He's very good with bow, axe and Ranger's knife."

"Is he your size?" Ingrid asked.

"He's slightly smaller... more agile than me...I take after our father... he takes after our mother."

"Funny how it all works," said Egil, "this business of blood and the inheritance of physical attributes and the genealogical tree. It's really fascinating."

They all stared at him without the slightest idea what he meant. He became aware of this, smiled and shrugged.

"What does your family do?" Lasgol asked.

"We're farmers in the east of the kingdom. I've spent all my life on the farm, working hard." He showed them his huge, leathery hands. There was no doubt they were the hands of a farmer. We're poor... the farm doesn't make much... the soil isn't good, and there are five of us brothers..."

"Five?"

"Plus my parents. It's tough in winter... That's why my oldest brother left to become a Ranger. My grandfather on my mother's side had been one. When my time came... I had no choice but to accept the invitation. We'd just gone through a horrible winter and only survived thanks to the goodness of our neighbors... we had no food left and we weren't going to get any more. It wasn't the first time. That's why I had to leave, I was a burden. My brother has his own family to take care of now. It's my turn to help. With a Ranger's pay I'll be able to help my parents, and their winters won't be so harsh."

"I'm so sorry..." Nilsa said, moist-eyed.

Ingrid nodded. "It does you credit."

"But did you want to be a Ranger?" Egil asked curiously.

Gerd heaved a deep sigh. "No, not really, no. I like being a farmer. Sow, cultivate the crops, gather in the harvest and live a quiet, simple life ... but I've got three younger brothers and the farm isn't enough for all of us. So I followed in my elder brother's footsteps."

"I gathered as much," said Egil. "If it's any consolation to you, I wouldn't be here either if I had the choice."

"I want to know something," said Viggo.

They all looked at him, knowing it would not be a friendly question.

"Fire away," said Gerd.

"Why are you such a coward?"

"Hey!" Ingrid protested at once. Nilsa glared.

"He told me to ask, and that's what I did. Come on, don't tell me you haven't wondered the same thing yourselves. He's the biggest and strongest of all. How can he be such a chicken?" Viggo was apparently unaware of any offense he might be giving.

"You're a troll!" Nilsa shouted at him. She could barely stop herself from attacking him.

"Okay, then," said Gerd. His cheeks were red. "I don't like to talk about it..."

"You don't have to if you don't want to," Lasgol said.

"I'd rather answer ... you're my team. I want you to know why I'm the way I am...You see..." He tried to go on, but the words would not come out of his mouth. He choked and began to cough.

"Is it because of some traumatic experience you had when you were little?" Egil asked.

Gerd, who was coughing uncontrollably by now, nodded repeatedly.

"I've read something on the subject in one of the books in my father's private library. Phobias derived from traumatic experiences during childhood."

Ingrid was completely baffled. "What kind of books do you read, then?"

"Oh, all kinds, of course. How else would I learn about everything?" He said it very seriously, as if it were the most natural thing in the world. They all stared at him incredulously.

At that moment Instructor Ben came back and signaled to them to follow him. They walked a good distance and came to a gully with a stream running down it. Ben raised his fist, and both teams crouched and froze. There was a strange silence, broken by a gust of wind which shook the branches and needles of the firs.

At that point they noticed before them on the other side of the gully, a pack of gray wolves was watching them. Lasgol's blood froze in his veins. To his horror, he realized that they were unarmed. Gerd, frozen with terror, started to shiver. Nilsa hugged him tightly in an attempt to make him stop. Ingrid found a thick stick to defend herself and grasped it firmly. Viggo put his hand to his waist and from a hidden compartment in his belt took out a small dagger. Lasgol's eyes widened in surprise. Viggo put his finger to his lips and gave him a curious look.

Ben hunkered down, very slowly, he started toward the gully, straight to the stream. *Where's he going? They're going to tear him to shreds! There must be at least a dozen of them!* Ben went on downhill, slowly, without any fear. Suddenly the largest and fiercest-looking wolf started down the gully on the other side.

"That's the alpha male," whispered Lasgol.

"The what?" asked Gerd.

"The leader of the pack," said Egil.

"It's going to kill him," said Viggo.

"Ben'll know how to defend himself," said Ingrid.

"Yeah, but the pack will jump at him," said Egil. "They'll kill him."

"This is terrible!" said Nilsa.

Ben reached the ravine and crouched down. The wolf approached from the other side of the water. It was showing its fangs and growling threateningly.

"It's going to attack him!" Nilsa muttered.

Lasgol held her firmly. "Shhh. Let's see what happens."

Ben put his hands to his chest and bowed his head to the wolf. The animal stopped growling and came even closer, although its fangs were still bared and threatening.

Ben took out his School of Wildlife medallion and stretched out his arms to show it to the wolf, without looking at it directly. Lasgol was spellbound, alert to every movement. His eyes were fixed on the medallion in front of the beast's snout. Suddenly the wolf growled and its aggression returned. And then something very strange happened. The wooden medallion gave out a green flash. At once the wolf stepped back and its aggressive attitude vanished.

Ben withdrew his arms and the medallion fell back against his chest. He stood up slowly and pointed to his right. The wolf followed his gaze, then went to stand on his right. Ben gestured to his left and the beast obeyed him once again. Everybody was watching, their mouths open.

"Go with your pack," Ben said to the wolf. The animal, as though understanding what the Ranger had said, went back to the pack.

"That's the most amazing thing I've ever seen," whispered Gerd.

"Truly remarkable," said Egil.

Ingrid dropped the stick.

"This looked to me like... like filthy magic..." Nilsa said. Her cheerful face had turned dark.

"Magic?" Ingrid asked. "Where did you see magic?"

"I don't know, that's the impression I had and I have a sixth sense with these things. I didn't like it at all. I don't like... that Ben. This had better not have been magic..." Her unrest grew. Her face was now red, the color of her hair, and her eyes were bright with fury. She did not seem at all her usual cheerful self.

"Take it easy," Egil said. "Rangers use arcane means, but I doubt whether anybody in the Camp has the Gift."

"That's what I hope too, for their sake," she replied, with deadly seriousness.

"Well, I think I'm really going to enjoy this School," said Gerd, breaking the tension.

Viggo put his dagger away. "Yeah, particularly if a snow panther or a bear bit off your face for being too confident and getting too close."

"Let's hope that doesn't happen," said Lasgol.

"Yeah... let's hope so..."

When they reached their cabin Lasgol could not stop thinking about the green flash. He had seen it with utter clarity. *But I'm the only one who saw it. But then of course I'm not exactly normal…* Thinking about the flash, something came to his mind: the egg. A similar flash, coming from the object, had left him unconscious. *Yes, the more I think about it, the more I believe it was very much like it.* He thought of getting it out and examining it, but stopped himself. *No, the last time it knocked me out. What if it kills me? I've no idea what I'm up against, it could end up badly.* He sat down on the floor in front of his trunk. He looked at his partners and saw that they were already asleep.

He sighed. He knew there was a risk, but even so, he put his hand in the trunk and took out the box with the egg. *I have to find out what all this means.* He opened the box and picked up the egg. No sooner had he done so than as if the egg had been expecting him, there came another golden flash. In his mind appeared a blurred image: two large eyes, those of a cat or perhaps a reptile; he could not make them out clearly. He concentrated, and as he did so there came another flash. He felt a terrible discharge, he began to convulse, and darkness took him.

Chapter 14

Master Instructor Oden woke them at dawn by playing his silver bell repeatedly, earlier than usual.

Startled, Egil opened his eyes.

"It's fascinating how such a small instrument is capable of emitting such a disturbing sound," he said aloud. "It seems to pierce the eardrums." He was about to get out of bed when he saw Lasgol on the floor, unconscious. "Lasgol!" he cried, and hastened to help him.

"What's the matter with him?" Gerd asked, looking frightened.

Viggo shook his head. "That boy gets weirder every day."

"Bring some water, Gerd, he won't wake up," Egil said.

Gerd fetched a glass of water, and they poured it over Lasgol's face. He opened his eyes wide and shook where he lay.

"Easy, it's us!" said Egil.

Gerd held him down until he relaxed.

Lasgol was still confused. "What happened?"

"You fell asleep on the floor again," said Egil, but something in his voice suggested that he suspected there was something more involved.

"Oh…"

"Is there anything wrong?" Gerd asked. "Can we help?"

"Huh?… No, there's nothing wrong with me."

"Tell that to somebody else," said Viggo. "You can't see your face, but you're as white as a ghost. You've been through something bad."

"No, no, it's nothing. I'll be better in a moment," said Lasgol. He tried to stand, but felt suddenly dizzy. Gerd had to hold him to stop him falling and hurting himself.

Viggo pointed to the egg on the floor beside him. "I bet my breakfast it has something to do with this."

"No, that's just a present."

"The know-it-all here will confirm it," he said with a nod at Egil. "Once is happenstance, twice it's something more, and you've been found unconscious twice beside that egg."

Lasgol looked at Egil, who nodded. "Viggo's right. You should trust us."

Oden's powerful voice sounded at that moment: "Fall in, in front of the cabins!"

"We have to go out," Gerd said, sounding unnerved. "Something's up. It's too early for them to call us to fall in."

"Okay, I'll explain everything," Lasgol said. "I just need some time."

Egil nodded. Gerd went to pick up the egg to give it back to Lasgol, but stopped. There was fear in his eyes. "Is it dangerous?" he asked.

Lasgol nodded twice, slowly.

Viggo grunted. "I knew it!"

"I'll get it," said Egil.

"No!" Lasgol shouted. But Egil had already reached out for it.

"Don't worry, an inert object can't harm…" he began. There was a discharge of energy and he was thrown back against the berths Gerd and Viggo shared, to land with a crash. He lay on the floor, bent double with pain.

"Egil!" Lasgol cried.

"Blasted egg," said Viggo, and threw a blanket over it.

Gerd, his eyes staring wide, murmured: "It's… magic… nothing good ever comes of magic, only pain and suffering…"

"Come out, now!" came Oden's final call.

"Go on," said Lasgol to Gerd and Viggo. "I'll take care of Egil."

Both boys nodded and went out. Lasgol did his best to help his friend to his feet. "Egil, come on, we've got to go out. Oden's called us to fall in."

Egil grunted with pain and tried to stand up. There was suffering on his face. He could not manage to.

"Coming…" he said. He tried to get up a second time, and failed once more.

Lasgol gave him his hand. "I'll help you."

Finally they managed to come out. Unfortunately they were the last to do so. Egil was holding his ribs. Ingrid and Nilsa noticed this and turned worried eyes on them.

"Are you all right?" Lasgol asked.

Egil nodded. "It's only the blow, it'll pass."

Master Instructor Oden gave them a stern look. "Traitor Dakon's son thinks he can be late for my call?"

"No, sir..."

"That's what it looks like, Traitor's Son."

"I'm sorry, sir..."

"No, you're not sorry yet, but you will be. After physical training, you'll go up to Vulture's Rock. I want you back by the end of lunch hour. If you don't make it back before lunch finishes you'll go without, and do two extra laps around the lake after dinner."

Lasgol swallowed. Vulture's Rock was half a morning away at the top of one of the peaks. He would never get back in time.

"Is that clear?"

"Yes, sir."

"It was my fault," Egil interrupted in an attempt to help him.

"Nobody asked you." Oden said.

"But.... it's not fair..."

Oden smiled. It was a cold smile. "Fair? Did I say it was fair?"

"No..." Egil said, looking downcast.

"Do you want to go with your friend? I don't see you raring to go..."

"I..."

Lasgol shook his head at him.

Egil gave in. "I don't think I'd be able to..."

"In that case, keep quiet and learn. All faults are penalized." Then he turned to the other initiates and said: "Any serious fault is penalized by expulsion. You've been warned."

He looked aside at Lasgol. "Traitor's Son," he called.

Lasgol bit his lip. He did not want to answer to that name.

"Don't make me repeat myself, or else I'll send your whole team to clean the stables for a month."

Lasgol swallowed the rage which was rising inside him. "Yes sir," he said at last.

"Your situation here is tolerated only at Dolbarar's express wish, against the general feeling among the Rangers. But don't try your luck too far, because not even he will save you if one of the Instructors decides to expel you."

Lasgol reminded himself of why he was there, why he had to put up with all this, and bowed his head. The fact that Dolbarar, the Camp Leader, had allowed his enrolment surprised him. Why would he do that? Was he obliged to do so by tradition? The sons of

Rangers had a right of entry by blood. Most probably Dolbarar was protecting that rule and not Lasgol himself, as Oden had hinted.

"Listen to me carefully. Dolbarar's told me to explain to you how our selection system works. I'll be delighted to do so. I enjoy doing it every year, though not as much as I enjoy escorting those who get expelled at the end of the year as far as the gate. I'll explain the basic regulations that'll rule your stay during this first year here. Pay close attention, because what's at stake is whether you stay with us or you're expelled."

Lasgol and Egil exchanged worried glances. Gerd's knees began to shake. Nilsa patted his back to calm him, although she could barely stay in the same place, she was so nervous.

Oden began to walk slowly, his hands behind his back. His cold gaze swept the faces of the initiates, who were hardly able to control their own nerves.

"At the end of each season there'll be two progress tests. The first will be the Individual Test. You'll be evaluated in the Four Schools, with a specific test in each. Every one of you is expected to be able to pass them. The grades you get in the individual tests in each School in the course of the year will be added up. According to the final score, you'll either go on to the second year or be expelled.

"Any questions?"

Ahart, the Captain of the Bears asked: "Then there are four tests?"

"Correct. The Spring Test, the Summer Test, the Autumn Test and the Winter Test. At the end of the year, the Master Rangers will decide who stays and who goes, according to the grades."

"If we fail one but pass the other three, will we be expelled?" asked Arvid, of the Falcons.

"In each test you'll receive one, two or three Oak Leaves." From his pocket he took an oval badge the size of a plum. It was made of wood and on it was carved an oak leaf. "If you're given one badge, it'll mean you haven't passed the test; you're a disgrace. Two means you've passed, but you need to improve. Three, that you've done well. That's what you must all aspire to, although I see a lot who won't manage even in their wildest dreams. Take note of what I tell you and let it sink in; excuses won't help you at all. You're expected to have a minimum of eight Oak Leaves in each School after the final test. Anyone with less than that will be expelled."

Nilsa raised her hand and waved it restlessly.

"Yes?"

"Suppose we get seven final grades in one School and twelve in each of the other three?"

Oden glared at her. He had not liked the question.

"You're a smartass, aren't you? If it were up to me I'd expel you, because you wouldn't have reached the minimum grades required in one of the Schools. But that's a decision the Master Rangers would make together. If I were you I'd make sure you have at least eight leaves in all four. And let me tell you, you don't look as if you could get twelve grades in anything. So you should start working hard."

Nilsa was red with shame. "Oh, yes, sir."

"Any more questions? If they're like the last one you can save yourselves the trouble."

Nobody dared ask anything else.

"Remember: eight Oak Leaves at the end of the year in each of the four Schools, or else expulsion. Nod if you've understood."

They all nodded. In many of their faces there was worry. A few, like Ingrid or Isgord, showed no doubt at all, but instead resolve and confidence. They would pass the tests, whatever they might be.

"On the day after the Individual Test," Oden went on, "you'll take the Team Test. This is a Test of Prestige. It consists of a team competition. It's a difficult test where you'll have to show everything you've learned up to that moment. The winning team will be rewarded with Prestige. Anybody know what Prestige is?"

Asgar, a boy from the Owls raised his hand at once. He was followed by others from various teams. Lasgol had no idea what this business of Prestige was. His Father had never explained anything about the Camp or the training. Confused, he wondered why. It worried him. He knew that everything that happened there was kept secret, but some of the other entrants seemed to have some information while he had none at all.

"Go ahead," Oden said, with a wave at the boy from the Owls.

"Prestige is a recognition for having won one of the tests or having performed an outstanding act for the Rangers."

"That's right. And what's it used for?" He pointed at another boy, from the Wolves team.

"It's used so that a candidate can opt for the Advanced Specialties."

145

"Good, and for anything else?" Now Oden gestured at another boy, this time from the Ferrets.

"It's used to save one of the team from being expelled."

"That's right. The team that gains prestige by winning one of the four tests will be able to save one of its members from expulsion. If there's more than one candidate for expulsion, the team will decide who it saves and who not."

Lasgol exchanged looks with his team. Nobody said anything, but they all knew it would be a very hard decision to make.

"Needless to say, the members of those teams who stand out will have a better chance of getting into the School of their choice. The first test will be at the end of spring. I recommend that you start working hard, from this very moment. Time goes by very fast here, and many of you are way below the minimum expected in order to pass the tests. There won't be a second chance for anybody. Work hard every day or you won't make it. The Summer Test will be more difficult than the Spring Test. In the same way, the Autumn Test will be still harder, and the final, the Winter Test, will take you to the limit of your endurance and knowledge. The Rangers don't accept anyone mediocre, the Rangers only accept the very best, those who stand out in all four Schools. You'll suffer, you'll learn, and the best of you will excel at the tests. For those who don't, a boat will be waiting at base camp to take you out of our domains."

Gerd and Egil exchanged a look of deep unease. They were very conscious of how much they would have to suffer and the hardships that awaited them if they were to go on.

"Any doubts about what I've explained?"

Nobody answered. Oden strolled back and forth, looking grimly at the members of each team, making sure they had all understood the seriousness of his words.

A worried silence, mixed with tension, floated in the air.

"All right then. Go and train, and bear everything I've told you in mind."

Lasgol struggled to reach the Vulture Rock in time, but it was impossible. The morning's effort had already punished his legs and the superhuman effort required to reach the rock had done the same to his lungs. The uphill approach through the woods to the mountain had finally broken him. As for the climb itself, it had been torture. The return to the camp had given him a little breath, but his body no longer responded. He arrived broken in body and spirit.

Oden was waiting for him in front of the canteen. And behind him, supporting Lasgol, was his team. Even Viggo was hanging around.

"You didn't make it," Oden said. "You know what's waiting for you this evening."

"I... I'll do it..."

The Master Instructor left without another word. Lasgol waited for him to disappear from view, then fell to the ground in exhaustion. His partners ran to help him. They laid him on one of the dining-room tables.

"He needs a massage," Egil said. "So his muscles can rest and he can get some relief."

"Okay," Gerd said. "Anybody know how to give one?"

Egil shook his head. "I just know what I've read. I haven't any practical experience."

"Yeah... as in everything else," Viggo commented.

"I know a little," said Nilsa.

Ingrid turned to her. "Then he's all yours."

Nilsa gave both his legs a thorough massage, then his arms, and finally his back. He fell asleep on the table and stayed there until the order came to go to the School of Nature class. They woke him up, and between them Gerd and Ingrid carried him to a field to the west where there was a huge garden and several wooden buildings.

Half-a-dozen Rangers were waiting for them. At their head was Erudite Eyra, Master Ranger of the School of Nature. At sixty, her curly hair was salt-and-pepper and her nose long and crooked. Her face was kind, but there was a touch of acidity in her gaze. Lasgol was pleasantly surprised to see that four of the six Rangers with her were women.

"My dear, if you'd be so kind," she said to one of them.

The Ranger came to stand in front of them to give them a good view of her. She was young, not more than twenty-five.

"This is Yria, Instructor in the School of Nature. Watch and learn."

Yria put her hand behind her back, and from a kind of leather satchel she brought out a trap made of branches and quills. She showed it to them, then placed it on the ground in front of her. She opened her cloak and the wooden medallion with the oak leaf was revealed. There was something else around her waist: a belt from which hung leather pouches and wooden and glass vials with corks. She took one, made of wood, uncorked it and poured a strangely colored liquid over the trap.

Nilsa was swaying from one leg to the other, with eyes that missed nothing. "What on earth can it be?"

"It must be a reactive ingredient with some specific function," Egil said.

"A what?" asked Gerd.

"Some preparation which reacts when mixed with others," Egil explained, as if he were an instructor.

"Look," said Nilsa.

Yria bent down, picked up two handfuls of earth and spread them over the trap. Lasgol was watching without missing the slightest movement. He was utterly intrigued, like everyone in his team. The Instructor waved her hand, and suddenly the trap melted into the ground and disappeared before everybody's eyes. Lasgol leant forward. He could not believe it. The most difficult part of setting a trap was hiding it so that it would not be seen, as he knew very well, having done it countless times. That had been amazing.

Nilsa clapped enthusiastically. "It's impossible!" she said.

"It's disappeared!" said Gerd. His eyes were fixed on the trap, but he could not see it.

"The earth has reacted to the reactive, presumably turning the trap a color imperceptible to the eye," Egil explained.

"Says the one who knows it all," Viggo commented. He was watching with one eye closed. "I can still see it. If you look carefully you can see it."

"Shut up and don't pester him," Ingrid said. "He always knows what he's talking about, unlike some other people."

Viggo made a face at her.

Yria took a step back and picked up a stone. She took another step back. Very slowly, she threw the stone at the trap. There was an explosion of smoke and earth. Half the initiates fell backwards with the shock. Yria smiled from ear to ear and went back to her place behind Eyra.

"Now that I really liked!" Viggo said with a smile. And for the first time it was a real smile, one of true pleasure.

"Impressive," said Egil, "I wonder about the composition of base elements and reactives that would create something like that. Very interesting. I'm going to enjoy studying this."

Gerd was shaking with fear on the ground. Nilsa was hugging him, trying to soothe him. He had received a massive shock.

Lasgol was stunned. He would have given anything to know how to set traps like that! He had to gain entry to this School!

"Now that I have your attention," Eyra went on with a laugh, "I'll explain what the School of Nature consists of and what you'll learn under my guidance. The first and most important thing is to know the world around us." She spread her arms wide and turned around fully. "This forest, those mountains, every plant and every tree, you need to know like the back of your hand. The Path of the Ranger teaches us that a Ranger needs to know the environment he must protect, and not just know it, he needs to be able to blend in with it and disappear, to belong to it. We Rangers live in the woods as if they were our very own home. Look at these mountains around us. Beautiful, majestic, and yet lethal. This School will teach you to survive in them, to live in their cold embrace as if you were their children. How many of you would survive in the high forests, up there in the mountains, for more than a week, if you were sent there without food or drink?"

Lasgol gazed up at the mountains. They were not particularly far away. He could see the frozen peaks and white flanks in the distance. Surviving for a couple of days was viable, but more than three would be complicated. More than a week he thought would be very difficult. Cold, hunger and thirst would be very hard to overcome up there.

Nobody answered. They were all aware of the difficulties.

"We'll teach you to survive up there, where Mother Nature is harsher with her children and only a few can prevail. And not just for a week, but all the time you need. A Ranger is in his or her element in the forests and mountains and can live in them like the wolf, the bear or the snow panther. You'll become lord and master, king predators. You'll dominate the environment and learn to hunt, to defend yourselves from other predators – including men – and survive on your own."

"I like that," whispered Ingrid.

Nilsa and Viggo nodded. Egil and Gerd did not seem so sure.

"Do any of you have any knowledge of healing?" Eyra asked. "Knowledge of what plants, roots, fungi, might be used for the treatment of illnesses?"

A few raised their hands and, to Lasgol's surprise, someone in his own team: Egil.

Eyra pointed at him. "Tell me, then. What healing properties does the dandelion have?"

"It's a common flowering herb. Its main properties are cleansing and diuretic. It cleanses the system of toxins. It cleans the skin and is good for constipation."

"That's right. For those who don't have that knowledge, don't worry, you'll acquire it. We'll teach you to recognize all the medicinal plants and their uses, so that you can heal wounds and illnesses, as long as they aren't too serious or deadly."

"That's wonderful," Nilsa said in a whisper.

"Egil knows so much!" Gerd commented, his face filled with admiration.

"Yes, he's a walking treatise," said Viggo.

"Just as we'll teach you to heal, we'll also teach you to use plants, fungi, and other substances with the opposite aim. The Rangers must be able to incapacitate, poison, and even kill the enemies of the realm, and in this School we'll teach you how to do that. For this we use traps, potions, poisons and other preparations, whose elaboration and effects you'll be taught as well."

Viggo rubbed his hands. "Well, at last things are getting interesting."

Nilsa rolled her eyes at him.

Ingrid's face, on the other hand, showed great interest.

"Poison?" Gerd said, shocked.

Eyra spread her arms and smiled. "Now I'll leave you in the hands of the Instructors so you can begin your training. Pay good attention: what they teach you will save your lives."

The Panthers turned out to have Instructor Yria, which pleased them all after seeing her demonstration. She took them to one of the wooden buildings, along with the Owls, Bears, and Snakes. On that first day she showed them different plants and their characteristics.

That evening Lasgol had to carry out the second part of his punishment. He went to the lake resignedly and did two exhausting laps. Oden was there to make sure he did as he had been ordered, and with him was Haakon. In their faces he could clearly see their enmity, and he knew that if it had depended on them he would already have been expelled. But he would not give them that satisfaction. He would comply with all the rules and punishments they saw fit to impose on him, no matter how exhausted he might be. They would not throw him out. He would fight until his body gave up.

He dragged himself back to the cabin. It was late, and he guessed his partners would already be asleep. But when he opened the door he found them all waiting for him, including the girls. Gerd picked him up in his strong arms and took him to his berth. Nilsa gave him another massage, and he fell into a deep sleep.

Chapter 15

Another week flew by with hardly anyone noticing. They were so occupied in overcoming the physical training and the learning skills that the days fled by. Now they all woke up before they heard Oden's silver bell, and were ready by the time he arrived at the cabins every dawn.

Gerd was the first to wake that morning. He stretched his sore muscles.

"Come on, guys, get up." he encouraged his cabin-mates as he searched for his clothes. "Let's not give that bossy Oden the slightest excuse."

Egil and Lasgol got dressed as fast as their exhausted bodies would allow. Gerd pushed them outside eagerly, with Viggo holding the door open for them. Ingrid and Nilsa were outside already, waiting for them. Lasgol did not know how they did it, as they must have been as tired as they were themselves. Gerd told him their secret: Ingrid got up early every morning to work out, so as not to lag behind the boys, and Nilsa had joined her. Now every day at dawn they exercised to improve their strength in arms, legs and torso. Lasgol had to admit that this was admirable. On the other hand, so that there would be no doubt that she did not fear anybody and would not tolerate any nonsense from anybody (least of all from a boy) Ingrid had beaten two more boys. One from the Boars, in Archery, and the other from the Bears, in the dining room. Now nobody fooled around with her anymore.

They fell in with the other teams: one knee on the ground, looking straight ahead. Lasgol glanced to one side and saw the Owls three cabins further down. Their leader Astrid, unmistakable with that black hair of hers which stood out among the fair heads of most of the initiates, glanced at him for an instant out of her enormous green eyes. Lasgol felt something flutter in his stomach. Astrid turned to say something to one of her partners. The Owls Team was unique in that it was similar to his own, with two girls in the team and one of them the leader.

Two cabins further away, Lasgol recognized the Eagles, led by

Isgord, who was watching him. No surprise there. Isgord was always watching him as though he wanted to strangle him for some reason he could not guess. Beside him were his four inseparable buddies: the twins Jared and Aston: two strong, athletic boys who looked like born warriors. With them, two shorter boys who looked like stoical bulldogs: Alaric and Bergen. Completing the group was Martha, a blonde girl with long curly hair. From what Nilsa had told them about her, she had a very bad temper and did not let anybody near Isgord, especially girls.

Master Instructor Oden addressed them all:

"Today you're coming with me to the Command House. Dolbarar's waiting to make an important announcement. Follow me."

He led them to the house on the lake. As they went through the inner area of the Camp Lasgol realized there was a lot of activity going on, more than usual. All the Rangers were going from one end to the other carrying weapons and supplies. They were assembling in groups in front of the stables, where the activity was even busier. He did not like the look of this. Something was wrong.

They crossed the bridge and arrived at the courtyard of the great house. Dolbarar was waiting for them in front of the door, and with him were the Four Master Rangers.

"Fall in," Oden ordered them.

Once they had one knee to the ground and were looking straight ahead, Dolbarar stared at them for a moment, then addressed the whole group:

"Today I have grave news to pass on to you. King Uthar has summoned all available Rangers to defend the realm."

A murmur of concern and shock spread through the initiates. Lasgol and Egil exchanged looks of unease.

"It's very unusual for King Uthar to summon all the Rangers," Egil whispered. "It hardly ever happens, only in times of grave danger for Norghana."

"The King has received reports that indicate the return of Darthor, Black Lord of the Ice. This is the worst possible news. Evil is on the prowl once again. The one who tried to kill our King and conquer our beloved kingdom has come back. For this reason the King is summoning all the Rangers to serve and defend the realm. The army is on maximum alert and the King is talking to all the

Dukes and Counts so they can strengthen their vigilance over their lands and prepare their forces. Unfortunately finding Darthor and his allies is a complicated task, as he is a master at hiding his presence. Hence the King is sending us Rangers to comb the whole kingdom and the neighboring lands until we find him. And find him we will. All Rangers will leave today with the order to find Darthor and his minions. We'll search the kingdom from east to west and from south to north until we find him. There'll be nowhere left for him to hide."

Egil half-closed his eyes. "The King'll have summoned my father Vikar…" he said in a whisper.

"Because he's the Duke of Olafstone?"

"Yes, but also to make sure that he doesn't support Darthor. To keep him under control. Remember they're rivals…"

"I get it."

Viggo raised one eyebrow. "So our know-it-all's really a nobleman."

"You shouldn't spy on other people," Nilsa scolded him.

"And you shouldn't interrupt conversations that don't concern you."

"Be quiet, all of you," said Ingrid. "Oden is looking at us and we're going to get penalized."

At their Captain's order they all stopped whispering.

Dolbarar went on: "It is the duty of a Ranger to protect the realm from internal and external enemies," he said, as though it were a creed. "Repeat it with me."

All the initiates did so. "Very good. The Rangers protect Norghana. This corps was created with this end, and with this end we live each day. We protect the realm in silence, from the shadows, for there are few of us, yet we are prepared for the task to us entrusted."

"There are few of us?" Gerd asked in puzzlement.

Egil nodded. "Compared to the Royal Army or even the personal armies of Dukes and Counts, yes."

"Do you know how many of us there are?" Nilsa asked.

"Roughly. My father's mentioned it once or twice. In all there are barely five hundred of us."

"As few as that?" said Gerd.

"Yes. This is an elite corps with specific tasks. The army's there to do the rest. Just consider that this is the only Camp where Rangers are trained. This year there are only eighty in the new entry, and about fifty will finish the training, with luck."

"We'll finish," said Ingrid with a wink. Egil smiled and nodded.

"You've forgotten to mention why they recruit every year," said Viggo.

"It's a dangerous profession," Egil admitted.

"A lot of Rangers die on missions in the King's service," Viggo said, "and they need to be replaced."

"Missions like this?" Nilsa asked.

"Yes, like this one."

"Don't be afraid," said Ingrid. "We'll learn to survive and face any danger."

"Let's hope so…" Gerd said, looking worried.

"The Rangers will carry out the mission entrusted to us by King Uthar," Dolbarar went on. "We won't fail, as we are guided by honor and our duty to our kingdom."

The faces of the Four Master Rangers were grave. It was obvious that they were worried, but there was no trace of fear in them.

"The *Path of the Ranger* teaches us that we serve the realm: in secret, in silence and without arousing suspicion."

Lasgol understood those words to be a dogma.

Dolbarar indicated the stables. "All the Rangers of the Shelter not assigned to teaching tasks will join the search. At this very moment they are starting to leave."

Lasgol turned and saw them moving off in a long line, with their hooded greenish-brown cloaks, on their faithful steeds. A feeling of abandonment came over him, as if they were now exposed and helpless. Then he turned to look at Dolbarar and the four Master Rangers. Their presence was so powerful, they emanated such force, that the feeling passed immediately.

"This situation won't affect your instruction, or that of the second, third or fourth year candidates. We'll go on with the training as we do every year. The Rangers are prepared to face any situation, no matter how dangerous or desperate it may be. I believe firmly that we'll prevail, as we've always done. May these words serve to soothe your hearts."

Gerd nodded. Nilsa smiled. In the Owls team, Astrid smiled encouragingly at her partners. Isgord on the other hand raised his fist to the Eagles, who replied by doing the same. The Boars did not appear particularly worried. The Wolves and Snakes were listening without revealing whether they were restless or not. Lasgol was sure they were, but did not want to show it in front of Dolbarar and the Four Master Rangers.

"Now you may proceed," Dolbarar said. "Go back to your instruction. And remember, we are what we learn. So learn, my Ranger Initiates, learn."

Oden ordered them to their feet and led them away. Before letting them go to their next lesson, he turned to them.

"The Rangers need to know their land like the backs of their hands," he said. "Leave the brainless fighting to the Royal Army. We use our heads. We study our environment, we learn, and we use this knowledge so that we can vanish in the forests and mountains as if we were a part of them. Remember that."

He led them to the western woods. In the center of an open area surrounded by firs Haakon the Untouchable, Master Ranger of the School of Expertise, was waiting for them. Lasgol felt nervous the moment he saw him. He did not know why; it might have been his appearance, or perhaps the somber air he seemed to emanate. He was tall and slender, with a truly sinister expression. His skin was black and his head clean-shaven, with small eyes above a beak-like nose. Lasgol felt uneasy at the sight of him.

"Welcome," he said in a low voice. "Sit down on the ground."

Nilsa sat down beside Lasgol, and judging by her expression she did not seem to find Haakon particularly pleasant. On the other hand there was a strange half-smile of pleasure on Viggo's face. Ingrid, as usual, was watching intently, as if she wanted to take in all the knowledge the Instructors could transmit to her.

"This School tries to expand what we might be able to do with our bodies and the five senses we have. I see by your expressions that you don't understand. We'll teach you to walk with the stealth of a predator, to vanish among the shadows like a night hunter, to camouflage yourselves like a chameleon, to walk unseen and unheard. You'll learn to fall on your victims without them knowing what's happened to them. And if confrontation becomes inevitable, we'll teach you to take your body to the limit of its possibilities to be practically unreachable and come out victorious. This will require you to be in perfect physical shape."

His gaze lingered on the members of each team, as if he were judging the worth of each one of them.

"You've been training now for several weeks, and Master Instructor Oden informs me that you're fit to begin instruction in the School of Expertise. Almost everyone, that is, with some exceptions."

His black eyes swept over the Panthers Team. They stopped on Gerd, then on Egil.

"We can't penalize everyone for the poor physique of a few, so those of you who are lagging will have to work doubly hard to catch up with the rest."

Gerd swallowed, and Egil let out a deep sigh.

"I think a personal demonstration will make you understand the concept behind this School more clearly."

He withdrew a few steps as far as the edge of the forest and moved between two trees. Very slowly he crouched down, and as he did so he wrapped himself in his Ranger's cloak and put on the hood. He hunkered there still as a statue, and then suddenly before their very eyes, he vanished.

Murmurs and cries of shock filled the clearing. Lasgol's mouth was hanging open and he could not manage to close it. Suddenly Haakon appeared beside a tree ten paces from where he had been and whistled. They turned their heads in his direction. They had not seen him move, nor had they perceived any movement in the undergrowth. Suddenly he sprinted at a demonic rate, zigzagged and returned to his original position before anybody could turn back their heads.

"It's not possible..." Lasgol stammered, stunned by the feat he had just witnessed. "How did he do that? It's unbelievable!"

Haakon addressed them: "I see you're beginning to understand. This School is not like the other three. It's more difficult. I'm not saying this because it's my own School. I'm saying it because it's a fact and that is what the *Path of the Ranger* calls it. Of the four Schools, that of School of Expertise marks the difference between the chosen and the mediocre. Great discipline is required, of both body and mind. For that reason, you'll suffer. I'm no friend of making things sound sweeter than they are. Get ready to work really hard, or else you won't manage to pass. If any of you believes he or she might enter this School in one of the elite specialties like Imperceptible Spy or Natural Assassin, you can forget it. It's a long time since I've seen anybody with enough talent to achieve it,"

"I'll make it," Ingrid murmured. There was a determined look on her face.

Lasgol turned his head toward her. He had to admit there was nobody in the whole Camp with more determination or who worked harder than Ingrid. He admired her for it, more and more. Behind her roughness there was a will of iron.

Haakon gestured, and from among the undergrowth there suddenly appeared five instructors.

Gerd rubbed his eyes. "Have they been there all along?"

"It looks like it," said Egil. "Camouflaged, like veritable human chameleons."

Haakon said: "The instructors will take charge of you now. I don't want to see you until you're able to walk over shadows." He turned and went into the forest. A moment later he had completely vanished.

"Fascinating," said Egil.

"Incredibly difficult, I'd say," Nilsa pointed out. Her shoulders were drooping, and for once she was not fidgeting restlessly.

"Well, I like this School," Viggo said.

They all turned toward him in surprise. They had not heard him say a positive word in all the time he had been with them. Not a single thing.

"What's the matter, can't I like something?"

Ingrid could not hold her tongue. "Sure, but we were beginning to think you had no soul."

Viggo bowed his head. "I do, beautiful, the thing is it's as black as coal."

"Don't call me *beautiful*, or I'll give you what for."

"I'm returning the compliment," Viggo replied with a provocative smile.

She frowned and clenched her fists.

"Besides, I'm not lying. You are beautiful, although it would do you good to take a little care of yourself. You look more like a boy than I do."

Ingrid raised her arm.

"And just so you know, you lose all your charm with that temper of yours, particularly the way you wallop anyone you see."

Lasgol got in between them before she could hit Viggo.

"We'd better pay attention to the Instructor. Here he comes." He indicated a tall Ranger with a wooden medallion around his neck bearing the image of a Snake. He signaled to three of the teams to come to him.

"You've been working on your physical condition. Now it's time to work on your balance. A Ranger must be able to walk without his feet touching the ground, so that the earth isn't marked by any footprint that might give him away. Today you'll begin to train in this new School."

He led them to a nearby gully. A small stream ran along it. The water was knee-high. Crossing it, from one side to the other, was the bare trunk of a pine tree.

"Get into your teams and cross it," said the Instructor.

"Walk on that trunk? But it's only half a hand-span wide," Gerd said despairingly.

"And if possible without falling and breaking your crown, big boy," said Viggo.

"I'd estimate there are a dozen small steps," Ingrid said.

Egil pointed at the far end, which looked wet. "Attention, team. They've smeared the end with something… I bet it's lard…"

"Great!" Nilsa protested, "As if it weren't difficult enough already. And the fall's more than six feet. I don't think the water's likely to soften the blow. We'll break our backs!"

"Or our butts!" said Viggo.

"Come on, get in line," Ingrid said. "Look at the Owls. They're not afraid, they're already on it, and so are the Wolves. We can't do less than that." She went to stand at the end of the line behind Borj, the strongest boy in the Owls.

Viggo and Gerd followed her. Nilsa grumbled, but she joined them, hopping up and down to try and ease her nerves. Lasgol came last. The experience turned out to be traumatic. Gerd and Egil fell before they reached the middle of the trunk, from the highest point. Just as Nilsa had anticipated, they hit the ground hard. Gerd ended up lying on his back in the ravine with his arms outspread. Egil fell on his backside, which struck the rocks at the bottom, and got up massaging his buttocks to try and ease the pain. Ingrid was on the point of reaching the other side, but on the slippery stretch she lost her footing and fell. She cried out with frustration, although she had not hurt herself as she had only fallen a foot and a half and struck the side of the gully.

"By the dark arts of Nocean Mages! Egil was right, they've smeared the end with lard, so be careful." Seeing her group's dispirited faces, she waved her fist. "Come on! We'll make it!"

Encouraged by Ingrid's enthusiasm, Nilsa started to cross determinedly. But no sooner had she taken three steps than she lost her balance. She fell off the trunk and landed on her face on the bottom of the ravine. She got up at once. She had a bump on her forehead which was beginning to swell.

"Right, back in line again!" the Instructor ordered. "You're pathetic. My grandmother would do better!"

"I don't think this School is for me," Nilsa said. Aware of her innate clumsiness, she waved a hand despairingly.

Astrid, the Captain of the Owls, helped her back to the line. "Why not?" she asked.

"I... well, I'm... a bit clumsy..."

"A bit, she says..." said Viggo, giggling, and started on the exercise.

Leana, Astrid's partner in the Owls, a slim blonde of unusual beauty, smiled at Nilsa. "Coordination and stealth aren't my forte either," she said, spreading her arms wide. "That School's for people like Asgar." She indicated one of her teammates, a thin, very agile boy with copper-colored hair who seemed to cross with no apparent effort.

"Don't give up," Lasgol said to her.

Viggo crossed the pole without any trouble, even the final part; he flew over it. Ingrid stared at him in perplexity. She could not believe it.

"Surprised? I have my own skills," he said from the other end. He spread his arms wide and made an elaborate bow. Then he winked at her.

Not knowing what to say, Ingrid replied with a frown.

"Let's see how Oscar does," said Astrid. She was watching her team-mates, including a very tall, strong boy with long blond hair and gray eyes. He reached the final part, but slipped and fell on his back. He grunted with pain.

"A demoralizing spectacle!" the Instructor shouted.

"My turn," Astrid said, and went at it with determination.

Lasgol watched her, every step of the way. She reached the final part, the slippery one, then as if she were on tiptoes, crossed it. The rest of her Team applauded and she raised her arms in triumph.

He was next. He took a deep breath, studied the trunk and made his decision. He crossed quickly, then when he reached the slippery end he picked up speed. He managed to cross it, but at the last minute the foot he was supporting himself with slipped. He had one foot on firm land and the other in the air. He tried to keep his balance with his arms and tilted sideways. He was going to fall into the ravine! A hand grabbed his wrist. Instinctively he gripped the arm. He was rescued by a strong tug. He looked up and saw that his savior was Astrid. His stomach gave a leap. The brunette smiled at him.

"You're welcome," she said, and went back to repeat the exercise with a smile on her lips.

Lasgol was left dumbfounded. "Thank...thank you..." he mumbled.

They repeated the exercise until it was dark. The Wolves withdrew, crestfallen. The Owls had not done so badly. Astrid and Asgar had managed to cross every time, and even Leana had done it too a couple of times.

At the bottom of the gully, under the fir tree, stretched out on both sides of the river, were the members of the Panthers. Egil, Gerd, Nilsa and Ingrid were so sore they could not move. Lasgol and Viggo, the winners of the day, were looking at each other, surprised at one another's skill. The one who was taking it worst was Ingrid. It was the first time she had failed at anything and she was furious at herself.

"Tomorrow's another day," Astrid told them from above.

"We'll all do better," Leana assured them.

Lasgol and Ingrid waved at them. The Owls went to rest.

The Panthers did not move.

"My father did warn me that this wouldn't be at all easy for me," Nilsa said, "but I didn't think it would be so hard. I'm sore all over. I'm going to have bruises that'll take weeks to wear off."

"Your father's a Ranger?" Gerd asked her. He did not move, to avoid groaning with pain.

"He was."

"I'm sorry."

Nilsa sighed. "A bloody Mage killed him."

They all stared at her.

"An Ice Mage?" Viggo asked with interest.

"No, not an Ice one, a worse one than that. Although in my opinion they're all just as bad. They should all be executed. Anybody who uses bloody magic, the Gift or Talent or whatever they want to call it."

"I'm sorry…" Lasgol said.

"Thanks. I've overcome it… I think… it was some years ago…"

Egil was intrigued. "If you don't mind my asking," he said, "how do you know it was a Mage? I thought the Rangers' missions were secret."

"They are. But Ethor, my father, had an ominous feeling before he left and told me."

"I see."

"He told me that if he didn't come back, then when the day came, if that was what my heart told me to do, I should join the Rangers. And that nothing would make him happier."

"So you're here to fulfill your father's wish," said Egil.

"Yes… but not just for that, for me as well… I want to become a Mage Hunter."

"The elite specialty of Archery?" Ingrid asked her in surprise.

"Yes. I want to kill all those bloody Mages and anyone who uses magic. Enemies, I mean…"

By the way she said it, Lasgol had the feeling that Nilsa was not going to make much of a distinction between friendly mages and enemy ones.

"That does you credit," said Ingrid.

"But my father warned me that it would be very hard for me to make it, because of my… my problems…"

"You'll make it," said Ingrid. "I'll help you."

"Thank you…"

"We'll all help you," Gerd said.

"We'll make your father proud of you," Egil added.

"Thank you, all of you. I really mean it."

Seeing again how his companions felt about everything magical, Lasgol knew he could not trust them with his secret, even if he wanted to. They would not understand. Better keep it buried inside.

The six team-mates stayed there at the bottom of the gully until the moon came up among the treetops, thinking about the few chances they had of achieving what they wanted for a variety of reasons, all of them valid and deep. The cold air of the night made itself felt, and reluctantly they got up and took their damp, suffering bodies to their cabin. The following day was going to be as tough, or even tougher than the one that was coming to an end.

Chapter 16

The days at the Camp were so hard, with so much to learn and do, that they did not even have time to realize that spring was nearly over. It was Egil who noticed one evening when they were coming back from their class in the School of Wildlife. They had spent the whole day in the fields behind the stables, learning everything to do with the anatomy, care and training of horses. Lasgol had enjoyed himself enormously with Trotter, although Instructor Ben had told him he did not ride well at all.

"The Traitor's son isn't a born rider," he had said, and spat at his feet. Lasgol had ignored it; it was not worth getting upset over. In any case, he very much enjoyed the company of his strong, cheerful pony. That was enough for him.

The instructor had not liked the fact that Lasgol had not reacted to his remark, so he had sent him to clean the stables for the whole week.

"That way the smell of traitor will be hidden by the smell of manure, which is a lot more pleasant."

Lasgol had not deigned to get angry. He had nodded and got down to the task. He would do nothing to get himself expelled, however much he was provoked.

On their way back to the cabin after dinner Egil, looking worried, commented: "We're getting near the end of spring."

"Wonderful," Nilsa said, "I love the summer." She did a somersault to celebrate.

Gerd rubbed his enormous hands together. "Me too. Nothing like a little warmth for a change."

Viggo shook his head slowly. "They don't get it."

"What is it we don't get?" Nilsa asked, looking puzzled.

"The Spring Test," said Egil.

Gerd looked terrified. "Already?"

"Oh!" Nilsa cried, and started to sway.

Lasgol had not realized either. Time went by too fast there.

"I'll go and ask Oden," Ingrid said. "We'll have to be ready." She walked away, looking determined.

The others sat under the cabin porch and awaited her return. Night was falling.

Ingrid came back, and her face told them she was not bringing good news

"Oden says the test is in two weeks and that we'd better work as if there were no tomorrow between now and the test, or else not do it at all. He says we're the most pathetic team he's seen in years…"

"Coming from him, that's quite a compliment," Viggo said scornfully.

Gerd gave a dispirited snort. "Two weeks…"

"The situation seems extremely complicated to me," Egil said.

"You can say that again," said Nilsa. "And we're not going to have time to improve very much."

A despairing silence fell on them like a slab of stone.

Ingrid broke the silence. "We won't give up!" she cried.

"Haven't you seen us? We suck!" said Viggo.

Ingrid turned to Lasgol and looked into his eyes with her own ice-blue ones. "Are you going to give up? After everything they're making you go through?"

Lasgol pondered for a long moment. The chances of passing the test were minimal. But something inside him told him to keep going, however great the difficulty.

"No, I'm not going to give up. Not without proving my father's innocence. Whatever the cost, however much I suffer."

Ingrid nodded several times. "If he's not giving up, and he has plenty of reason to, are *you* going to give up? Without even trying?" Her voice was so harsh that Gerd almost fell backwards.

The Panthers glanced at one another.

"No, I'm not going to give up," said Egil. "I won't give my father that satisfaction. If they must throw me out, let them. But I'm not quitting."

"If you carry on, so will I," Nilsa said. There was conviction in her voice. "I know the specialty of Mage Hunter is practically out of my reach, but I'm going to give it a try, for my father's sake."

When he saw his teammates' reactions, Gerd took courage. "I won't give up either. Otherwise what'll be the point of all the bad moments I've been through?"

All gazes turned to Viggo.

"All right, but if we have a group hug now, I'll throw up."

And for the first time Ingrid burst out laughing.

He gave a triumphant smile. "I knew my charm would have its effect on you sooner or later."

"Oh yeah, your nonexistent charm. Don't push your luck." She gave him a frown and an icy glare.

Viggo winked at her. Seeing that this infuriated her, he raised his hands in a conciliatory gesture and stepped back. Ingrid gave him a look full of hatred, but held back.

"We'd better get some rest," Lasgol said. "We have a lot of work ahead of us."

The others nodded, and they withdrew inside the cabin.

At midnight Lasgol was woken by a dull, repeated noise. It sounded like a woodpecker pecking at the bark of a tree. He got up and went to the door, thinking that perhaps the noise was coming from outside. No, apparently not. He spun around.

Egil stretched in his bunk. "What's that noise?"

"I don't know," said Lasgol. He was trying to locate the origin of the noise in the darkness.

"Turn on the lamp," Viggo said from the other bunk. "You're not going to find it like that, and you've already woken us up." He sounded annoyed.

"Not Gerd," Egil said. He gestured towards their friend, who was peacefully snoring in the bunk below Viggo's.

"He wouldn't wake up even if a party of Red Usik savages broke down the door and attacked him," Viggo said.

Egil burst out laughing.

Lasgol lit the oil lamp. The sound was getting stronger all the time, a steady tapping. He went around the inside of the small cabin. "Where's it coming from?"

Egil indicated Lasgol's trunk. "I think... it's coming from the trunk..."

"Oh..." said Lasgol. If it was coming from the trunk, he had a pretty good idea of what it must be. The sound grew louder. He picked up his father's box, and there was no doubt now. The sound was coming from inside: it was the egg.

Viggo came closer to watch. "I bet it's that weird egg of yours."

he said. Egil followed him.

Lasgol opened the box. A golden flash dazzled them.

Viggo covered his eyes with his arm. "What the hell?"

Lasgol squinted and looked at the egg in the box. The rapid tapping went on. It was coming from inside the egg.

"How weird," said Lasgol.

There came another sudden flash.

Egil had bent over to get a better view of it. "The egg's giving out golden flashes at intervals!" he cried.

Viggo stepped back. "Well, I don't like this at all!"

"Why not?" said Egil. "It's fascinating!"

"Because that can only mean one thing: magic."

"So?"

"So? What d'you mean, *so*? Magic's very dangerous, or hasn't anybody told you already, know-it-all?"

"There's a lot of superstition and exaggeration around this arcane subject."

"It's not a 'subject', it's bloody magic, and magic is bad in itself," Viggo concluded, and folded his arms across his chest.

Gerd had just woken up. "Magic?" he asked in alarm. "Who said magic?"

"Look," Viggo said. He indicated the egg in its open box in Lasgol's hands.

"Oh! That's magic!" He sat up in his bunk so quickly that he hit his head. "Ouch!" he muttered. He stood up and hid behind Viggo. "Don't touch it, shut the box! It could kill us all!"

"What do I do?" Lasgol asked Egil.

"Hmm…. we need to analyze what's happening. It's obvious that this is an ongoing process. In my humble opinion it might be either a call or a process of birth."

Lasgol stared at the egg. The tapping went on, and the flashes filled the cabin.

"Well, if it's calling someone, it's going to be bad news," Viggo said. "Magic just brings trouble, massive trouble."

Lasgol was beginning to feel a curious sensation. It was as if something inside him were telling him to pick the egg up in his hands. *That's a bad idea. The last time it almost killed me.* He resisted, shaking his head. But the feeling was becoming more and more pressing. Perhaps it was because of the steady tapping.

"Shut the box and we can bury it outside," Gerd suggested.

"No way!" said Egil. "We have to study it."

Lasgol remembered something his father had often said: "In difficult moments, be guided by your instincts. They won't fail you." He made his decision. He took the egg in his hands and put down the box. And when he did so the tapping stopped.

"It's stopped," Egil said. "It must feel you."

Lasgol looked at him blankly. "What do I do now?"

There came a new flash, but this time it was localized. It bathed Lasgol from head to foot as if it were examining him. In his mind there appeared those large eyes he had seen before. Suddenly they heard a crack, and the top of the egg broke open.

"By the Ice Mages!" Gerd cried out in terror.

"Don't drop it!" said Egil.

Lasgol glanced at his friend and clasped the egg firmly. He was frightened, but trying to stay calm. Something inside the egg pushed the cracked surface and it broke off completely. Pieces of shell fell to the floor, and a hole appeared at the top.

"What the hell!" Viggo said. He reached for a small dagger at his belt, ready to defend himself.

Lasgol realized that his hands were shaking. He took a deep breath and managed to calm down. Another piece of shell, a bigger one this time, fell to the floor. They were all watching tensely. Inside the hole appeared two huge eyes, round and bulging. He recognized them. The eyes looked at him. They were reptilian eyes, yellow, with a blue slit in the pupil. He swallowed. After the eyes came a head. It was flat and oval, with a crest around it. It was covered with blue scales with silver dots on them. The mouth appeared to be smiling and the nose was simply two round holes. Suddenly it opened its mouth and a shrill sound came out of it, like a question.

"What on earth is it?" Gerd screamed.

The animal shrieked again. Lasgol stared at it, not knowing what to do.

"It's some kind of reptile," said Egil. "A very exotic one,"

Suddenly, with a lightning movement, it emerged from the egg, and climbed up Lasgol's hand. The shock made him drop the empty shell, but it did not break. It rolled between Viggo's feet and struck Gerd's foot.

He leapt back. "Argh!" he shouted.

Lasgol took a closer look at the creature on his wrist. It was not very big, the size of his own palm. It resembled a lizard, but all four of its legs were long and strong and its tail too was very long. Its most outstanding feature were its eyes, which were relatively large in comparison with its body, as were its feet, especially the fingers and toes, which were not only large but wide and rounded. They seemed to adhere to Lasgol's wrist. Two crests ran down its back from head to tail.

"It's very cold," Lasgol said as he turned his hand over. The animal wrapped its tail around his wrist and sat on his palm.

Egil looked closely at it. "Really curious," he said. He touched its back. When he did so, the creature turned toward him and opened its mouth threateningly. It had no teeth, but its tongue was wide and blue.

"Be careful!" Gerd cried. "It might be a dragon chick!"

"Nonsense!" Viggo snapped back. "Dragons went extinct thousands of years ago."

"It's some kind of reptile," Egil said, "but I've never seen one like it before." He tried to stroke it.

The animal, becoming aware of this, opened its mouth threateningly and shrieked. Immediately it started to change color until it matched Lasgol's skin. Then it mimicked this until it vanished.

"Unbelievable!" said Gerd.

"It has the ability to camouflage itself, like a chameleon," said Egil.

Viggo came closer. "It can't be. I can't see it. Is it on your hand?"

Lasgol nodded. "I can't see it, but I can feel a cold body there."

"I don't like this," Viggo said. "It's one thing to be a chameleon, but that thing's practically invisible. This can only be magic."

Gerd shuddered. "And if it can do this, what else d'you think it'll do? And suppose it's poisonous and kills us with a bite, or turns us to stone with its gaze? There are stories of creatures that used to do that…"

For some reason Lasgol could not fully comprehend, the little animal did not arouse any sense of danger in him. Instead, he felt the need to protect it, to look after it.

"It's not dangerous," he said, more to himself than to the others. "I'm going to keep it."

Egil clapped. "Excellent!" he said. "We'll study it. Tomorrow I'll

go to the library and look in the tomes and parchments on the School
of Wildlife, and I'm sure to come across something. Maybe I'll have
to look through treatises on Magic… I've heard they have several
volumes on it, although you need a special permit to study them. I
don't know whether Dolbarar will allow me one."

Viggo pointed his dagger at Lasgol's hand. "That's a very bad
idea."

"I don't like the idea one little bit either," said Gerd.

"I'll take care of it," Lasgol assured them. "Nothing bad will
happen, I promise."

"Let's move away a little and see what it does," Egil said. Viggo
and Gerd went with him reluctantly to the other end of the cabin.

A moment passed, then all of a sudden the color began to return
to the little creature. It became visible. It looked at Lasgol with its
large eyes and let out a squeal. Lasgol smiled at it. He tried to touch it
with his finger. The animal bent its head, and he stroked it. The
silver-blue scales were soft to his touch. The creature squealed again,
apparently pleased, and licked his finger. He stared at its eyes in
surprise. Suddenly he felt something in his mind, like a blurred image,
except that it was not an image, it was more a feeling… of hunger.
He was puzzled. The feeling was not his own; they had just come
from their dinner in the dining room… and then he realized what
was happening. The little animal was projecting its own feeling.
Definitely, whatever that creature might be, it had some form of
magic.

"I think it's hungry," he told his roommates.

"What d'you think that thing eats?" Viggo said.

Egil scratched his chin. "Reptiles, generally speaking, eat insects,
unless they're herbivores. And if my memory serves me right, they
also eat fruit. I'll go and fetch some lettuce from the dining room. I'll
be back in a moment."

Lasgol went on stroking the creature. It was fascinating.

"I'm going to get the girls," Gerd said. "They ought to see this."

Ingrid and Nilsa came in and were struck dumb when they saw
the little animal in Lasgol's hand.

Ingrid raised one eyebrow. "What is it?" she asked.

"I think it's a baby dragon," said Gerd.

"It can't be," Ingrid said. "It hasn't got any wings."

"How cute, look how it's smiling," Nilsa said. She rushed forward to touch it.

"Better not –" began Lasgol. But the warning was too late.

Nilsa was enchanted with the little creature. She touched it, at which it opened its mouth defensively and began to change color.

"Look what's happening now," said Viggo.

The creature vanished from Lasgol's hand. Nilsa cried out. Ingrid came to look closer and rubbed her eyes.

"Where did it go?"

"Nowhere. It's still in my hand."

"But I can't see it," she said incredulously.

"Oh, oh, this smells of unholy magic!" Nilsa said, and stepped back as though she had seen a demon.

"I told you," said Gerd.

Ingrid shook her head "I don't like this…"

"If that thing's magic," Nilsa said, "I don't want to have anything to do with it. Magic just brings misfortune. I hate it." She moved further back.

At that moment Egil came in through the door with some lettuce leaves in one hand and half an orange in the other. He gave them to Lasgol, then asked everyone to step back and keep quiet so that the creature would come out of its invisible state. They waited for a moment, and finally it reappeared. Lasgol offered it a piece of lettuce. It took a bite and swallowed it, then squealed and nodded. Lasgol took this to mean it wanted more. He fed it little pieces of lettuce until there was none left.

"It's an herbivore," said Egil. "Now try with the orange."

Lasgol did so, and Egil turned out to be right again. The creature licked and nibbled the orange. It ate until it was full. Once again he felt that strange sensation in his mind, like a blurred image that was transmitting a need. This time the need was for sleep.

"I think it wants to sleep."

"Are you seriously going to keep it?" Viggo protested.

"I agree, I don't think having a magical creature with us is a good idea," Ingrid said. "We've got enough problems as it is, and surely that thing'll bring us even more."

"I think it's a phenomenal discovery," said Egil. "We need to study it, no doubt about that."

"Relax," Lasgol said. "I can understand your worries, I really can, but I don't think it represents any danger. I'll take care of it and make sure that nothing happens. I promise."

For a moment Ingrid, Viggo, Gerd and Nilsa exchanged doubtful looks. In the end Ingrid nodded. "All right then, but if anything happens, we get rid of it."

"And if it does any more magic, you'll make it disappear, or else I will," Nilsa said. Something in her voice caused a shiver to run down Lasgol's spine.

But he accepted. "Thanks," he said. "Don't worry."

They all went back to their bunks for the rest of the night. Lasgol stowed the creature in his father's box and put this beside his head, on the bed. Egil came closer to take a look.

"It's fascinating," he whispered. "We have a chance to study quite an extraordinary specimen."

"Let's hope it's not dangerous."

"We'll be careful. You don't realize what we've got here, do you?"

Lasgol looked at him in puzzlement.

"It's very rare to find people who have the gift, as there are so few of them, but to find a creature with the gift, now that really is very rare."

"Ah …"

"And there's something even more intriguing. This creature has a reason for being. A reason why it has those qualities."

"Any idea what?"

"No, but there's one significant element."

"Is there?"

"Yes. You."

"Me? Why?"

"You had the egg. And the creature only seems to want dealings with you."

"It could be coincidence."

Egil smiled. "Coincidences are very rarely anything of the kind. Who gave you the egg?"

Lasgol hesitated over whether to confide in him or not. He had not told anybody anything personal. He considered the idea, and decided to trust him.

"My father gave it to me. Well, they sent it to me along with his belongings."

Egil stroked his chin. "Curious… they sent it to you… Who did?"

"The Rangers."

"And you think the Egg belonged to your father?"

"Well, I don't know whether it was his. I think he sent it to me."

"This is getting more and more interesting. Why do you think it was for you?"

Lasgol told him what had happened when the egg began to spin under his finger, and how he had seen his name in the spots on it. He said nothing about the flashes and the vision of the creature's eyes.

"Certainly very intriguing... and fascinating."

"I need to know why my father sent me the egg, what for... and if it's got anything to do with what happened to him."

"That's a mystery we need to investigate."

"It might be dangerous."

"There's probably danger around you already, whether we can see it or not, and an understanding of what's going on might help us prevent it."

Lasgol nodded. "Thanks."

Egil smiled. "You're most welcome. Now rest, we have a lot to do and find out."

The cabin relapsed into the silence of the night. Lasgol fell asleep watching the creature with a feeling of apprehension. Something bad was afoot. He could sense it.

Chapter 17

For the next two weeks the six team-mates tried as hard as they could, with a single purpose in mind: to pass the Spring Test. They put everything they had into it, Lasgol more than anyone. Despite the fact that the other pupils' and Instructors' rejection of him was more and more open, he kept on. The booby traps, dirty tricks, half-whispered insults, even being spat at, were his standard fare, but he did not complain or flinch. He just kept going. With one single goal: to pass the tests. What especially annoyed and frustrated him was that the Instructors treated him differently, much worse than they did the others, instead of being impartial. That was not fair. And he remembered Ulf's words: Life isn't fair. There's no use crying about it. You simply must keep going.

A group of third-year pupils tried to provoke him into fighting beside the library. He bore the insults and shoving. He did not offer any resistance, as he knew that confrontation was what they were after. Two Rangers saw what was happening but decided to ignore it. He was not surprised. He could not expect any help from them. When they saw they were not going to get what they wanted, one of the bullies, tall and red-headed, launched a hard punch at him. He took it in the eye. The burst of pain made him take two steps backwards. But he did not flinch. He shook his head, regained his ground and raised his chin defiantly. Another of the boys hit him in the stomach so hard that he was winded. Lasgol bent double with pain, unable to get his breath back. Next came a knee that made him roll on the ground.

He lay there in a sea of pain. Other Initiates walked past him but no one helped him. It took him a moment to recover. He was very sore, but he stood up slowly. He turned to face his attackers and lifted his chin. He would receive the beating without giving them any satisfaction.

He was about to get another punch when Ivana, the Master Ranger of the School of Archery, saw them on her way to the Command House. She called out, came up to them and demanded an explanation. The third-years said it was nothing, just an exchange of opinions, and Lasgol did not give them away. He was no snitch. Besides, he knew it would not solve anything. Ivana told them to move away and went on to the Command House. Lasgol resigned himself and went on training and doing his best.

Gerd and Egil, with Ingrid's help, were working on their strength and endurance after training every evening before dinner. In addition, Egil, Gerd and Viggo, with Nilsa's help, were trying to improve their archery skills before lunch every day. Lasgol helped them all with his knowledge of tracking. He would draw the different prints of all the animals he knew on the ground and explain everything he knew about them and how to tell them apart. Egil gave them masterly lessons on medicinal plants and poisonous fungi. Lasgol taught them how to make traps. Viggo explained how to cross the pine-trunk which had been smeared with lard and they spent days trying, with varied results. Every night they went to bed exhausted and aching, knowing they had not made much progress and that the following day would bring them more suffering and frustration. Still, none of them would give up. They all had their reasons, different in each case, which drove them on and would not allow them to give up in the face of adversity.

In addition to this Lasgol and Egil were spending their few free moments studying the creature and trying to unravel the mystery which surrounded it. Why had Dakon had it? Why had he sent it? What powers did it have, and how did they work? Lasgol had told Egil more of his own story as he came to trust him more and more, and they were becoming inseparable friends.

Many evenings they shut themselves in the library with the excuse of studying plants and their medicinal benefits for the Instruction of Nature. But they were really looking for tomes which dealt with exotic animals on the shelves devoted to Instruction of Wildlife. The Library was bigger than Lasgol had imagined. In the form of a five-story tower, it must have been converted from an old military building. It was one of the few buildings in the whole Camp which was made of stone, from the foundation to the battlemented roof. Against the inside walls of bare rock were shelves filled with countless tomes and parchments. Each floor was dedicated to one School, with long oak tables between the bookshelves. There was a labyrinth of shelves and tables which Lasgol enjoyed exploring, and where Egil, who was fascinated, seemed to have found his home. The building was in the middle of an oak wood between the canteen and the Command House. From the outside, since it was covered in creepers and moss, looked like a huge tree.

They had not found anything remotely similar to the creature, so they were still looking. Meanwhile the little being was growing and scuttled all over Lasgol's body, as if he were its parent. It slept most of the day, but when it woke it was full of energy. Little by little it was growing used to the cabin's environment and its inmates, although Viggo, Gerd and Ingrid did not go near it. Egil wanted to stroke it, but it shied away from him. At least it did seem to tolerate their presence. Nilsa watched it with visible distrust, as if she expected it to do something which involved magic. Lasgol was delighted with the smiling little thing who fed it and looked after it as best he could. When they were at their Instruction he put it to sleep inside the trunk.

Finally the dreaded day of the Spring Test arrived. They got up before Master Instructor Oden's silver bell sounded.

"Nervous?" Lasgol asked Egil as they got dressed.

"Yes, quite a Bit. I don't want to be expelled. I couldn't bear the shame it would cause my father."

"You put too much pressure on yourself. You should be whatever you want, not what your father tells you."

"You don't understand, my friend. If I fail, it won't just mean humiliation for my father the Duke of Olafstone, but he'll have to 'yield' one of my two brothers to the service of the King. And that would be adding insult to injury."

"Oh, I see…"

Ingrid came into the cabin, followed by Nilsa. "Come on, keep your spirits up! We'll manage this!"

Gerd smiled. "We'll manage this," he repeated to himself, clenching his fists and trying to encourage himself.

"We've trained a lot," Nilsa said. "We'll pass, you just wait and see." But then she stumbled on the bearskin and almost fell.

Viggo grumbled under his breath but said nothing.

The sound of Oden's voice, followed by the bell, brought all thirteen teams out to fall in before the cabins.

"There's been another drop-out this morning," Oden announced as he walked back and forth in front of the kneeling initiates. "That makes four since we began instruction. If anybody else wants to withdraw and avoid ridicule in the Spring Test, they can step forward." He stopped before Lasgol and stared at him, waiting for him to give up.

Lasgol swallowed. He was not going to give up. He looked away to his left and met Isgord's gaze. He was smiling. But further along he saw Astrid. She shook her head almost imperceptibly. Lasgol looked Oden in the eye and let him see the resolve in his own. He would not give up.

"You're still in time to save yourself from ridicule, Traitor," Oden said to him.

Lasgol bit his lip and swallowed his rage. He shook his head.

"Very well, as you wish." He turned to the others. "Follow me! And remember what's at stake today!"

Dolbarar was waiting for them outside the Command House. He was wearing formal dress, which underlined the power he emanated.

"Welcome to the Spring Test!" he said cheerfully, looking up at the tops of the trees as he spoke.

When they heard the Camp leader's voice everybody stood to attention.

"Today we have the Individual Tests, where each one of you will be able to show all you've learned. I know you've done your best, and today is the day you can validate that effort. I can assure you that in these tests we're not looking for you to fail. Far from it: we want to establish that you've managed to assimilate what the Four Schools have taught you in body and mind. So I want you to be at ease. You'll be assessed by the four Master Rangers themselves."

Lasgol looked at Egil, who opened his eyes like saucers and gulped. He was not the only one to gulp and look fearful.

"When the assessment is over," said Dolbarar, "the Master Rangers will give you one, two, or three Oak Leaves. He showed them the oval wooden pins. "Three means that you've excelled in the School. Two, that you've done well but you need to improve. One leaf means you've failed to pass the test."

Lasgol swallowed again. The idea of getting one Oak Leaf and failing unsettled his stomach. His fellow initiates also wore expressions of concern.

"Tomorrow, after you've rested and recovered your strength, we'll have the Test by Teams. It will last all day and all night. It's very special; it will test you as a team, so you will have to help one another. The team must cross the finishing line in its entirety. If one of the members fails to, the entire team will be penalized. The penalty for not completing the Team Test in the specified time is the loss of one Oak Leaf from the individual tests. On the other hand, the winning team will receive a Leaf of Prestige, and will be able to use it to save one of its members in the final expulsions." He showed them the Leaf of Prestige, which was much larger than the others.

"We could do with one of those," said Ingrid.

"We'll have all we're likely to if we manage to pass the test and don't lose any Leaves," said Viggo.

"Oh ye of little faith!"

"I'm a realist."

Dolbarar spread his arms wide. "Now breathe deeply, relax and go! The Individual tests are waiting for you!"

The initiates withdrew, a minority of them full of self-confidence, most nervous and worried.

Oden announced the order of the teams. The first four moved off to the Master Houses of the School of Expertise. The Panthers had to wait. They sat in front of the cabins and waited nervously. Nobody spoke. At mid-morning Oden called them. At the Master House of the School of Archery, two instructors were waiting at the door.

"The Captain can come in," said one of them.

"And not a word, either before or after the test," the other warned them.

Ingrid went in decisively, as the person she was. She came out shortly afterwards and nodded at them with a gesture of triumph. This encouraged the others. Nilsa went in, and when she came out she was smiling. Gerd was next. When he came out there was a mixture of fear and relief on his face. Then it was Lasgol's turn. He went in and found Ivana waiting for him, sitting behind a great oak table. Her gaze and her beauty were intimidating. He went up to a chalked line on the floor in front of the table and clasped his hands behind his back.

"Team?"

"Snow Panthers."

"Name?"

"Lasgol." She wrote it down in a tome. "I'm going to ask you fifteen questions about this School which you should know the answers to. Answer me quickly and exactly."

"Yes, ma'am."

He answered all the questions. There were only two he hesitated over, although he answered them anyway, even if he was not sure he was correct.

"Now the practical test," she said, and indicated a table against the wall to her left. On it was a bow which had been disassembled. Beside the bow was an arrow, also in separate parts.

Ivana indicated another table, against the opposite wall. "The tools are over there."

Lasgol saw several tools on the other table. He was beginning to guess what was coming next.

"I want you to put the bow and the arrow together in the shortest possible time and present it to me for inspection. You may only use one tool at a time and you must put each back on the table after using it."

Before he could say anything, the Master Ranger gave the order: "Go!"

Lasgol ran to the first table and looked at the parts of the bow for a moment. His heart was beating hard. He turned and ran to the table with the tools, grabbed the first one and ran back as fast as he could. He repeated the operation six times and managed to complete the task. He ran to the Master Ranger's table and handed both to her. He was breathless, and his heart was ready to leap out of his mouth.

Ivana glanced at the bow and arrow and gave her approval with a nod.

"Now the shooting test," she said, and indicated an open window to her right where a bow and quiver full of arrows had been placed. "Stand on the mark on the floor."

Lasgol saw an X chalked in front of the window.

"Do you see the target?"

Lasgol squinted and saw it, in the middle of the field outside the building, at two hundred paces.

"Yes, ma'am."

"You have ten shots. Don't waste them."

Lasgol took a deep breath. He had to stay calm, because what with running to and from and his nerves, he was not going to hit the target. In any case, two hundred paces was a considerable distance, more than he had trained for. *I've got to relax, then I can do it. I can't afford to fail this test.* He released ten times. He missed three, and the seven which hit were not very good shots, but at least he reached the target.

"Leave the bow and quiver where they were. You may leave."

"Yes, ma'am."

He turned to leave, and as he went out he saw an instructor taking the bow apart and placing it back on the table, while outside, another picked up the arrows and wrote down the results.

When he came out Egil gave him a worried look.

"Not a word," said one of the instructors.

Lasgol winked at Egil and made an encouraging gesture. Egil went in, and they waited for him in silence. When he came out again he looked deeply worried.

From there they went to the Master House of the School of Wildlife. Tamer Esben, Master Ranger, was waiting inside. As in the previous test they went in one by one, starting with the Captain. The test went similarly. Esben began with fifteen questions about wildlife. Being the person he was, as big and ugly as a black bear, he was intimidating, particularly his face, with its large brown eyes and snub nose. The Panthers answered without letting themselves be intimidated, at least not too obviously. The practical tests were hard. First a circuit on horseback, with jumps over fallen trees and a trot through a forest with low-hanging branches, then fording a river where the water completely covered their mount, and finally a race against an instructor. The results were not very promising. Nilsa fell off her horse during the jumps. Gerd sank with his horse in the river because of the young giant's weight and both horse and rider almost drowned. Egil had suffered in the race, arriving some way behind...

And as if that had not been disaster enough, next came the tracking test. Esben made them identify five different types of prints in the forest. Then he watched them while they followed a trail as far as the lair of the animal they had to identify. Only Lasgol and Egil managed to finish the tracking test.

Afternoon came, and things did not improve for the Panthers. They were taken to the Master House of the School of Nature. Erudite Eyra, Master Ranger, was waiting for them there. Lasgol had a soft spot for the old woman; of all the Rangers she was the only one who showed any sign of sweet nature. On this particular day however, she was not sweet at all, rather the opposite. With her curly salt-and-pepper hair and her long crooked nose she looked like a witch, though a good one. At the same time her expression, which was usually pleasant, was very serious.

The first part of the test was a set of questions about plants, roots and fungi and their healing properties. Egil did not fail a single one of them. Lasgol and Viggo did not do too badly either. But the others suffered.

For the practical part of the test the Erudite took them to a nearby forest and made them search for a healing root and a poisonous mushroom. This time Egil was the one who had a hard time finding them. Lasgol had no problem. The others took too long, but in the end they managed it.

As a final test, the old lady made them prepare a trap and hide it as quickly as they could. Lasgol was the only one who shone.

Finally it was time for the test they all feared the most, that of the School of Expertise. The sinister Haakon the Untouchable, Master Ranger, was waiting for them at his Master House. In this test there were no questions, only the practical part.

He sent them to do five laps around the lake as fast as they could. One by one they set off, accompanied by an instructor who set the pace. Egil and Gerd had put a lot of effort into training and had improved, but five laps at that pace was likely to be too much for them. And so it turned out. Ingrid and Lasgol made it. Viggo made it with enormous effort, and Nilsa, after tripping and falling twice out of pure exhaustion, managed to finish. Egil and Gerd reached the finish shattered, but at least they reached it. They did not give up, even though they knew they had taken too long.

That in itself had been hard, but what followed ended up breaking their spirits. Haakon had prepared the pole test, but on this occasion half the pole had been smeared with lard, and the height was greater so that the fall would be even more painful. He gave them until midnight to complete it. The six of them tried again and again, but they kept falling into the river, battering and bruising themselves in the process. They were too tired to get it right. Egil was the one who realized this. They rested until they had got some of their strength back, then tried again. Viggo was the first to manage it successfully. Then Lasgol did the same. This encouraged the others. Lasgol and Viggo stood under the pole to break their partners' fall, but the instructor who was watching them would not allow it.

They did not give up, even in the midst of pain and exhaustion. They reached the middle without any trouble, but nearer the end they skidded and fell. Nilsa was the next to cross. She did it in a rather unorthodox way by running, slipping with both feet and falling on her face on the pole. But using her own inertia she was able to slide along the pole and reach the end. The instructor conceded the point. Seeing this, Ingrid did the same, threw herself on to the pole and slid to the other end. At the fifth attempt she crossed. Gerd and Egil were left lying in the river, without strength for another attempt, their bodies aching and bruised. Their friends shouted encouragement at them.

The instructor gave warning that the test was about to end. Egil and Gerd got to their feet, walked up the gully as far as the pole and made one final attempt. Gerd went first. He fell into the river two paces from the end. Egil took a deep breath, removed his boots, straightened his thick woolen socks properly and tried. To everybody's surprise he managed it. The instructor conceded the point, and the test came to an end.

They picked up Gerd from the bottom of the gully and went back to their cabin. He was so bruised that Viggo and Lasgol had to carry him. Ingrid helped Egil, who could barely walk. As they left the field they passed a couple of posts where other teams were still enduring the final part of the test in the School of Expertise.

They reached the cabin and slumped on to the porch.

"What a nightmare," Gerd said. He was lying on his back on the wooden floor. "I've done really badly in all the tests. I'm not going to make it."

"The same as yours truly," said Egil. "It was a farcical display."

"And what do you care if you're expelled?" Viggo said, sounding annoyed.

Egil looked at him seriously. "I care quite a lot."

"Don't know why, seeing who you are…"

"How do you know who I am?" Egil asked in surprise.

"I know a lot of things. I have that skill."

"Who are you?" Gerd asked.

Viggo pointed his finger at Egil. "He's the son of a Duke. And not of any Duke, oh no. The most powerful in the realm."

"Are you Duke Olafstone's son?" Ingrid asked in surprise.

Egil sighed deeply. "Yes…" he said heavily.

"Wow!" said Gerd. "It's almost unreal for a farmer like me to be in the presence of a nobleman."

"A nobleman…" Nilsa said, and sighed. "The riches you must have seen…"

"Let me remind you that once we're part of the Rangers we renounce our past. Now I'm just like you, neither more nor less."

"Okay," Gerd said, "but you've got to tell me more about the life of the nobility."

"Yes, yes…" Nilsa said, swaying impatiently and clapping to encourage him.

Egil jerked his finger at Viggo and said: "If there's anyone who needs to tell us about his life and origins, it's him. He hasn't said anything up to now, and as a rule anyone who keeps quiet is doing it for some good reason."

"That's true," Ingrid said. "What are you hiding?"

They all looked at Viggo, who had stiffened. His face turned somber, sinister. The expression lasted a moment, one in which Lasgol felt a latent danger emanating from him. Then he smiled, a forced smile, and his body relaxed.

"I'm the complete opposite of our little friend the nobleman," he said.

Ingrid half-closed her eyes. "And what would that mean?"

"I mean exactly what I said. He belongs to the highest social class. I'm the opposite. I come from the lowest."

"The lowest? What are you, then?"

"I was born and grew up in the streets of Ostangor."

"That's the second biggest city of the realm," Nilsa said. "They say that some filthy Ice Mage of the Court lives there." Her good mood had vanished. Her usual smiling face was now so grim it was scary.

"Yes. In the dirty streets of the poorest neighborhood, that's where I grew up, among the mud, rats and garbage." He lowered his gaze in shame.

"But… aren't you the son of a Ranger?" Ingrid asked.

"Grandson. Unfortunately my father wasn't what you'd call a model citizen. He is doing time in the silver mines. Sentenced to life. He got drunk and killed a man in a bar brawl."

"Oh, I'm so sorry…" Gerd said.

"It would seem that Ranger blood, although it passes from

fathers to sons, doesn't always transmit the good qualities. My father preferred to rob, drink and have fun rather than serve the king, so he didn't accept the invitation. Then he had me, and when my grandfather died, he abandoned us and left my mother and me in the street. He'd lost the house and everything we had because of gambling and drinking."

"That's terrible," said Gerd.

"So I grew up in the dirtiest, poorest streets. I learned many things there, let's say it was another kind of training to prepare you for life, a hard, pitiless life, which is what it is for the less fortunate. My mother died of fever some time afterwards and I had to make do as best I could. When the invitation came to train as a Ranger, I accepted. I had nothing to lose."

"I had no idea…" said Egil, feeling guilty at having forced an explanation from him.

"Don't apologize, I messed with you and you defended yourself. There's nothing to feel bad about."

"Your story is horrible," said Gerd, shaking his head.

"Don't pity me. Nobody's going to pity me! I've been less lucky than others, but I'm not ashamed of who I am. I know what I am: a sewer rat, but one that knows how to bite, scratch and survive. The same way I survived in the sewers of the great city, I'll survive here. I can assure you that I'm better prepared for that than a lot of those who're competing here."

Lasgol took a long look at Viggo's sinister gaze and with the certainty from his expression, he knew he was not bragging. He was telling the truth. There was a long silence. They were all dispirited and broken.

"We'll do better tomorrow," Ingrid said. "None of my team's going back home. Come on, everybody go to sleep. Let's rest."

They all went to bed. Lasgol played a little with the creature, which had now taken to jumping non-stop on his chest, as if trying to gauge how far it could reach. *What are you? And what do you want with me?* It suddenly jumped so high it stuck to the bottom of the upper bunk. The creature squealed, as if celebrating the fact. Lasgol knew that when it grew bigger it was going to give him something more than a headache.

What a day, he thought, and sighed. *And tomorrow we have the Team Tests. Please let nothing happen to us.* And with that thought he fell asleep.

Chapter 18

The morning was crisp, the sun had just come out, and Oden had called them out of their cabins and taken them in front of the Command House. Dolbarar was waiting for them in his formal dress. On his face was a friendly, good-humored smile.

"Welcome, everybody! I hope you enjoyed a good night's rest. It should be enough for you to have recovered from yesterday's individual tests, and to be able to face what awaits you. Today we have the Test by Teams. Let me remind you that it will last all day and all night. Let me warn you that it is essential to pace yourselves well, otherwise you won't make it. The test is devised to test you as a team, which means you will have to help each other. This is vital. Form up your teams. Captains, please step forward."

The thirteen teams grouped themselves in the order of their cabins, with their captains in front of them. An Instructor gave each captain two rolled parchments, a satchel and a water-skin.

"The rule of the test is as follows: when I give the signal, you will open the parchments and follow the instructions written on them. You can only take with you what the Captain has been given. Nothing else. You'll then complete the test indicated in the parchments. You must cross the finishing line, which will be right here, with all the tests completed, before the sun rises tomorrow morning. Every member of the team must cross at the same time. If one fails, you all fail. The entire team will be penalized. You know the penalty for not completing the test in the time allowed: you will lose one Oak Leaf from your individual tests. This may lead to expulsion, so be brave, but above all, be intelligent."

Ingrid turned and looked at Gerd, then at Egil, as if telling them that she expected that of them.

"The winning team, the one that completes the test in the least time, will be awarded one Leaf of Prestige. This acknowledgment has two important uses. On the one hand, it can be used to save one of the members of the team who may be facing expulsion on the day of the Acceptance Ceremony, which will take place on the last day of the course, once all four major tests are completed. At the

Acceptance Ceremony it will be decided who will go on to the second year and who will be expelled. All the points received in each School will count, and the opinion of the Four Master Rangers will be taken into account as well. Those who fail to gain eight points in each will be expelled."

Lasgol shuddered to hear Dolbarar speak about expulsion. Nor was he the only one; many became very nervous, Nilsa among them. She could not stay still and her hands and feet were shaking.

"On the other hand, those of you who wish to enter the Elite Specialties will need one Leaf of Prestige, which means you'll have to compete for first place in order to gain them."

Isgord turned to Ingrid and gestured to indicate that he would fight for first place. Ingrid, unflinchingly, returned the gesture. Astrid was watching them, but made no gesture.

"Right then! Time flies, it's time to start the Test by Teams. At my signal, open the parchments." Dolbarar waited a moment, then pointed up at the sky. "Now!"

The Captains opened the parchments, and their team-mates gathered around them trying to see what they said.

"So what is it? What does it say?" asked Nilsa. She could not control her nervousness in the midst of the buzz of questions from the members of the other teams.

Ingrid was studying both parchments with close attention. "Give me a moment to look at them properly."

"That looks like a map," said Gerd.

"Yes, this is a map with a route marked on it."

"And the other one?" asked Egil.

"It looks like instructions: *Follow the map to the marked place. Find the Green Ranger's Scarf. Solve the test and go on. There are three tests to be solved before you come back.*" Ingrid shook her head. "I don't quite understand."

Viggo tried to take hold of the map: "Let me have a look."

Ingrid tugged it back, "I'm the Captain. I'll say who takes the map and when."

"The rest of us need to know what it's about, though, don't we?" Viggo protested.

"Don't argue," Lasgol said. "We have to work together. You heard Dolbarar."

"Maybe if you could be so kind as to put them on the ground, that way we'd all see them," suggested Egil.

"All right then." Ingrid bent down and put the two parchments on the ground, with a couple of stones to hold them in place.

They all looked at them, trying to work out what it all meant.

"We have to follow the map to the indicated point," Lasgol said.

Egil nodded. "Yes. I'd guess once we get there, there'll be a test to pass."

"But it talks about three tests," said Nilsa.

"Let's focus on the first one, then we'll see." Viggo said.

Gerd pointed north. "Hurry up, the first teams are already setting out."

Lasgol craned his head and saw the Eagles start running. After them came the Boars and Wolves, but in different directions. This puzzled him.

"Then let's be on our way!" cried Ingrid.

"Which way?" asked Lasgol.

Egil took a look at the map, then at the distant mountains. "Northeast. We have to reach Ogre's Peak."

"Right," Ingrid said. "Let's go!" She broke into a run.

The other five followed her at once. They passed the Owls as Astrid was giving her own team-mates the order to run. In front of them two other teams were already going into the forest, and further ahead were the majority of teams who had already left.

The race across country was both fast and chaotic. Everybody ran as if they were being chased by ravenous lions. They leapt over obstacles and around the edges of buildings. On leaving the Camp however, each team went in a different direction.

Ingrid went into the forest and set a brisk pace. Nilsa followed closely behind her. Viggo came third, with Gerd and Egil behind them. Lasgol took up the rear. They ran for almost two hours, crossing forests and rivers and going around lakes. Soon, the effects of tiredness began to be felt. Little by little Gerd and Egil began to lag. Lasgol was slowing his pace to stay with them. At one moment they came out of the forest on to an open area as the other three were already entering another stretch of forest.

"Wait!" Lasgol called out.

Ingrid heard him and stopped. They looked at each other, separated by five hundred paces of open land. The Captain gestured at them to hurry.

Egil had his hands on his waist and was panting from the effort. "Tell... her... to go... on ..."

"But we'll lose them."

"We know the location... of the first test..." he said breathlessly. "If they get there first, they might be able to pass the test. And they'll be able to go on. We'll gain time."

Lasgol understood. "Go on! We'll catch up with you at the first stop. If you pass the test, keep going, and leave a clear trail. We'll follow behind you."

"Okay, understood!" Ingrid said. She waved and went on, Nilsa and Viggo with her.

Gerd and Egil rested till they got a little strength back, then set off again. They ran, but at a slower pace, which soon turned into a quick walk rather than a gentle trot. They followed their partners' trail. When they reached the first slopes they were forced to slow down. The hills became very steep as they went up, and soon they were climbing amid snow and rock. The cold began to take its toll on their bodies; the more they climbed, the more snow they found and the lower the temperature fell. The punishment on the body was tremendous.

It took them half the morning to reach Ogre's Peak. Lasgol helped Gerd and Egil to climb. He encouraged them and showed them where to put their feet and fingers, helping them as they climbed, as the way became very difficult toward the end. When they reached the top they found their three team-mates still there. Their serious faces and sunken eyes indicated they were not happy at all.

"But... what are you doing ... still here?" Gerd asked, panting. The icy breeze of the top whipped at them. The temperature up there was very low and the wind was cutting.

Ingrid snorted in frustration. "We can't pass the first test."

"I think we ought to look for a shortcut," Viggo suggested. "I'm freezing."

"We can't cheat!" Nilsa said angrily.

"Sure, it's much better not to pass the first test and be last than catch pneumonia up here and die."

"The Green Ranger's scarf ought to be here," Lasgol said.

Gerd and Egil sat on the ground, trying to regain their breath.

"Yes," Ingrid said, "but we've searched the whole top and ... nothing."

Lasgol looked around thoughtfully. In front of him was the rocky peak in the horrible shape of an ogre's head. Behind him were mountain ranges higher, whiter, purer and more beautiful. The ground was white except where he and his partners had trampled it. There was nothing there. Not a thing.

"What if it isn't visible?" he said.

"We wouldn't miss a green Ranger's scarf," Viggo said.

"Let's search for something hidden, something we can't see," suggested Lasgol.

Ingrid was not prepared to give up and was willing to try anything. "Good idea."

They started to feel around them with their hands and feet. Then they moved out, trying to cover the whole surface.

Viggo trod on an innocent-looking lump of snow. "I think there's something here."

Ingrid and Lasgol turned and at the same moment they heard a *click*. The trap hidden under the mound of snow became activated. Suddenly an enormous cloud of smoke came out of the trap and rose into the sky.

Viggo fell backwards with a yelp.

Nilsa ran to his side. "Are you all right?"

"Yes, yes! It just scared me to death!"

"That's funny," said Gerd. "I'd say it was a smoke signal."

"And you wouldn't be wrong," said Egil. He pointed toward Eagle Peak, to the north. Another column of smoke was rising there.

Nilsa pointed to the west. "Look," she said. Three other clouds of smoke had been activated on different summits of the endless range which surrounded the entire Rangers' Camp.

"We're not the only ones who've passed the first test," Ingrid said.

"Looks like it," said Viggo.

Nilsa pointed at the trap. "Look!"

Something had become visible once the smoke had vanished. A green scarf was fixed to the ground with a spike. Beside it was something long, wrapped in leather. Lasgol bent to pick it up.

"The green scarf!" Nilsa cried in delight.

"This is the first one," Ingrid said.

Lasgol unwrapped whatever it was.

"A bow!" cried Gerd.

"What would we want a bow for?" Viggo asked.

"No arrows?" asked Ingrid.

Lasgol shook his head.

"That's strange."

"These tests are really weird," Nilsa said.

"There's something else," Lasgol said. He showed them the inside of the leather the bow was wrapped in. It was tattooed.

"Another map!" said Nilsa.

Lasgol studied it. "Yes, and it marks the spot for the next test."

"Right," Ingrid said. "On we go to the second position."

Egil was more or less recovered by now. "Which location do we have to reach now?" he asked.

"It marks Fisherman's Cabin, to the east."

None of them knew the place, but at least it was not on a mountain. Judging by the drawing on the map it looked like a flat area in the middle of the forest.

"All right," said Lasgol. "You go ahead, I'll guide Egil and Gerd."

"Right then," said Ingrid. "Off we go."

"Be careful on the way down, don't crack your heads open," Viggo said. He looked aside at Nilsa. "Especially you."

She poked her tongue at him and made a rude gesture.

As soon as Gerd was well enough he, Lasgol and Egil left. It took them a while to get into a rhythm, but they finally made it. They went as fast as they could, straining their bodies. They could not run, but they walked as fast as their legs would allow.

At the cabin they found Ingrid, Nilsa and Viggo waiting inside. Their faces were a poem.

Ingrid swallowed hard. "We can't find the scarf. We can't go on. We've gone over the whole cabin, but we haven't found anything. It's a well-kept cabin, it seems as though someone uses it."

Egil dropped in front of the door in exhaustion. "What... does the map mark?"

"The middle of the frozen lake, but there's nothing but ice there."

"If that's what it shows, we'll have to go to the middle of the lake," Lasgol said.

"Are you sure?" Viggo objected. "There's nothing there, and the ice might break."

"Lasgol's right," Egil said. "These tests are designed to test us. We can't let ourselves be guided by the obvious. I fear we need to

190

think the exact opposite."

They reached a decision and moved forward carefully on the ice. After a few steps Nilsa skidded and landed on her backside. Viggo roared with laughter.

"Good thing it's not thin ice, or else..."

"You're an idiot!" she said from the ground. Ingrid helped her to her feet, but it was so slippery that they both went down.

Viggo laughed so hard that his laughter echoed all around the lake.

"The biggest idiot of all!" Ingrid grumbled.

When they reached the center of the lake they found to their surprise that someone had drilled a round hole in the surface. Looking down at the bottom of the lake through the hole and the blue water, they could make out something red.

"It has to be that," Lasgol said.

"I'll get it," Gerd said.

They all looked at him blankly.

"You?" Viggo said. Disbelief was written all over his face.

"Yes, me."

"Aren't you afraid?" Nilsa asked him.

"No, not of this."

"How come you're scared of your own shadow, but not of getting into a frozen lake where you could freeze to death?"

"Because I've done it before. My brother and I always went fishing in a frozen lake like this one every winter, since we were little. It's not too far from my parents' farm. It was one of the few sources of food in winter. We spent plenty of afternoons there fishing. We drilled a hole very much like this one, then sat down and fished. In fact we had a good time talking about what we wanted to do when we grew up, the latest gossip in the village, what we'd caught that day, which usually wasn't very much ... anyway, one day as we were walking where the ice wasn't so thick, it broke and my brother fell in."

"How awful!" said Nilsa.

"So what did you do?" Lasgol asked.

"For a moment I was paralyzed by fear. I couldn't react. I was so afraid I just stood there like a stone statue. Luckily after a moment I recovered and without thinking twice I dived in to save him. It was a horrible experience, the cold and the fear almost killed me, but I

PEDRO URVI

managed to get him out."

"And you're willing to do it again?" Ingrid asked.

"Someone has to do it. And I know I can survive this. I won't let any of you take the risk. You might not make it … and I'd never forgive myself. I'll go." He began to take off his clothes.

"In that case, let's get a fire ready in the cabin," Ingrid said.

"And a restorative tisane, the way they taught us to in School of Nature," said Egil.

"Great idea!" said Nilsa. "I'll look for the plants."

Gerd, in his underclothes, took a deep breath and his chest swelled. He looked at Lasgol and Viggo as though trying to summon up courage. He nodded, then got into the freezing water of the lake.

Lasgol saw the body sinking and felt an enormous anxiety. He knelt down beside the hole, and Viggo joined him. A long moment passed. There was no sign of Gerd. They began to worry.

"He ought to have come up already," Lasgol said.

"Give him a moment more."

They waited, but Lasgol could not bear it any longer.

"Something's wrong, I'm going in to get him." He began to take off his clothes.

At that moment a hand emerged from the water. In it was a long box, an intense red. It was followed by Gerd's head. His face was completely purple.

"Help me get him out!" Lasgol cried.

He and Viggo lifted him and dragged him out. Ingrid joined them, and they carried the giant to the cabin. He was so cold he could not speak, only shiver.

"Sit him by the fire," Ingrid said.

Egil wrapped him in a blanket he found in the cabin.

Nilsa handed him a hot tisane. "Are you all right?"

Gerd took it with shaking hands and nodded.

The rest of the team looked at Gerd with concern, until at last his color began to change and he stopped shivering.

"Better?"

"A l— a lot …don't ever… let me do it … again …"

"Ha, ha, ha, easy, buddy," Egil assured him. "I won't allow it."

Nilsa had opened the box. "The green scarf is in the box! And a quiver with three arrows!"

"Okay," Viggo said with a sneer, "we have the bow and three

arrows for it. Now all we need is a dragon to slay."

"Don't be stupid!" Ingrid said.

He raised one eyebrow. "You wait and see what we have to kill with those three arrows..."

"Surely not a dragon."

"Well then, it'll be a huge Troll, or some other Magical Creature."

Nilsa's face turned white. She clenched her fists tightly. "There'd better not be any magic involved!" she said furiously.

"Easy... don't pay attention to him, he's joking," said Ingrid when she saw her face.

"Sure, just joking... well, we'll see," Viggo said.

"Well, we have the bow and arrows," said Ingrid. "Isn't there a map?"

Nilsa examined the inside of the box and realized that it was made of tanned leather. She stripped it off, and on the other side she saw the tattoo.

"The map!" she cried triumphantly.

Ingrid studied the map carefully. "Good. We'll have to set off for the third test. We need to go to the Lonely Warrior. We'll go first. Judging by the map, it's quite a long way. We'll be running for most of the night. We'll leave you food and water, we've already eaten. When Gerd's well enough, you follow us."

Lasgol nodded. "All right."

Ingrid, Nilsa and Viggo left as quickly as they could. A good while later, with Gerd now recovered, the three laggards set off in their turn. Lasgol set the pace, Gerd and Egil followed. They were so tired, and their bodies were so sore from the effort, that they did not even speak. They needed every bit of strength to keep going. The journey took them through forests, which made the going more difficult. Lasgol was aware that they would have to rest, or else Egil or Gerd would collapse and not get up again. They were exhausted. They came out of the forest into a clearing. In the middle of it was a white boulder in the rough form of a warrior. It was like a huge monument dedicated to some warrior god.

"Here we are," Lasgol said. "This is the Lonely Warrior."

Ingrid, Nilsa and Viggo were waiting beside the boulder with looks of resignation.

"You haven't... found... the scarf, then?" Gerd asked. He was holding his sides, trying to breathe.

"Very smart," Viggo said with a grimace of annoyance.

Ingrid pointed behind her. "The map marks this boulder. But we've looked everywhere around it and found nothing. We even felt with our hands, in case it wasn't visible."

"Nothing at all," repeated Nilsa.

Lasgol and Egil looked thoughtfully at the place, puzzling over what could be done. Gerd dropped to the ground and began to snort like an exhausted horse. After a moment Lasgol had a sudden hunch.

He went up to the boulder. "Help me," he said.

"What are you going to do?" Ingrid asked.

"I'm going up there. Unless you've done that already."

"No... it didn't occur to us to try climbing." She sounded embarrassed. She went to the base of the boulder. "Climb on to me."

Lasgol climbed on to her back and began to scramble up the boulder. It was not easy as there were no points where his hands could get a grip, but he had a talent for climbing; it was something he loved to do. With a little effort and perseverance, he managed to get to the top.

"Are you sure you didn't grow up among monkeys?" Viggo said, not without a certain respect.

"Is there anything up there?" Egil asked.

"Yes. I've got it. It's more instructions." He jumped down.

"What does it say?" Nilsa asked eagerly.

Lasgol read out: *"Three shots, one target, one reward."*

Viggo looked all around. "I don't understand ... what target?"

Lasgol pointed to the east. "You can't see it from here. It's behind that stretch of forest, at the top of a pine tree. You can only see the target from up there."

"My, they're devious!" Viggo protested.

"And we were looking everywhere," Nilsa complained.

"Who's going to shoot?" Egil asked.

They all looked at Ingrid, as she was the best archer in the group by far.

"All right. I'll do it," she agreed without hesitation.

This time it was Lasgol who helped Ingrid climb up the boulder. When she reached the top she waved at them.

Lasgol watched her. It was the dead of night, but the moon was bright, nearly full. There was some visibility, but that shot was only for champions, and he knew it.

Ingrid assembled the bow. She took a deep breath and aimed. Up there, with the bow ready, she looked like a warrior goddess. There followed a tense moment. Then she let out her breath and released the arrow smoothly. They watched the flight, willing it to hit the target.

She missed, and protested with a curse.

"Don't be discouraged," Gerd said.

"It's the wind." She pulled out a couple of hairs and let them fall in front of her nose to determine the direction of the wind. "From the east. I'll adjust my aim."

Nilsa clapped. "Courage!"

Ingrid gestured sharply to her to calm down.

"Sorry… the excitement…"

Ingrid repeated her movements methodically. She adjusted, and released. The arrow flew straight to the target. At the last instant, it veered a little and she missed.

"Nothing," she muttered in frustration.

The team's enthusiasm was beginning to ebb.

Viggo said: "Not to make you nervous, but we've only got one arrow left."

Ingrid gave him a look of hatred. He smiled back at her.

"I overcompensated. This time I won't miss."

She repeated the shot, but this time the compensation was less. The arrow flew toward the target. They all held their breath.

It found its mark.

"Yes!" she shouted jubilantly.

A leather pouch fell to the ground when the arrow hit the target.

"You're the best!" Nilsa said, and the Captain smiled.

"Go and see. Something fell to the ground when I hit the target."

Nilsa and Viggo ran through the trees to the leather pouch. When they found it and opened it, inside it was the map wrapped around a stone, along with the third Ranger's Scarf.

"It marks the end! Now we know where we have to go!" Nilsa cried with a leap of delight as they came back to the others.

Ingrid scrambled down the boulder. "We'd better hurry. We haven't got much time. Remember we have to be back before sunrise, and all together."

They suddenly realized that Lasgol had lagged behind.

"Lasgol, what's the matter?" Egil asked.

Lasgol did not speak.

"What's up? Are you all right?" Ingrid asked him.

He fell to his knees.

"Lasgol!" cried Nilsa.

They ran back to him. When they reached his side they saw what the matter was. There was an arrow buried in his arm!

They were struck dumb.

"What happened?" Ingrid cried.

"I don't know …" he muttered. "I turned... felt a blow and… a sharp pain…"

"An accident!" Nilsa said, looking at Ingrid's bow.

"Some other team in the area… a stray shot…" Gerd suggested. His eyes were wide with fear.

Viggo was looking all around. "No, this is no accident, there's something wrong here…"

"If it hit his arm as he moved," Egil said, "we can assume the shot was aimed at his heart." He gestured towards the forest to the north.

Viggo pulled Lasgol down flat on the ground, practically covering him with his own body. "They might try again!"

Ingrid reacted. "Everybody down! There's an archer somewhere!"

They all dropped to the ground at once and stayed still, watching in silence. In the middle of the night however, with only the light of the moon, they could not see further than a dozen paces.

"Lasgol, how are you?" Ingrid asked.

"It hurts… but not too much."

"In cases like this we need to make a tourniquet, to stop the loss of blood," Egil said.

"I'll do it," said Viggo. He took off his belt and tied it tightly about four finger-breadths above the wound. "Don't breathe now, I'm going to break off the arrow."

Lasgol nodded.

With a sharp snap, Viggo broke the shaft of the arrow. "There. It'll stop the wound from getting any worse. We can't take the head out here. We'll have to wait till we get to a safe place."

"Then let's get out of here," said Ingrid. "Lasgol, can you run?"

"I… think so."

"He'll be able to now," Viggo said. "He's in shock, but that'll soon pass."

"How do you know all this?" Ingrid asked him.

"Let's say I've been through this before, my past life has been quite *interesting*." He showed them a scar on his right shoulder.

Ingrid sighed. "Right then, off we go. Follow me!"

The six partners set off at a run, keeping their heads down, seeking the shadows as they had been taught. Ingrid led the way, following the map. They had to go eastwards to the Blue Ravine, and from there due south to the Camp. For a long while they went on without a word, fearful of being attacked from the shadows, glancing warily in all directions. They ran as fast as they could, in single file, with Lasgol in the middle. They did not stop until they reached the Blue Ravine. It was unmistakable; both sides were covered with blue plants with large petals.

"We're here," Ingrid said.

"How are you, Lasgol?" Egil asked.

Viggo and Gerd were watching the rear in case anybody had followed them.

"Okay... it hurts... but I'm fine..."

"We have to get to the Camp," Nilsa said.

Ingrid was looking at Lasgol with concern. "We still have a long way to go."

"We'll have to hurry," said Egil. "He's losing blood."

"On we go," said Ingrid encouragingly. "We're going to make it!"

They walked because they could not run any more. They were heading south. Ingrid, Nilsa and Viggo set the pace, and it was a brisk one. Egil and Gerd accompanied Lasgol, and to everyone else's surprise, as well as their own, even though they were exhausted they were keeping up. Their legs were in agony, their lungs were burning, they could barely think, but their concern for Lasgol, who was in the center of the group, made them keep going. Ingrid glanced back over her shoulder to check they were following, and surprisingly, they were. Egil and Gerd were not prepared to give way to exhaustion.

"We're almost there!" Ingrid cried. "One last effort!"

The lights of the Camp were in sight. And at that moment, Lasgol collapsed.

"Wait!" Egil shouted.

Ingrid stopped and turned around, followed by Viggo and Nilsa.

"Lasgol!" Gerd said to him. "Keep going, we're here!"

"He's lost a lot of blood," Egil said. "He can't go on."

"Then we'll carry him," said Ingrid.

"I'll give you a hand," said Viggo.

Ingrid looked at him in surprise, but Viggo ignored her. They took Lasgol by the armpits and headed to the Camp with Egil, Gerd and Nilsa closely behind them. They were so worried that they forgot their own exhaustion.

The group crossed the finishing line, just before sunrise. The Instructors were waiting for them.

Master Instructor Oden was unable to hide his great surprise. "The Panthers Team has completed the Test by Teams within the allotted time," he announced.

"Please help us!" Ingrid cried. "We have a wounded man!"

"What the hell's happened?" he asked as he came up to them with several other instructors.

Viggo pointed to the wound. "Someone tried to kill him."

Oden looked at him in bewilderment.

"He has an arrow in his arm, and he's lost a lot of blood," said Egil.

"To the infirmary! Quickly!" Oden ordered.

While the instructors were carrying him at a run, half-conscious, Lasgol saw the sun rise. *We did it,* he thought proudly. Suddenly he felt the icy touch of death.

His heart stopped.

He breathed out and died.

Chapter 19

The creature was disconsolate. Egil was trying to soothe it, but there was no way he could. It shrieked and hopped from one place to another. He tried to catch it, but it was impossible; it was running all over the cabin as though it had gone crazy. Gerd, frightened at all the little animal's shrieking and scampering, climbed up on to his bunk,

"We ought to set a trap for it," Viggo said. "That's what they taught us for."

"How can you be so heartless!" Ingrid exclaimed. "Can't you see it's like that because of Lasgol?"

"All the more reason to capture and 'tranquilize' it."

"You're not going to 'tranquilize' anybody," Ingrid said, arms folded, bringing the discussion to an end.

"Wet blanket ..."

Nilsa watched the creature from a distance. She did not want to do anything about it. That thing was magic, and magic was her personal enemy.

"Egil," Ingrid said, "you'll have to get it to calm down. It's going to attract Oden's attention, or else the other teams'. It's making too much noise."

By now Egil was breathless from chasing the creature all over the cabin. "I'm trying... don't think I'm not trying..."

"Poor little thing," Gerd said from his bunk. But as he was afraid of it, he did not get any closer, just in case.

Egil managed to corner it and made to grab it. It made itself invisible.

"Oh.... I lost it."

"Well, at least it's not screaming," Viggo said.

Tears welled up in Gerd's eyes. "Poor thing."

Lasgol woke up with a terrible headache. He did not know where he was or what was happening. He tried to focus his vision. He was lying on his back, and he could make out a wooden ceiling. But it was not the ceiling of his cabin. He tried to get up, but his strength gave out and he fell backwards on to the bed.

"Stay still," said a woman's voice he did not recognize. "You're too weak to sit up."

"Where…. where am I?

"In the infirmary. You've been here for three days."

"Three days?"

"Yes, since you were brought here at death's door."

He turned his head and managed to focus his gaze on the woman's face. She was old, and was not dressed like a Ranger.

"Who are you?"

"My name is Edwina Sommerfeld. I'm a Healer of the Temple of Tirsar."

"Oh…" he mumbled. He shut his eyes and remembered what his father had told him about the order of Healers with their base in the Kingdom of Rogdon, the western realm, home of the silver and blue mounted Lancers

He opened his eyes again. Without stopping to think, he asked: "What's a Healer of Rogdon doing in the Rangers' Camp in the Kingdom of Norghana?"

Caught by surprise, the healer began to laugh.

"I see your body is weak, but your mind's still wide awake."

"I… I'm sorry, ma'am."

"There's nothing to be sorry about. It's a logical question. The kingdoms of Rogdon and Norghana are rivals, they've always been. The lords of the green western plains and the lords of the frozen north compete for the supremacy over our beloved land of Tremia. But the order of Healers of Tirsar serves all men equally. We're there where we're needed. Dolbarar asked our Leader many years ago for a Healer to come and help at this campsite. There are very few of us who have been blessed with the Gift of Healing and we can't accept all the requests for help we get, but this one was granted, and I was sent here. Since then this has been my home. I help to heal all who pass through this camp. I've been here for many years, and I must say you all keep me very busy year after year."

He was still trying to make sense of what had happened. "I…. don't know… what happened… an accident... another student during the last test…" he muttered.

"Don't think about that now. You rest and recover. Drink this. It's something to help you do just that."

Lasgol accepted the bowl and took a swig.

"Ugh," he moaned, "it tastes horrible."

"Yes, but you need it. Take it. Your body's very weak."

He did as he was told, and an instant later he was fast asleep. He woke up two days later.

"How do you feel today?" Edwina asked him.

"Better... I think..."

"Try to sit up. Slowly."

He leaned on his hands. This time his strength held and he made it.

"Much better," Edwina said, and smiled broadly. "Now take this tisane. It'll help."

Lasgol obeyed. It tasted as bad as the other one, but he said nothing.

"And my partners?"

"They're all well, don't worry. They've come every day to ask after you, but you were too weak to have visitors. If you're better this afternoon, I'll let them come in."

"Thank you," he said, and smiled.

A little while later the door to the room opened and Oden came in, looking serious. As usual, his copper hair was gathered in a queue. He looked at Lasgol with his intense amber eyes.

"Initiate," he said with an abrupt gesture.

Lasgol saluted him in return. "Master Instructor."

"I need to ask you a couple of questions about what happened."

Lasgol nodded.

"Did you see who shot you?"

"No, sir... it was too dark."

"Didn't you see anything, a figure, a movement? Anything?"

"No, sir... I was watching Ingrid take her shot and moved to follow it better ... and that's when I felt it... a sharp blow and then a pang of intense pain..."

"That movement saved your life. The arrow was aimed at your heart. And didn't you see anything that might help us catch the culprit?"

"Culprit? Wasn't it an accident? Another team doing the test too close by?"

Oden frowned and shook his head.

"There were three other teams, yes, but it wasn't them."

"How do you know, sir?"

"We found the bow at the place where the arrow was released. The trajectory from that place to where you were hit shows that it was aimed at your heart."

Lasgol swallowed. "I see..."

"There's one more thing."

"There wasn't a second shot?"

"You're smart. Pity you're Dakon's son."

Lasgol frowned, but said nothing. It was not worth it.

"There was no second shot because there was no need. The arrow was poisoned."

Lasgol's face turned white with the shock of this. "Poisoned?"

"A slowing-down poison," Edwina said. "I don't know how you've survived, you ought to be dead. Well, to be exact, you were."

Lasgol's eyes were like saucers. "What? Dead?"

"That's what it looks like," Oden said. "When I brought you to the Healer your heart wasn't beating any longer. You were dead. She worked a miracle."

Lasgol looked at Edwina like someone who has seen a ghost.

"The poison slows the heart down until it stops beating," she explained. "When Oden brought you to me you were dead, your heart had stopped beating a moment before. Luckily it wasn't too late. I used my Gift of healing to start your heart, and once I had it beating again I focused on fighting the poison. That was more complicated. It's taken me days."

"I... can't believe it..."

"Well you might as well," Oden said.

Edwina examined her patient. "What's surprising is the fact that you didn't die before you reached the camp. The poison was a powerful one. The only rational explanation I can find is that because of the tremendous effort you were making to reach the finishing line, there was less slowing-down. That, or else you have the heart of a horse." She smiled.

Lasgol recalled the tremendous effort. "Yes... we were running flat out ..."

"And running with all your heart. When you stopped, the poison finished doing its job."

Lasgol nodded. He could not believe anyone could have tried to murder him.

"Dolbarar wants to see you."

"Now?" Edwina asked.

Oden nodded.

"Let me make sure there are no traces of poison in his body."

The Master Instructor's face showed intense disgust. "I'll wait outside while you do… what you… have to do," he said, and went out quickly.

Edwina smiled. "The Ranger doesn't like my Gift. Well, he and most of them. They don't understand it, and man tends to fear what he doesn't understand."

"You mean your magic?"

"Yes, although we don't call it that. For us, the few who have been blessed with it, it's the Gift, or the Talent, as it's called here in the North. It's funny, they can't even see it, but even so they fear it. You're not afraid, are you?" she said with a mischievous smile and a trace of suspicion.

Lasgol realized that she had analyzed him, with her Gift, and in the process had found out his secret…he shook his head.

"They don't know about it, do they?" Edwina asked him.

"No, nobody does…"

"All right, don't worry, it'll be our secret," she said, and winked.

"Thank you…"

Edwina made him lie down and placed her palms above his chest. She closed her eyes and concentrated. Suddenly he saw a blue flash issuing from the healer's hands and enter his body. He felt a trace of warmth in his chest, and for a moment he panicked. But then he glanced at Edwina's face and knew that nothing bad would happen to him. After a long while, she opened her eyes and withdrew her hands. Lasgol saw the flash disappear and followed it with his gaze. She noticed this.

"You can see it, can't you?"

"Yes…" he admitted. He knew that only those with the Gift were able to perceive the flashes and its energy when it was being used.

The healer looked into his eyes for a moment, then smiled.

"I don't see any trace of the poison in your system. Everything's all right. You can get dressed and go to Dolbarar, but then come back and see me so I can give you some potions to help you.

"Thank you so much, ma'am…. I don't know how I can thank you…"

"There's nothing to thank me for. It's my vocation," she said, and smiled.

Oden was waiting for him outside. He gestured to him and they set off. The infirmary was at the south end of the Camp, at the opposite end to the stables. Lasgol had never noticed the small white building surrounded by a garden. There were still many things he did not know about the place.

As he crossed the great hall of the Command House, he saw the Four Master Rangers seated in conversation in front of a low fire. When they noticed that Lasgol had come in they stopped talking and their eyes turned to him. Oden greeted them respectfully and they returned the greeting, but they did not say anything else. Oden led him into Dolbarar's presence, in his private office on the second floor.

"Thank you, Oden," said Dolbarar in dismissal.

The leader of the Rangers was sitting behind a huge oak desk. On it were several parchments, with an inkwell and a white quill pen at one end. He closed a tome he had been consulting and looked Lasgol up and down.

"Do sit down, you must still be very weak."

"I'm fine, sir."

Dolbarar smiled. "That's the spirit. You've been lucky. That poison nearly killed you."

"The Healer saved me."

Dolbarar nodded. "She's an old friend, and her work here is invaluable. This is a very ugly business and it has me very worried. An attempt at murder... is something very serious. It's not often that anything like this has happened before. Accidents, many. Fights, some. Expulsions for bad behavior too. But attempted murder very, very seldom... very worrying..." His gaze was distant.

Lasgol watched him, not knowing what to say. Despite his age, almost seventy, he emanated agile energy and power. Lasgol had never seen him from so close. His intense emerald eyes caught the boy's attention. His face was kind, yet determined. His long straight hair came down to his shoulders and was completely white, and his well-tended beard trimmed one finger's-breadth thick made him unmistakable.

"Any idea who would want to see you dead?"

"No, sir..."

"As the person you are, or rather as your father's son, you must have many enemies."

"Not on my personal account. Some do hate me, that's true."

"We must never underestimate men's hatred. It's a very powerful feeling, capable of driving them to unthinkable acts."

"Like killing me…"

"Exactly. There are many here who don't want you to graduate. You know that perfectly well. Both among the initiates and the second, third and fourth years, and also among the Rangers. Don't think I'm blind. I may be old, but my senses and my instinct work perfectly. At least for the moment."

"I don't think it was any of them… I honestly don't."

"A list would help me eliminate suspects."

"Sir, I couldn't…"

"All right, I understand. It does you credit. Let's leave it, then. But if you see anyone going further than he should, you must tell me at once."

"Yes, sir."

"What concerns me is the poison. It's one of ours. It's taught in the fourth year, in School of Nature. And this means the assassin is one of ours."

"A Ranger?"

"It could be anyone of our people. From an Instructor to a student from any of the four courses. But it's someone in this Camp. With knowledge of or access to the poisons which Erudite Eyra, Master Ranger of the School of Nature, keeps under lock and key. That complicates the situation. It indicates that there's a rotten apple among my people. That's something I particularly loathe, although it's true that you can never tell whether a young person will turn bad and leave the Path of the Ranger over the years. Rangers rarely go bad, very rarely indeed. Here we teach loyalty to the kingdom, honesty, discipline, service. Not all who come here are great men and women, but all of them we mold and give the tools to attain greatness. If one of them betrays us…"

"I see… that would be a black mark on the corps."

"If what I fear is confirmed, yes. I've informed Gondabar, the King's Master Ranger, our Supreme Leader. He's in the capital, Norghania, at the court. He serves Uthar there. I'm sure this business will worry him."

Lasgol was thoughtful. If there was a treacherous Ranger, and if the Supreme Leader of the Rangers had been notified, that meant he was in deep trouble.

"I can assure you that I'll do everything in my power to unmask the murderer. And we'll make sure you're watched at all times so that no harm comes to you. You may rest assured. It's my responsibility."

"Knowing that makes me feel safer. Thank you."

Dolbarar stood up and went to the window. He looked outside with nostalgia in his eyes. "I knew your father Dakon very well," he said.

Lasgol was suddenly tense. "Did you?"

"He was an exceptional Ranger. He was the youngest to become First Ranger. He excelled in all four Schools, nothing was too much for him. He was a first-rate student all the years he was here. The Master Rangers of the Schools vied to have him in their specialties. He was really an outstanding student."

"I didn't know that, sir."

"Do you know which specialty he chose?"

"No sir. He never told me much about his life as a Ranger."

Dolbarar nodded. "That's how it should be. As it is laid out in the Path of the Ranger. A Ranger must always keep the secret of the Path, as only by following it by himself or herself can the initiate understand and assimilate its teachings as a dogma of life. But I can tell you the truth. He chose to be a Mage Hunter, of the School of Archery. There was nobody better with a bow. He could hit a moving target at four hundred paces. He was exceptional. He chose that specialty above all others, not because of his great ability with the bow, but because of his wish to protect the king from mages and other enemies with the Gift. Because those are the most difficult to neutralize."

"I see… Magic…"

"A Mage Hunter is capable of killing a Mage because the range of a bow is greater than the range of the enemy's magic."

Lasgol half-closed his eyes. That was interesting. He had always thought that Mages were more powerful than all the rest: infantry, cavalry, archers, Rangers…

"Did you know?"

"No… I didn't."

"But if the Mage comes within two hundred paces, then the Mage

Hunter is lost because the Mage is far more powerful, and at that distance he can use his magic on him."

"I see…"

"I myself recommended Dakon to King Uthar. There was nobody better suited to defend him against enemy mages and sorcerers, and he turned out to be an asset. The King and your father became fast friends. Uthar wanted him at his side at all times. He never left Norghania, the capital, unless Dakon went with him. He became the King's personal bodyguard. He only rarely sent him on missions, as he wanted him beside him. And in those years their friendship grew, they were like inseparable brothers. Every year the King attends the Acceptance Ceremony, here at the Camp, at the end of winter. He always came with Dakon. I remember the long conversations the three of us used to have… right here, by the fire in the common room, drinking Nocean wine… such good memories," he finished sadly.

Lasgol kept his eyes on Dolbarar. He wanted to ask him what had really happened; he must know, or at least he would have some insight into what might have happened to his father. He did not dare, and kept silent.

Dolbarar came back to reality and smiled. "Forgive me, I let myself drift… Memories sometimes take us back to better times."

Lasgol took a deep breath, gathered his courage together and asked. He would never have a better opportunity.

"Sir, what happened to my father?"

Dolbarar bent his head and gazed at him with sadness in his eyes.

"I've asked myself that same question a million times. I'd like to be able to offer you an explanation, but unfortunately I don't have one. The last time I saw your father it was right here, at the Acceptance Ceremony, with the King. Everything seemed completely normal. I never noticed anything unusual in him. We enjoyed the Ceremony immensely. Uthar was delighted with the visit. He confided in me about the threat of Darthor. The Corrupt Mage was growing, the reports indicated that he would soon attack to take the kingdom away. The threat was real, and it would soon strike. It had him in a constant state of alarm, and the Ceremony had provided him with a few days of rest and quiet which he was deeply grateful for. Dakon took advantage of the visit to talk to the Master Rangers and some Instructor friends. He even took an afternoon off, with the

King's leave, to roam outside the Camp and reminisce about old times. They left after the Ceremony finished. Five days later, it happened…"

"The betrayal…"

Dolbarar nodded slowly and reluctantly. "Your father led King Uthar to an ambush in the Gorge of the Frozen Giant."

"My father didn't necessarily know that Darthor had prepared the ambush in that particular pass."

"True. But your father insisted on going that way. There are three passes that cross the frozen mountains of the northeast. Darthor was gathering his forces on the coast, beyond the mountains. The Generals suggested taking the pass further to the south, the Orator's Pass, but Dakon insisted on taking the one north of that, the Gorge of the Frozen Giant. Uthar ignored his generals and heeded your father. He took the most dangerous pass, and it was there that the ambush took place."

"It's not proof enough for me…"

Dolbarar sighed. "There's an additional proof that is irrefutable, and you know it. Although you may not want to accept it, your father shot an arrow at the King. He tried to kill him. He hit him and almost killed him. That's incontestable, and an irrefutable proof. If it hadn't been for Sven, Commander of the Royal Guard, who pushed the King off his horse when he saw Dakon's attack, Uthar would have died. The arrow hit the king on his left collarbone. It was meant for his heart."

"It could have been an accident."

"If it had been any other man, I might consider that hypothesis… but as it was Dakon, First Ranger of the Realm, I can't." Dolbarar shook his head. "If he released, he did so intentionally. He would never have done it by mistake. I'm sorry to crush your hopes, but that's how it is."

Lasgol bent his head. He did not know what to think. There was a lump in his throat and tears in his eyes.

"We all wish our parents were perfect, but the truth of life teaches us that it's not so. They're human beings, and humans have faults, whether we want to see them or not. In some people those faults drive them, in the course of time and under extreme conditions, to commit unthinkable, incomprehensible acts."

"What… drove him to do it?" he muttered. A tear ran down his cheek.

Dolbarar shook his head slowly. "I don't know. I wish I had the answer, believe me. I'd sleep much better if I did. But I don't have it."

Lasgol swallowed and composed himself.

"They say one of the King's Ice Mages killed him. Is that true?"

Dolbarar nodded. "I'm afraid so. It was Oltar, Royal Mage. He was riding on Uthar's right and defended his King. He killed Dakon with ice lightning."

"He killed him... but there was no funeral..."

"Those condemned lose that honor. The king was beside himself over the betrayal. He's never recovered, either from the wound or from his best friend's betrayal."

"What happened to my father's body?"

"I don't know. I would guess he was buried in a common grave with all the others who fell in the battle against Darthor."

"I see..."

"You must leave the past behind you. Those are not your acts, they're your father's. You can't carry that load on your shoulders, or else you'll sink under it. Forget, look to the future, your own future. If you wish to be a Ranger, of your own free will, not because of your father, I will not oppose it. You'll be treated the same as the other candidates. But if you're here because of your father, I can tell you that you won't make it. The weight of the load will crush you, and you'll fail."

Lasgol nodded and looked down at the floor.

"Difficult times are coming once again. There's a rumor that Darthor has returned to the North, beyond the impassable mountains. They say he's gathering forces to attack the kingdom. And this time he has the help of powerful beings."

Lasgol looked up. "Powerful beings?"

"These are only rumors, there's no proof, but there's talk of Elementals and Ice Giants. It's said that they serve him. He drives them along with his army of men and beasts from the Frozen Continent."

"He has beasts in his army?"

"Yes. Snow Trolls, corrupt Ogres and other beasts. Or so it's said."

"How can Darthor control them?"

"He's a great Mage. He has a great deal of power."

"I thought he was an Ice Mage who had been corrupted by evil."

"No, my young initiate, you must not believe everything the rabble says. Darthor is no Ice Mage, he's something different… powerful… very powerful."

"So is he a Sorcerer?"

"He might be, I don't know. The type of Magic he uses is something unknown to us, but if he can dominate beasts and magical creatures, then he's no common mage. He's said to be more powerful now than last time, and on that occasion he nearly defeated us. The King survived the ambush thanks to the quick action of Sven and Oltar, who took him out of there alive. A week later, still injured, he gathered the royal troops and crossed the pass to the south. He fought Darthor and his forces and defeated them, but Darthor managed to escape. This time it'll be harder to defeat him."

Lasgol was thoughtful, taking in everything Dolbarar had told him.

Dolbarar noticed his serious face. He spread his arms wide in a friendly gesture.

"You needn't worry about these things, they're no concern of yours. The King, the Generals and the Rangers will deal with Darthor. You, my young initiate, must focus on passing the tests, and keep alert. If you notice any movement against you, I want you to come and tell me at once. Agreed?"

Lasgol sighed. "Yes sir, agreed."

"Very well. Now go back to your team, and tomorrow go and see the Healer so that she can make sure you're all right and can go back to your training."

Lasgol nodded and left without another word. His mind told him that everything pointed toward his father's guilt, even more now after what Dolbarar had told him, but his stubborn heart refused to accept it. That was a greater torture for him because he could neither leave the painful past behind nor move on to a better future. More importantly, it did not let him concentrate on the danger: there was someone in the Camp who wanted to kill him.

Chapter 20

Lasgol's reception was something he had not expected. His team-mates were waiting for him in the cabin. As soon as he came in, they hurled themselves at him and hugged him amid cheers and laughter.

"What a scare you gave us!" Ingrid said as she squeezed him tight.

"I'm so glad you're well!" Nilsa said, and kissed him on the cheek.

Gerd lifted him from the floor in a bear-hug. "You scared me so much! I thought you'd died!"

"You'd better put him down on the floor, big guy," Egil said, "or his stitches'll come loose."

"Oh, of course! What a brute I am," Gerd said. He put Lasgol down gently.

Egil gave him a heartfelt hug. "We were very worried," he admitted.

Even Viggo smiled and patted him on the back.

Suddenly they heard animal shrieks coming from the far end of the room. The creature came down from Lasgol's bunk and crossed the room at top speed, then jumped on to his chest with a tremendous leap.

"Hi there, little one!"

The creature crawled up his chest and curled around his neck. It began to lick his cheek.

"He's been acting crazy," Egil said. "Shrieking and crying all day."

Viggo frowned. "And most of the night too."

"We couldn't soothe him."

"He still won't let anybody touch him," Gerd said, sounding upset. "Although you know I'm scared to."

"Of course, you're a mountain beside it, it's totally logical you should be scared of it," Viggo said sarcastically. "I'm sure if a rat came into the cabin you'd jump on to the bed."

Gerd looked terrified. "A rat? Where?"

Viggo slapped his own forehead. "I just can't believe it…"

Lasgol meanwhile was stroking the creature's head and ridged back. "I'm back, little one, everything's all right."

He took it to his bunk and sat down. The others came to stand around him. The creature calmed down. It did not stop licking Lasgol with its little blue tongue.

"How are you?" Ingrid asked him.

"What did they tell you?" Nilsa asked. "There are all sorts of rumors running around."

"If Dolbarar called you," Viggo said, "he must think there's been foul play."

Lasgol sighed. "Relax. I'll tell you everything. Sit down."

They all did so, on the bear rug in front of his bunk. He told them everything that had happened and what he now knew. When he finished, there was a long silence.

"You've come back from the dead," Egil said at last. "That's fascinating!"

Nilsa's face twisted. "There's a Healer in the Camp and we didn't know anything about it?"

"Don't get started on magic," said Viggo.

"Healers: they may pursue good, but they use magic, they use evil, to reach that goal. I can't approve of it."

"Well," Lasgol put in, "if it hadn't been for her I'd be dead."

"Well…." she began, but found she had no argument to make. "Even if it's for good it's still magic, and in the long run it'll only bring trouble."

"I think it was Isgord," Viggo said. "That guy has it in for you."

"Dolbarar admits that the poison is the Rangers'?" said Gerd. "That's terrible! It points straight to one of our people!"

"We must protect you," said Ingrid. "This could happen again."

Each of them went on with a different thread of conversation. Lasgol relaxed and played with the creature. He was too tired to answer them all, and their ideas were becoming stranger and wilder. He was happy to be back with his team-mates. Very happy.

He fell asleep with his partners' voices in the background. When he woke up the following morning they had already left for Instruction. He was so tired he had not even heard the bell and Oden calling. He went to see the Healer and noticed that when he passed the Rangers they stopped what they were doing to watch him. He looked over his shoulder, and one of them waved at him in greeting. *Dolbarar's orders*, he thought.

Edwina gave him potions and beverages to take every night for a week and gave him permission to go on with his instruction, except for the morning physical training. For that he needed to wait another two weeks. He thanked the good woman for all her help.

She raised her finger in admonishment. "Don't ever let me see you again in such a bad condition."

"You mean dead," Lasgol joked.

Edwina laughed. "Take care and be careful," she said, with a wink.

"I will, and many thanks for everything."

He joined his team-mates at dinnertime in the dining room. Previously everybody had turned a hostile gaze on him, but now it was worse and more intense, if that were possible. He saw Dolbarar and the Four Master Rangers at his table and greeted them with a slight nod. They returned the greeting. Their faces were grave. He was aware that it was because of what had happened.

Gerd was devouring a roast turkey leg. "What did the Healer say?"

"Tomorrow I'll join you for Instruction, but not for Physical Training in the morning."

"Great!" said Nilsa.

Gerd looked at him enviously. "You don't have to do laps around the lake. Lucky you."

Lasgol was lost in thought for a while.

"Is anything the matter?" Ingrid asked.

"No ... it's just that I've just realized I don't know what happened with the Spring Tests." He looked at his friends apprehensively, waiting for the bad news.

There was a silence. His team-mates looked at each other, and no-one said anything. Their faces were serious. He took a deep breath and prepared himself.

"As bad as that? I don't remember what happened in the Test by Teams... it's all vague in my mind... I have some..."

Nobody spoke.

"Five teams didn't manage to finish the test in time," said Viggo. "They've been penalized with the loss of an Oak Leaf from their individual tests. They're ripe for expulsion."

Lasgol tensed. Without meaning to, he bit his tongue.

"And what about us?"

A gloomy silence followed Viggo's words. Lasgol clenched his jaw, readying himself for the bad news.

"We weren't penalized!" Ingrid said, and smiled proudly.

Lasgol looked at her in disbelief. Then he turned to Egil and Gerd, who were both smiling from ear to ear.

Nilsa nodded. "It's true."

"But how?"

"We passed the Test by Teams," Ingrid said. "We arrived just in time. That's why we weren't penalized with the loss of an Oak Leaf for our individual tests."

Lasgol breathed out in relief. "Thank goodness..."

Viggo shook his head. "Although on the other hand, we already know the results of the individual tests."

"Very bad?"

Viggo nodded heavily. "Very."

Ingrid sighed. "These are the results," she said, and handed him a note.

	School of Archery	School of Wildlife	School of Nature	School of Expertise
Ingrid	2	2	1	1
Nilsa	2	1	1	1
Gerd	1	2	1	1
Egil	1	2	2	1
Viggo	2	1	1	2
Lasgol	1	2	1	2

Lasgol saw the results and his stomach took a turn. They were very bad. Really bad. Worse than he had expected.

"Phew.... they're terrible..."

"You can say that again," Viggo said. "We're a disaster."

Lasgol looked at his partners in embarrassment. He felt terrible. But Egil, Gerd. Nilsa and Ingrid seemed unable to hold back smiles. He was dumbfounded.

"You're .... smiling?"

The four nodded and began to smile from ear to ear.

"I don't understand..."

Ingrid put her hand on his shoulder. "Dolbarar has awarded each of us an additional Oak Leaf to use wherever we might need it, for exceptional behavior during the test, for saving the life of a fellow initiate."

"Seriously?"

"Yes. You nearly died, you see," Viggo said, "and that helped us with the individual tests."

There was the trace of a sarcastic smile on Lasgol's face as he raised one hand to his wound. "Wow, I'm glad..." he said. "But even with one more leaf, they're not exactly brilliant results."

"Well, that's not all," Ingrid said. "The reason we were smiling is because Dolbarar made all the Initiates fall in and announced it officially so that everybody would know."

"We were heroes for a day!" Gerd said proudly.

Nilsa smiled. "And the envy of all."

"And with the help of the extra leaf," Egil added optimistically, "we might be able to recover and not be expelled at the end. It gives us another chance."

"Hey, you're right," Lasgol agreed. "It is a reason to smile." He felt better.

They had dinner and enjoyed the conversation and the laughter. The only bad news was that Isgord and the Eagles had won the Test by Teams. On the other hand Lasgol had expected it; they were the strongest team, they, the Boars and the Bears.

He was finishing when the Owls got up from their table and started to leave the canteen. Astrid and Leana stopped beside them.

"How are the heroes of the Test by Teams today?" Leana said mockingly, but immediately smiled.

"We're great!" Gerd said with his mouth full.

"Nothing like being heroes to make you feel great," Nilsa said with a broad smile.

"Enjoy the honor. You've earned it."

"We're doing that, believe me," said Egil.

Astrid looked at Lasgol in concern. "And how's the dying patient?"

"I'm all right, it wasn't that bad…" Lasgol said, waving it aside.

She frowned. "Are you sure? The rumor is that you've come back from the icy realm of death."

Lasgol turned red. "Well…. come back… not really…"

"But you were dead when you got to the infirmary, weren't you?" asked Kotar, the dark, quiet introvert from the Owls. "At least that's what they're saying…"

Lasgol did not know what to answer. Asgar, Borj and Oscar too came close to listen. He had the whole Owls team behind him, watching him, waiting to hear what he would say.

"It was only a moment. Then I was reanimated."

Borj turned to his partners. "You see? He was dead! Pay the bet."

"Hey, I won too," said Oscar.

"No way, you bet that he'd crossed the finishing line dead. But he died on his way to the infirmary, right?"

Lasgol shrugged and shivered. He had no desire to remember.

"You're brutes, the lot of you!" said Astrid. She gave Borj a push. "Let him be. He's been through enough."

"But the bets…" Asgar protested.

"You heard the Captain," Leana said. "Get out, blockheads."

Leana led her team mates away amid recriminations as they

argued about who had won the bet.

Astrid glanced at Lasgol for a moment. "Don't pay any attention to them."

"Thanks, Astrid," he replied, and even dared to glance at the brunette's green eyes. He felt something stir in his stomach.

"You'd better be careful," she warned him. "If you were *famous* before, you're even more so now."

Lasgol snorted. "I will be, thanks."

She smiled and left.

That evening, as he played with the creature, Lasgol could not stop thinking about the possible expulsion at the end of the year. He had to find some way of avoiding being expelled, either himself or any of his team-mates. But at the same time he needed to be very alert: someone had tried to kill him, and he had no idea why. Suddenly Astrid's face came into his mind. Every time he saw her he felt nervous, and he did not know the reason for that either. He fell asleep wondering how to solve all these riddles.

The following days were strange. He went back to Instruction, recovered from his wound by now, and everything seemed normal, but it was not. When he ran around the lake he was constantly checking the forest shadows or turning to see if anyone was following him. He was restless. He saw shadows and danger where there were none. Egil had told him this was absolutely normal, that it was called a state of paranoia, and that it was the result of the dramatic effect of having undergone a murder attempt. It was amazing how much Egil knew about any subject. He even took Lasgol to the library and showed him in a tome. Viggo recommended him to stay in this state for life, as it was the only way he would be able to avoid *accidents*, as he called them.

It was not only Lasgol however who was behaving oddly, it was his partners as well. Ingrid had become over-protective; if anybody gave Lasgol a black look or made any kind of comment, she downed them with two right hooks. Master Instructor Oden had already had to intervene on two occasions, and had warned her. Another altercation and she would lose her Oak Leaf. Gerd was more frightened than usual, and Nilsa more nervous each moment. Lasgol knew that in both cases it was because of what had happened. The Instructors watched him far more closely now. It was at Dolbarar's order, but it made him nervous because the murderer might be one of them. Although it could be one of the other Initiates, or even someone from the other years.

To make things worse, the instruction was becoming increasingly difficult. In School of Archery they started training with knives. The Path of the Ranger dictated that a Ranger must be a master in the use of the knife. First, as a survival tool. Second, as a weapon in one-to-one fighting and as a throwing weapon. The Path of the Ranger stated that the best companion a Ranger could have was his Ranger's Knife. Lasgol did not know how to use the knife, and he was having a hard time with the instruction, but there was someone in the team who excelled at it. Lasgol had not imagined it, but when he thought about his origin and the life he had led it made perfect sense. It was none other than Viggo. He was a magnificent fighter with the knife, and not only that, he threw with unbelievable precision. Even the instructor Ivar congratulated him. Ingrid, who was good, was furious to see that Viggo was better than she was.

In the School of Wildlife they progressed from horses to mastiffs and wolfhounds. Faithful companions of the Rangers, except that gaining the trust of those huge animals which could bite your head off was not at all easy. They smelled fear. Paradoxically, the only one who was not afraid of them was Gerd. The giant treated them as if they were puppies and the animals not only let him approach and stroke them, they obeyed him. He said he had grown up surrounded by dogs at the farm and that there were no better animals, and that deep down, these gigantic dogs were no more than puppies. Gerd's fears and non-fears were beginning to be a complete mystery. A mouse would scare him, but not wolfhounds. Lasgol could not fathom the giant.

Lasgol now felt a special interest in the School of Nature, but it was not in the incredible traps they were learning to make and hide. No, it was in the potions, particularly the poisons. Unfortunately they were learning a lot about healing potions and ointments and very little about poisons and toxins. But he kept his wits about him in case he was able to learn something to help him decipher the mystery of his attacker and the poison which had been used.

The subject he was enjoying most and the skill he was beginning to realize might be most helpful in his own situation, was the School of Expertise. Haakon had started to teach them the art of walking among shadows and disappearing into them, as well as avoiding missiles by making zigzagging movements. These two skills would have prevented him from being hit that night. He was trying his hardest in this School, as he was very aware that his life was still in danger and that those skills might save his life at any given moment.

In fact it was during instruction in this School that Isgord approached him.

"I see you've made a good recovery."

Lasgol flexed his injured arm. "Yes, as good as new."

"You try very hard. Some might say too hard."

"And what's it to you?"

"Nothing. But it won't save you."

"Is that a threat?"

"It's a fact."

"And why is that?"

"You'll know when the time comes."

Ingrid and Gerd noticed the exchange and came over at once. Immediately the twins Jared and Aston of the Eagles came to stand beside Isgord.

"Get out, and take these two muscular morons with you or else you'll regret it," Ingrid said with such conviction that Lasgol's skin turned to gooseflesh.

Isgord smiled. A cold smile, full of self-confidence. He made a sign to the twins and left.

"If I had to bet on someone," Ingrid said as she saw him leave, "I'd bet it was him."

Gerd's face turned pale. "Do you think so?"

"Yes, I do. He hates Lasgol, he's cold and very good. I don't know the reason, but the rest fits. It's him."

"Thanks for your help," Lasgol said to his partners.

"You're welcome, but be careful with that one," Ingrid said.

Lasgol had an ominous feeling. A very real one.

Chapter 21

The days flew by at the Camp between physical training in the mornings and instruction in the afternoons. The fact that the periods of instruction alternated every day confused some and appealed to others.

"I don't understand why we can't have a whole week of Archery and then one of School of Wildlife and so on," Viggo grumbled one afternoon when they were on their way back from chopping wood as an extra task Oden had given them, just because they were the team of the "Traitor's son".

"That's just what I think," Gerd agreed, though he was an exceptional woodcutter; with his strength he could almost fell a tree with a single stroke.

"Or a whole month of each School, that would be much better," Nilsa said. She was also very good, although her style was the complete opposite of Gerd's. The big guy did not make many strokes, but very precise ones; she on the other hand made a multitude of smaller strokes at great speed.

"I'm sure they do it to confuse us," Viggo said.

Egil chuckled.

Viggo, who had heard him, turned to him. "What do you think, know-it-all?"

"They do it so we can make progress in all the subjects at the same pace. But you're not entirely wrong. Alternating subjects every day increases the difficulty of learning."

"See? I was right!"

"But it also improves it. You learn more because learning is an emotional thing. If we were to study one subject for a whole month we'd get bored at certain stages and learn much less. Alternating everyday forces us to stay alert, interested and even a little fearful, which makes us learn better."

"Bah! Nonsense!" Viggo said.

Egil smiled at Lasgol, who smiled back.

The days flew by, and with them the pleasant summer. Lasgol had enjoyed the season, it was his favorite. In Norghana it was always cold, but in summer you could almost enjoy the heat as much as in the southern realms of Tremia. He loved the feeling of the sun warming his body, the scent of the woods in summer, being able to swim in the lakes without the fear of freezing, the clear, intensely blue sky, so unlike the rest of the year. And with the end of the season came the Summer Test.

The Snow Panthers had made enormous efforts: all six of them, but particularly Egil and Gerd, who were very much aware that they had the greatest problems. Would all the work they had put in be enough for them to pass the tests? Lasgol hoped so, but his upset stomach said otherwise.

Dolbarar made the test official with a speech full of words of encouragement and cheer. The members of the thirteen teams listened to the Leader of the Camp's words with restless hearts, for there were many others like Lasgol who were unsure how well they could do. But Dolbarar knew how to instill courage into their fighting souls, and many spirits were raised.

When their turn came, the Snow Panthers made their way to the Master House of the School of Archery to begin the Individual Tests. As they had expected, these were much more difficult. Master Ranger Ivana's questions made Lasgol sweat over the answers. Not only did they need to know more about the subject, but the concepts themselves were more difficult. Lasgol answered the thirty questions as best he could, explaining and amplifying everything he could remember from what he had learned. Ivana's cold face showed no feeling, so that there was no way he could know whether he had done well or not.

The practical test was even more difficult. He had to fight against one of the instructors with a long knife. If he could not manage to touch his opponent on one of the areas marked on his protective breastplate, he would fail the test. He tried, and received a good beating. The instructor defended himself vigorously and punished him with forceful blows whenever he dropped his guard. By the gleam of satisfaction in the eyes of the instructor every time he delivered a blow, Lasgol knew this must be one of the many who hated him for being the person he was, and was taking advantage of the situation to punish him. He took strength from his anger and kept fighting; no matter how much the blows might hurt, he was not going to give up. He finally managed to catch his opponent with a feint he had been rehearsing with Viggo. He ended up with one black eye, aching ribs and a split lip, but he was exultant.

The second practice test was first in archery, then in knife-throwing. He had improved considerably with the bow, but he had some trouble hitting the targets, which were now at a distance of a hundred and fifty paces, but he did not do at all badly. With the knife, on the other hand, he had more problems. The target was at six paces, and he failed four throws out of ten. The ones he did make were not particularly accurate. He had a long way to go yet. He resigned himself, hoping he would still have the chance to improve.

Next, they went to the Master House of the School of Wildlife, where Master Ranger Esben, the Tamer, was waiting for them. Ingrid went in first, then the others one by one. Lasgol entered in good spirits. Esben began with thirty questions about wildlife, and he realized these were much more complex than the ones in the Spring Test. Some he found hard to answer, but in the end he did quite well, or at least so he thought himself.

The practice test was even more difficult. First they had to show their ability with bloodhounds, mastiffs and wolfhounds. Only Gerd and Ingrid did well in this. Gerd handled them with kindness and affection, and the animals loved him in their turn and followed his instructions. Ingrid dominated them with her firm authority; the animals respected her and did what she wanted. The rest of the team had difficulties.

The tracking test that followed was very difficult, even for Lasgol. Esben made them identify and follow ten different trails in the eastern forest. As it was summer, the prints were not as clear on the hard terrain, which made it difficult to make them out and identify. Following the trail caused them many headaches. Lasgol and Egil did well, but the rest of the team had a great many problems.

After lunch they went to the Master House of the School of Nature, where Erudite Eyra, Master Ranger, asked them thirty complicated questions about which plants to use for healing different illnesses and ailments. Lasgol answered quite well. Egil did not hesitate over any question and answered all with aplomb. The rest of the team suffered, but they all managed to answer as best they could.

For the practical part of the test they had to prepare a paralyzing poison, which was something Lasgol enjoyed doing. It was a complex formula which involved measuring and mixing the ingredients well, then cooking them and letting them cool on a neutral base. Luckily they had been practicing potions and similar preparations all season. They all did quite well, except for Nilsa, who made a mess of mixing her components and had to start again twice from scratch. The poison was capable of paralyzing the affected area of the body, so that it was perfect for smearing arrows and knives.

To end the day of tests came the test of the of School of Expertise. Haakon the Untouchable, Master Ranger, was waiting for them. Judging by the faces of the members of the teams who had preceded them, and who looked like beaten ghosts, the test was going to be tough. Haakon was no friend of asking questions, so he went straight to the practical test. He much preferred to see the results of his teaching in action.

He sent them to complete five laps around the lake, following the murderous pace set by one of their instructors. Egil and Gerd suffered unspeakably but kept up with the others. They knew what to expect and had been training hard. For the first time in this type of test Nilsa did badly, not because of tripping – which she did – but because of the tremendous pace. Ingrid, Lasgol and Viggo, who had improved, did well. Nilsa, Egil and Gerd finished exhausted, but made it.

The next test was the absolute opposite; it required calm and concentration, so that it was even harder to complete. They had to surprise an instructor by attacking him from behind, using shadows and stealth, a skill they had been working at all summer. The instructor turned at regular intervals and scanned the shadowed area they had to approach him from. If he caught them in movement, or heard them, they were eliminated. They had to reach him and touch his back. Lasgol did not do badly. Seeking the shadows always and intent on making no noise, he managed to get within three paces of the instructor, but the latter turned and caught him moving. Viggo just managed to pass the test, and Nilsa was eliminated half-way when she stepped on a twig which broke with a loud crack.

To finish, Haakon gave them a test of strength. In teams, they had to fell an enormous fir, using only their short axes. It was quite difficult, and they had to work in coordination and in turns. Once it was felled they stripped it until not a single branch was left. When the trunk was clean, Haakon ordered them to take it to the top of Beaver Hill. The Panthers exchanged looks of horror; they were exhausted, and lifting that huge trunk without the help of pulleys was going to be a complicated business. As for reaching the hill, that would be a miracle. Ingrid encouraged them with her own determination. She took one end, with Viggo, Lasgol and Egil taking the middle and Gerd and Nilsa the other end. At the count of three they lifted the trunk on to their shoulders, and with Ingrid calling out the pace they set off. The effort they had to make was brutal. On the hillside ledges they almost had to abandon the attempt, but they were saved by Gerd's colossal strength. Like a titan the giant held the entire weight at the change of level. Thanks to him they reached the top and passed the test.

Broken by the effort, they made their way back down. They had something to eat and went to sleep at once. The Test by Teams would start at dawn, and they would need all the strength they could gather together. Nobody spoke; they were too tired and demoralized by the tests and the fear of what would be waiting for them the next day.

At sunrise they set off: tired, with aching bodies and low spirits. Lasgol sighed. He did not feel confident. They fell in before the Master House.

Oden gave a map to each team. This time that, and their Ranger Knives, were all they had.

"The rule for passing this test is simple," he said casually, as though a child could do it. "Follow the instructions and reach the end before sunrise."

The captains consulted the map, and at once the teams set off, each in a different direction. Isgord and the Eagles went first; once again they would strive to come first. Lasgol's eyes went to Astrid, who was already disappearing toward the east at the head of the Owls.

Ingrid pointed to the west and gave the order: "Let's go, Panthers! Follow me to victory!"

Lasgol knew they had no chance of winning, but he had to admit that Ingrid's spirit was unbreakable. She was worthy of admiration; nothing brought her down, and she always kept going. He envied her for it. He wished his spirit was as strong as hers.

They ran through the woods and plains in a westerly direction for half the day, then stopped to drink at a ravine and eat some wild berries they found. Ingrid and Egil examined the map.

"It's over there," said Egil.

They looked ahead of them and saw a great lake of blue water. They could not make out the opposite shore.

"What do we have to do?" asked Nilsa.

It was Egil who answered. "We have to cross the lake. By swimming, I very much fear…"

"You can't be serious," said Gerd.

"That's what the map says," Ingrid pointed out.

"But you can't even see the other end!" Viggo protested.

Ingrid spoke up confidently. "Come on, we can do it."

Lasgol studied the lake. Viggo and Gerd were not good swimmers, the former because he had grown up in the streets of a city and the latter because of his massive body. They would have problems crossing it. During the morning routine of physical training in the summer Herkson had added crossing the lake to the obligatory laps around it, and many of them had had trouble in the water.

Reluctantly, Gerd and Viggo went in. It was less cold than they had expected, and they started to swim. Lasgol was not wrong. Halfway across the lake they could now see the other side, but Gerd and Viggo started to get into difficulties. Ingrid gestured to Nilsa and Egil to go on and stayed behind to help the laggards. Lasgol did the same. He was a good swimmer, his father had taught him when he was a little boy, and he had often gone to Green Lake behind the village, particularly in summer.

Gerd was having a hard time, and there was panic on his face. Lasgol fell back and began to swim beside him. He had to stop panic taking hold of the giant, or else he would sink. He was gradually beginning to understand Gerd's fears. He was afraid of the unknown, of what he could not touch, of what might be: not so much of things he knew, even if they were dangerous. Drowning was in the former category and terror would make itself felt. Lasgol encouraged him and smiled as if this were nothing, as if he could never drown. Seeing Lasgol at his side, Gerd grew calmer. Lasgol made him slacken his pace. And thus, gently and slowly, they managed to swim across.

Viggo, on the other hand, reached his limit and began to drown. Gripped by panic, he thrashed his arms and yelled, swallowed water and began to sink. Ingrid went to his aid and both of them disappeared under the water. For a moment it seemed the lake had swallowed them, then suddenly Viggo resurfaced. After a moment

Ingrid came up too. She took Viggo by the neck and with a tremendous effort, dragged him to the shore. He was unconscious, and she was left lying on the grass. Nilsa blew air into Viggo's lungs, so that he started to cough and bring up the water he had swallowed. They put him on his side so that he would throw it all up.

"Only just…" said Egil.

At last Viggo managed to gasp: "Thanks…"

"You're welcome," Ingrid replied. "Next time try to drown a little closer to the shore, will you?"

Viggo frowned. "Next time… don't save me…I don't want to owe you anything… particularly you."

Ingrid looked offended at this. "It was a reflex act. Next time I'll leave you to drown."

"You're always the same," Nilsa said. "You're like cats and dogs."

"He's such an idiot."

"And you're so bossy."

"You're both hopeless," Nilsa said. She went away, raising her hands in frustration.

Egil and Gerd were smiling. Lasgol could not help but smile too.

They found a Ranger's Scarf on the shore, under a rock, with a map.

Nilsa made a victory sign. "We've got one now!"

When they had recovered, without waiting for their clothes to dry, they went on toward the next point on the map. They reached the foot of a mountain and climbed up to the top. Nobody spoke; they were all concentrating on not losing their foothold. They reached the summit as night was beginning to fall. They were very tired. The climb had been tough, and what they saw at the top left them frozen.

Tied to a stake they found the second green scarf and the next map, and something else…

Viggo waved his arms angrily. "A rope? Seriously?"

"That's what it looks like," Nilsa said. She was looking at the way down on the other side of the peak and the thick rope firmly tethered to a rocky outcrop.

Gerd was staring at the vertical wall, smooth as marble, and the bottom of the abyss in the distance below, his face white as snow. "We have to go down that rope?"

"Don't be ninnies," Ingrid said. "We've already done that in

Expertise."

Viggo too was looking down. "We've trained in small descents," he growled. "This is a bloody mountain!"

"We're Rangers and we fear nothing!" Ingrid cried. "Keep going, follow me!" And before anybody had a chance to complain, she started to climb down the rope.

Lasgol smiled and followed her.

Leaning her feet against the side of the mountain, she guided them down. The others followed her example very carefully. When they had gone down some way, they realized that the distance was not as great as it seemed from the top, it was an optical illusion. Even so, the descent was slow and hard on their arms. When they reached the bottom they lay down on the ground. They needed to rest their bodies and let the fear they had experienced recede.

Ingrid did not let them rest for long however. When she and Egil had studied the map, she made them get up and go on. They set off toward a very dense forest. They were supposed to cross it, and it looked as though it was going to be arduous undertaking.

The forest seemed not to want intruders in its domains. They had to use their knives to clear a way for themselves, as if they were in a jungle. They were getting more and more scratched and cut by the wild vegetation they had to make their way through.

"First we swim across a lake," Viggo commented. "Then we climb a mountain and now we cross a forest. This has to be Oden's idea."

"Or rather Haakon's," said Gerd.

They reached an open area in the middle of the forest and cheered up a little. They stopped to rest for a moment.

"At last, some quiet," said Nilsa. She was sucking blood from several scratches on her arm.

Egil came forward and gazed up at the sky. "According to my calculations, there's not much left. We'll soon get out."

Lasgol heard a rasping sound, then branches snapping, to his left. The undergrowth at the edge of the forest started to move. Surprised, he stopped to watch. Suddenly the bushes were pushed apart and a beast came out into the clearing. A long snout in a round head and a great deal of fur were the first things he noticed. The animal was more than three feet across, with four strong legs and a thick body.

They stopped where they were, petrified with fear.

A bear! was what Lasgol's mind shouted at the sight of those terrible, threatening jaws.

The beast had long, brownish-gray fur with a streak of silver-pointed hairs down its back. It rose to its hind legs and gave a deafening roar.

"Nobody move!" Ingrid whispered urgently.

Lasgol was remembering what he had learned in the School of Wildlife about chance encounters with wild beasts in the mountains. "Don't run, face it and don't make any sudden movement," he said.

The animal was huge, more than six feet standing erect, and must have weighed as much as three men. Lasgol took note of its limbs and claws. One swipe and it could tear the head off a man, or split him in two. Even if all it did was drop on to one of them, it would mean death under its enormous weight.

Once again it roared menacingly and shook its front paws, revealing its claws and open jaws.

Nobody moved. Gerd's knees began to tremble. But he did not run, even though his panic-stricken face showed clearly that he wanted to get away from there as fast as he could.

"It's a Gray Bear of the high mountains," Egil whispered. He had recognized the beast by the great hump on its back. From what they had learned, the hump was really a muscle that gave extra power to the beast's front legs, which were not as strong as its hind ones, and helped it in digging out lairs in the mountains.

"What do we do?" asked Nilsa. She was trying to hold back her fear and making a tremendous effort to stay still. "Maybe it doesn't want to attack, just frighten us."

"Gray Bears are very aggressive and dangerous," Egil said. He was as still as a statue. Only his lips moved, and that barely. "Because of their size they can't flee or climb or get up a tree."

"And that's why they attack and fight," Viggo said, understanding what he meant.

"That's right. We must withdraw all of us together, without turning away from it. As if we were a great enemy."

"All right then," Ingrid said. "On the count of three, step back. One, two... and... three."

They took a step back as one. The beast roared, but did not move.

Gerd gasped.

"Now then. One, two… and… three."

They took three steps and suddenly, from among the trees, another creature appeared: the bear's cub.

Lasgol realized this was not good. Not good at all. The bear would attack them to defend its cub, which by now was in the open. *What bad luck!* The little cub looked at them curiously and moved toward its mother.

Egil had come to the same conclusion. "It'll attack us to protect its cub."

"Run!" Ingrid cried. "Climb a tree!"

They fled. The big bear got down on all fours and started to run after them. For such a big and heavy animal it was running at an amazing speed. Panic took over the group. They were running for their lives, and fear rose in their throats. Ingrid and Viggo ran ahead, followed by Egil and Gerd. Lasgol and Nilsa brought up the rear. The bear was gaining on them, it was faster than they were. Gerd yelled in terror and Nilsa let out a cry of horror: "Noooo!"

Ingrid reached a tree and climbed up the first branches with cat-like ease. Viggo climbed up after her. Egil and Gerd tried to do the same with another, lower tree. Egil could not manage to reach the branches. Gerd was shaking with fear, but he grasped his friend and lifted him by the armpits so that he could reach the lower branches. Egil managed to grasp the lowest branch and started to climb. Gerd did a two-pace run-up and with a leap, reached the lowest branch and began to climb. A roar behind him told him the bear was underneath him.

Egil reached down to him. "Don't look! Climb!"

Gerd managed to lift himself up. The bear clawed at him and took one of his boots off. He cried out in terror.

Lasgol and Nilsa feinted and ran to a huge, steep-sided rock. The bear saw them and went for them. Lasgol reached the rock and with a leap began to climb. Nilsa did the same, but tripped and slammed against the rock. She fell backwards and was left stunned on the grass. The bear was fast approaching.

"Here!" Ingrid shouted, trying to draw the bear's attention. "You smelly beast! Here!" The animal stopped a single pace away from Nilsa and looked at the tree where Ingrid was shouting and gesturing like a madwoman. It roared and focused its attention on Nilsa, who by now was on all fours, trying to get to her feet. The bear attacked.

Lasgol leapt off the rock and got in between her and the beast.

When it saw him, the bear rose again on to its hind legs and gave a deadly roar. Lasgol knew that if the animal fell on him it would be his death. The others were looking on in terror.

Lasgol knew he only had a single chance of getting out of there alive. He must break the promise he had made to himself after his father's death. He must use his Gift, or else he would die. He did not want to. He wanted to go on being normal, like his friends. But he had no choice. He would have to use it and face the consequences. His great secret would be out, and he would never be normal again. His attempt to go unnoticed would end there. But it was that or die. Besides, it was not only his own life, which was at stake, it was Nilsa's too. If the Gift gave them a chance, he would use it. Otherwise he and Nilsa would die, torn to pieces by a wild beast.

He shut his eyes for an instant and searched for his inner energy. He found it in his chest, like a calm lake of blue waters. He had to decide in the blink of an eye which skill out of the ones he had developed he could use in that situation. If he was wrong, they would die.

He spread his arms wide and used his Gift. A green flash ran through his body. The bear was about to claw him, but it felt the magic and hesitated. This gave him time to use his skill of Animal Communication. He opened his mouth and gave a tremendous roar. Not a human roar but that of a bear, identical to the one the beast had just given. This puzzled the animal even further.

He stretched out his arm and raised his right palm. Focusing, he caught the mind of the beast, an aggressive reddish-brown aura. He communicated with it: *Leave. Go away.* The bear shook its head and looked around, trying to understand where this message was coming from. He concentrated even more and tried with his whole being. Nilsa's life was at stake as well as his own. *Go away. There's no danger. Go.* The bear looked at Lasgol and understood that it was the young human speaking to it. It looked at him, undecided. He tried again. *Take your cub and leave. Go.* The bear hesitated, now totally baffled. It got down on to all fours and looked at its cub.

Nilsa seized her chance to recover. She climbed up on to the rock and was safe.

Lasgol forced the order. He did it aloud as well as in his mind.

"Go, now! *Leave and don't come back!*

The bear gave him a look of submission and left. It went to its cub, and both retreated into the forest.

Lasgol lowered his hand and gasped. It had worked. He felt an immense relief. He had not thought he would make it.

"What we've just seen can't have happened," Egil said to Gerd, who was staring blankly.

Ingrid rubbed her eyes. "My eyes are tricking me," she said to Viggo.

"They're not your eyes, it's Lasgol who's tricked us," Viggo said. His eyes were half-closed in a stare of hatred.

"I don't understand..."

"He's one of those bastards with magic. That's the only explanation for what he just did. He should've ended up torn to pieces."

Ingrid threw her head back and shook it hard.

Viggo climbed down from the tree. "You're a sorcerer! You've lied to us!"

Lasgol shook his head. "I'm no sorcerer."

"Well, a mage, then." Ingrid accused him.

Lasgol shook his head again. "Not that either..."

"But you have the Gift," Egil said. "You possess the Talent."

Lasgol nodded and bent his head.

"That means he can do some kind of Magic, doesn't it?" Gerd asked, looking worried.

"I think that's been made more than clear," Viggo said.

Gerd was shaking his head in a mixture of fear and sadness. "Magic is very, very dangerous."

Viggo pointed at Lasgol. "People like him, you mean."

"You've lied to us," Ingrid said accusingly.

"No, I haven't lied..."

"But you've kept this hidden from us," Viggo said.

"Yes... I didn't want my secret to be known..."

"You should've trusted us, you should've told me," said Egil, and in his eyes was the pain of betrayal.

"I didn't want anybody to know... I'm stigmatized enough for being who I am. This is only going to make things much worse..."

"That's exactly why," Ingrid cried furiously. "We've protected you, we've helped you, and you haven't told us the truth about who you are and what you are."

"I'm sorry... I truly am. Forgive me... I just wanted to be normal... I thought I could keep it hidden until I became a Ranger."

"I can't forgive it," Ingrid said.

"Me neither," said Viggo.

Lasgol sought Gerd's gaze, but the giant shook his head.

"Egil..." he begged.

"I'm sorry, Lasgol," he said with deep sadness. "I trusted you with who I am and my reasons for being here, my fears, my doubts, and you've kept something really important back, the most important thing."

Nilsa came up to Lasgol. Her face was as red as a tomato and her eyes seemed about to pierce him. She was holding back her anger as best she could.

"You saved my life. I'll never forget that, and if I can I'll repay you by saving yours. But you know very well what I think of that accursed magic and the unscrupulous beings who use it. Don't you dare come near me. Keep well away. I won't say this again. If you come near me or use magic in my presence ever again, I'll bury this knife in your heart." She showed him her weapon.

Lasgol swallowed. Speechless, he looked away from her furious eyes.

Egil was shaking his head. "You ought to have told us," he repeated

"What other secrets are you hiding?" Viggo asked. "What other arcane powers do you have?"

"None, I swear... I'm not dangerous."

"We can't believe you, not after this," Ingrid said.

"He's probably in Darthor's service," Viggo said. "Just like his father."

"I'm not! And neither was my father!"

"That we can't know, and we can't ever trust you again," Ingrid said. "After doing everything we could to save your life... what a real disappointment..." She turned her back on him.

"Let's finish the test," said Egil. "It'll be the best thing to do."

"Please..." Lasgol begged.

His plea was ignored. They set off. Lasgol knew he had lost his partners' friendship and felt as if a mountain had fallen on him. They finished crossing the forest. They found the green scarf and the last map with the direction to take toward the Camp.

Ingrid set a tremendous pace toward the end. The incident with the bear had delayed them considerably, and if they were already behind, now they were considerably worse. Lasgol went last, following his partners. Egil suffered badly in his attempt to keep up the pace. Gerd, being fitter, was standing up better to the punishment; his body, after all, was a strong one. At a thousand paces or so from the Camp Egil collapsed in exhaustion and was unable to get back up. Lasgol tried to help him, but he could not take a step further.

"I'll carry him," Gerd said,

"Are you sure?" Ingrid asked.

"I'm the strongest. You lot couldn't carry him on your backs."

"What about between two of us?"

Ingrid was calculating how much longer they had left. "We wouldn't get there in time. The sun's just about to rise."

"Lift him on to me, quick," Gerd urged them.

Viggo picked Egil up and lifted him on to Gerd's back.

"Hold on tight," he told him.

They ran. Gerd carried Egil on his back and went as fast as he could. The girls led the way and Lasgol brought up the rear. Seeing Gerd struggling to finish the test, with Egil on his back, Lasgol felt enormous admiration for him. Nobody else could have done anything of the kind. Gerd's spirit was as immense as his body was powerful.

They arrived with the sun already peering over the horizon. They crossed the finishing line and Gerd fell to his knees. Egil rolled several paces and stayed lying where he had fallen. They had finished the test just in time. Oden counted the Ranger Scarves and approved. They were exhausted, with their bodies cruelly mistreated by the effort, but they had made it.

And Lasgol had lost his partners' trust and friendship.

Chapter 22

Lasgol's spirits were at rock bottom, His teammates were not speaking to him. They ignored him as if he were not with them. Even Egil. He let out a long sigh of resignation. His father had already warned him about the fear and intolerance the Gift aroused in people. *Man fears the unknown, the thing he's unable to understand. It's in our nature. The more arcane the reason, the greatest the fear and rejection it generates. The Gift is feared and rejected by the great majority. Only a few understand and accept it. You must be wary of exposing yourself openly, or else you'll suffer for it.* And so it had come to pass.

He lay down on his bunk and started to play with the creature.

"You and I, we're both different... and they fear us because of it."

The creature flexed its long legs, bouncing without moving from where it was, which meant it was happy. Little by little Lasgol was learning what his little friend was trying to convey to him.

"Always keep up this playful, happy spirit of yours."

He sighed deeply. He let his memory fly back to the day when he had discovered he had the Gift, just after his seventh birthday. Or rather, it had been his father who had noticed. It had started innocently and naturally enough, playing with his dog Warrior. He was trying to make him understand he had to fetch and bring back the stick he was throwing for him. Unfortunately Warrior was an extremely rebellious dog and had his own ideas. He had been like that since he was a puppy. When Lasgol threw the stick for him in the backyard, the dog ran away with it and hid it.

One day, after dozens of fruitless attempts, Lasgol was stroking the dog's head.

"Why don't you understand me? Why are you so naughty?" he was saying as he petted him.

Warrior was enjoying the stroking, but his lively eyes revealed that he was going to go on doing what he wanted to. Lasgol wanted him to understand him. He was feeling more and more frustrated, trying with all his might to make the dog understand and do what he was told.

"Bring me the stick," he told Warrior, shutting his own eyes hard as he held the dog's head in his hands. "Don't hide it." He touched his forehead to the dog's.

Then something unheard-of happened. He felt something strange, like a tingling which ran all through his body. A green flash issued from his head and hands. For a single instant his mind was aware of a greenish aura around his companion's head. Later on he would realize it was his mind. Without knowing how, he connected with it and the order was transmitted. *Bring the stick, don't hide it.* Lasgol felt it and received a deadly shock. He was left speechless, not knowing what to think. Warrior, still as a statue, was looking at him with big eyes. He barked once and ran off. After a moment he came back with the stick.

Lasgol was petrified with the surprise.

"You understood me? No, no, it couldn't be." He was convinced it was all a figment of his imagination.

It occurred to him that it had been nothing but a coincidence. Yes, it had to be that. So he repeated the order. He took Warrior's head in his hands, looked into his eyes, concentrated and ordered: "Bring me the rag doll."

Again there was a flash. He connected his mind with that of his four-legged friend and transmitted the order. Warrior barked and disappeared at a run. To Lasgol's enormous surprise, he came back with the doll in his mouth.

The dog had understood! He could communicate with him! He did not know what that strange green flash was or why he felt the tingling, but what happened next was unbelievable. He tried several times more before telling his father, and the same thing happened every time.

When he explained what had happened to Dakon, his father's face shadowed and the light in his eyes went out, giving way to a look of concern. He made Lasgol repeat the test, changing the orders Warrior was given. The dog understood every time and did what he was told. Lasgol's father was now deeply worried.

"Has any other skill manifested itself?" he asked.

"Skill?"

"Being able to do something a normal person can't do, or which would be almost impossible for him."

"No... just this."

"And this green flash you say you see… have you experienced it before?"

"No... you don't see the flash, Father?"

"No, I believe it's only visible to those who have the Gift."

"Oh… I see."

"You don't have any strange object on you, with powers? Charmed?"

"No, Father."

"Hmmm… then it can only be one thing."

"What's that?"

"You've got the Gift, the Talent."

Lasgol did not know what he meant.

"A few people, a fortunate minority, are born with the gift of the Gods of Ice: the ability to develop skills which are impossible for the rest of us. It's commonly known as magic among the people."

"Magic? You mean I can do magic?"

"Not exactly. I'm saying that what you've done with Warrior is considered magic by common people, and it's not something that produces a positive reaction. That's why you must be very careful and keep it secret. People are afraid of what they don't know or don't understand. Particularly magic. Those with the Gift are persecuted and rejected. I fear for you."

"Don't worry, Father. I'll keep it secret. Nobody'll ever know."

"Very well. It'll be our secret. I'll help you develop skills with your Gift, and you must promise me you'll be very careful."

"I promise, Father."

And so it had been. During the following years until his death, Dakon had helped Lasgol to develop a few skills, practicing in secret and without anybody's help. He would bring home books from the Library of the Rangers' Camp or the Royal Library of King Uthar's Palace and they would study them together, seeing how they might apply what others had already learned about the Gift to his own particular case. It was hard to understand because every person with the gift, were all different in abilities, skill levels and power. Dakon did not want to risk consulting the Ice Mages, or any other experts in magic at the Court, at least until Lasgol was a little older and could fend for himself. He wanted to protect him from rejection, superstition and envy. He would be neither the first nor the last to be burnt at the stake or stoned for having the Gift.

So they experimented on the basis of trial and error. They did not advance much, and Lasgol did not make much progress in the few skills he had found, but he enjoyed every moment he shared with his Father. He treasured those memories in his heart. When Dakon died, and what with everything that happened afterwards, he decided to bury the Gift with his Father. He would never use it again. It would only bring him more trouble, and without his father he had lost his interest in developing it. He swore on the memory of his father never to use the gift again and to keep it secret. Up until now, he had kept that promise. And he had kept his promise. He had not used his Gift, not deliberately, and had not told his secret to anyone until the attack by the bear. He did not regret breaking his promise; Nilsa's life had been in danger and he had no choice. Now he would have to pay the consequences, and just as his father had warned him, people did not understand, not even his team-mates.

He sighed. The creature felt his sadness and licked his hand.

"At least I've got you."

The creature smiled, or so it seemed to Lasgol, although he could not say for sure, since its mouth had the form of a smile and hence it looked as if it was always smiling.

"I should give you a name. Yes, you need a name. Let's see…"

The creature stared at him with its huge eyes, round and bulging, fixed on him.

"What sort of name would suit you? Let's see… how about Fighter?"

The creature did not move. It just went on staring at him.

"Right…. what about Smiley?"

There was no reaction from the creature.

"Let's see…"

The creature started to camouflage itself with its surroundings until it vanished before his eyes.

"You do like to camouflage yourself and disappear. Camouflage…. I'll call you Camou… Camu… How would that be, Camu?"

The creature suddenly reappeared. Flexing its four legs, it began to bounce in place.

"I see you like it. Wonderful, from now on you'll be Camu."

The creature jumped on to his chest, staring at his face.

"I wonder if…" Lasgol thought. "Now I've broken my promise, I could try." He concentrated and sought for his Gift inside him. He found it and used it. He wanted to communicate with Camu. He felt the tingling, followed by the green flash. Suddenly he saw the creature's mind like an intense green aura around its head and sent it an order: *Turn invisible.* Camu looked at Lasgol. A moment later it did what he had asked it; it camouflaged itself and became invisible.

"Yayyy!" Lasgol cried, thrilled by the success.

He sought the creature's mind again and tried to perceive something, to see if Camu could communicate with him. Unfortunately he could not. It was as though he could send a message to the creature, but not the creature to him. Or at least, for now he did not know how to manage it. *Turn visible again,* he ordered, and the creature reappeared.

"Very good," Lasgol said, and scratched its head.

Camu licked his finger and gave a squeal of delight.

Three days later, after the customary deliberations among the Four Master Rangers, the Initiates were summoned to the Command House.

Dolbarar gathered all thirteen teams and called the Captains of each team one by one. When they stepped forward he gave each one the dreaded parchment with the results of the Tests. Viggo called it "The Will" because it was proof that they were dead and ready to be buried. Ingrid came back to the team and showed them what they had got.

	School of Archery	School of Wildlife	School of Nature	School of Expertise
Ingrid	2	2	2	1
Nilsa	2	2	1	1
Gerd	2	2	1	1
Egil	1	2	2	1
Viggo	2	2	1	2
Lasgol	1	2	2	2

Once again the results were pretty bad. A little better than the previous ones, but they all had problems in one or two specialties. If they did not manage to improve, they would be expelled at the end of the year at the dreaded Ceremony of Acceptance, when Dolbarar would hand out the badges. Wooden ones granted passage to the second year. Copper ones meant expulsion. Lasgol had frequent nightmares in which Dolbarar handed him a copper badge in front of everyone, even King Uthar. He would wake up with a start, covered in sweat. The worst thing was that they had already had two tests and there were only two more in which to regain the lost points. Either they managed to obtain three points in the next tests or they would be unable to improve some of the results. The concern was beginning to take its toll; faces were long and spirits low.

To make his life even worse, the days went by and Lasgol's situation with his teammates was not improving. Now he did not even try to start a conversation with them. Every time he had tried he had failed. They did not want to speak to him. So he decided to wait until things improved a little. Perhaps with a bit of luck something would change, things would improve and they would trust him again.

A couple of weeks later they were on their way back from dinner when they found the door of their cabin open.

"Gerd!" cried Egil, as he went in.

They found Gerd on the floor unconscious. His head was bleeding.

Egil cradled the giant's head in his hands. "Hey, wake up!"

At the sound of the uproar, Ingrid came in with Nilsa. "What happened?"

Viggo indicated the trunks, which were open with all their contents spread out on the floor. "He's unconscious. And we've been robbed."

"I… my head…" Gerd said as he came to.

"Who did this to you?" Ingrid asked.

He put his hand to his head. "I didn't see… I came in… saw the mess and something hit me hard on the head. For once, I came back early from dinner…"

Viggo was kneeling beside some wet footprints. "He didn't see him, he was waiting behind the door. A big foot, a man's, leather boot, not military, not a Ranger's …"

"Curious… not a Ranger's…" Ingrid wondered.

"Or he wants us to think he's not a Ranger…" Viggo said.

"It could be that…" Nilsa said. She was looking everywhere

nervously.

"He knew what he was doing," Viggo said. "It's not easy to knock the giant down."

They helped Gerd to his feet. He was still stunned.

"Let me have a look," Ingrid said. She examined the wound. "It's not serious, it's bleeding quite a bit but the cut isn't deep. With a few stitches you'll be as good as new."

"Thank goodness," Nilsa gasped. "You gave me quite a shock."

"You and me both," Gerd said with a grin.

When they saw him smile they were relieved.

"Hold this cloth, press it on the wound," Ingrid said. "Nilsa, go and see what our side's like."

Worried by what had happened to Gerd, Lasgol had not realized that the trunk where he had left Camu was overturned on the floor beside his bunk.

"Where are you, little one?"

He looked among the mess scattered across the floor, but could not find it. The others looked on without a word. He began to put his things back in the trunk and noticed that his father's gift was missing.

"The box... the egg... they're not here."

Viggo jabbed his finger at Lasgol. "This guy is sure to have something to do with it."

"We can't say that for sure," Egil protested.

Suddenly the creature appeared on Egil's bunk. It gave a gigantic leap and landed on Lasgol's chest.

"Hi there, little one! You had me all worried."

The creature climbed up to his face and began to lick his cheek.

"And the little beast appeared," Viggo said with an expression of disgust.

Nilsa came back. "Our side's the same, they've gone through everything."

"All right. Don't touch anything," Ingrid said. "Nilsa and I will take Gerd to the Healer and we'll tell Oden everything that's happened. Wait for him to come." Immediately they left.

The Master Instructor appeared with three other Rangers. They inspected the cabin from top to bottom. Lasgol had his hands behind his back and in them was Camu. He used his Gift to communicate with the creature: *Still. Quiet. Not visible.* It was becoming easier. Camu did as told. It remained still as a statue and became invisible. When Gerd, Ingrid and Nilsa came back, Oden questioned them one by one for some time.

Oden was furious. He paced from one end of the cabin to the other. He tried to minimize what had happened and suggested that it was no more than a bad joke by one of the other teams or one from the fourth year, who were prone to such pranks. The footprints, he said, had been intended to be found, and whoever it was had lost their nerve when Gerd walked in on them. He was going to find out who it had been and expel them.

Lasgol was not convinced by this explanation, and by the faces of the others nor were they. But of course they had said nothing to Oden about the disappearance of the box and the egg that had belonged to Lasgol's father. Viggo was the only one who protested against Oden's theory, but the Master Instructor silenced him.

When Oden left, Viggo turned to the group. "You don't believe that, do you?"

Ingrid shook her head.

He pointed at Lasgol, accusingly. "It's got something to do with him and his dark arts, I'm telling you."

"They're not dark arts," Lasgol said, trying to defend himself.

"You shut up," Viggo snapped. "Nobody's talking to you."

"Has anybody else been relieved of any belongings?" Egil asked.

Gerd, Viggo, Ingrid and Nilsa shook their heads.

"Nor me," Egil said. "That means we can assume that it has to do with Lasgol or his creature, because the object which has been stolen is the box with the remains of the egg."

"Just what I meant!" cried Viggo.

Ingrid gave Lasgol a long, deep look. "This has got something to do with you, with who you are... with what you are... keep away from us. You're a danger to the rest of us, you put us at risk."

Lasgol felt Ingrid's words like whiplashes of fire on his face. But he knew that deep down she was right.

"Okay, I understand..." he said, and bowed his head.

With that, all his hopes that things would get better, died. If they had not trusted him before, now that Gerd had been wounded they would do so even less. He sighed. And the worst of it was that they were right. He was sure that what had happened had something to do with him, and he felt terrible for putting his teammates at risk. He would have to do what Ingrid had said and keep as far away from them as he could. If anything should happen to them because of him, he would never forgive himself. *Please don't let anything bad happen to them because of me,* he prayed to the Gods of Ice, but unfortunately he had an ominous feeling about the whole business.

Chapter 23

Autumn painted the beautiful forests in tones of ochre. The leaves turned from their youthful green to the ochre-browns of maturity, then little by little they shriveled and fell, helped by the winds that were beginning to blow more strongly. The forests and lakes were dazzling in their beauty. Then the first snow arrived, painting the high mountains white and descending as far as the great valley and the Camp at their feet.

All the same, Lasgol's heart was deeply saddened. He had spent the whole season with Camu as his sole company. He gave thanks to the Gods of Ice for the creature, which cheered his evenings when he came back exhausted from Instruction. His team-mates ignored him and only spoke to him when absolutely necessary. Outside of his team, everybody avoided him. There was one exception though: Astrid, who was the only person to say a kind word to him, which he greatly appreciated.

Now the days went by slowly for Lasgol and the season became interminable. The temperature began to go down, the sky turned gray. Autumn was ending and Winter was fast approaching. Once Autumn was gone, the dreaded Autumn test came. With the passing of the days, the Autumn Test was finally upon them. The Autumn Test was upon them. Lasgol knew it would be hard, harder than the two previous ones, as was required by the Path of the Ranger, according to what Oden had told them: "Each test needs to be more difficult than the one before. Rangers must be able to overcome every difficulty they encounter on their way."

The thirteen teams gathered before the Command House, and Dolbarar took his place to give the test its official start. On this occasion his speech was mainly concerned to encourage them. They had already been through three-quarters of the year, they only had to pass this Test and they would enter the final stage: Winter. He encouraged them and tried to calm their nerves. Nobody must fail now, not after all the efforts they had made, but they knew that some would not pass and this weighed heavily on their spirits. He wished them good luck and declared the Autumn Test under way.

They began with the individual tests, Lasgol and the other Snow Panthers made their way to the Master House of the School of Archery. The questions Master Ranger Ivana had for them were not only more difficult, but they contained traps; they had to keep their wits about them or they would fail, as the reply they gave might be the opposite of the one required. This time, the number of questions on the test doubled from thirty to sixty. Lasgol had a hard time.

The practical part of the test began with a combat. They had been practicing handling the short axe all autumn, both as a tool for building weapons, shelter and other useful things, and as a fighting weapon. "A Ranger always carries a Knife and an Axe at his waist", as was laid down in the Path of the Ranger. These were special weapons. designed for the Rangers' own purposes: the blade of the knife had a straight edge on one side, a serrated one on the other. The axe was light and could be thrown. The handle was of steel and could be used as a hammer.

Lasgol had to fight with long knife and short axe against an Instructor. He did not do too badly, although he found it hard to touch the Instructor, who gave him quite a beating and made him pay for every mistake. Lasgol was tempted to use his Gift, but he was determined not to do so except in an emergency. Besides, he felt that using it for the Tests would be cheating, since the other Initiates did not have this advantage. *No, I won't cheat by using my Gift. I'll either pass, or be thrown out on my own merits.*

The second Archery test was particularly complicated. They had been practicing archery against swinging targets for weeks. They would hang a pumpkin from a branch and make it swing. It was already difficult enough to hit the target following the movement of the pendulum, but in the test there were now two pumpkins swaying in opposite directions. Lasgol had to concentrate; he only had six shots and three targets to be hit. He missed his first two shots. The movement in reverse was spoiling his concentration. He made an effort to focus. He concentrated on following the movement of one of the pumpkins, forgetting about the other, and released. He hit it! He repeated the process, but missed. He could not afford another miss. He was about to fail the test; he could see the smile of satisfaction on the Instructor's face. He took a deep breath and became calmer. He aimed carefully, following the swinging, and released. The arrow hit the target. He gasped in relief. He repeated the shot with infinite care. He hit the target! The Instructor cursed under his breath. He had passed the Test.

Esben the Tamer was waiting for them at the Master House of the School of Wildlife. The test began with another sixty questions about wildlife, and they were not easy ones. This time Lasgol had trouble answering a couple of them.

The practical part of the test was something he enjoyed, even though it was very difficult. First they had to demonstrate their skill with hawks. They had been learning to tame these wonderful birds all autumn. There was no faster or more skillful hunter in the skies than a hawk. It was the fastest animal on Tremia, Esben said. The complicated thing was making them understand and obey. The specimen allotted to Lasgol during the test was beautiful: a large female hawk with a blue-gray back and white chest with dark spots. The head was black, with black whiskers. A spectacular bird.

The Test consisted of hunting with the hawk, but it was a special kind of hunting: the hawk was trained to hunt pigeons and ravens in flight and bring them back to the Ranger, as this was a way of intercepting the enemy's messages. The bird responded well to Lasgol's commands and brought him a carrier pigeon and a raven, each with a message tied to its foot. He passed the test. They did not all have the same luck. Viggo's hawk would not obey him and Nilsa's decided to treat itself to its prey instead of bringing her the body with the attached message.

They rested a little and had lunch, then went to the Master House of the School of Nature, where Erudite Eyra was waiting for them. The sixty questions she gave them about plants, herbs, roots, mushrooms and their healing or poisonous properties were complicated, but Lasgol answered quite well.

There were two parts to the practical test. The first involved preparing an ointment against infections and another to heal cuts and bleeding wounds quickly. It was a demanding, elaborate process, but they had practiced it already, and this time Lasgol made the two ointments blend properly.

The second part of the practical test was to create a trap with nothing but the materials laid out on a table: twigs, wooden sticks, a piece of cord and a Ranger's Knife. Lasgol did this very well.

As he was leaving, the old woman told him to take the ointments and traps he had made with him. They were genuine, and throwing them away would be an unpardonable waste.

To round off the day of tests, came the test of School of Expertise. Haakon the Untouchable was going to make sure they remembered this day. He sent them to do ten laps around the lake. Lasgol managed to finish. He saw several initiates lag behind and fail. Egil and Gerd ended up being sick, but managed to finish out of sheer pride. Nilsa too was broken. Ingrid on the other hand seemed indestructible.

For the second part of the practical test they had to camouflage themselves in the undergrowth using only their knives and whatever they found around them, and stay still so that the instructor would not spot them. They had been perfecting the camouflage and the *Way of the Chameleon* for the whole season. Lasgol went to the river, took off his red cloak and covered his body with mud: particularly his face, head and hands. Then he used his knife to cut ferns, branches and grasses and covered his body with these so that it would be difficult for him to be recognized. He crouched down among the undergrowth and remained still as a statue, blending in with the environment. The Instructor passed beside him, stopped three paces away and scanned the area with his gaze. Lasgol did not even blink, held his breath and managed to deceive the instructor, who failed to spot him. However, because of the effort at the start, and the tension of having to stay still for so long, his body failed him. He shifted his position and had to recover quickly. The Instructor spotted him, but accepted the test as good enough. Lasgol breathed out heavily. He could not take a single step further.

Once they had finished the test, they dragged themselves back to the cabin. They were so tired they were unable to speak. Ingrid, who seemed indestructible, went to the dining-room and brought them food. They could barely eat, but they had to get their strength back. Lasgol fell asleep with Camu in one hand and a piece of bread in the other. Gerd fell asleep with a piece of smoked meat hanging from his mouth.

The Test by Teams began at dawn, which arrived in the blink of an eye. Oden woke them up with his infernal silver bell and led the thirteen teams to the front of the Command House. He made them fall in and summoned the Captains.

"For this test, the members of each team may only carry their Ranger's Knife and Axe. Nothing else." He gave each Captain a map.

"When I give the signal, the test will begin. You know the rules, I'll be waiting for you at the finishing line. You have to get there before dawn." He raised his arm and a moment later let it drop.

Ingrid spread out the map, studied it and pointed to the east.

"Let's go, Snow Panthers!"

They left the camp behind, crossed a forest, then skirted a lake and finally crossed a plain. Suddenly they came to a great river.

"Do we have to swim across?" asked Gerd.

"Search for the Ranger's Scarf," said Ingrid.

They searched the area and found some prints beside the river. When they followed them they found a scarf half-buried in the mud. At any other time it would have gone unnoticed, but their training was paying off. Now they were able to detect the tracks and the objects that were out of place leagues away, almost by instinct. Wrapped inside the scarf were the next map and a set of instructions.

"What does it say?" Viggo wanted to know.

"We have to build a vessel to cross it," Ingrid told him.

"A boat? Are we crazy?" he cried.

Egil confirmed this. "That's what the instructions say. They're very precise."

"By the Gods of Ice!" Viggo cried.

"Well," Nilsa said, "not really as outrageous as that. We've studied all kinds of Norghanian vessels in Instruction. We know how they're built."

"But we don't have the tools," said Gerd.

"Or materials," said Ingrid.

Egil was thoughtful. "Hmm... that's not completely true. We have our axes and knives, they're tools, and we have a whole forest behind us, with materials."

"But how are we going to build a boat with that?" Viggo insisted.

"By being intelligent," Egil said. "The instructions say a vessel, but don't specify what kind."

Ingrid arched a blonde eyebrow. "What are you thinking?"

"We'll build a raft. It's a simple vessel and it will allow us to cross."

"You're so smart I could kiss you!"

Egil blushed. "It's nothing..."

"Let's get started, then!"

Between the six of them they felled eight trees which were not too thick but sufficiently strong to hold one of them, stripped them of branches and joined them together. Then they found lianas to use as rope. They also used the boys' cloaks and tunics, to tie the trunks together. Finally they checked it for soundness; it seemed to hold. They put the raft in the water and very carefully lay down on it, first placing their weight on the outside, then on the inside. The stream began to carry them downriver. They rowed with their arms as best they could, and the raft traced a long diagonal until they reached dry land on the other side. The six clambered ashore, and as they did so the raft came apart and was carried away by the river. They lost their cloaks and tunics.

Viggo watched the tree-trunks and their clothes vanish downriver. "We're going to freeze tonight."

Gerd smiled broadly. "I'll give you a bear hug and keep you warm."

"Ugh! No way!" Viggo moved away from the giant, who was spreading his arms with his bare chest revealed.

Ingrid laughed heartily. "Here, take my cloak."

Viggo took it and wrapped it around himself.

"And mine," said Nilsa.

"For Egil," said Gerd. Lasgol nodded.

"I can make a tunic with the Ranger's scarves," said Lasgol.

"Well then, we're just left with a half-naked giant," Viggo said.

"We'll think of something," Ingrid said. "Come on, let's go!"

They found the Ranger's Scarf with the next map held down by a knife on a stump very close to the river. Lasgol took the scarf and tied the ends to another, and so began to make a tunic.

Viggo was suspicious. "They've left it too visible," he said.

"Let's see what's waiting for us now," said Ingrid. She studied the map.

"Where does it say we have to go?" Nilsa asked.

- "Nowhere," said Ingrid.

"What?"

She showed them the map, which marked their present position and... nothing else.

"This is too much!" said Viggo. "They've lost their minds. What are we supposed to do without a map?"

Egil studied the map and the concise instructions on it.

"It says: *Follow the trail of the Ranger.*"

248

Viggo looked around. "What trail?"

"What Ranger?" Nilsa said. She was scanning the horizon looking for a person. Lasgol crouched and studied the soil around the stump. At first he could see nothing, but after a moment he managed to make out half a footprint. He bent over and felt it with his hand.

"It's the print of a Ranger's boot. Two days old."

"They want us to follow a trail that's two days old?" Viggo protested. "How are we supposed to do that?"

"By paying a lot of attention," Egil said with the trace of a smile.

"But he'll have done his best to hide his trail," Nilsa suggested.

"Well then," Ingrid said, "we'll find it, whatever it takes."

"We'll do best to stay a couple of paces apart and go over the area so as to cover more land," Egil said. "Let's go slowly, all six of us together. Anyone who spots anything, call out."

"All right then," Ingrid said. "You heard Egil, get in position."

Very slowly, the six partners started scanning the area, moving toward the forest. Nilsa was right: the Ranger they had to follow had hidden his tracks, and he had made a good job of it. They only found a clue hidden here and there at wide intervals. Lasgol was able to find the trail whenever they seemed to have lost it. A footprint, a bush with snapped twigs, a mark on a tree. Egil, for his part, worked out that the clues had been set at fixed intervals. This was a great help to them, since they knew when the next one was due to appear. Between Lasgol and Egil they managed to get as far as a waterfall with a small pond.

"And now what?" Ingrid demanded.

"The next track should be here," said Egil.

"It disappears in the water," Lasgol said. He pointed to one last footprint on the edge of the pond.

"In the water?" Nilsa repeated. "And what do we do?"

"Get into the water?" Gerd said with a smile. He was already naked from the waist up.

Egil nodded.

Gerd plunged into the water and swam under it for a long while. He resurfaced with water-lilies and weeds covering his head and shoulders.

Nilsa burst out laughing. "What a scene!"

"Anything there?" Ingrid asked.

"Nothing, just mud and weeds,"

"Look in the waterfall," said Egil.

"In the waterfall?"

"Behind the waterfall, to be more exact."

Gerd stared at him blankly, but turned to look at the waterfall. He nodded and swam to it, dived and vanished. A long moment went by and he still had not resurfaced.

"Do you think he's drowning?" Nilsa said apprehensively.

Egil shook his head.

"I wouldn't be so sure," Viggo said. "The giant isn't exactly a mermaid in the water..."

"I'm going to get him," Ingrid said, sounding concerned. She was about to dive in when Gerd reappeared with a large leather satchel in his hand. He swam toward them.

"There's a cave behind the waterfall!" he announced, spluttering.

Egil grinned. "That's what I thought."

Gerd came out of the water and handed them the satchel. "Here you are," he said. They opened it. Inside they found the Ranger's Scarf and a glass phial.

Egil opened it. "There's a map inside."

"At last!" said Ingrid.

While they were examining it, Lasgol cut the satchel in two and with the last Ranger's scarf made a jerkin for Gerd. It did not cover him completely, but it protected him from the cold.

Nilsa burst out laughing when she saw him. "You look like a giant beggar," she said, giggling, as she ran around him.

Ingrid gave each of them a despairing glance. "We certainly are a pitiful sight."

"Appearances can be deceptive," Egil said, and winked.

"Come on, team! On we go!" Ingrid cried.

They followed the map for some time. They arranged themselves in a line with Ingrid at the front setting the pace, Nilsa and Viggo behind, Egil and Gerd in the middle and Lasgol at the rear. They had grown used to this formation and it was now almost natural to them.

They reached a huge empty area with two solitary boulders in the middle.

Viggo looked around. "Where's the next clue?"

Egil too was looking around. "The map indicates this position."

"But there's nothing here," Nilsa said. "Except those two big rocks."

"Let's have a proper look," Gerd said. He went toward them.

Lasgol searched the area and discovered something out of place: on one side there was a lonely tree, an oak, and yet the forest was of firs, He found this strange, and went up to the tree. Apart from its species there was nothing wrong. He studied the branches and autumn leaves. Nothing. The position ... the roots ... He bent over, following a hunch, and he found something among the roots: the Ranger's Scarf and the map with the instructions! He called his teammates.

"How did you do that? Did you use any of your *special* skills?" Viggo asked accusingly.

Nilsa threatened him with her fist. "You'd better not have used any filthy magic!"

"I haven't. The rocks were the most obvious place. Too obvious. It's a trick to make us waste time."

"You've probably been using your Talent to pass the tests from the start," said Viggo.

"I haven't. And I'm not going to either."

"Sure, and I believe you!"

"If you don't want to believe me, that's your problem, not mine."

"But the thing is that you are our problem," Ingrid said. "You're a Snow Panther, and that makes you our problem."

"I don't want to be anybody's problem."

"It's a little late for that," Viggo said.

"What does the test say?" Egil interrupted, trying to stop the argument.

"We have to prepare an antidote for the bite of a silver snake."

"That's not going to be easy," Gerd said. He was trying to remember the instructions Erudite Eyra had given them.

"Does anybody remember the ingredients?" Ingrid asked. They all looked at Egil.

The thin boy reddened. "Yeah, I know them."

"Very well. Let's divide up the tasks," Ingrid said.

Egil told them what they had to find, and they all set off. He stayed to prepare a fire. One by one they came back, the last being Viggo, who had had trouble finding the resin they needed.

"I had to cover nearly half Norghana to find it!" he protested.

"That's because you're blinder than a mole," Ingrid said.

Viggo made a face, Gerd and Nilsa laughed.

Egil used the glass phial they had found at the waterfall to mix the ingredients, then put the mixture on the fire.

"What now?" Ingrid asked. "How long do we have to wait?"

"We have to stir it until it turns blue," Egil said.

Ingrid looked up at the sky. Time was running out. "We can't stay here stirring this and wasting time. It's already starting to get dark."

"I can stay behind to stir it," Lasgol put in. "When it's ready I'll catch up with you."

"All right. You finish this and then come join us in the east, at the first lake. Don't delay. If I have to come and get you you'll be sorry."

"Don't worry. I'll catch up with you presently."

Gerd gave him a worried look before they left.

Night fell on the forest and Lasgol began to feel hopeless in the midst of all that solitude and quiet. But at last the antidote was ready, and he felt more cheerful. He took it off the fire and put it aside to cool.

"I see your partners have left you behind," came a sudden deep voice at his back. "This makes things a lot easier for me."

Lasgol turned and saw a figure coming out of the bushes, wrapped in a dark hooded cloak. It was not that of a Ranger.

"Who are you?" he asked. He had an ominous feeling.

"You and I already know each other," the stranger said.

The voice was vaguely familiar. Lasgol racked his brains, but could not manage to recognize him.

The stranger pushed back his hood. "Do you remember me now?"

"Nistrom! What are you doing here?" Lasgol was amazed to find the mercenary there. The last time he had seen him had been at the village, in Skad, when he had won the competition for fighting with sword and shield, and he and Ulf had given him the winner's trophy.

"What do you think someone like me would be doing here?" he said with a dangerous smile.

Lasgol was thinking hard, trying to find an answer to that question. There was only one that made sense: the mercenary was there because of him. To kill him.

"You were always kind to me…"

Nistrom nodded. "I had orders to watch you closely. And that's what I did."

"That's why you moved to our village?"

"Yes."

Lasgol shook his head. "And now?"

The mercenary bowed his head and made an apologetic gesture.

"You should never have joined the Rangers to poke your nose into what ought to stay dead. It would've saved us this last unpleasant encounter."

Lasgol was trying to find a way out. "You don't have to do this."

"It's too late. You've meddled in things you should have stayed out of. It hasn't been well-received. I've been ordered to kill you."

"Who by?"

"Someone very powerful."

"The poisoned arrow. Was it you?"

"Maybe yes, maybe no. They want you dead, they might have paid someone else…"

Lasgol raised his hands in a pacifying gesture. "I don't know what I've done, but I can stop doing it. There's no need for you to kill me. I haven't found out anything. I promise you."

"I'm sorry. I like you. But you have very powerful enemies. I must kill you. If I don't, it'll cost me my life." He drew a sword and a dagger.

"Nistrom… please…"

"Don't resist. I'll give you a quick death. You won't suffer."

Lasgol took a good look at the mercenary. He knew at first hand that he was an excellent fighter. He himself had no chance against him. He felt a terrible knot in his stomach. *I'm not going to let him kill me without a fight. Never. I'll fight!* He took out his short axe and the long Ranger's knife.

Nistrom shook his head slowly.

"That'll only make things worse for you."

"I'm not going to let you kill me. I'm going to defend myself."

"As you wish," Nistrom said. He advanced toward Lasgol with a lethal look in his eyes.

Lasgol sought his Gift, found the blue energy inside his chest and used it. *Cat-like Reflexes,* he summoned. A green flash ran though his body. Nistrom did not waste a single moment; with a leap he attacked with a stroke aimed straight at Lasgol's heart. With his reflexes enhanced by the Gift Lasgol moved to one side, dodging like a cat. Nistrom's sword found nothing but air. Immediately he made a sideways cut with his dagger, searching for Lasgol's neck.

Instinctively the boy retreated from his position, dodging the dagger which passed near his face.

Nistrom realized that something was not right. "What's going on here?"

Lasgol did not answer. He flexed his feet and waited for the next attack. This time it was a feint: a deceptive move carried out by an excellent swordsman. The mercenary sought Lasgol's thigh with a fleeting stroke, and when the boy drew back his leg the sword went toward his chest like lightning. He threw himself back, but the trick had worked and he was an instant too late. He felt a cold painful sting in his shoulder.

"How did you manage to avoid that feint? I've killed many men with that move, men much better prepared than you."

"Ranger training," Lasgol said, trying to gain time. His shoulder was bleeding.

"That blood ought to be from your heart. There's something going on here. No Ranger can move like you do, least of all an Initiate. What are you hiding from me?"

"I'm just Lasgol, son of Dakon. And I'm not going to let you kill me."

"I can smell foul play, and there's some of that here. I've been fighting and killing for years, many years."

Suddenly he launched a tremendous thrust at Lasgol's face. When he saw the sword coming straight at his face Lasgol ducked instinctively. The sword passed close to his head, cutting several hairs in the process. Crouching, he sought his Gift. A green flash ran through his hands. He used a skill he had developed with his father's help: *Throwing Dirt*. He buried the tip of his dagger in the ground and with a twist of his hand threw earth at Nistrom's face. Through his Gift the earth that flew up was charged with blinding intensity. The mercenary covered his eyes with his forearm as a cloud of earth and dirt hit him in the face.

"I'll get you!" he cried as he staggered back, trying to clear his vision.

Lasgol seized his chance, without rising, he reached for the back of his belt, where he carried the trap he had made for the individual test. Quickly he set it on the ground and used his Gift again: *Trap Hiding*. A green flash covered it. The trap vanished and was now ready.

"You've left me half-blinded!" Nistrom cried. "The game's over!" One of his eyes was closed, the other watering. He moved forward, ready to run his opponent through. Lasgol stepped back. Nistrom prepared to wield his sword and stepped on the trap. There was a metallic noise, and the mercenary looked down. Half a dozen sharp spikes pierced his right foot. He groaned in pain.

"Let me go," Lasgol said. "There's no need for this."

"I have orders to kill you, and that's what I'm going to do," the mercenary said. With a strong tug he freed his foot from the spikes of the trap. He roared to high heaven with the pain. "I'll tear you to pieces for this!" He roared again as he set his foot on the ground to move toward his victim. He was lame in one leg now and blind in one eye. But that would not stop him. Not someone so experienced.

Lasgol moved back, wondering how to defend himself. He activated the Gift of *Monkey Nimbleness*. Nistrom lashed out with his left hand, and his dagger flew straight for Lasgol's neck. It was too fast, so there was no way he would be able to dodge it, even with heightened reflexes and agility. He could only bend backwards to avoid it. He flexed his legs to the limit until his body was parallel with the ground. The dagger passed close to his belly and face, but he could not keep his balance and fell flat on his back.

"I've got you now," Nistrom said. He moved forward, ready to run him through.

Lasgol raised his hand from the ground. "Don't do it."

Nistrom's arm moved back ready for the final blow.

Lasgol felt that he was lost. He was about to die.

Then something unheard-of happened. Instead of coming forward, the arm dropped.

Lasgol blinked hard. He did not understand what had happened. Two strong arms appeared holding Nistrom's in a bear-hug.

"Get up, Lasgol, quick!" Gerd urged him.

"Gerd!" Lasgol cried in amazement. He leapt back to his feet.

"Let me go!" Nistrom growled. He was struggling with Gerd, who had him in a tight grip from behind. The giant was too strong and the mercenary could not free himself. Suddenly he bent forward.

"Be careful!" Lasgol shouted in warning.

Gerd did not see it coming. Nistrom straightened up again swiftly and butted his head against his captor's nose. The giant felt his nose explode into an intense pain. His eyes started to water and blood gushed from his nose. He put his hands to his face and staggered several steps back.

Nistrom was free. He raised his arm to attack Gerd. Ingrid arrived at a run and pushed herself between them.

"What do you think you're doing?" she said to Nistrom.

"I'm going to kill you all."

She turned a determined gaze on him. "You're not going to kill anybody, not while I'm in charge."

"Well, I'll kill you first," Nistrom said, and went for her. She fought back like a lioness, blocking the mercenary's sword with her axe and knife.

"I see you can fight, but that's not going to save you."

Lasgol led Gerd away. The giant could barely see, and was an easy target. Ingrid kept her attacker at bay as best she could, but she was no rival for the mercenary. With a master-twist of his wrist he sent her axe flying out of her hand. Then he feinted and cut her wrist so that she lost her knife. She was left disarmed.

Nistrom smiled. He was about to run her through when suddenly something metallic struck him in the arm from behind. He grunted. A small dagger was buried in his arm.

"To hell with you!" he shouted and carried through the strike.

A shadow flew over Ingrid, throwing her down. Nistrom's sword found flesh, but not Ingrid's. Viggo had leapt over her to protect her and taken the blow in the shoulder. He and Ingrid rolled across the ground, out of the mercenary's reach.

Nistrom weighed up the situation. He was lame and could not see properly. He had a dagger buried in his right arm. He turned to Lasgol.

"I've got to kill you. It's your life or mine."

Lasgol prepared himself. At a distance, coming out of the forest, he saw Nilsa and Egil running toward them. They were doing so stealthily, blending with the shadows of the night, exactly as they had learned in School of Expertise. Nistrom had not even seen them. There was a moment when Nilsa seemed to trip and lose her balance. If she fell, Nistrom would hear and become aware of them. In an uncommon display of skill she managed to control her balance and avoid falling.

"If you insist on killing me, here I am," Lasgol said. He spread his arms wide and showed the Ranger's Axe and Knife, trying to draw the mercenary's attention to himself.

Nistrom advanced. With a swift movement he slipped his sword from one hand to the other and launched a stroke with his left. Lasgol, caught off guard, ducked, and the blow cut his left ear. *He's ambidextrous! Is nothing going to finish him? He's ready for anything!* The mercenary used his left hand with almost as much skill as his right. Lasgol dodged the thrusts and feints as best he could, but he was certain that he would be caught any moment now and he would die.

He gambled. He took a step back and raised his dagger ready to throw. Nistrom saw the move and got ready. His deep eyes, charged with experience, shone with confidence. He knew he would be able to dodge Lasgol's throw.

"Now!" Lasgol cried, and threw the dagger with all his might.

Nistrom avoided Lasgol's throw, just as he had expected. But what he had not foreseen was that two other knives were seeking his back. Nilsa and Egil had thrown at the same time as Lasgol, from the shadows. Nilsa's knife hit him in the middle of his back. Nistrom spun around like lightning, and Egil's knife brushed past his face.

"You vermin!" he cried, arching backwards.

"Axe!" said Lasgol.

"No!" Nistrom shouted.

The three axes flew toward him. Nistrom was caught where the three trajectories crossed. He avoided Egil's, but Lasgol's axe buried itself deep in his back, Nilsa's in his chest. The mercenary took a single step sideways, dropped his sword and fell on his side.

For a moment nobody moved. They were watching Nistrom, waiting for him to get back up, but he didn't. Lasgol went over to him warily. He picked up the sword, and with it in his hand crouched down beside the mercenary. He was dying.

"Who sent you?" he asked the dying man.

"You... won't survive..."

"Who wants to kill me? Why?"

"You're ...dead..." Nistrom said with his last breath, and died.

Lasgol gave a deep sigh.

"We... we've... killed him?" Nilsa asked in disbelief. She was looking very frightened.

Egil was examining the body. "Yes... he's incontrovertibly dead."

"Thank you all," Lasgol said gratefully. "If it hadn't been for you ... it'd be me in his place now."

Ingrid was kneeling beside Viggo. "Keep your gratitude for later. This moron needs bandaging."

"Moron? Me?" Viggo protested indignantly from the ground. "After I've just saved your life!"

"I had him," Ingrid said. She was tearing her shirt to bandage the cut on her wrist.

"Oh yeah, with that irresistible personal charm of yours."

Egil went to help Ingrid with Viggo. Gerd was coming too, with his head thrown back.

Nilsa ran to him. "Are you all right?"

"It hurts like fury, but it's not bleeding any more. I think it's broken."

"Could be twisted or dislocated, but broken? I'm not sure…"

"Put it back in place."

"Are you sure? It's going to hurt a lot."

"I'm not afraid of pain, get on with it."

Nilsa looked at him in puzzlement. "You're not afraid of pain?"

Gerd shook his head and got down on his knees. "It's only pain. It'll pass."

"My, you're weird… all right." She shrugged, took hold of his nose and with a sharp tug set it back in place.

Gerd screamed in agony. After a moment, his face became calm again.

"I really don't understand what frightens you," Nilsa told him. "You're scared of your own shadow, but not of pain, or diving into a frozen lake." She shook her head.

Gerd shrugged. His face showed that he had no answer to this. "And what about you? You're delightful most of the time, but if someone mentions magic or anything arcane, then you turn aggressive, irrational, as if you were somebody else…it's as if there are two people in you."

Nilsa looked at him in astonishment. "I'd never realized that…I'm… just a… I…"

Lasgol was staring at the mercenary's lifeless body, unable to believe what had just happened. He was shaking his head, unable to come out of his trance of amazement.

"Search him, you might find something," Viggo said, and grunted with pain from the dressing Ingrid and Egil were putting on.

Lasgol searched the body. Nothing. Then he remembered where

he had come out of and went over to look. He found the satchel behind a tree. He brought it back to his mates and emptied it. Inside were Ranger's clothes, some food and a box.

"Isn't that the box the egg was in?" Egil asked.

"Yes…" Lasgol picked it up and inspected it.

"Then it was him who attacked me in the cabin." Gerd said.

"Looks like it," Nilsa replied.

"But why did he want the egg-box?" asked Ingrid.

"I think he was looking for what was inside," Egil said.

Lasgol was puzzled. "The egg? Camu?"

"I think so," said Egil.

"He wanted the egg and to kill Lasgol," said Viggo.

"Are the two connected?" Nilsa wondered.

"Everything points in that direction," said Egil.

"How? Why?" Lasgol asked blankly.

"That's a mystery you'll have to solve, unless you want to end up like him," Egil said.

They were all silent, gazing at the body of the mercenary.

Unfortunately he found nothing that would explain things.

"Lasgol," Nilsa said, "you're bleeding."

"Oh, yeah, I hadn't realized."

They finished dressing the wounds as best they could.

"Use the ointments from the individual Nature Test," Egil said. "They'll help us."

"We need to get back to the camp," Ingrid said. She turned to Viggo. "Are you up to it?"

He frowned. "Of course I am."

"And you?" she asked Lasgol.

"Yes, my wound isn't that deep."

"All right then. Off we go!"

They walked all night. They had to stop several times to adjust the dressing on Viggo's wound. Lasgol was still unable to believe that Nistrom had tried to kill him. He was baffled.

"Thank you…" he said to his team mates again as they rested before the last stretch to the Camp.

Egil nodded. Nilsa smiled fleetingly, then frowned.

"You didn't think we'd let him kill you," Gerd said. He was feeling his tender nose.

"But the fact that we helped you doesn't mean everything's

forgotten," Viggo said with a grimace of pain.

"We'd better not fail the Team Test because of this," Ingrid said.

Lasgol said nothing. There was a lump in his throat. He was touched and grateful. Tears pricked at his eyes.

They ran to the Camp and crossed the finishing line just as the sun was appearing.

Oden looked at the sun, made a gesture to show how close they had cut it and was about to grant the test. He went up to Ingrid to ask her for the scarves when he saw everybody's wounds. He exploded.

"What the hell's happened now? Can't you complete a test without bloodshed?"

Ingrid shrugged and looked innocent.

"Follow me to the Healer! By all the winds of winter! And not a single word!"

Chapter 24

Dolbarar was very serious. He scratched his snow-white beard as he stared at the six members of the Panthers Team. He had summoned them, and they were now standing in a row in the middle of the great common hall of the Command House. The leader of the Camp was sitting at the long meeting-table where all important matters were discussed. flanked by the four Master Rangers.

"Thank you for bringing them, Oden," Dolbarar said, and the Master Instructor withdrew, leaving them alone.

"Are you all better?" the Leader of the Camp wanted to know.

Ingrid answered as Captain. "Yes, we're all better, sir."

"Very well." Dolbarar nodded. He studied the six companions one by one, as if he were evaluating them in his mind. "I've summoned you to this meeting because I want to get to the bottom of this ugly business. I've asked the four Master Rangers for their assistance, given the extreme gravity of the situation." He bowed his head respectfully toward them, and the Masters returned the bow. Their faces were stern, somber.

The six companions bowed in turn, feeling uncomfortable and restless.

"The best thing would be for you to tell us what happened. We'd like to hear from each of you, as your vision of the facts will probably be different and complementary. Let's begin in reverse order of the confrontation. Who was the last to arrive at the scene?"

"It was Nilsa and yours truly, sir," Egil said.

"Very well. Tell us what happened, from your point of view, with as much detail as you can recall."

Nilsa and Egil did so, trying not to leave anything out. When they finished it was Viggo's turn. He was followed by Ingrid and then Gerd. Finally Lasgol told his part, which was the most complete as it covered the whole incident.

When he had finished there was a long silence, which was broken by Dolbarar.

"What happened yesterday is proof of something... terrible and regrettable. It's the second time there's been an attempt on Lasgol's life. Here, within the borders of our Camp. Something unthinkable…deeply worrying…"

"It's unacceptable," said Ivana, the Master Ranger of the School of Archery. "Nobody should be able to enter our domains undetected. I've reproached the watchmen. There will be punishment. Severe punishment."

Lasgol could not take his eyes off this woman's cold, lethal beauty. He felt sorry for the watchmen.

"The area to be watched is a very wide one," said Erudite Eyra, Master Ranger of the School of Nature, apologetically. "Our wonderful shelter, the Secret Valley as they call it, is a hidden place, but vast. From the Camp in the center you'd need at least one week on foot in any direction to reach the limits of the valley."

"Yes," said Esben the Tamer, Master Ranger of the School of Wildlife, "but we're almost entirely surrounded by mountains, except for the entrance via the River of No Return. As long as we watch that entrance we ought to be able to keep an eye on everyone who enters our domains."

"Have you found that mercenary assassin's trail?" Dolbarar asked him.

"Yes. I followed it. Everything indicates that he came into the valley through the northern pass."

Lasgol threw his head back in surprise. This caught his attention. He had not known there was a northern pass. The mountains to the north were both majestic and impassable.

"I'll hang the Northern Pass watchmen by their big toes!" Ivana muttered.

"We mustn't be hasty in our conclusions," said Haakon the Untouchable, Master Ranger in School of Expertise. "Until now we thought he might have been one of our own people, going by his knowledge of the camp and the use of a Ranger poison in the first attempt on Lasgol's life. Although there's no evidence that it was stolen."

Eyra bowed her head. "The poison was stolen from my store."

"How's that?" Esben asked. "You said nothing was missing."

"At first I didn't notice, as he hadn't taken a container. Nothing was missing, the inventory account added up properly. Everything seemed to be in order."

"And so?" Haakon prompted her.

"What he did was much more intelligent. I found that some containers were missing a little of their contents."

"Very intelligent indeed," Haakon said. "He filled his own container by taking a little out of several of yours. A nice trick."

"How long have we known this?" Ivana said, sounding annoyed.

"We've only just found out," Dolbarar admitted.

Eyra nodded. "When I found out what had happened with the mercenary I couldn't sleep, so I went over all my potions and poisons, one by one. That's when I saw it, and I told Dolbarar at once."

"A very smart mercenary," Haakon said. "Perhaps too smart…"

"And one who knew the Camp very well," Esben said. "Which worries me, and worries me greatly. How can a stranger know our land, our ways, and move among us without being detected?"

"That's exactly my concern," Dolbarar agreed. "How did he know where to get the poison and how to fool our watchmen?"

"We have a traitor," Haakon stated.

"That's a strong claim," Eyra said.

"It's the most logical explanation. Someone must have helped him, and it must have been one of us. I don't think it would be possible otherwise. We'd have hunted him down."

Dolbarar turned to Lasgol. "Did he tell you who he was working for? Whether he had an accomplice inside the camp?"

"No, sir… I tried to make him tell me, but I couldn't manage to."

"Were you able to guess anything about it?"

"Nothing, sir," said Ingrid. "Except that he was an excellent fighter and had plenty of experience."

"And he knew Lasgol," Viggo put in, "so they've probably been watching him for a long time."

"And it's only now that they've decided to kill him," Egil added. "That indicates that the fact Lasgol is here now is a clue to the reason for the attack."

"The young initiate is right," Haakon said. "He's tried to kill him twice – within our Camp, no less – when he could easily have killed him in his own village."

"Very true," said Eyra. "But why now? Why here?"

Dolbarar half-closed his eyes. "That, my dear friend, is the key question, or rather questions."

"In any case," Ivana said, "the problem should now be no more after the excellent performance of the Panthers Team, who neutralized the threat."

Dolbarar nodded several times. "And so it should. But we must not lower our guard, just in case. I won't rest until I find out how he managed to steal the poison and avoid being detected within our domains. On the other hand" – he looked at each of them in turn – "I must congratulate you for eliminating the threat and saving your partner. Two actions which do you credit."

"Great credit," Eyra said.

"When an enemy dies," Haakon said," we Rangers don't celebrate it because it's our duty to eliminate threats. When a brother is in danger we defend him, always. We Rangers never leave anyone on their own. Never."

"What you've done, and how you've done it, all of you together," Esben said, "is an example for all of us to follow."

The companions looked at each other, and in their eyes was a certain shame at having left Lasgol on his own, at the way they had treated him.

"I need to be sure we have no more intruders," Dolbarar said. "Important days are upon us. I can't risk the Ceremony of Acceptance. King Uthar himself is coming to preside over it, as he does every year. It's one of his favorite ceremonies and it's not often he misses it. I can't afford uncertainty, I need to be sure there's no murderer marauding when the King arrives with his retinue. I can't risk exposing His Majesty to any possible danger. If I must cancel Uthar's presence because of this, I will, even though it will be a dishonor for the Rangers. I don't know how I'm going to explain to the King that he can't attend because we're incapable of ensuring the safety of the Camp. Particularly this place, the home of the Rangers who serve him, somewhere which was intended from the start to be secret and safe. The dishonor will be terrible … I'll have to resign from my post…"

"That will never happen," Ivana said in a voice of conviction.

"There's still time," Eyra said. "We'll sort out this mess."

"We'll guarantee the safety of the Camp and the whole valley," Haakon said. "And as for the possibility that there's a traitor among us, I'll take it on myself to find him and execute him."

"Nobody will leave a mark on the Rangers' honor," said Esben, "not as long as we're here to protect it."

"Thank you all. The King's visit is the most important event of the year. It's a true honor that Uthar bestows upon us with his presence."

"Will Gondabar come with him?" Eyra asked.

"I believe so. The King's Master Ranger will attend. As our leader he wouldn't dream of missing the event."

"We see him less and less," Ivana protested.

"The duties at the king's court are many," Dolbarar said.

Esben smiled. "I think he prefers life at court to life at the Camp."

"Don't let him hear you say that, he'll deny it and make you pay."

Esben smiled. "No, I won't."

"Gondabar has a hundred Rangers with him in Norghana," Haakon said, "as well as Gatik, First Ranger. Isn't that too many just to watch over the city? Shouldn't they be watching over the realm?"

"That's what Uthar requires. Darthor's threat is growing. The King only trusts the Rangers for his personal protection. That's why he's asked Gondabar to strengthen the protection in the capital."

"Darthor may be powerful," Esben said, "but he won't reach Norghana. The King's army would stop him."

"The King fears a surprise attack in his home. That's why he's summoned his most faithful servants, the Rangers, to protect him."

"Darthor would never get as far as the Royal Castle," Ivana said confidently.

"We shouldn't underestimate him. The King doesn't. He's an extremely powerful enemy, an unequalled mage who now has a fearsome army in his service. An army of men and beasts: the wild men of the ice, trolls of the snow, corrupt Ogres and other beastly beings, reinforced with Elementals and Ice Giants."

"Has that been confirmed?" Haakon asked.

Dolbarar nodded heavily. "Our Rangers have located it. They've landed on the Ice Coast, a long way to the north. Our brothers are keeping an eye on them. It's an enormous army. Thousands of men and beasts."

"If they're so far north," Eyra said, "either they attack now or else they'll have to wait until spring. They won't be able to cross the passes in winter."

"True, but Uthar isn't counting on this. Besides, there are rumors that some of the King's rivals might be thinking of joining Darthor to bring down the King."

Ivana was outraged. "Our nobles? How can that be?"

"They're only rumors, but not all the Dukes and Counts are faithful followers of the King. Some want the crown for themselves…"

Lasgol looked at Egil, who swallowed. They were talking about his father and his allies.

"Traitors!" Ivana cried. "I'll put an arrow between their eyes!"

Dolbarar made a calming gesture.

"Politics is not for us. We serve the King and follow his orders. For the moment, let's focus on the problem at hand. We must ensure the safety of the Camp, still knowing that the King is to attend the Ceremony of Acceptance, and that Darthor is getting closer and seeking his death."

"I've been around the camp with the bloodhounds, and they haven't found any unfamiliar trails," said Esben.

"You'd better set Gretchen loose," Dolbarar said. "We can't afford to take risks."

"Very well, I'll let her loose tonight. If there's a human lurking out there in the high forests she'll find him and bring him to us. What's left of him."

Lasgol glanced at Egil, who shrugged.

"We'll impose a curfew," Dolbarar said. "With Gretchen loose, nobody will be able to leave the camp until she's back."

Lasgol could no longer hold back his curiosity. He decided to ask a question. "Gretchen, sir?"

Dolbarar smiled. "Don't worry. As long as you're within the boundaries of the Camp, nothing will happen to you. And now, get back to your cabin and rest. If you see anything strange, out of the ordinary, you're to tell me at once."

Lasgol glanced at his companions; nobody said a word. Nobody spoke during the walk to the cabin, or when they got into their bunks to sleep. They all had too many things in their heads which they needed to digest: Lasgol more than anyone else. He had the grim feeling that the danger was not over with Nistrom's death. Not even the company of his playful little friend who was licking his hand, would comforted him. Could he be right? He could only do one thing: go on and see what would happen. He would keep all his senses alert. They would not catch him unawares again. He petted

Camu, and with the creature's cold touch on his cheek, he fell asleep. He found no rest however. His dreams were plagued by nightmares, of corrupt Mages and huge murderous beasts.

Chapter 25

Their wounds did not take long to heal. The Healer worked miracles with her Gift, or as she said, "helped Mother Nature with her hard work". She could not heal deadly wounds or terminal illnesses, but she was capable of healing, and accelerating the recovery time for wounds and non-lethal illnesses..

Lasgol was back training with all his companions within a week, and Viggo a week later. Gerd's nose healed well, although he swore every time he looked in the mirror that it was a little crooked. He complained that the "incident" – as they called it – had ruined his good looks. Viggo maintained that what had gone crooked was, his brain.

But the "other" wounds however, would not heal so fast. Perhaps they never would. They had killed a man. It was a traumatic event which would mark them forever. They had no choice, but even so, it was an event of such magnitude and significance that it would take their young souls a long time to come to terms with. Each one of them coped with the dramatic experience in a different way.

For Ingrid, it had been a decisive step in her evolution toward the leader she wished to become. It had been tough but necessary, and she had acted correctly in a very difficult situation. She had no regrets. Viggo complained about his wound, but as for the killing of the mercenary, he had not the slightest remorse. Far from it: he boasted of it. If any other mercenary or assassin tried again, he would find a dagger in his right eye.

The rest of the team did not handle things so well. Gerd was more frightened than usual. Some fears which he had already overcome had returned and the giant was constantly scared all over again. Nilsa was much more nervous and restless than usual, and this brought on more "accidents". Her clumsiness had increased tenfold.

The one most affected by what had happened was Egil. He could not believe he had killed a man. For the scholar, killing was unthinkable, something atrocious, evil in itself. He had taken some tomes on philosophy out of the library and was reading them in an attempt to overcome his remorse. There were nights when he woke up in the middle of a nightmare, drenched in perspiration. They all knew it was because of what had happened. Inevitably he tried to rationalize what had happened and come to some explanation or understanding that would allow him to move on.

Lasgol was tremendously grateful to his companions. They had saved his life. It hurt him to see them so affected by what had happened. After all, it was because of him, however he felt neither remorse nor guilt. He had defended himself, it had been his own life or the mercenary's, and he was happy it had not ended up being his. Still, he felt bad for his friends, for the fact that they had to live through an ordeal like that.

While they were recovering from the experience, winter arrived at the Camp. The cold, which had already been intense in autumn, suddenly turned icy. The snowfalls was constant and the whole valley was covered by a thick white blanket that would not leave until the spring. The landscape was terrifying, with a white and dangerous beauty. The woods in winter, and particularly the mountains, became beautiful as well as lethal in Norghana. A single mistake meant falling down a cliff. A bad calculation or losing one's way, meant freezing to death in a forest trapped by a blizzard.

The instruction became even more arduous, not because the instructors had increased the difficulty of the exercises, but because of the added harshness of the adverse weather. Oden made them fall in every morning, no matter how cold it might be, even if they were amid the worst of blizzards. They had been given winter clothes which, so he said, were more than enough, although the hunched bodies, chattering teeth and shaky knees suggested the opposite. Haakon made them run around the lake, even though it might be freezing or snowing, a lashing wind or even an icy fog which nothing could be seen. The worse the conditions, the more the instructors seemed to enjoy themselves, and the more the initiates suffered.

The only good thing about winter was getting back to the cabin after a hard, freezing day of instruction. The cabin, covered with snow, welcomed them with the smoke of the chimney and the heat of a low fire inside, which comforted body and soul. Lasgol always stopped at the entrance to look at the wooden cabin, half-buried in snow, with the warm light of the fire shining through the windows. He found it an idyllic image, one he cherished.

Inside though, things were far from idyllic. He had thanked his companions one by one for saving his life, but the reactions he had received had not been as warm as he would have wished. Gerd was the only one who was now closer and friendlier. The others kept at a cool distance. At least they were speaking to him now instead of ignoring him completely. Things had improved, although he would still have to work hard to regain their respect and trust. He knew it, and though it saddened him, he did not lose heart and tried to keep up a positive attitude. Somehow he would manage to restore the broken bonds.

He was aware that Egil was the coldest, and most distant towards him. This surprised him because he felt that out of all of his teammates, Egil would be the first he could re-establish friendship with, but he was mistaken.

"I'm not one to forgive a betrayal," he had told Lasgol.

"I was wrong, I know that now," he had replied. "I should've told you everything."

"My body may not be strong, but my honor and determination are."

"I'm really sorry, I had no intention …"

"And I'm not one to forgive or forget for the sake of a few nice words either."

That was all they had said about the matter. Lasgol felt terrible, but he did not want to antagonize Egil any further, so he gave him space in the hope that they would gradually regain their friendship. He could only wait and see. And not put his foot in it again.

Camu kept growing. He was also getting more playful and taking more liberties. He ran all over the room and gave ever greater leaps. Now he had taken to chasing Viggo, who kept calling him "vermin" and had added "of the frozen abysses". Gerd was gradually losing his fear of the creature. Every day he faced his fear of the unknown, of magic, and tried to overcome it. Lasgol could see the internal struggle reflected in the giant's face. He interacted with Camu with an enormous effort. And the surprising thing was that Camu had started to obey him now and then. This had left everybody open-mouthed with amazement, because the creature always did what it wanted and never heeded anybody. What was undeniable by now was that Gerd had a special skill with animals, even magical ones.

Nilsa, on the other hand, did not accept Camu. If he was in the room, she could make a great effort and bear it for a while, but then she would leave the room and walk away from the cabin. Lasgol watched her from the window until she disappeared into the night. He wondered how he could resolve the situation. Ingrid begged Nilsa to stay, but most nights she left.

Ingrid went on acting as Captain with the same authority and determination as always, but now that the end of the year was approaching it seemed that the pressure was beginning to take its toll. She was more churlish than usual, and even had an altercation during the School of Expertise session with Jobas, the Captain of the Boars. Jobas was a huge boy, almost as big as Gerd, and had a very bad temper. Almost all the Boars were the same in this. In one exercise he had brought down a girl with a vindictive shove and then made fun of her, even though she was half his size.

When Ingrid saw this she leapt in at once. But far from cowering, Jobas had stood up to her. Haakon, watching from a distance, allowed things to follow their course. This time however, Ingrid had lost. Jobas was too big and strong for her. She ended up on the ground with a split lip. Viggo leapt to her defense, and Nilsa followed. There was quite a brawl. Ingrid was not punished because Haakon did not report the incident, which surprised Lasgol.

One evening he was looking at the snowy cabin before going in, as he liked to do. He knew that the warmth of the fire, his teammates and Camu were waiting for him inside, and he wanted to savor the feeling a little longer before going in. A voice behind him brought him back to reality.

"Two murder attempts, you're a real celebrity all across the Camp," said the voice, which he recognized at once.

"Astrid..." he said, turning toward her. When he saw her face, her green eyes and jet-black hair, he was speechless. "I... oh well... not exactly a celebrity ..."

Her smile was deeply sarcastic. "And as eloquent as ever."

Lasgol went as red as a tomato. "Speaking... isn't one of my strong points."

"Attracting trouble seems to be, though," she replied with a broad smile.

He smiled. "Well... I certainly can't deny that."

"And to think that when I first saw you and they told me who you were, I thought you were in for a really bad time... but who'd have expected this?"

Lasgol gave a comical wave, trying to make light of it. "Yeah... not even in my worst nightmares."

"Well, at least it looks as if it's over now."

"I hope so."

"They say you knew him. D'you know why he tried to kill you?"

"I did know him, from my village. I don't know why he did it. He said he was under orders from someone very powerful."

"Darthor?"

"Looks like it..."

"Yeah, the rumors about him grow with every passing day, and the news isn't good. They say he has a great army of horrible creatures."

Lasgol was thoughtful. "Army? Does he have soldiers?"

"I see you're not very up-to-date."

"Nobody tells me anything."

"I can help you with that."

"Thanks. It means a lot to me. Lets just say my personal relationships aren't going very well right now..."

Astrid laughed. "All right, I'll tell you. Darthor has an army of Wild Ones of the Ice."

"Wild Ones of the Ice? Aren't they a myth, Norghanian folklore?"

"No, they're very real. I can assure you. My grandfather fought against one of them. Way to the north, when he was young."

"What happened?"

"He died. He was cloven in two with an axe."

"Oh! I'm sorry."

"Don't worry. To be honest, I don't even remember, but my grandmother always spoke about them, the Wild Ones of the Ice. It's etched in my memory. Huge men, over six feet tall, with amazing strength and muscles. Beside them, the biggest of the Norghanians, like my grandfather, look like children. Wild Ones of the Ice, with smooth skin, without any wrinkles so they don't seem to age, and an amazing ice-blue color."

"Their skin is ice-blue?" Lasgol interrupted, trying to visualize them.

"There's more. Their hair and beards are bluish-blond, as if they'd been frozen in a winter storm, but the most remarkable feature is their eyes: such a pale gray it seems to blend with the white of their eyes, almost lacking life. Anyone who sees them suffers from nightmares. They keep to themselves and don't wish to be disturbed. They dress in white bearskins. They don't know anything about swords. They get what they want with the axe, and their enormous physical power. They say that one of them can kill ten Norghanian soldiers, even several of the King's Invincibles of the Ice, the elite infantry."

Lasgol was left speechless.

"They're the People of the Ice. They live in the Frozen Continent to the north, but not all of them. One part lives to the north of our realm, on Tremian soil."

"I thought all of them lived beyond the seas."

"No, several of their tribes are on this continent, at the far end, further north. In fact it's said that Norghana, our realm, used to belong to them a thousand years ago, before they migrated to the frozen continent. As far as they're concerned, this land we walk on is theirs."

"That's not good."

"That's right. They don't often cross the northern mountains and enter our territory, but when they do…"

"I see… And why have they joined Darthor?"

"That's a good question. Some say that Darthor dominates them with his arcane arts. Others say that they're tired of being bullied and want to get Norghana back for their tribes on the frozen continent."

"And what do you think yourself?"

"That there's some truth in both theories. My grandfather met them because he went to the far end of our land to find them, with others like him. They may not have been the only ones. They must have sent expeditions beyond the mountains. The Wild Ones of Ice won't have liked that. And I think Darthor controls them in some way, dark or otherwise."

"As Egil would say, this is all very fascinating."

"And very dangerous."

"You're telling me."

"King Uthar is putting his army together. They're expecting a great confrontation by the thaw."

"At the end of winter?"

"Yes. The northern passes are closing because of the bad weather. They'll soon be impassable. The snow and ice will shut them completely until winter's over and the thaw begins in spring. Darthor won't be able to cross the mountains and move south. Everyone thinks that'll be when the two armies face each other."

"Everyone?"

"The teams. It's the main topic for conversation these days. Well, that and the attempts on your life."

"I can imagine there are bets…"

"And pretty big ones too! I'm making a fortune!"

Lasgol looked puzzled.

"I'm one of the few who've bet you manage to finish the year. Alive, of course."

"Oh, I see …" He arched an eyebrow. "Well, I intend to make them lose all their money."

"Wonderful! That way I'll end up with a bag full of coins."

"What other rumors are there?"

"Something troubling…they say the mercenary couldn't have acted alone, that there's a traitor in the camp."

"Do you believe that?"

"I don't like the idea at all, but I must admit it makes sense. Otherwise how can you explain how a mercenary could enter the Camp, steal poison from Eyra and attack without his presence being detected? Somebody who knows the Camp and its workings well. One of our own people."

Lasgol was thoughtful. "It might've been one of the students… someone from the fourth year? Someone who'd infiltrated us?"

"It might be… but to stay hidden, the mercenary had to know the whole place very well so as to be able to move freely…"

"Maybe a Ranger?"

"I think someone higher, an instructor perhaps. Someone who's been here for a long time and knows the place to perfection."

Haakon's face came to Lasgol's mind, and he could not get rid of it.

"That would be very bad news for Dolbarar."

"And for everybody. Having another traitor among us would be another terrible stain."

Lasgol became serious. The comment was a reference to his father.

Astrid realized this. "I'm sorry, I spoke without thinking."

"I'm who I am."

"Yes, but you're not your father, and they shouldn't judge you for him, and nor should you have to justify yourself because of him."

"I'm my father's son. I'll carry that load. I won't renounce who I am."

"It does you credit. I'm sorry about everything they're making you go through."

"Is that why you speak to me when most of them don't even deign to say a word to me?" Lasgol said, wounded. "Because you're sorry for the traitor's son?"

Astrid looked him in the eye and said nothing for a moment. "Yes. Because of that and because you have something special. I don't know what it is, but it's something that makes you interesting." She gave him a seductive smile and left, keeping her intense green eyes fixed on his own, which were wide in amazement.

The days went by, and the six Snow Panthers trained as if a winter storm would carry them away at any moment. Ingrid spurred them on day and night, as if the instructors did not do it enough already. The improvement in everybody was clear, particularly because in such adverse terrain and conditions, the slightest mistake was paid for dearly. Lasgol watched Egil and Gerd running on the snow in the midst of a blizzard like indefatigable wild hares and could barely believe it. Nilsa leapt over fallen trunks and climbed trees almost as well as Ingrid. Even he himself could now use the bow as never before. It was truly surprising what willpower and sacrifice could achieve.

As the final test approached, Ingrid grew more and more restless. She made hasty decisions and acted almost by instinct instead of with her head, which was not good in a leader. Lasgol believed it was because of the enormous pressure she placed on herself. They were risking a lot, it was true; if they did not do well there would be expulsions, and not only that, many would find the doors to the elite specializations closed to them. This meant that the thirteen teams would push themselves to their limit, and rivalry would be a killer.

Ingrid wanted the team to triumph, wanted all of them to triumph, and that pressure was affecting her. Master Instructor Oden's motivating speech the week before the date of the Test did not help at all.

"The Winter Test will be different from the others," he told them at dawn when they assembled in front of the cabins. "It'll be more difficult, more competitive…harder." He stopped to look at the faces that were watching him with restless eyes, as he liked to do, watching for whether any sign of fear appeared in the Initiates' eyes. "There won't be individual tests, only a great team test. An elimination test."

The murmurs of surprise among the teams became audible.

"Taken by surprise, are you? Well, that's what the life of a Ranger is like. You must be ready for any eventuality, as is taught in the Path of the Ranger. You'll be competing for the three positions of honor. Only the three best teams will be rewarded and only one will achieve glory."

The murmurs became cries of surprise. The Eagles, the Boars, and the Wolves were shouting with joy, sure they would be the winners. Other teams, like the Owls or the Foxes, took it with controlled euphoria, as they knew they had some chance against the more boastful teams. But the others, including the Snow Panthers, stared at the ground with an air of defeat. They did not feel they were capable of beating the stronger teams.

Ingrid pushed them to train even harder. There was not much time left and the team's chances were very slight.

Chapter 26

And so the great day of the Winter Test arrived, the one which crowned the year. It was decided which teams would achieve glory, which of the initiates would pass on to the second year and which had not made it and would be expelled. The week had been intense, not just because of what was at stake but because the King was to attend the event. They had been working without respite on the preparations for the royal visit: all the years, first, second, third and fourth. The Camp was wearing its finest ceremonial dress, and everything shone.

Dolbarar assembled the thirteen teams in front of the Command House. It was an icy winter morning. Snow covered the whole camp, and a layer of ice had formed in many places during the night. The Four Master Rangers took their places behind him.

"Good morning to all this year's Initiates," Dolbarar greeted them with a kind smile. "I see from your eager faces and the nerves you can barely hold in check that you are all aware of the importance of today's test. For a whole year you have been instructed in body and mind, under the guidance of the best masters." He indicated the Four Master Rangers behind him with a gesture, and they acknowledged the honor with a nod. "Today is the day when you must use everything you've learned and be successful in the culminating test."

Nilsa was unable to keep still. "I'm so nervous I'm going to pee myself," she whispered.

"I'm terrified," Gerd admitted.

Ingrid shushed them. "Let me hear what he says. I don't want to miss a thing."

"As if that's going to help," muttered Viggo.

Dolbarar went on with his explanation. "This test is a competition by elimination. You will compete against the other teams in eliminatory rounds until only two teams remain: the finalists. That is, two teams compete against each other, the winning team goes on and competes against the winner of another eliminatory round. And so on until there are only two teams left."

"As long as we don't have to compete against the Eagles," Nilsa said.

"Or the Bears," added Gerd.

Viggo grimaced. "Or against most of them."

Dolbarar indicated the preparations being made in front of the Command House. "Tomorrow will be the great final, on this very spot. It will take place before King Uthar. His Majesty will arrive at the Camp this evening and will preside over the final himself."

Murmurs and whispers ran through the thirteen teams. It was a great honor, but at the same time it added a great deal of pressure to the test.

"Without fear and without nerves," Ingrid encouraged them.

"And now it's time to begin the drawing of lots," Dolbarar said. He signaled to Oden, who approached the Camp Leader and showed him his leather pouch.

"Inside this bag are the badges of all the teams. I'll bring them out one by one and call the selected teams. The team of the White Eagles has won two of the three tests already, and therefore do not need to participate in the first two eliminatory rounds. Their position is recognized, and they will enter the competition in the third round."

"Good!" Isgord said with a swagger, and the members of his team looked self-satisfied. They were the favorites and they knew it.

Dolbarar went on: "First eliminatory round. Your attention, please." He put his hand in the bag and took out a badge. "The Bears," he announced. There followed a moment of silence while he put his hand in again and took out another badge. "Against the Wolves."

There were comments from both teams as they tried to intimidate their rivals.

The drawing of lots continued. "The Owls against the Snakes," Dolbarar called out next. He went on taking out badges. "The Foxes against the Boars."

They all waited on edge to find out their luck, and at last their turn came.

"The Snow Panthers against the Falcons," Dolbarar called out.

"The Falcons, that's good!" cried Ingrid.

Viggo nodded. "Yeah, it could've been much worse."

Gerd was unconvinced. "We'll see."

Dolbarar finished pairing off the rest of the teams. "One last note," he said with a mischievous smile. "To make the eliminatory rounds more exciting, they'll take place on different kinds of terrain, each a little more complicated than the one before. The winning teams on the first area of terrain will fight in the second, and then the winners in the third. I think you know what I mean."

Viggo grimaced. "As if it wasn't 'exciting' enough already."

"Shut up, you dimwit," Ingrid scolded.

"The first rounds will take place in the forests on the low mountains to the north. Oden will lead you there and the Four Master Rangers will act as umpires."

At a gesture from Dolbarar, they set out toward the mountains in silence, concentrating on what was waiting for them. When they arrived, Oden explained the rules.

"You'll all be given white hooded cloaks, a short bow, and a quiver with twelve arrows with marking tips. A knife and an axe, also with blunt marking edges." He took a bow and released an arrow at a tree. As the tip made contact with the wood, there was a hollow sound and a red stain appeared, the size of a fist. He threw the knife and axe with the same result. "I think you understand how the marking weapons work." He looked around and the Initiates nodded.

"Each team will enter at one end of the forest. The winning team will be the one any of whose members crosses the forest, reaches the other end and takes hold of the opposing team's badge. It will be tied to a spear stuck in the ground at each team's starting point. If a member of the team is caught and marked, he or she will be eliminated. Bodily fights are allowed. Grave injuries are not. Mark, don't break. Keep a watch on brutality or else you'll be penalized." His hard gaze swept over the initiates, leaving no doubt in their minds. "The winner will be the first to seize the opposing team's badge. What strategy you follow is up to you to decide. There's a set time. At the end of it, if neither team has taken the other's badge, the captains will fight a duel until one touches the other and breaks the tie."

"Nice little test," Viggo commented to his companions. "It's going to be a real show!"

Ingrid was silent. She looked worried.

Oden repeated the rules, so that everybody was clear about them. The eliminatory rounds began with the confrontation of Bears and Wolves. The former went into the woods on the mountain from the east, the latter from the west. Ivana stayed by the Bears' badge and Eyra by the Wolves'. Haakon and Esben went in with the teams to act as umpires. The other teams waited their turn nervously. There was a long, tense period of silence, then suddenly shouting broke out: shouts as real as if this were a fight to the death. Suddenly a competitor in white appeared running toward the Bears' badge, leaping over snowy trunks and vegetation. It was the captain of the Wolves. An arrow sought his back, but he ducked and it brushed his head in passing. He zigzagged, dodging another arrow, and made off with the Bears' badge.

"The winners are the Wolves!" cried Ivana.

The members of both teams came out of the snowy forest. Most of their cloaks were marked with red. The Wolves congratulated their captain, while the Bears, who were one of the favorite teams, could not understand how they had lost and were arguing agitatedly among themselves.

The eliminatory rounds went on. The Owls beat the Snakes, and Lasgol was glad on behalf of Astrid and her team. The Boars beat the Foxes easily.

And then came the turn of the Snow Panthers.

"Come on," Ingrid called out to encourage them. "We're going to make it!"

Lasgol took a good look at the Falcons as they took their positions. They were a good team. To be honest, all the teams were good compared to their own. He looked at his team-mates' faces and was aware of the fear and unease in them. Ingrid gave the badge to Ivana, who put it in its place, and they went into the forest.

"And now begin!" Oden said.

Ingrid beckoned the team around her.

"What strategy should we follow?" the captain asked. "Defensive, or attack straight away?"

"I'd attack," Gerd said. He was checking his weapons. For some strange reason, he was showing no sign of fear.

"Hm…" Egil said thoughtfully. "I disagree substantially. I don't think attacking is our best option, given the circumstances."

"You don't think so?" Viggo said. "Of course not! They'll make mincemeat of us if we attack."

"Oh ye of little faith!" complained Ingrid.

"I'm a realist."

"I'd say more of a pessimist," said Nilsa.

"Be quiet and don't point that at me, or you'll eliminate me by mistake, clumsy!"

She poked her tongue at him. "I've improved a lot, I'm not half as clumsy."

"All of you, shut up," Ingrid said. "We haven't time for this. Egil, what do you suggest?"

"The most prudent thing to do, and I would venture to say the most intelligent, is to defend our position. We'll have more chance that way than if we try to beat them in the offensive. Or that's my conclusion, considering all the variables at play in the situation we find ourselves in." He was looking around him at the snow-covered forest.

Ingrid gave her judgment. "Well, we'll defend, then."

"What formation do we take up?" Viggo asked.

"I have an idea," said Egil. He beckoned them to come closer, took a twig and drew their position on the snow.

"Take up your positions," said Ingrid. "Be careful with your breathing," she warned them. "The steam will give you away."

The wind blew icily among the trees with an ululating sound. It swerved toward the side of the mountain which it brushed against. A strange sound followed: the sound of footsteps on the snow. Wary footsteps. A silhouette covered in white moved forward and hid behind a fir tree. In the snow it was barely visible. It was followed by two others which took up their positions to the right and left. There was a moment of silence, then three more silhouettes appeared a little to the rear. The Falcons were a hundred paces from the Panthers' badge.

There was no sign of the Panthers. It was as if the earth had swallowed them. The first silhouette crouched down, gave a sign and began to move forward, bent double, in the direction of the badge. At fifty paces, a face suddenly appeared from behind a tree. It was Nilsa, who had managed to stay hidden like a statue of ice. She released an arrow against the assailant. It caught him in the side, and the red stain appeared on his cloak. They heard a curse.

"Arvid, eliminated. On the ground." Esben said. They could not see him, but they knew he was there, watching.

The member of the Falcons team did as he was told.

His companions moved forward and shot at Nilsa, who protected herself behind the tree.

"Surround her," said Gonars, the captain of the Falcons.

Two of the Falcons obeyed and moved to surround Nilsa so that she would not be able to move or else they would get her.

Like lightning Ingrid appeared behind another tree five paces to Nilsa's right and took a shot. She hit one of the assailants.

"Rasmus, eliminated. On the ground," came Esben's voice again.

The other Falcon released an arrow at Ingrid, but she hid behind the tree.

"Come out and fight!" Gonars shouted furiously.

As if in answer to his request, Gerd appeared behind another tree five paces to Nilsa's left and took a shot.

Gonars threw himself to one side and avoided the arrow.

Immediately three arrows sought Gerd's body, but he hid behind the tree just in time.

"Go for the big guy!" Gonars ordered. Three of his people hurried to Gerd's position.

Nilsa tried to defend herself, but she was hit by the Falcon who had been stalking her.

Ingrid got him in turn.

"Both eliminated. On the ground."

Suddenly Gerd came out from behind the tree with one axe in each hand, like the personification of a Norghanian demigod of war. The three attackers raised their bows. Three arrows sped toward Gerd. With a powerful lash, he sent the axes against the two nearest Falcons. The arrows hit him, but his axes eliminated two enemies.

"No!" cried Gonars. "Cover me, I'm going for the badge!" he said to his teammate, and started to zigzag.

Ingrid came out to block his way. She launched an arrow. But Gonars was very nimble and dodged it. His teammate tried to get Ingrid, but she covered herself.

Gonars moved like lightning, sliding across the snow.

He was five paces away. He was going to make it!

Suddenly, from behind the two last trees in front of the spear with the badge, Egil and Lasgol appeared with their bows at the ready.

"No!" cried Gonars in frustration.

Two paces away from the badge, their arrows got him on both sides.

"Gonars, eliminated," came Haakon's voice.

Jacob, the last Falcon took a shot at Ingrid and was about to move forward when he heard a noise at his back. He was about to turn, but it was already too late. The two knives Viggo had thrown got him in the back.

"Jacob, eliminated," Haakon said.

"The Snow Panthers win!" Ivana proclaimed.

Lasgol and Egil looked at each other in disbelief. They had made it! The plan had worked! They had won! The whole team fell on one another amid cries of delight.

The eliminatory rounds went on. Once the twelve teams had faced off in the forest, six were left as winners and were led to the lakes. The losing teams remained on the mountain and competed among themselves.

At the lakes, Dolbarar awaited them to continue with the eliminatory rounds. This was the second piece of terrain where the teams would have to confront each other. He drew lots for the fights once more. Who would they get this time? The six teams looked at each other nervously. Lasgol noticed that the other teams were very strong. They, and the Owls, were the weakest. But anything might happen, they could not allow themselves to be discouraged.

"Next series," Dolbarar said. He put his hand in the bag and took out the first badge. "The Wolves," he announced. "Against the Tigers."

The two teams took each other's measure. Their strength was similar. Both had good archers and several strong individuals. The fight would be very much between equals.

Dolbarar went on: "The Owls against the Gorillas." That would be interesting. The Gorillas were six strong and powerful boys, giving them a physical advantage, but with Astrid and Leana the Owls were more skillful. Lasgol wished Astrid and her team good luck; they were going to need it. And on the subject of needing luck, their own turn came.

"The Boars against the Panthers," Dolbarar said, and the teams were finally paired off.

Lasgol felt as if they had poured a bucket of icy water over his head. The Boars, together with the Wolves, were among the strongest teams. His teammates' faces were a poem to watch. Even Ingrid looked downcast. Apart from the Wolves, this was the worst possible pairing. The Boars were smiling and congratulating each other as if they had already won, sure of their superiority. Gerd drew himself up to his full height and went over to them. He folded his arms over his huge chest, without showing so much as a trace of fear.

"That's the right spirit!" Ingrid said enthusiastically. "Good for you!"

"Those bigheads are going to find out a thing or two," Viggo said. He sounded more positive.

"Exactly!" said Nilsa.

Lasgol felt his spirits rising.

The second eliminatory round was certainly more complex than the first, for everyone. Not just because of the terrain, but because of the competitors' skill and their eagerness to triumph. All the teams included someone who risked expulsion if they were eliminated and failed to reach the positions of glory.

The Wolves got rid of the Tigers, but not without difficulty. It was a result that surprised nobody, as the Wolves were one of the strongest teams and were expected to be in the fight for the final victory. But in the next face-off something unexpected happened. The Owls managed to defeat the Gorillas, thanks to the skill of Astrid and Leana. Three strong boys who were also good archers tried to stop them, when at the end of the test the two girls threw themselves on the Gorillas' badge, but failed. Astrid and Leana moved like gazelles chased by predators amid the forest. Leana was thrown to the ground a hundred paces from the badge. She fought like a fiend, but she was marked. At the same time Astrid leapt over a fallen trunk and with a somersault managed to avoid the Captain of the Gorillas. She seized the enemy badge in an exhibition of agility and swiftness.

The next competition was between the Boars and the Panthers. The Boars made a strong start. The snow was not so heavy by the lakes. There was less opportunity to camouflage themselves, which was in their favor. They were big, strong and very well prepared, and they had the advantage. Ingrid, Gerd and Viggo came out to meet them as their six rivals advanced in a line. Confident in their abilities, they showed no fear of their opponents. Egil stayed hidden, defending the Badge in case a rival tried to reach it. But as expected, the Boars were far superior, and Gerd was the first to fall. Nilsa followed shortly afterwards. Viggo and Ingrid managed to hold their own, but they had to risk a lot, and Viggo was eliminated. Ingrid fought like a tigress and brought down another opponent, but in the end she was beaten. While the fight was under way, the Panthers put in place the stratagem Egi had devised.

Defying the cold, in a move that only fools would attempt, risking freezing to death, Lasgol got into the lake and swam under water until he was past the enemy lines. He resurfaced at their rear and dragged himself out of the water, shivering with cold. While the Boars were destroying his team-mates, he got to his feet as best he could and ran, forcing his frozen body, to steal the badge. The Boars were so sure of their superiority they had left no-one defending their badge. They finished off Egil and were about to seize the Panthers' badge when Lasgol took their own.

The Panthers won. Haakon conceded their victory despite the complaints of the Boars that it had been a trick. The lake was a part of the terrain, and as such it could be used as any team saw fit.

The Panthers jumped and shouted in jubilation for a victory not even they could believe they had won. Lasgol was on the verge of catching pneumonia, but it had been worth it. They had to dry him at once, give him dry clothes and make a fire so that he could get warm. Ingrid gave him a vigorous massage to get the process started.

The winning teams were led from the lakes to the flat land, the third area of terrain chosen by Dolbarar for the last rounds. The leader of the camp received the three winning teams on the flat land. Here there were neither mountains nor lakes they could use as allies. With Dolbarar, the Eagles were waiting.

"These will be the last fights today," he announced. "The two finalists will come out from here, and tomorrow they will compete in the grand finale before King Uthar and his retinue."

Lasgol and Egil exchanged a disbelieving look at having got that far.

Ingrid clenched her fist tightly. "We have to reach that final."

"That'd save us from expulsion," said Egil.

"We need it," Gerd said.

"It would be a real bind to have gotten so far and then not make it," said Viggo.

"Don't be a bird of ill omen," said Nilsa.

Lasgol was looking closely at Isgord and his team-mates. They had no chance of beating this team; they were too good at everything.

They had no weak spot. They would not let themselves be tricked. Isgord was intelligent and Marta very shrewd.

"Last draw of today," Dolbarar announced.

They all paid absolute attention while the leader of the Camp took out the first badge. It was the Owls'.

"Owls against…"

They all waited tensely. Lasgol's eyes turned to Astrid. He had no desire to confront her, but on the other hand, hers was the most manageable team. The Eagles and the Wolves were formidable adversaries. While he was debating inwardly whether to fight Astrid or not, Dolbarar made his decision for him.

"Owls against Eagles."

He gasped. Neither the one nor the other. It was the Wolves who had been drawn against them. At least he would not need to feel bad.

"Wolves against Panthers," Dolbarar finished.

Both teams exchanged tense looks. The Wolves were not conceited, and nor would they be over-confident. They were good, every single one of them: agile, strong, good fighters with bow and short weapons. A powerful team.

Oden pointed to the area where they were to confront one another. "Get ready. First round: Owls against Eagles."

The two teams entered the cleared forest and took their places. The terrain, flat and with few trees, left the contenders in view of one another. Haakon and Esben followed as umpires. Ivana and Eyra would do the same from beside the spears which bore the badges.

The encounter was shorter and less even than Lasgol had expected. Inwardly he was cheering Astrid and the Owls, but the Eagles' superiority was apparent. They worked thoroughly, coming very close to being penalized at times, and defeated the Owls easily. Astrid and her team ended up beaten and defeated.

Lasgol cursed inwardly. The other Panthers, seeing how soon the Owls had come out of the forest, lost all courage. The Wolves were going to destroy them.

Ingrid noticed this. She called her team-mates around her.

"The Wolves are very good. We all know that, but we have a chance to reach the final. We must grab it. This is no time for doubts, no time for fears, it's time for willpower and spirit. We're risking expulsion. We've got to give everything we have. Everything!"

"Yes!" said Nilsa, carried away by the Captain's passion.

"Are you with me?"

"We're with you, Captain," Viggo said. Gerd and Lasgol nodded.

"We'll make it," Egil said, affirming Ingrid's message.

"Let's go for them!" cried Ingrid.

The Panthers arranged themselves around the spear which carried their badge. They studied the forest. There was not much vegetation, and the snow only came up to their ankles. In the middle was a large clearing and a rocky formation.

"They have to cross over to reach our side," Egil said thoughtfully. "It's like a little sea with an island in the middle."

"That's right," said Ingrid. "So what do we do?"

"It's better to defend," Egil said. "I think it's been made absolutely clear that offensive action is not our forte."

"Got a strategy?" Viggo asked.

"With this open terrain I can't think of anything. We'll have to fight."

"Well then," Ingrid said, "we'll fight."

The starting signal sounded. The Wolves set out at a crazy run.

"They want to get to the center!" shouted Ingrid. "Run!"

The Panthers raced across the snow, leaping over roots, bushes and undergrowth. Ingrid and Lasgol were the first to arrive at the edge. The Wolves were already racing across the clearing toward the rocks in the middle. Ingrid nocked an arrow and released as Lasgol did the same. Luca, the Captain of the Wolves, was already climbing the rocks in search of the advantage the height would give him. Ashlin, the only girl in the team, was climbing after him with amazing agility. The rest of the team took refuge behind the massive rock. A moment later three arrows flew toward the bodies of Ingrid and Lasgol. They took cover behind two trees.

"They're very good!" said Ingrid. She indicated Nilsa and Viggo, who were approaching at a run. They threw themselves down on the ground.

"They certainly are," Lasgol agreed. He glanced swiftly around and hid behind the tree again.

Gerd and Egil arrived last and Ingrid sent them to their positions. They took up a line of defense behind the trees at the edge. There was an exchange of arrows. Unfortunately the Wolves were better archers, as well as being better positioned. Luca got Gerd, who was unable to hide his enormous body completely.

"I've been hit!" he called out to his team-mates.

"Take cover!" Ingrid said as an arrow flew near her head.

Suddenly the four Wolves behind the rocks started to run in a zigzag. Two toward the east, two toward the west.

"They're attacking our flanks!" said Egil.

"Drive them back!" cried Ingrid.

They all loosed arrows, trying to hit them. Viggo hit one of them, but Luca hit him in turn when he broke cover to shoot. The same thing happened to Nilsa, who received a double hit from the two archers in their elevated position.

"Hell!" Ingrid cried.

Egil crawled over to Ingrid and Lasgol. "They've got our flanks."

Two arrows, one from the east, and one from the west, confirmed his warning. Ingrid and Lasgol crouched down.

Ingrid looked to either side. "We're not going to get out of this."

Egil grimaced in Lasgol's direction. "He could… with his skills…"

Ingrid shook her head. "No, we won't cheat. If we lose, we lose."

"It wouldn't be exactly cheating… it's what I am…"

"You're right. But I don't want to win at any price. No, no magic."

Lasgol nodded. "All right, I won't use my skills."

Egil nodded, and the pact was sealed.

Four arrows sought their bodies.

"We have to retreat," Lasgol said after a brief glance. "We can't hold this position. They're getting too close to our flanks."

Egil shook his head. "If we retreat, their last two archers up there will get us."

"So?" Ingrid asked.

Egil smiled. A mischievous smile, as if he had an idea. He made a sign to Lasgol to follow, and they both crawled toward the east.

"I'm not much good at combat, but I'll get an advantage for you," Egil said. "Use it well."

A hundred paces away, one knee on the ground and his bow at the ready, their rival was waiting. Egil and Lasgol waited for him to release. He missed.

"Now! shouted Egil.

They got to their feet, dropped their bows and ran to the archer of the Wolves. At fifty paces he caught Egil in the chest. He was running in front, covering Lasgol, who went on after Egil's sacrifice with all his might. At ten paces the Wolf released. Lasgol threw himself forward and the arrow passed close by his head but did not impact. He rolled across the ground, stood up in front of the Wolf and unsheathed knife and axe. His rival threw aside his bow and unsheathed his in turn. He did it a single moment too late. Lasgol's weapons marked his chest with two crossed thrusts.

Lasgol drew back to Ingrid's position and saw that the Captain had advanced and taken down a Wolf who was flanking them from the west. He looked up at the rock. Luca and Ashleen were not there. *Oh no!* he thought, and an instant later they both fell on him. The three rolled across the snow-covered ground. Lasgol got to his feet and received a powerful punch from Ashleen. He took a step back, stunned. Luca thrust at him with his knife. He threw himself to one side by instinct and managed to avoid the thrust. Ashleen's axe sought his chest, but he blocked her with his own. He received a kick in the stomach from Luca. He bent over, his lungs empty. Luca was about to finish him off when Ingrid appeared. With an enormous leap she brought Luca down so that he was left rolling on the ground.

Lasgol managed to catch his breath, and Ashleen jumped on him. He tried to free himself from her, but there was no way he could. She was almost as tough and fierce as Ingrid, and he was half-stunned and breathless. In that state he could fight and most likely lose, or he could risk it all in one move... he did not stop to think twice, he would take the risk. He lunged at Ashleen just when she threw her knife. With eyes wide as saucers she saw Lasgol's axe leave his hand and head straight to her chest. The knife marked Lasgol, and the axe marked Ashleen.

"Both eliminated," came Esben's voice.

Lasgol smiled. Now it was all in Ingrid's hands. Those who had been eliminated from both teams formed a circle to watch the fight and cheer on their captains.

Both contenders, knife and axe in hand, eyed each other as they moved in a circle.

"Our deal as Captains ends here," Luca said.

"It's a fair deal," Ingrid answered.

"And it's been respected. There's been no bad blood or tricks between Wolves and Panthers, as we agreed."

"That's true, you've kept your side of the bargain."

"And now this deal has to be broken, because one of us has to win."

Ingrid nodded.

"Good luck," said Luca.

"Likewise."

At once they launched into the attack. Ingrid fought Luca like a lioness, but he defended himself like a tiger. They exchanged blows, thrusts and reverses with impressive swiftness and agility. Neither seemed to have the advantage, and in that moment a mistake tilted the scales. It was not made by one of the Captains, but rather by one of their team-mates.

"Are you going to let a girl beat you?" said Bjorn, a boy of the Wolves, big and not too bright.

It was with that comment that caused the end of the Wolves.

An irrepressible fury came over Ingrid and she turned into an unstoppable whirlwind. She destroyed Luca. The Captain of the Wolves ended up on the ground, beaten and marked.

Dolbarar made his proclamation: "The Snow Panthers are the winners!"

The Panthers threw themselves on Ingrid and lifted her to their shoulders amid shouts of joy. The happiness of the team was uncontainable.

Ashleen went over to Bjorn and hit him in the stomach. "You idiot! You made us lose!"

The Panthers had achieved the unthinkable. They were to reach the grand finale.

Chapter 27

The arrival of King Uthar Haugen and his retinue at the Camp was quite an event. One section of trees and brushwood that made up the impenetrable wall around it was cleared to let them through, as if by magic. Lasgol knew it was not magic but hidden pulleys, but it certainly created an arcane illusion.

For the King's reception they had been made to form two long lines and fall in. They were all required to be present to welcome his Majesty. They assembled from the entrance to the Command House. On the right, all the pupils of the four years; on the left, the Rangers and Instructors: all in their official uniform. In front of the house Dolbarar and the Four Master Rangers were waiting in their ceremonial dress.

The long procession passed through the entrance. First came a column of light cavalry: the King's explorers. They wore light scaled armor and high riding boots. They were followed by a full regiment of Invincibles of the Ice, the Elite Infantry of Norghana.

Ingrid was unable to contain her awe when she saw them. "Wow!"

"They're impressive," Gerd said when he saw them in their heavy armor. They were not big men, but they looked hardened and agile. Expert swordsmen. They were dressed all in white: winged helmet, chainmail jerkin and cloak. Even their shields were white. Only the steel of their Norghanian swords was not.

"They're the best infantry on the continent," Ingrid said. "They say nothing can defeat them in close formation."

"The heavy cavalry of Rogdon, the Lancers, might," Viggo said.

"Certainly not their infantry," Ingrid stated flatly, and grimaced with disgust. Viggo smiled, happy to have irked her once again. "Leave me out of it, because I'm not in the mood for your comments."

"You'll have to bear with it. Remember, I saved your life."

"You remind me of it every day. I still don't know what prompted you to do it."

He gave her a mischievous smile, with a brightness in his black eyes. "Your beauty, hidden under that northern roughness."

Gerd choked, and Egil smiled from ear to ear. Lasgol had to swallow a guffaw.

Ingrid turned as red as a tomato and showed him her fist. "When we break ranks I'm going to give you a going over."

"No need, I'm handsome enough already," he said, and winked at her.

Ingrid could not restrain herself. They were all grinning.

The infantry was followed by a company of Royal Rangers in their green hooded cloaks. Leading them was Gatik Lang, the First Ranger. The six watched him pass, open-mouthed, with enormous admiration and envy.

"They're the best among us," Egil said. "The ones who protect the King."

Ingrid's eyes were fixed on Gatik. He was a tall thin man of around thirty, with blond hair, a short beard and a stern, determined face. He did not look like one of nature's jokers.

"I'll be the first woman to be First Ranger," she assured her teammates.

They all waited for Viggo's satirical response, but it did not come. She had spoken so convincingly and so naturally that he did not want to hurt her feelings, so he said nothing.

Bringing up the rear was none other than Arvid Gondabar, the Leader of the Rangers. Lasgol was surprised to see how old he was. Dolbarar was well advanced in years, but Gondabar was at least ten years older. He did not look as though there were many springs left for him. He was gaunt, with a long sharp nose. He barely had any hair left and his face, shriveled by age and the harsh outdoor life of the Rangers, was sullen; Dolbarar's, in contrast, was much more amenable, but there was goodness in this man's deep gaze.

After the Royal Rangers came the Royal Guard. The Invincibles of the Ice might freeze one's blood, but these melted it. They were huge, all as big as Gerd, hardened men, covered with scars, their faces marked by war. They were impressive; they could kill a man with a single blow. They carried swords and short axes at their waists, but what caught Lasgol's attention was the double-headed axe they all carried behind their backs.

"Those double-headed axes weigh as much as a man," he said, remembering Ulf's.

"Surely Gerd could manage one," Nilsa said.

The giant smiled. "Wouldn't mind trying."

"First master the short axe, then we'll talk about it," Viggo said. "Just in case you knock someone's head off by accident. Which with Nilsa at hand might happen at any moment."

"Dimwit!" the redhead said, and poked her tongue out at him.

At that moment King Uthar came past them on a great albino thoroughbred courser. Lasgol watched him, spellbound. He was just as he had imagined him: a formidable man, bigger even than his guards. He was as broad across the shoulders as two men, and half a head taller than Gerd. He must have been in his early forties. His blond hair was worn loose under a jeweled crown and fell to his shoulders. His eyes were large and blue on a hard face. His armor was exquisite, in silver and gold, with inlaid jewels. A long red and white cloak hung at his back.

The six friends, one knee on the ground, watched the king out of the corners of their eyes as he approached with regal poise, awed by his imposing presence and the regal aura which surrounded him. On the king's right rode Sven Borg, Commander of the Royal Guard. Lasgol was surprised by the Commander's appearance. He was not big and strong, like the King and the royal guards. Instead he was thin and not particularly tall. His horse was dark, like his eyes. In fact he seemed out of place.

"They say Sven is the best warrior in the whole North," Viggo said.

"Is he a Norghanian?" Lasgol asked.

"Yes, he's from the south, from the border. Hence his features. He's won all the sword-fighting competitions. He's said to be invincible with a sword and a dagger. He moves so nimbly and has such mastery of swordsmanship that his opponents fall just like that."

"I'd love to be like that myself," Nilsa said.

Lasgol was interested in this man. He was the one who had saved the King from his father's attack. And though this man caught his attention, the one riding on the King's left did so even more: Olthar, Royal Mage. He wore a snow-white robe without any decoration. The Mage's hair was long and white, his eyes gray and icy. His body seemed frail, but there was something in him which radiated power, like a latent, veiled threat. Yes, this man was powerful. Very powerful. Lasgol looked closely at the staff he carried; it was exquisite, white as snow, inlaid with silver. That powerful mage, with that weapon, was the one who had killed his father Dakon.

There they were, just going past Lasgol, the three men involved in the death of the one person he loved more than anybody else in the world. He longed to talk to them, to ask them what had happened, why his father had ended up dead. He knew the answer, but he longed to hear it from their lips in case he could find something that did not fit, in case there was some gap in their stories. Yet seeing them there in flesh and blood, so powerful, in front of him, his hopes began to vanish.

The procession reached Dolbarar and the Four Master Rangers. King Uthar, Commander Sven, the Mage Olthar, the Leader of the Rangers Gondabar and the First Ranger Gatik dismounted, saluted and entered the Command House, together with their hosts. The Royal Guard surrounded the building, and the Royal Rangers took up their positions. The light cavalry and infantry withdrew.

Master Instructor Oden gave the order and they all broke ranks. Lasgol and his teammates went back to their cabin and spent the afternoon chatting animatedly about everything they had seen and the grand finale which awaited them at dawn. They talked for hours until night came.

"Tomorrow we'll beat the Eagles!"

"I won't say I'm not a little bit scared of them," Gerd said. "The King and all those important people'll be there watching…"

"What tends to happen to you, my friend," said Egil, "is that you're apprehensive in the face of the unknown. Because it's an abstract idea or concept, that's what prevents your mind fully understanding or accepting it, and hence it defends itself by causing you this fear of something which is not necessarily bad."

"Wow, you're smart," Gerd said, and slapped Egil's back. The blow nearly split him in two. "So tell me, what do I do to get rid of the fear?"

"You've seen them all, they're real. Imagine them sitting at the dining-room table eating, drinking and chatting, the way we all do. That should help."

"Thanks pal, that's what I'll do."

Nilsa was very interested. "What would you recommend for me so I don't put my foot in it tomorrow?"

"There's no solution for you," Viggo said.

"Be quiet and listen," Ingrid said. "You'll learn something."

"For you..." Egil said thoughtfully, "I think what you ought to do is concentrate on a single task each moment and tackle it calmly. You tend to try and do several things at the same time, and that's why your mind jumps from one thing to the next: you get nervous and make mistakes."

Nilsa nodded. "My head's always full of ideas. I'll try to focus more. Thanks."

"And what do you recommend for the unceasing toothache that is Viggo?" Ingrid asked him. They all laughed, except Viggo, who wrinkled his nose.

Egil shrugged. "I think that requires a much deeper and more exhaustive study. But he'll do whatever is necessary for the team, that I know for sure."

"For all except for Miss Bossy-Boots," said Viggo.

Ingrid made a face at him.

"There's something in what he says, though," Egil said to her. "Sometimes... you tend to impose your opinion without asking first... or taking feelings into account..."

"I know, but I'm not going to admit it to him," she said, and made a comic face, which was something she very rarely did.

They all laughed heartily.

Ingrid indicated Lasgol. "Since we're on the subject, what can you say about him?"

Egil sighed. "He needs to be honest, first with himself, then with all of us afterwards," he said, still sounding resentful. Very resentful.

"I... I'm sorry," Lasgol said. "Really sorry."

"It'll be enough for me if you shine tomorrow at the final," Ingrid said.

"I will," Lasgol assured her. "You can count on me."

"Right then. Tomorrow we'll fight, and despite our faults and limitations, we'll win!"

They all applauded her words.

Lasgol withdrew to play with Camu, who had now taken to stealing the others' clothes and bringing them to him. He was scolding the creature when he saw Nilsa through the window going off on one of her night-strolls. He felt guilty. He knew it was because of the creature.

"Take his sock to Gerd," he told Camu.

Camu flexed his legs and wagged his tail, happy, but did not obey him. Lasgol concentrated. Using his Gift, he gave it the order: *Return it to Gerd.* This time Camu looked at Lasgol and obeyed.

"Here it is!" Gerd said to the creature. "I've been looking for it for days." The creature flexed its legs again and wagged its tail.

"You ought to shut your trunk," Lasgol said.

Gerd shut it quickly, and Camu jumped on top of it.

Gerd wagged his finger in front of Camu's smiling face. "It's mine. No stealing."

While Gerd was trying to avoid Camu, who was chasing him thinking he wanted to play, Lasgol looked out of the window. He saw Nilsa beside a tree and noticed that she was beckoning to him. So he went out and pointed at himself, she nodded. He went over to her.

"Everything all right?" he asked her.

"Yes, it's just that I need to talk to you."

"Sure. What's up?"

"Let's go where we can't be seen and we can be by ourselves."

Lasgol followed her to the firewood cabin. It was a place set apart, with only a single huge building covered with snow where they kept all the firewood for the winter. It was surrounded by oaks. Inside it was dark, with the light of the moon coming in through a window as the sole source of light. There was a strong smell of damp wood.

"What is it?" Lasgol asked, puzzled.

"He wants to speak to you."

"Who does?"

"Me," came a voice from the shadows.

Lasgol turned and glimpsed a silhouette coming towards him. When it was near the window he recognized it.

"Isgord!"

"He's told me he wanted to make peace with you. For me... so we can be together, him and me."

"You can leave us now, honey." Isgord said to Nilsa.

"Honey? Be together?" Lasgol asked blankly, "What does this mean?"

"Well, you see, Nilsa and I have established a nice little friendship. We usually meet here at night."

"Friendship?" Nilsa asked, sounding offended. "You told me it was much more than that, that I was the princess you were searching for and couldn't find."

"Ah, yes… well…there are things you say when you need something from someone … don't take it personally."

"What did you need from me? You said you wanted to see me, to be with me."

"Well, you see, it's really not you I want to see, it's him." He pointed to Lasgol. "Unfortunately he's always surrounded. There's no way of catching him on his own."

"You've used me!"

"I'm afraid so," Isgord said, and he launched a lightning punch at Nilsa's chin. The redhead, caught by surprise, fell unconscious like a sack.

"Hey!" Lasgol cried. He pushed Isgord hard, so that he moved several steps back, and bent down to see how Nilsa was.

"You and I have some unfinished business," Isgord said. "The time has come to settle it." He unsheathed the Ranger's knife.

Lasgol got to his feet. Nilsa was all right, though unconscious. He saw the threat and took his own knife out. "This is a mistake. Think what you're doing."

"I've been thinking about it for a long time. It's time to settle the score."

"What score? What d'you have against me?"

"I'll explain so that you understand. Do you know what happened the day of Darthor's ambush at the northern pass? The day your father led the King to the ambush and then tried to kill him? Right?"

Lasgol nodded, frowning. "Everybody knows the story."

"The trouble is they don't know the whole story. A few details have been lost, left out. The story all Norghanians know is all about King Uthar and the treacherous Ranger Dakon, and how Commander Sven and the Mage Olthar saved the king that day. But what very few people know is that they'd all have died and Darthor would have been successful if it hadn't been for a forgotten hero."

"What hero?"

"Exactly. Not even the traitor's son knows who it was that stopped his Father's plan from succeeding."

"Explain yourself."

"I see I have your attention. Good. Your Father was leading the King's forces to the ambush. Darthor's forces were stationed at the pass. It would've been a bloodbath. The King and his people wouldn't have survived. Then at the last moment, when they were entering the gorge, a messenger arrived and warned the King about the ambush.

"Does that ring a bell?"

"Dolbarar told me something…"

"That messenger was a Ranger. His name was Tomsen D'you know who he was?"

"No…"

"It was my father! Tomsen Ostberg!"

The truth gradually dawned on Lasgol. "What happened to him?"

"He died in the ambush. He defended the wounded King's retreat and was killed."

"I'm so sorry…"

"You see the irony, don't you? The Ranger who saved the King died unnoticed. Nobody knows about his sacrifice, nobody knows what he managed to do with his courage and daring. Yet everybody knows the traitor Dakon."

"I didn't know anything about this. I'm sorry."

"Oh yes, that's something you're really going to be. My father died as an anonymous hero, but destiny has given me the chance to avenge him." He showed Lasgol his knife.

"If you take your revenge and kill me, you'll condemn yourself. They'll hang you from a tree for it."

"You're right. That's not the revenge I'm seeking."

"I don't understand."

"I'm not going to kill you. I'm going to do something worse, I'm going to maim you. You won't be able to be a Ranger. Whatever the reason you're here – and I know it's very important to you or else you wouldn't put up with all you've had to – that'll be the end of it."

"You'll be expelled if you do that."

"I don't think so. Not over the Son of the Traitor. They all know there's bad blood between us all and that the level of competitiveness here is insane. I'll say that the argument got out of hand, that you took out a knife and I had to defend myself. Who will they believe, the Traitor's Son or the Captain of the Eagles?"

Lasgol shook his head. "It's not too late. Stop this madness."

"I'll tell you something else. Even if they expel me, which I doubt very much, it'll have been worth it. I can always enlist in the royal army. They don't look too closely at people who come knocking."

Lasgol saw the spark of determination in Isgord's eyes and knew that he was completely serious. He was going to maim him for life.

Isgord's attack was so fast and furious that Lasgol could barely evade him. Seeing the danger he was in, he decided to use his Gift to defend himself. A thrust caught him in the forearm. The pain of the cut did not allow him to concentrate enough to activate a defense.

"Don't resist and you'll suffer less. I'll be quick. A swift cut in your Achilles tendon and everything'll be over."

"You're crazy if you think I'm going to let you," Lasgol said, and called on his *Cat-like Reflexes*.

Isgord intensified his attack. He was very good with the knife, which did not surprise Lasgol. Isgord was good at almost everything. Lasgol dodged accurate thrusts and attempts to disarm him. His opponent tried to throw him down after a feint and almost succeeded. Lasgol used his Gift to increase his agility and avoid being brought down.

The other boy began to suspect that something strange was going on. He could not beat Lasgol. He hurled himself on him in a savage leap, Lasgol avoided him by turning half his body with dazzling speed. He hit his opponent on the head with the handle of his weapon as he passed in front of him. Isgord rolled on the ground and got up on to one knee. He felt his head and saw it was bleeding.

"How can you defend yourself like that? You're not that good. I've been watching you, ever since that first day."

"We all have our secrets."

"I don't know whether you've been fooling us in the tests and you haven't made an effort to stand out, or whether something's going on now, but I can tell that whatever it is, it's not normal. I don't like it."

"Go away and let's forget about this. It doesn't need to go any further."

"Throw the knife down and surrender, or she'll be the one who pays," Isgord said, and went to stand over the unconscious Nilsa.

"Wait! Don't hurt her!"

"The knife…"

Lasgol threw down the knife.

"Lie down on the ground, face down."

Lasgol looked at the helpless Nilsa and did as he was told.

"That's the way I like it," Isgord said, and grabbed his right foot.

"Don't do it."

"Your compassion's your weakness. I never would've done anything to Nilsa. She's innocent, and a girl. She can cope with a punch – after all, she's a Ranger. But injure her seriously? No way. I'd never do anything like that."

"I thought so, but I didn't want to take the risk."

"You won't suffer," said Isgord, and got ready to slash Lasgol's tendon.

At that moment a voice sounded.

"What's going on in there? Come out at once."

Isgord turned his head.

There was a moment of hesitation. Lasgol was about to cry for help but Isgord threatened him with the knife. The door of the cabin started to open. Isgord ran to the back of the building and disappeared into the shadows. The moment a figure entered from the front door, Isgord fled out through the back.

Lasgol let out his breath in a gasp. He had been saved by the skin of his teeth. The figure came in and Lasgol recognized him. He was unmistakable, with that brown skin and shaven head.

It was Haakon!

He was glad, then changed his mind. His feeling of relief had been too hasty. What was the man doing there? Why had he seen him following him? A realization struck him: Haakon was the traitor. It made complete sense. He knew the camp and all the surroundings like the back of his hand. He could move without being seen thanks to his mastery of Expertise. He knew how to prepare the poison… he was following him… he was a grim character and he was here now. Lasgol felt cold sweat running down his back. Haakon had the perfect opportunity and excuse to finish him off.

The Ranger bent over Nilsa to examine her. "What have you done?"

"It wasn't me," Lasgol said. He moved to pick up his knife.

"Leave that knife where it is," Haakon said. With a lightning move he took out his own and pointed it at the boy.

Lasgol looked at Haakon's dark eyes, and read mortal danger in them. He took his hand away from his knife.

Haakon got to his feet with his knife raised. In the dimness the sinister figure looked like a spirit of death sent to end his life. Lasgol swallowed.

"You shouldn't have joined the Rangers."

Lasgol shivered. He had heard this before. "The mercenary Nistrom told me the same…"

"Wherever you go, danger follows you."

"Like now?" Lasgol said. He took a step back and called on his Gift of *Cat-like Reflexes* once again.

Haakon watched him for a long moment, as if weighing up the situation.

"Don't get me wrong, Initiate. I'm here on Dolbarar's orders, not to kill you."

Lasgol froze. "On Dolbarar's orders?"

"Dolbarar charged me with following you, so that no more harm would come to you in the camp."

"I thought you were the traitor…"

"You thought wrong. I'm trying to stop you from being killed, not the opposite, but if you sniff around… if you don't let the dead lie… they'll come and take your soul."

"I can't. I have to find out the truth about what happened to my father."

"Everybody in Norghana knows what happened to him."

"But it's not the whole truth."

Haakon threatened him with the knife again. "I don't like you. You don't listen and you're stubborn. I'd rather you weren't here. Trouble follows you, and it's trouble that affects us all."

Lasgol shuddered at the threat.

"But I'm going to do my duty as a Ranger. Pick her up and I'll come with you to your cabin."

Lasgol hesitated.

"Come on, boy, I haven't got all day. If I'd wanted to kill you, I'd have done it already."

Lasgol sighed. He picked up Nilsa and slung her over his shoulder.

"Come on, Traitor's Son."

Chapter 28

The following dawn, at Nilsa's request, Lasgol told their teammates what had happened the night before. The freckled redhead was so embarrassed that she could not manage to get a word out.

Egil looked as though he could not believe it. "Unpardonable! She's lost her head over somebody who's full of hate!"

"I'll beat him to a pulp!" Ingrid cried furiously. "By the time I've finished with him, not even his own mother'll recognize him."

"I'll help you," Gerd said, striking his palm with his fist. For the first time there was hatred in the giant's eyes.

Viggo mimicked cuts in various parts of his body. "If you like I can maim him, in several different places, just like that." He said this as if it were the most natural thing in the world, which gave Lasgol gooseflesh.

"Honestly, sometimes you scare me," Ingrid said.

Lasgol tried to calm them. "No, please, no fights."

"Anyway, he'll have to wait until after the test," Viggo said, "'cause the King and all those stuffed shirts are expecting their show and wouldn't want to be deprived of their entertainment."

"The great winter final, the one that crowns the best team?" Egil said. It was a rhetorical question, since he already knew the answer. "And which, contrary to all predictions, the six of us have reached?"

"Well, yes, that too," Viggo said. He shrugged and smiled.

Ingrid was looking out of the cabin window. "Let's go out. I can see Oden coming to get us."

Before they left Lasgol said goodbye to Camu, who had been very active lately and was beginning to come out of the cabin to explore when they were outside, which made him very uneasy.

"No exploring till I'm back, understood?"

Camu watched him, smiling, and flexed his legs.

"No, we can't play now, and you can't leave the cabin. The King's arrived with all his entourage, there are too many people around in the Camp. It's dangerous."

The creature gave a shriek of happiness and began to bounce

around the room.

Lasgol breathed out heavily. *Don't leave the cabin*, he ordered, using his Gift.

The creature stopped, looked at him and gave a forlorn cry.

"I'm sorry, but it's for your own good."

Lasgol went out to join his team. He wondered whether the order would last long enough in Camu's mind. Taking into account that he had little control over his own skills as yet, he was afraid not. No, it would probably not last long enough. *I'll just have to hurry back.*

The Master Instructor led them to the great square in front of the Command House. A raised platform had been placed there; on it were benches and a large armchair which from a distance looked like a real wooden throne with comfortable cushions. Seated on it, waiting, was King Uthar. He was chatting animatedly with Gondabar, Leader of the Rangers, who was seated beside him in a much more modest, though still comfortable, chair. On the benches were all the Instructors of the camp. Beside Uthar were Commander Sven and the Mage Olthar. Further back was Dolbarar, and with him Ivana, Eyra, Esben and Haakon. The First Ranger Gatik was at the King's side with the Royal Rangers.

Oden indicated to the finalists where they were to stand, then withdrew.

Dolbarar stood up and presented the two teams to the audience. Surrounding the square were all the other Rangers and the students of all three years.

"Let the White Eagles team stand forth," he announced

Isgord led the team as Captain. He was followed by the twins Jared and Aston, two strong athletic boys who looked as if they had been born to be warriors of the royal guard. Then came Alaric and Bergen, shorter but stoical, hard as rock. Bringing up the rear was Marta, a blonde girl with long curly hair. They knelt before King Uthar.

"Let the team of the Panthers of the Snow stand forth."

Ingrid led her team with a determined stride, her chin raised, followed by Nilsa and Gerd. After them came Lasgol and Viggo, then Egil. They knelt before the King.

Uthar rose to his feet. He was so big and radiated such strength that he was impressive. He addressed them all with a smile.

"This is a final I always enjoy a lot. The best of the new blood. A sample of the future our Rangers have in store for us. Dolbarar assures me you're the most brilliant, that you haven't reached this final by chance. Much is expected of you, true, but I can assure you that the reward for your efforts will be greater than you can imagine. The elite specializations await those who are outstanding. The Four Master Rangers miss nothing, and they are already choosing possible candidates." He waved toward Eyra, Ivana, Esben and Haakon, who bowed with great respect.

Lasgol glanced over his shoulder at the great square. Where there had always been a clearing with only a few trees, a kind of complicated labyrinth with tall wooden walls had now been placed.

"Someone might be even selected for a position in my personal escort. It is made up of the best among all the Rangers."

Lasgol looked at the Royal Rangers lined up to the King's right and had no doubt that they were the best.

"Or might even become First Ranger. Something not at all easy to achieve. But if I remember correctly, my champion started by winning this competition in his first year. Isn't that so, Gatik?"

The First Ranger stepped forward. "It was a memorable day, your Majesty."

"Who knows, perhaps among you is the next First Ranger. More than that, maybe even the next Leader of the Rangers. My dear friend Gondabar wishes to retire." The King smiled at him, and the Leader of the Rangers bowed.

"It would be an honor to retire after a life of service to the crown, your Majesty."

Uthar laughed. A loud, deep laugh. "We'll have none of that. You still have many days in which to serve me. You won't get away from your duties so easily."

Lasgol's eyes turned to Isgord, who gave him a look of hatred mixed with conviction. *Today I'm going to defeat you*, it said. Lasgol shivered.

Uthar turned to the two teams and gave a loud clap.

"Now let the final begin! I'm anxious to see what these young people are made of!"

Dolbarar directed them to their positions.

"The Eagles will start from the eastern end and the Panthers from the west."

They took up their positions beside the spear which carried their badge and studied the battlefield. It was surrounded by a wooden palisade, with corridors opening in different directions.

"They've created a wooden labyrinth," Ingrid said in puzzlement.

Gerd pointed to a ditch filled with water at the end of the central corridor. "With obstacles."

"Just in case it wasn't difficult enough already," Viggo protested.

They all looked at Egil.

"Let me think for a moment…"

"Let the final begin!" Dolbarar announced.

"Let's move forward together." Ingrid said.

Egil shook his head. "No. There are three corridors that start from our badge. We'll have to separate into pairs and go down them. That way we'll have more options. If they don't do the same, one corridor will be left free and we'll have a chance to reach their badge and win."

"Hey, that's really smart of you!" Nilsa said, and kissed his cheek.

Egil blushed to the roots of his hair.

"All right then," Ingrid said. "Egil, with me, on the right. Lasgol and Nilsa, on the left. Viggo and Gerd down the middle."

"When you come across the enemy," Egil said, "shout out how many there are."

"Let's go, Panthers!" Ingrid shouted to her team. "We're the best!"

Lasgol and Nilsa moved along the corridor, crouching, with bows at the ready. They could only see what was ahead of them and in the distant heights, the treetops and lookout-points of the camp. Everything else was blocked by the high walls of the labyrinth and the surrounding palisade. They came out to a wider area with two barrels on one side and a pile of logs on the other. In the middle was a passage. Lasgol made a sign to Nilsa and they both hid behind the barrels.

"Two!" came Ingrid's voice.

"Be careful," Lasgol said to his partner.

Suddenly two large figures appeared crouching in front of them. Lasgol stood up and shot. The first figure rolled across the ground and hid behind the logs. The second shot at Lasgol, who took cover behind the barrels.

"Two!" came Viggo's voice.

Nilsa shot at the second figure, but it took cover by retreating into the passage.

"Two!" shouted Lasgol.

"They've separated like us," Nilsa said to Lasgol as she took cover beside him.

"These two are the twins, Jared and Aston. If they get close they'll destroy us. We've got to keep them away."

Dolbarar's voice reached them: "Egil, down."

"Hell!" yelled Nilsa, and shot at Jared. At the same time Lasgol shot at Aston.

"Gerd, down!"

"They're crushing us!" Nilsa said, her eyes full of uncertainty.

Lasgol shot again, first at Jared and then at Aston, but missed. All of a sudden the twins dropped their bows, grabbed knife and axe and leapt over the logs toward the barrels.

"They're coming!" said Lasgol.

Nilsa stood up and shot, but missed. Jared ran her down.

Lasgol took a shot and hit Aston in the chest.

"Aston, down!"

Nilsa received a powerful punch in the eye and lost the axe she was holding. Jared, on top of her, was about to mark her with his axe when Lasgol flung himself at the raised arm and stopped the blow. He took an elbow in the temple, which threw him down and left him stunned on the ground, but Nilsa took the chance to spin around like a panther and marked the twin with her knife as he was coming to deal with Lasgol.

"Jared, down!"

Nilsa helped Lasgol to his feet. "Come on, get up!"

Lasgol, half-dizzy, picked up his bow.

"We… have to… seize the advantage," he muttered. "We've won this corridor."

"True. Ingrid and Viggo are holding on in the other two."

"Or maybe they've retreated to defend the badge."

Nilsa's eye was swelling all the time and beginning to close. "What do we do?"

"We go on to victory," Lasgol said, sounding determined.

They went along the next corridor, always turning left at the crossings. They passed two open areas with obstacles, dodging wooden barricades, trenches, posts and ramps. Nobody came out to meet them.

"Viggo, down!"

"We've lost the center," Lasgol said. "Run, we have to get there first!"

They reached the end of the labyrinth, where he saw the Eagles' badge. *It's right there, nobody's defending it. It's ours, we're going to win.*

He ran toward it.

When he was only a single step away from it, Isgord appeared on his left and intercepted him with a tremendous two-footed kick. He was thrown outside the labyrinth, rolled across the ground and lost his bow. Isgord unsheathed his knife and axe and went after him.

"Nilsa, the badge!" shouted Lasgol. He was retreating to draw Isgord away.

"She won't make it," Isgord said with a smile as he advanced toward Lasgol. "Marta's defending it."

"Alaric, down!"

Isgord shook his head and cursed. He launched himself at Lasgol, who retreated once again.

"I'm going to defeat you, in front of everybody," Isgord said. He pointed behind Lasgol's back.

Lasgol turned and saw that they were now in front of the tribune. The King, along everybody else, was following the final stage of the contest with great interest. He felt the weight of all the nobility's gazes on him.

Isgord attacked. Lasgol blocked him and slid away out of his reach.

"Bergen, down!"

Lasgol knew that would have been Ingrid, who must be defending the Panthers' badge. Isgord attacked with a feint, but Lasgol moved away from his reach one again.

"Nilsa, down!"

Isgord smiled triumphantly. "We're going to win."

"I wouldn't be so sure. Ingrid will finish off Marta."

"Not if I help her."

"You can go whenever you want..."

"And turn my back on you? No way."

Suddenly an intense feeling of alarm came over Lasgol. He looked at Isgord. But no, it was not because of his rival. He gave a swift worried glance around, but saw nothing unusual. Out of the corner of his eye he saw Isgord's knife seeking his stomach. He dodged the thrust with a backward leap. The knife attack was followed by the axe. He leapt to one side and dodged it.

"Fight me, don't avoid me!" Isgord shouted in frustration.

The feeling of intense danger struck him again. But it was not coming from within him. It was not something he himself was causing, like when he felt he was being watched. No, this was different, something un-natural, arcane and external. *What's going on? What is this?* He was puzzled, and nor was it caused by the fight, which was giving him a familiar feeling of elation and fear. Something churned in the pit of his stomach every time Isgord attacked.

"I'm going to defeat you. You can dodge and block all you want, but I'm better than you are, and you know it. I'll mark you, you won't be able to stop me."

No, it was definitely not coming from Isgord. The feeling was of urgency, of danger, very intense, but it was not his stomach, it was his mind. *Something very bad is going on, but I don't know what or where.*

"I'm going to enjoy defeating you in front of the King, in front of everybody."

Lasgol did not allow himself to be disturbed by his enemy's words. He was deeply worried. He needed to understand what was happening. *It's something related to my Gift. It's external. The alarm's being sent to me, like a message.*

Isgord launched a combined attack with knife and axe. Lasgol rolled across the ground and avoided it. He dug in one knee and was about to stand up again when in his mind there appeared a distorted image. Someone or something was sending it to him. He saw a blurred aura, with an image inside it which he could not make out clearly. He shut his eyes for an instant, at the risk of being hit. And it was then that he was able to focus it. The image showed him a Ranger in one of the lookouts. The contours of the image were distorted and the image itself blurred, but there was no doubt that it was a Ranger with his hooded cloak, and a bow in his hands.

The sound of a heavy footstep made him open his eyes. Isgord was hurling himself at him in a great leap, with his weapons in front of him. *I've got to dodge him!* He somersaulted twice and nearly bumped into Commander Sven's feet.

"Coward!" cried Isgord, who was growing more and more frustrated. He got to his feet again nimbly.

The feeling of alarm struck him again, this time with extreme urgency. He shut his eyes and concentrated on the face of the image which was being sent to him. The Ranger was raising his bow and taking aim. As he did, the sun lit up his face.

Lasgol recognized him!

It's Daven, the Recruiter! What's he doing?"

He was completely at a loss. He needed to understand who or what was sending him that image. He used his Gift. He called upon his skill to detect hidden beings. Right then a golden flash showed him someone he knew very well.

Camu.

The creature was under the lookout. Its body was taut, its tail pointing at the Ranger above.

It's Camu sending me the image and warning me of the danger! And if it was Camu, that could only mean one thing...*Magic! There's Magic at play! Magic! Danger! Daven!* Quickly, his mind joined up the loose ends in a moment of clairvoyance.

He closed his eyes. He saw Daven release. The arrow took off at great speed.

At that moment, Isgord came down on him.

He used his Gift. He called upon his Cat-Reflexes agility. He took one step for support and launched himself into the air.

Isgord's weapons reached him in the back as he flew through the air.

"Treason!" Lasgol shouted.

"What's this?" cried Sven, but he had no time to draw his sword.

The arrow meant for the King's heart struck Lasgol in the shoulder with a dull sound. With a grunt of pain he fell on Uthar, who grasped him, wide-eyed.

Lasgol pointed to the lookout.

"Archer!" he said.

"By the abysses of the ice!" Uthar cried.

"Protect the King!" Sven ordered with all the force of his lungs.

A second arrow flew, heading to his face.

Olthar reacted. He raised a wall of ice in front of the King. The arrow struck it and was unable to pass through it. A moment later the whole Royal Guard was surrounding the King, forming a defensive circle with their shields held up. Mage Olthar raised a sphere of ice about himself and came to stand beside the King to strengthen the wall of Ice.

Sven, sword in hand, was pointing to Daven on the lookout. "Gatik! Royal Rangers! Bring him down!"

First Ranger Gatik and the Royal Rangers released their arrows against Daven. With a swift defensive movement he crouched down out of reach. But one arrow struck him with terrible force in the foot he was supporting himself with, so that he fell from the lookout. He hit the ground with a dull thump very close to where Camu was. Seeing the Royal Rangers running toward him, the creature camouflaged itself and vanished.

"Don't kill him!" Uthar shouted at his men. "I want him alive!"

In an instant the murderer was surrounded by the First Ranger Gatik, who had hit him, and about thirty Rangers with their bows aimed at his chest. But Daven was not moving. He had lost consciousness with the impact.

"He's knocked out," Gatik said. "We need to search the Camp. There might be a second assassin."

"Invincibles! Comb the camp!" Sven ordered his infantry. Coolly, martially, the Invincibles of the Ice sealed the exit and began to search the entire camp, sweeping all four directions in two long lines.

Lasgol, lying on the ground beside the King, was struggling not to moan aloud with the intense pain. "How are you, lad?" Uthar asked him.

"Fine... your Majesty..." he muttered untruthfully.

The King bent over and checked the wound. "It almost went right through. It's a miracle you're alive. Don't move or you'll lose that shoulder. We need a surgeon!"

Dolbarar came running with the Four Master Rangers. The Royal Guard let them through.

"We need to call Edwina, quickly."

"I'll do it," Haakon said, and ran off.

Uthar let out his breath. "You've saved my life, Initiate. That's something I'll never forget. What's your name?"

"Lasgol... your Majesty."

"He's Dakon's son," Dolbarar whispered to the King.

Uthar's face showed immense surprise.

"The Traitor's son has saved my life?"

"That is so, my liege," Dolbarar said.

The King was dumbfounded for a long moment. His expression changed from surprise to concern.

"I want this whole business analyzed with the greatest care," he said to Sven and Olthar. "I want to know what happened and why."

"Of course, your Majesty, but for the moment you need to take cover. There might be more assassins."

"Very well," Uthar said. "To the Command House. Bring the boy and the murderer. Let them be tended to inside, and secure the Camp and the surroundings. This is Darthor's doing."

Chapter 29

"How is he?" King Uthar asked Edwina. The Healer had been working on Lasgol's wound for some time as he rested on a stool in front of the common room fire. She had healed him with her Gift, applying unguents to prevent infection and accelerate the formation of a scar. Now she was immobilizing the shoulder with a tight bandage to prevent the wound from re-opening.

She let out her breath abruptly. "You've been very lucky," she said. "The arrow failed to touch any vital organ, but only just."

Uthar nodded several times. "He threw himself forward to protect me with his body. The arrow might have hit him anywhere."

"In that case, I repeat that he's been very lucky," Edwina said. "The wound will heal, but he's going to need more than a month of absolute rest, plus another to restore movement in the shoulder and arm. An arrow from such a long distance… causes a lot of damage."

"So it shall be done, Healer," Dolbarar said.

"A heroic act," Sven added.

King Uthar turned to Lasgol. "You did very well."

"It's his duty as a Ranger," Gondabar, leader of the Rangers, pointed out.

"Even so, it was heroic. Fortunately, the luck of the brave has saved you."

Lasgol did not know what to say. "I saw he was going to shoot and I acted without thinking."

"That leap you took was awesome," Sven said.

"True, he flew more than five paces," Olthar said. "You prepare them well here," he added to Dolbarar.

The Leader of the Camp nodded. "He's one of the best of this year."

"How come you saw it?" Gatik asked. "He was more than two hundred paces away, on a watch-lookout, at the top of a tree."

Lasgol thought about telling them everything, but seeing the room filled with people he hesitated. Better to be prudent; he did not know them. He would tell the truth, but not all of it.

"During the fight I had a bad feeling… I felt something was

wrong... I thought it was because I was going to lose, but then I saw something that... caught my attention... I caught a glimpse of the raised bow, aiming. I realized the feeling was very real. And I acted."

"You did very well in following your instinct," Uthar said. "Your King is grateful."

Edwina went over to the big table where Daven lay, still unconscious, guarded by the Four Master Rangers.

"I can't believe Daven was the traitor," Dolbarar said, shaking his head. "He's the best Recruiter we have."

"What an affront!" Gondabar muttered. He was plainly deeply affected by what had happened. "One of our own people is the traitor in the camp. It's a terrible stain, your Majesty ... unpardonable."

"We'll discuss that later," said Uthar. "At the moment I want to understand this." He turned to Edwina. "Don't let him die. I want to interrogate him."

"I'll do what I can, your Majesty."

The Healer began to treat the arrow-wound in Daven's leg. All eyes were on her, but they let her work in silence. Lasgol watched the blue energy issue from Edwina's hands and enter Daven's body. He wondered whether anybody else was able to see it. Then he met Olthar's icy eyes. Yes, the Mage could see it too. He remembered his father's words: *Only those blessed with the Gift are able to see it when someone else is using it, and not always even then.*

When Daven was out of danger, the King ordered him to be awakened.

Edwina warned them: "When I examined his body I found something strange..."

"What do you mean by strange?"

"He has a Rune of Power on his chest."

The King looked at her blankly. "Show it to me."

Edwina unfastened Daven's tunic. On his lower torso a round rune was stamped on his flesh, the size of an apple. It was made up of three strange sentences in an unknown language, which made up three concentric circles around an open eye. It shone with a golden tinge.

"That's Darthor's mark!" cried the King.

"The rune emanates power," said Edwina.

Olthar bent over to study it. He put his hand over it and

concentrated.

"Nothing. I can perceive nothing. But in me the ability to perceive the Gift isn't very strong. Still, I agree with his Majesty, it's Darthor's mark, no doubt about that. We've found it on several of his agents."

"Why do they mark themselves?" Dolbarar asked. "For what purpose?"

Sven too came over to look at the mark. "Yes, it's the same mark. We believe it's some arcane ritual of obedience, of servitude to Darthor. They burn the rune with fire on the flesh as proof of loyalty."

"Yes, that would make sense," said Dolbarar. "In many primitive cultures tattoos, marks made with knives or fire, are used as proof of membership and loyalty."

"It's the same rune we found stamped on the traitor Dakon's chest," Olthar said.

Hearing that, Lasgol tensed. He leaned forward and looked at it.

"Yes, exactly the same," Commander Sven confirmed.

"There's no room for doubt," the King said. "It's Darthor's mark, and he's one of his agents. Now wake him up. I wish to interrogate him."

Edwina put her hands on Daven's head and closed her eyes. When she opened them again, Daven opened his own. The Healer withdrew to the table while Daven pushed himself up to a sitting position. Ivana, Haakon, Esben and Eyra, who were watching him in silence, tensed. They approached the table like the shadows of executioners beside a prisoner condemned to death.

Daven looked straight at the King, who with Sven and Olthar by his side was also watching the Ranger with a deep gaze, one of hatred.

"You've failed in your attempt, murderer," said Uthar.

Daven's eyes were fixed on the King's. "Your days are numbered."

"You dare threaten me? Me, the King!"

"Of course I dare. Your end is near. My army is preparing itself. Soon I'll tear out your rotten heart and put an end to all your evil acts in the lands of the north."

"Be careful, there's something strange going on here," Dolbarar put in. "This isn't the Daven I know."

Uthar looked at Olthar and Sven in puzzlement.

Olthar raised one eyebrow. "Who are you?" he asked Daven.

"Doesn't the King's great Ice Mage know who he's addressing? It hardly matters. You'll die beside him. You'll pay with your life for what happened at the Northern Pass."

"He's not in his right mind," Sven said.

Daven fixed his eyes on him. "Of course I am, Commander. You'll be the first of the three to die, because you saved the King at the pass, and with that act you sealed your fate."

"Do you speak for Darthor, then?" Uthar asked in confusion.

Daven laughed: a deep, distorted laugh.

Lasgol was watching all this, not knowing what to think. Daven looked like a different person. Even his voice was different.

"I don't speak for Darthor," Daven cried. "I *am* Darthor!"

Uthar tensed at once. Haakon and Esben held Daven's arms and legs down and Ivana put a knife to his throat.

There was a flash of understanding in Edwina's eyes. "Do you mean you've possessed this man?"

"Of course I possess him. He's mine. His thoughts, his will, are mine." He pierced Lasgol with his gaze. "Just as once I possessed the father of the one who saved you today."

Lasgol came closer. "You possessed my father?"

"Yes, the great Dakon Eklund, First Ranger and personal friend of the King. And he almost managed to accomplish my plan."

Lasgol felt a mixture of pain, rage and relief. The first two were for the loss of his father, the third for confirming what he had always known: his father was innocent.

"You'll pay for this! I'll burn you alive! You won't defeat me!" Uthar said furiously.

Daven laughed again, and Uthar hit him hard repeatedly.

Sven stopped him. "Your Majesty, it's not him!"

The King managed to recover his poise. Daven, bleeding from the mouth and nose, went on laughing.

"We've got to stop this," Sven said. "Darthor may well be watching us through Daven's eyes. We can't give him this advantage."

"What can we do to stop it?" the King asked Olthar.

"We must break the spell. Or kill him."

"Do you know how to break it?"

"Unfortunately it's not my specialty."

Uthar's eyes went back to Daven. "I don't want to kill him, but Sven is right. He's a spy and he's just one pace away from us. I'm not prepared to risk it."

"Your Majesty," Edwina interrupted. "Perhaps I might be able."

"Lay him down."

Haakon, Esben and Ivana held him down on the table, and the Healer put her hands over the rune. Lasgol could see it flashing golden. Edwina's healing energy began to act upon it, and Daven arched in pain.

"Hold him fast. This will be painful for him!"

Edwina's blue energy was fighting the golden of Darthor's Rune. Daven began to yell with pain, writhing under her hands. They held him firmly down on the table and gagged his mouth. The Healer's forehead was damp with perspiration and her eyes were shut. The struggle went on for a long time. All of a sudden the rune began to fade from Daven's chest, and he fainted. Little by little it became fainter until it had completely vanished. Edwina opened her eyes and drew her hands away. She took a step back and almost fell from exhaustion. Eyra guided her to the fireside so that she could rest in an armchair.

Suddenly Daven's eyes opened wide. He looked around him anxiously.

"What...? What's happening...?"

"Who are you?" Uthar asked him with his eyes half-closed.

Daven looked utterly lost. "Daven Omdahl, your Majesty, Recruiter Ranger, my liege."

"And Darthor?"

"Darthor? I... I don't know, your Majesty."

"You don't know? Or are you trying to deceive me?"

"I don't know what's going on, my liege. I don't understand what's happening ...what am I doing here? How did I get here?"

"What's the last thing you remember?" Olthar asked.

"I was leaving for the east.... for the coast, on a reconnaissance mission."

Olthar and the King looked at Dolbarar. "That was three months ago," said the Leader of the Camp.

"What season is this?" Sven asked Daven.

"Mid-autumn, sir. What's going on?"

"What's the last thing you remember before you woke up on this table?" Olthar asked. "Think, the last detail you remember."

Daven puzzled over this. "A stranger. He asked me for directions at a crossing near the city of Sewin."

"And?"

"Nothing else… the next thing I know is waking up here."

"The stranger, what was he like?" Sven asked.

"I never saw his face. It was hidden under a hood."

"That was Darthor, curse it!" Uthar thundered.

"That means he's crossed to this side of the mountains," Sven said.

"Not necessarily," Olthar said. "It might have been one of his sorcerers."

Uthar indicated Daven. "Whatever the case, it's clear that he dominated this poor unfortunate."

"That means the rumors are true," Sven said. "Darthor is not only a corrupt Mage of the Ice, but a Dominator."

"And a very powerful one," Olthar commented, "as we've just found out. He's had this Ranger under his control for months, and from a long distance away."

"It doesn't matter how powerful he is," Uthar said, "we'll defeat him. He won't have his way with Norghana. When the thaw comes in spring, we'll cross the passes and put an end to him in the North. You have my word as King!"

"Hail King Uthar!" cried Sven.

"Hail!" they all cried in unison.

Chapter 30

In the course of the next few days the King's forces turned the Camp upside down. They searched every cabin, every hut, every wood, every bush, and even under every rock. They questioned every single Ranger, but they could not find any assassin or any plot to kill the King, or anything suspicious or irregular. The Rangers co-operated at all times and secured the boundary. At last King Uthar was satisfied and decided to return to the capital, Norghania, to prepare an offensive against Darthor's forces.

Before leaving, he asked Dolbarar to have all the Rangers of the Camp assemble in front of the Command House. He wanted to speak to them.

"What has happened here shows the danger the realm is in. Darthor has dared to attempt against my life, and of all places, in one which is sacred to me: the Camp. This place is the Rangers' heart, where they are trained, where they operate from. You are the protectors of the crown, the defenders of the lands of the realm. The fact that he's dared to do it here sends us a clear message: he'll stop at nothing to get hold of the kingdom." He glanced aside at Dolbarar, Leader of the Rangers, who nodded with a look of grave concern.

A murmur of unease rose among the Rangers, most of whom were upset at having failed their King in not discovering and preventing the attempt on his life.

"I don't want this incident to be misinterpreted as a dishonor on this glorious corps. No. The enemy has attacked where we never dreamed it could be possible, and that shows unmistakably that he's very powerful and intelligent. An enemy who will be very difficult to defeat, but whom between us all, we will nevertheless defeat. I won't rest until he's executed. For Norghana! For the crown!"

The Rangers shouted as one: "For Norghana! For the King!"

Uthar nodded, acknowledging the cheers. "There is a mistake from the past which I must correct, justice must be done. Because a king, above all, must be just and impartial." He turned to Sven, who handed him a parchment with the royal seal. "It has been proven that the First Ranger Dakon, my friend, did not commit high treason, but was dominated by Darthor through a rune stamped on his flesh, and was unaware of the acts he committed against the crown. Therefore I proclaim his proven innocence, and in order that it may be so confirmed, I have written this royal pardon. Dakon is exonerated of the crimes for which he was condemned. His titles, lands and goods will be returned: in this case, to his heir. Thus I proclaim as King of Norghana."

The murmurs were now cries of surprise and astonishment which interrupted the King's words. Mage Olthar waved at the crowd to be silent. At his gesture everyone became quiet, such was the fear aroused by that person and his magic.

The King smiled. "Let Initiate Lasgol Eklund, son of Dakon, come forth!"

Lasgol came forward to stand before the King, knelt and bent his head. The eyes of all the Rangers were fixed on him.

"As for you, Lasgol, for the services rendered to the crown, for saving the life of the King of Norghana, risking your own, for the valor and honor shown, I grant you this badge of courage. It's the highest honor a soldier can obtain."

Sven handed the king his own.

"Stand, Lasgol," Uthar said.

Lasgol stood up and swallowed a grunt. His shoulder hurt with every movement.

"As we have no badge for you here, Sven's will do the honors," Uthar whispered into Lasgol's ear as he fastened it on.

Lasgol was so excited about all that was happening that he could barely hold back his tears.

"Thank you... your Majesty... it's an honor..." he stammered.

"My thanks are due to you. You saved my life."

"And... thank you ... for restoring my father's good name..."

"It's only fair. I never understood what happened to him. We were like brothers. Now I understand everything."

Lasgol nodded. He bowed and went back to his team.

Uthar gave way to Dolbarar with a wave. "It's time for the Ceremony," the king said to the Leader of the Camp.

Dolbarar looked at the front rows where the first-, second-, third- and fourth- year Rangers were standing.

"This year has turned out to be a strange one. The finals have been suspended because of events. The first year's final test is declared invalid, and the other year's tests have not taken place. It's the first time in more than twenty-five years that anything like this has happened. But tradition must be respected, despite everything. We must continue with the Ceremony of Acceptance."

The initiates shifted uneasily, as some needed the points to avoid being expelled, others in order to reach the elite specializations.

"Therefore I declare the Ceremony of Acceptance under way, where the merits of each one of you will be decided, and also who will continue with us next year and who will be expelled."

A funereal silence followed these words. Nilsa was so nervous that she stepped on Gerd. The giant was paralyzed with the fear of being expelled and did not even notice. Egil watched with concern. He had calculated his chances, and they were minimal. Ingrid was sure she would pass, whereas Viggo, his arms folded over his chest, looked like someone who was sure he was not going to make it.

"After discussing it with the Master Rangers for a long time, since it is a difficult decision in many cases" Dolbarar went on, "we've decided that the finals have ended in a tie. There's no winner, but neither is there a loser. The two teams who reached the finals will receive the Leaf of Prestige as if they had both won. We've decided this is the fairest thing we can do under the circumstances."

Eyra, Ivana, Esben and Haakon, who were standing behind Dolbarar, nodded with a slight bow toward their leader. The gasps of relief among many, and of frustration among a few, rose among all who had taken part.

"Master Rangers, the first-year list," Dolbarar said.

Haakon approached solemnly and handed him a parchment with the names of those who had passed and those who were to be expelled.

"The results of all the tests, and the merit points achieved during the entire year, have been considered in putting together the list of those who will stay and those who face expulsion. When I read your name, come up here and you will be given a badge. If the badge is wooden, it will mean you have passed. If the badge is copper, it will mean you have not succeeded."

Dolbarar began to read out the names. Isgord was the first to go up and pass. Exultantly and proudly, he showed his team the wooden badge. One by one, all of them followed him. In each team there were one or two who had not succeeded. Their disappointment, and in some cases their tears, were heartbreaking. And at last came the turn of the Snow Panthers. As captain, Ingrid went up first and was given the wooden badge. She raised her fist in a sign of victory and cheered on her team.

"Yes! Go Panthers!"

Nilsa followed. She was so nervous that she dropped her badge when Dolbarar gave it to her. It took her a while to get it back and realize it was wooden.

"I passed!" she shouted, looking utterly incredulous.

Dolbarar called Gerd in turn. The giant went up slowly, his limbs shaking. He received the badge; it was copper. With a great effort he held back his tears and without a word he went back with Ingrid and Nilsa, who hugged him to comfort him.

Viggo was next. To the surprise of many, including himself, he passed. He went back to his place, staring at the badge as though he could not believe it was really made of wood. He even looked back in case they called him to say it had been a mistake.

Egil was called and went up looking worried. Dolbarar handed him his badge. It was copper. Egil let out a cry of dismay, shook his head and went back to his place with his shoulders sagging. His partners tried to comfort him with affectionate words and hugs, but he was still disconsolate.

The last one to be called was Lasgol. He approached fearfully, with his nerves churning in his stomach. He was on the point of throwing up; seeing what had happened to Gerd and Egil he feared the worst, but Dolbarar smiled at him and handed him a badge. He looked at it warily and realized that it was wooden. He muffled a cry of joy and ran back to his team.

The last to be called were the Owls. Astrid passed, and Lasgol sighed in relief when he saw this.

"Come forward, team captains," said Dolbarar.

Ingrid hurried to his side. Astrid and Isgord went to stand beside him, as did the captains of the other teams after a moment.

"The rule establishes that you have a chance to save someone in your teams if you have obtained a Leaf of Prestige for having won in one of the four tests by teams. The Eagles have two Leaves of Prestige for winning both the Spring and Winter Tests. The Wolves have one for winning the Summer Test. The Bears, one, for winning the Autumn Test. Finally the Panthers, one, for winning the Winter

Test. Go back with your teams and discuss the matter. Come back with the name of the person you wish to save from expulsion."

Ingrid explained. They had to choose between saving Gerd or Egil with the Leaf of Prestige they had received for the tie in the Winter Test. It was an impossible decision.

"How can they ask us to choose? It's awful!" moaned Nilsa.

Viggo was looking upset. "The best thing is to toss a coin."

Lasgol too was upset. He did not want to lose either of his friends.

"Gerd ought to be saved. It's the right thing to do. He needs it, and I don't."

"No, Egil, that's not fair," Gerd said immediately.

"Yes, it is, my friend. I'm the son of the most important Duke of the realm. Nothing will happen to me. You need this, I don't."

"But your father... the dishonor..."

"I'll get over it. It's decided. Gerd stays. I go."

Nilsa threw her arms around Egil and hugged him tightly, nearly knocking him down with the momentum. The rest joined in a group hug. Egil, in tears, thanked them.

"The decision?" Dolbarar asked.

The Eagles and the Wolves, having no-one facing expulsion, saved their Leaves of Prestige to keep the option of going on to the prestigious schools. The Bears saved Polse, the only one they had facing expulsion. Ingrid gave Gerd's name.

"In that case," Dolbarar said, "Egil, of the Panthers of the Snow, will be expelled."

Egil drew himself up to his full height and wiped away his tears. He nodded, accepting his fate.

Isgord, smiling from ear to ear, was looking at Lasgol, whose eyes were moist.

"Just a moment, Dolbarar," said King Uthar.

"Yes, your Majesty?"

"I have a request. I would like to ask for an additional Leaf of Prestige to be awarded to the Snow Panthers, for having helped save the life of the King."

Dolbarar looked at the Four Master Rangers. "It's not a usual request. There's no precedent..."

"Nobody has ever tried to kill the King of Norghana in the Camp before," Uthar said, emphasizing the fact, "and he was saved by

Initiates."

Dolbarar indicated the other Master Rangers. "We could grant it, but it must be a unanimous decision."

The King nodded in acceptance of this. Dolbarar and the other Master Rangers conferred in a circle. After a moment, the Leader of the Camp turned to speak.

"It's unanimous. We hereby grant the Leaf of Prestige to the Panthers of the Snow by royal request, for exceptional behavior."

"Could they use this Leaf of Prestige to save the one who has been expelled?" King Uthar asked. This had been his intention all along.

"That is so, your Majesty."

"That would please me greatly."

"In that case," Dolbarar said, "Egil is saved from expulsion."

The Panthers were astonished. This was something they had certainly not been expecting. Nilsa gave a cry of joy, and the rest of the team joined in cheers, leaps, embraces and general unbridled merriment. They were all saved!

Isgord stared at Lasgol, red with rage. He was on the verge of exploding with anger.

The Ceremony continued with the handing of badges to the second-, third- and fourth-year students. The six members of the Panthers of the Snow Team were so delighted that they could not restrain themselves, so that the rest of the Ceremony went by like a dream. Gerd could not believe he had been saved. The color had come back to his face, displacing the fear. Nilsa hugged everyone and smiled non-stop, full of both happiness and nerves. Viggo stared at his badge in disbelief. Ingrid thanked Egil for all the good he had done and his impressively scholarly brain. Lasgol too was smiling from ear to ear. Not only had he managed to restore his father's good name, but he had graduated. And not just him, but his five new friends as well. He could not believe it. He was so happy he would have liked to shout to the sky like a madman.

Dolbarar brought the Ceremony to an end with some words for all the Rangers.

"You are the future. The survival of the crown and the kingdom depend on you. Always remember: *With loyalty and valor the Ranger will look after the Kingdom and defend the Crown from enemies, both internal and external, serving their country with honor and in secrecy.*"

All the Rangers repeated this mantra as one: *"With loyalty and valor, the Ranger will look after the Kingdom and defend the Crown from enemies, both internal and external, serving their country with honor and in secrecy."*

King Uthar nodded, smiling.

"Another year, another great ceremony."

He embraced Dolbarar and took his leave of the Four Master Rangers with a salute. Then he gave the order and his retinue assembled in formation. In the same way as they had arrived, they began to leave the Camp in a single long column of armed men.

The Rangers sang the ode to the brave while the King mounted. They sang while the procession left the Camp.

Oden ordered everyone to go back to the cabins to make the column's exit from the grounds easier.

The Snow Panthers hurried back to their own cabin, from where they watched the retinue leave.

"Let me see the King's medal," Ingrid said to Lasgol.

He handed it to her, and they all huddled around to look.

All except Nilsa. She went over to Lasgol and with sincere repentance in her eyes said: "I'm so, so sorry… Will you ever be able to forgive my stupidity?"

"Everything's forgiven. Isgord tricked you. It wasn't your fault."

"It was really, but thanks all the same."

"Well," Viggo said, "in the end the moron didn't get what he wanted and he's seething with rage"

Gerd winked at Lasgol. "How does it feel to be a hero?"

He shrugged. "I'm just happy that everything's ended well."

"Weren't you afraid?"

"Yes, Gerd, I was. But I acted on pure instinct and training, probably…"

"I'd like to be able to do the same one day," the giant said hopefully.

Lasgol gave him a slap on the shoulder. "Don't worry, when the moment of truth comes you'll just go ahead. I'm sure of it."

"Thanks, my friend."

At that moment King Uthar, accompanied by Mage Olthar and Commander Sven, passed out into the distance.

All of them watched with respect and admiration. Suddenly, Camu appeared on Lasgol's shoulder. He stood rigid, pointed his tail toward the King and his two companions and started to shriek into

Lasgol's ear.

"Make him shut up, or else we'll get into trouble," Viggo warned him.

"Easy, Camu, it's okay," Lasgol said as he scratched the little head.

Camu however, kept pointing his tail as the retinue went by.

"Yes, Camu, I know you can feel magic, I know. Its Mage Olthar, he's very powerful. Relax. He's a friend. Now hide before they see you."

Camu looked at Lasgol with his bulging eyes. He did not seem very convinced. But he obeyed and vanished.

Egil came up to Lasgol. In the scholar's eyes Lasgol read that he was still wounded by what had happened between them.

"Will you forgive me some day?" he hastened to ask.

Egil took a deep breath and looked sternly at him. "Will you promise there won't be any more secrets between us?"

"I promise. I give you my word."

The scholar breathed out heavily. "All right," he said, giving way, and the two friends joined in a heartfelt embrace. The smiles returned to their faces.

Viggo made a face. "You're going to make me throw up with all this touchy-feely stuff."

"Shut up and say something positive for once," Ingrid said.

Viggo arched his brows. "Today you look very nice with those braids," he said to her, and for once he meant what he said to her.

She blushed to the roots of her hair. Then she paled. Finally she launched a right hook at Viggo that knocked him down.

Everybody laughed, while Ingrid went into the cabin muttering rude comments about Viggo.

"That girl has a problem," he said from the ground, rubbing his chin. "There's no understanding her."

Gerd stretched out his hand to him, unable to stop laughing, and he got to his feet.

"You really are an idiot," Nilsa said, shaking her head and smiling.

Lasgol looked in the direction of the Owls' cabin and saw Astrid there. The girl gave him a nod, then smiled broadly at him. He returned the nod, feeling butterflies in his stomach.

"What are you going to do now the mystery of what happened to your father's been solved?" Egil asked.

Lasgol was thoughtful for a moment. "I need to go to my village, to Skad, to claim the titles and possessions that were my father's, and make sure his name is cleared."

"I see. And about becoming a Ranger? There's no reason any longer for you to go on here…"

"Hmmm…" Lasgol said. He considered this. "It's funny. I never really wanted to be a Ranger. I came here because of what happened to my father. But now…"

"You're not going to tell me you want to go on with us?" Egil said, trying to drag the words out of him.

"Well… you're not going to believe it, but yes, I do. That's exactly what I want to do."

Egil gave him the trace of a smile and arched one eyebrow. "You sure? Knowing that next year it'll be even harder?"

Lasgol nodded. "I want to be a Ranger. Like my father was. Now I don't have any doubts. It's what I want to be."

Egil smiled from ear to ear.

"Well, then," Viggo said, "you'd better use the weeks of vacation we've been given until the start of the second year. I'm going to enjoy myself as much as I can, I recommend all of you do the same."

His companions smiled at the prospect and went into the cabin. Lasgol saw the last components of the royal retinue go by. A tear ran down his cheek. He had done it. He had succeeded in exonerating his father. He had cleared his name. That was the reason why he had come here, and in spite of everything, he had done it. He sighed in relief. He had always believed that if he managed it he would feel joy, pride even, but no, all he felt was an immense relief, as if his soul had been enveloped in a balm of peace. He smiled.

For you, Father. Thank you for everything, I'll always love you.

---THE END BOOK 1---

Acknowledgements

I'm lucky enough to have very good friends and a wonderful family, and it's thanks to them that this book is now a reality. I can't express the incredible help they have given me during this epic journey.

I wish to thank my great friend Guiller C. for all his support, tireless encouragement and invaluable advice. This saga, not just this book, would never have come to exist without him.

Mon, master-strategist and exceptional plot-twister. Apart from acting as editor and always having a whip ready for deadlines to be met. A million thanks.

To Luis R. for helping me with the re-writes and for all the hours we spent talking about the books and how to make them more enjoyable for the readers.

Roser M., for all the readings, comments, criticisms, for what she has taught me and all her help in a thousand and one ways. And in addition, for being delightful.

The Bro, who as he always does, has supported me and helped me in his very own way.

Guiller B, for all your great advice, ideas, help and, above all, support.

My parents, who are the best in the world and have helped and supported me unbelievably in this, as in all my projects.

Olaya Martínez, for being an exceptional editor, a tireless worker, a great professional and above all for her encouragement and hope. And for everything she has taught me along the way.

Sarima, for being an artist with exquisite taste, and for drawing like an angel. Please visit her website: http://envuelorasante.com/

Special thanks to my wonderful collaborators: Christy Cox and Peter Gauld for caring so much about my books and for always going above and beyond. Thank you so very much.

And finally: thank you very much, reader, for supporting this author. I hope you've enjoyed it; if so I'd appreciate it if you could write a comment and recommend it to your family and friends.

Thank you very much, and with warmest regards.

Pedro

Author

Pedro Urvi

I would love to hear from you.
Thank you for reading my books.

You can find me at:
Mail: pedrourvi@hotmail.com
Twitter: https://twitter.com/PedroUrvi
Author Page Amazon:
https://www.facebook.com/PedroUrviAuthor/
My Website: http://pedrourvi.com

Again, thank you so much for reading my books.

☐

The adventure continues:

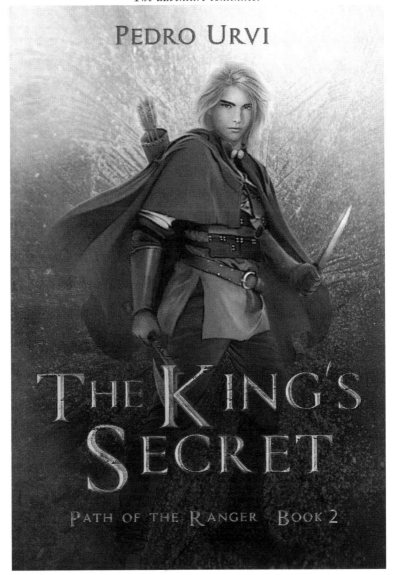

PEDRO URVI

THE KING'S
SECRET

PATH OF THE RANGER · BOOK 2

Printed in Great Britain
by Amazon

71299963R00196